The Mind Thief Murders

Neversleep Scrolls

Phillip Walton

The Augury, Inc.

Neversleep Scrolls: The Mind Thief Murders
A Fantasy Mystery Series in the Realm of Galhadria

"From the Archives of the Great Library of Arathes, Golden City of Elves, The Wise Scholars of Graysage present: The unlikely and highly questionable account from those who were avowed witness... these are the suspenseful investigations of the human, Fraenk Neversleep. The story begins. "

Cover Art: Braden Maxwell

Published by The Augury, Inc.
Murfreesboro, TN

Paperback ISBN: 979-8-9914937-1-0
Hardcover ISBN: 979-8-9914937-0-3
eBook ISBN: 979-8-9914937-4-1
FICTION / Fantasy / Mystery

CONTENTS

Part 1

    Part 1 ... 1

    Chapter 1 ... 3

    Chapter 2 ... 9

    Chapter 3 ... 17

    Chapter 4 ... 25

Part 2

    Part 2 ... 39

    Chapter 5 ... 41

    Chapter 6 ... 49

    Chapter 7 ... 57

    Chapter 8 ... 67

    Chapter 9 ... 75

    Chapter 10 ... 87

Part 3

    Part 3 ... 97

    Chapter 11 ... 99

    Chapter 12 ... 107

    Chapter 13 ... 117

Chapter 14   127

Chapter 15   139

Chapter 16   149

Chapter 17   157

Chapter 18   165

Chapter 19   175

Part 4

Part 4   183

Chapter 20   185

Chapter 21   193

Chapter 22   203

Chapter 23   215

Part 5

Part 5   223

Chapter 24   225

Chapter 25   235

Chapter 26   245

Chapter 27   259

Chapter 28   269

Chapter 29   277

Part 6

Part 6   289

Chapter 30   291

Chapter 31   301

Chapter 32   311

Chapter 33   319

Chapter 34   327

Part 7

Part 7   335

Chapter 35   337

Chapter 36   347

Chapter 37   357

Chapter 38   365

Chapter 39   375

Chapter 40   383

Chapter 41   391

Part 8

Part 8   399

Chapter 42   401

Chapter 43   411

Chapter 44   419

Chapter 45   427

Chapter 46   437

Chapter 47   447

Chapter 48   457

Chapter 49   467

Chapter 50   475

THE END   483

Epilogue   485

More from the World of Galhadria   487

Part I

W

HEN THE SOMBER TOLL of the nursemaid's bell rang in the humid night air, marking the hour, the city of Arathes had quieted to a hum. It was a momentary lull. A pause between breaths before it all came roaring back to life again like a sleeping dragon—vigorous, shining, and hungry.

Arathes was the Golden Crown of the Elven kingdom. It wrapped its way around the mountain that bore its name and was surrounded on three sides by Lake Ewyn. Its tawny, elegant buildings were a harmonious symphony of brick and marble, clay and wood. They grew like mushrooms, partially carved into the hill itself in an engineering second only to the University in Marien, which was an actual floating island fixed to the ground by a massive chain.

The city was a prosperous nexus of trade with merchants from every part of the world arriving in ox carts and caravans or up the Maxsarmattis River with heavily-laden barges and sleek sailing ships carrying exotic cargo. Wealthy travelers and distinguished dignitaries from every corner of the map made Arathes their chosen destination for its arts and culture.

It was also a holy city that was home to the Seven Crystalline Cathedrals to the Divines—a popular pilgrimage site for the devout. At its summit sat the Summer Palace of the Monarch, currently occupied by his young nephew, the beloved High Lord Krispen Whiteleaf.

Yes, fair Arathes! A beacon of abundant wealth, just governance, and unquestioned military power in the region. Across the kingdom of Sarmatti, bards sang odes to the City of Gossamer Dreams, a paradise second only to the heavens themselves. Elvish officials boasted the streets were safe to walk day or night without fear of being accosted. A city where nothing bad ever happened or ever could.

Of course, only suckers believed all that elvish dreck. And they were exactly the kind of fool that the city feasted upon and spit back out with just the rags on their back and an empty coin purse. Behind the golden gleam of Arathes hid dark shadows. It was the kind of place where someone could get away with murder, so long as you killed the right sort of guy—like a human.

In the garden of Blackroot Manor were ancient silverwood trees with their trunks fat and smooth, pale bark neatly lining the outer wall. Exotic flowers from across the kingdom grew in manicured riot around the shallow stream that wove its way down the length. Glowing fairy lights floated like dust motes in the air, giving the scene an otherworldly feel.

But it was all an artifice that only those with extravagant means could create. Tons of rich soil was hauled up in carts and landscaped by armies of gardeners. Even the bubbling stream of clear, sapphire blue was carefully carved out of the stone and fed by ancient cisterns deep in the mountain. The elves prided themselves on their connection to the natural world and those with enough gold could recreate it even in the challenging altitude of the upper city levels.

At this hour, the garden was empty, save for the one dark specter of a man who sat on a stone bench in front of the Ancestral Pool. Despite not being more than ankle deep, the ink black water was so still that it mirrored a second set of stars in the ground, like a vast rectangular gate to a parallel world below. It was said that under certain conditions, an elf could speak with their forebears across time through its ominous reflection. But this man was clearly not here for divination. He sat with his back to the pool, facing the stone wall behind it.

This haunt of the elven garden, Arch Preceptor Fraenk Neversleep, unstoppered a small bottle and took a long drink. The liquor burned pleasantly in his chest, sending warm prickles across his skin. Fraenk shook the bottle, noticing it was getting light. It wouldn't do to run out. Fortunately, he knew plenty of taverns open all night, and he always kept a few of his own bottles secreted away in stashes around the city.

A lithe black shape sprang up onto the bench beside him and gave a soft chitter. It was a skrate—one of the feral lizard cats that seemed to infest the city. They were certainly a nuisance, but the elves were too enamored with all of nature to see any harm done to them. Fraenk found they had other uses too.

He replaced the bottle in his cloak and retrieved a small dried fish from an inner pouch. Only while being fed would the creature let Fraenk retrieve the contents of the small pouch around its neck. It smacked noisily as it ate, and when it saw Fraenk had no more fish, the skrate gave an annoyed yowl and disappeared back into the darkness.

He unfurled a small scrap of paper and examined the irregular black symbol—a crude circle crossed with several hash marks, probably done in the charcoal from a burned stick. For those who could decipher this dispatch, it spoke of death.

Fraenk frowned and re-folded it.

"*Shalokar's teeth,*" he cursed.

It was nearly a quarter of an hour later when Fraenk finally heard his underling arrive. An air current sent a ripple of motion through the fairy lights, and they quickly blinked out. Then followed by a weighty scuff of foot on stone.

Fraenk turned to see Preceptor Nimuth Stonebridge coming along the garden path, looking disheveled and a bit drunk. His face bore some of the features distinctive to half-elves—the sharp angle to the corner of his ears, tapered nose, and smooth beardless chin—but he was stocky, with wide shoulders, a thick neck, and meaty hands; a telltale sign of human parentage. Traits that would keep him from ever rising high in elven society.

The boy grew up an outsider to both worlds. Too elf to be human, too human to pass even with the other half elves, who typically received some kind of patronage from their elven families. Instead of seeking a life of leisure and scholarship, he turned his talents to the happenings of the city's underworld. He ran with gangs, stole, scammed, and collected debts. Nim had a reputation for being fair but fearless, which allowed him to rise quickly. But he ran afoul of the partisans so many times that Fraenk knew he'd have to recruit him to his preceptor service, or the half-elf would end up a guest of Kylerla, floating face down in the lake.

To his credit, Nim Stonebridge didn't require much convincing to join. After all, there was a fine line between being a spy and a criminal. Both were the lives of whispers, secrets, and knives in the dark. The half-elf said he preferred to be on the more honest side to begin with. Fraenk found much to like about the half-elf; he was earnest, cool-headed, and inquisitive. But Nim had a storied history of bad luck in the gambling den—a pressure point that could be squeezed. Fraenk sensed he was keeping secrets, but as the old Aruthien saying goes, "Trust *is a bridge, built one stone at a time.*"

"How much did you lose tonight, Nim?"

The half-elf stopped beside the bench and sighed. Fraenk caught a whiff of tobacco smoke, bitter ale, and fish, flavored with a savory mix of Gazean spices served at a particular dock-front watering hole.

"That much, eh? Well, I warned you, the dice at The Skive Toad have a foul taint. Bedeviled, some would say."

"Those low-eyed cruks are cheating, more than like," Nim muttered.

"And I was just about to win it all back when some page boy come tugging at me elbow. He looked like you roused him out of a dead dream."

"You know, there's several brothels on Canal Street. It's a little more fun to lose your coin there," Fraenk said.

Stonebridge sat heavily on the bench beside him.

"If I didn't have foul luck, I'd have none at all," Nim complained.

"Come on. We've got work," Fraenk slapped his thighs and stood. Nim sighed again.

When the light caught his face, one could see that Fraenk was human—and a handsome one at that. He had light brown skin, high cheekbones, and an angular jaw. Fraenk was no longer a young man, yet only wisps of gray had begun to sprout in the thin, dark stubble on his chin. His brown eyes were deep and seemed to view all the lies and secrets a man had in his soul. But he also bore a playful smile that threatened to appear with every wry remark. While some men bore the marks of a life fighting with their hands, Fraenk's preferred weapon was his mind. His scars couldn't be seen with the eyes.

Fraenk adjusted his dark green wool cloak. Torch light glinted off the Arch Preceptor's pin, displaying prominently on his lapel: emblems of a parchment roll pierced with a dagger. These were the only articles considered proper uniforms for the job. It meant they were on official business.

Stonebridge stood again with some effort and stretched. Fraenk handed Nim the scrap of paper.

"What's this? You finally teach one of those skrates how to draw?"

Nim turned it, trying unsuccessfully to find an orientation that would make the symbols yield a meaning.

"Rat runes. Language of the streets," Fraenk answered. "It means our duty hearkens. And we have no more time to waste."

"At this hour? Gods... You really don't ever sleep, do you, Arch Preceptor?" Nim yawned.

"The business of the Blackroot family never sleeps, either. And we are its eyes and ears."

Fraenk slipped on a pair of black eel skin gloves and turned. Stonebridge started to follow, then was caught by a realization. He turned back to the bench where Fraenk had been sitting.

"Might I inquire about something, sir?"

"By all means. Our job is to ask questions."

"Forgive the personal nature, but most elves come out here to stare into the night pool—search for wisdom from the ancestor or somesuch... But that's not how I find you. So were you here just staring at a wall? Is that a weird *human* thing?"

Fraenk gave a bewildered look back over his shoulder.

"Oh yes. You mean that wall. It is quite intriguing. Do you recognize it?"

"I've seen a wall before, sir. Possibly two."

"But have you actually *looked* at it?"

At first glance, the masonry remained merely tan blocks crawling with delicate vines; perhaps etched with some kind of decorative flourish. But then he saw it: the worn bas-relief carving of a battle, or more accurately—a siege. The stylized figures of elven heroes at the top of the city firing arrows down at the grotesquely proportioned humans below. In one panorama, the scene told the tale of the nigh-unstoppable human army with vastly greater numbers, storming the gates of Arathes and being completely slaughtered by the tiny garrison of elves as they bravely defended their home. Now, after centuries passed and a thousand rainstorms, their features softened and chipped with slender vines crawling through the cracks.

"It is, of course, the great myth of our city. The Siege of Arathes. According to records, during the First Crusade, Monarch Lochlain Blackforger the Hard-Bitten called in old General Eloain Windgrass, who was said to possess the wit and courage of a recently topped chicken. This was the very same commander who couldn't be trusted to command a regular army, mind you, and the Monarch tells him to establish a frontier outpost to reinforce the armies fighting the wicked Ozreus of Tigrean. But what does Windgrass know about building castles? Enough to know he should get someone else to do it. So in order to build this critical fortification, the general, using all his aforementioned headless-chicken wisdom, contracted none other than—"

"—Lysorian the Clever. Yes, I know this. Every child in the city does."

"Of course. The great genius who designed Arathes as an elaborate trap. Each level rising to rain hell down on those below. And it worked devastatingly well. An entire army grew feathers that day and met their heathen dirt gods. No surrender, no quarter. Killed them to a man. Killed their horses too, which I think was excessive."

"It seemed like you were going to tell me something I didn't already know, sir," Nim scratched his shoulder.

"Well, did you know that early manuscripts call him Lysorian the *Chaos-Touched*? By those accounts, he was quite mad and did more than dabble in the dark arcane. Rumored to have even made a pact with the Infernal, Hylarr, to grant him his genius mind for murderous traps. The Graysages have worked hard to keep that bit buried in their vault at the Great Library. Add on another thousand years of various construction, and you get the wonderful mess that the city is today."

"Wait. Do they even have a vault in the Great Library?" Stonebridge's eyes narrowed, skeptical.

"My point being, you've probably passed these carvings for years without notice. But they're <u>everywhere</u> when you choose to look. Built into the very fabric of Arathes."

"It's just a... decoration. A flourish on a wall," Stonebridge waved dismissively. "Like you said, they're everywhere."

"Indeed. As if we all need a reminder."

Fraenk strode away in the direction of the entrance of the estate, leaving Nim standing to contemplate the wall. Even though the stones didn't change, the details of it seemed to emerge. The elves, almost godlike in their tower, were raining their wrath down. Their faces were placid, not fearful. Mouths curled up in the slightest smile.

"Huh. So walls are not just a place to piss," Nim shrugged, then followed after Fraenk, out of the garden and into a city that would soon awaken.

2

AFTER A WINDING RIDE down through the streets of Arathes, Fraenk and Nim slowed their mares on the vast main avenue that gave onto an impressive view to the harbor of Lake Ewyn. When the imposing entrance of the Lower Market came into view, they dismounted and led their horses closer. The iron gate was typically closed and locked at this hour, but they could see it was cracked just wide enough to admit a man.

Someone must be inside.

The Lower Market Bazaar of Blackroot district lacked both the upscale offerings and high-end clientele that the Grand Market of Arathes in Hardoak district had, but in terms of the variety of goods from across the world, it was second to none. During the day, it was home to hundreds of stalls that commenced brisk commerce, voices ringing out in a babel of languages. Both elven kind and humans alike came to barter for Gazean hot spices, skeins of rough woolen yak yarn from Vigabrock, dragon-fired crystal dishware from distant Sho, aromatic tobacco, beer by the barrel, white-stringed Kamlyn lyres, dark Tigraenian cutlery, and ripe, aromatic fruits from Ophidaaran isles, all on offer. Not to mention countless other goods that weren't strictly legal but had vendors just the same. For a city so obsessed with one's status, it seemed to be one of the few places where both elves and humans met on equal terms, without an air of pretense, family, or station.

The bazaar was nestled in a wide stone courtyard, hemmed in on three sides by tall buildings, where the merchants and their families lived and carried out business. In the center was pressed with an assemblage of canvas stalls for the transient vendors. Those with imported goods fresh from the docks had to be carted in every morning and out every night. The gate was locked at the night bell, but traders knew it was far from secure.

"Wait here," Fraenk said, handing his reins to his underling. "I'll put an ear to the whispers. See what's amiss."

Nim had no sooner lashed the pair of horses to one of the potted palm trees that lined the avenue when a tiny scream came from overhead. Nim scrambled back startled by a pair of feuding, or perhaps coupling, skrates, which tumbled noisily from the fronds. They twisted midair, landing lightly feet-first on the stones, nearly raking Stonebridge with their sharp claws.

"Ulf's Hammer!" Nim cursed, taking a few more steps away from their nasty teeth and mildly poisonous saliva. The larger one narrowed his yellow eyes and seemed ready to charge him until he clapped his hands and shouted, making it retreat. It rose into a two-legged run, scrambling across the courtyard and then wedging its body into an open drainage pipe. The other gave its scaly skin a few irritated licks, then with a screech, it clambered up the wall and out of sight. The creature's delicate claws could be heard clicking across the clay roof tiles as it ran.

Nim looked back to see Fraenk standing near the alley across the thorough-fare. A cluster of filthy street kids in ragged garments gathered around him, and he was speaking in an urgent tone with them. All had patchy, close-cropped hair, which made it hard to determine their gender. They were stick-thin and probably crawling with lice and fleas. The residents of the city rarely, if ever, spoke to these kids except to clout them away when they begged for a spare copper coin or suspiciously sidled too close to an unguarded trader's cart.

To the criminal element of the city, street kids were seen as a nuisance on a level with the skrates. Pickpockets and barrel bandits who were too small to take anything important, but an annoyance nonetheless. Nim watched with curiosity as Fraenk spoke to them like he would another citizen. They gestured. Fraenk nodded. He asked something, and they pointed. And when they concluded their business, Nim heard the distinctive clink as Fraenk dropped a trio of copper coins into the tallest boy's hands. The kids quickly scampered off down the street, the youngest among them calling out with delighted whoops.

After Fraenk returned, Nim folded his arms and waited for an explanation. When none was forthcoming, he asked:

"Getting a line on the best begging corners, sir?"

"It's part of how I stay so well informed. There's none who sees more than the alley rats."

"Ah. So it was them that sent you the cipher."

"I taught them a few shapes to mark if they needed to pass a message. And of course, it's important to keep your informants eager to share."

Fraenk proceeded up to the market gates, where a loose gathering of humans and a pair of curious Firbolgs stopped to peer through the bars and whisper rumors to one another. Seeing the preceptors, the conversation stopped entirely until after Fraenk and Nim had slipped inside. Fraenk pulled the gate shut behind them.

"The 'rats' said there's two partisans already in there already. But they raised the summoning call and more are likely on the way. We need to go quickly."

"They say what happened?" Nim asked.

"Nothing good."

As they strode quickly past the long list of canvas stalls and shuttered shops, Fraenk felt a dark foreboding begin to creep into his chest. This was no place for real trouble, least of all in the early hours of the morning. During the day, there was always the heated and almost athletic bartering over overpriced goods. This sometimes devolved into verbose curses involving impossible violations to the other's bodily orifices, but this wasn't meant to be taken literally nor as an affront. Cursing and haggling for an immaculately struck bargain was, in fact, one of the Lower Market's charms. This spirited deal-making rarely came to violence, however. There was occasionally the random scuffle over an allegedly rigged scale or counterfeit good. Even a hard cuff to a would-be pickpocket or alley rat. And any true criminal in the market got a definitive beating by the merciless partisans assigned to its security.

Now walking past these closed and darkened stalls felt like a midnight stroll through a mausoleum. It was all dark shadows and blind corners. Fraenk looked back to make sure Nim was still behind him. He spied the half-elf a few booths back, having paused to admire the lurid painting on a shop canvas that sold women's erotic night garments.

Fraenk whistled softly through his teeth to get Nim's attention. When he had caught up, Fraenk indicated back over his shoulder with a tilt of the head. The flickering glow of orange light bounced off the facades of the building just around the corner.

"Sorry, sir. I was just..."

"Nevermind that. Stay close and don't let these partisans tell us our business," Fraenk said.

"Yes sir," Nim set his lip and gave a single, determined nod. Fraenk was surprised by a feeling of strength with having the half-elf at his side. He returned the nod, and they strode forth.

They rounded past a stall with tall draping silks slung on cane poles, and the far corner of the plaza came into view. And then Fraenk knew why he was feeling this sense of dread, for there ahead of them were two men visible under the light of a lantern and, at their feet, a lifeless body on the ground.

The boy crouched on his heels in the alley, angry and waiting. The deep gash on his chin had finally stopped bleeding. Dried blood on his neck cracked and flaked to the ground. The throb of pain from the cut pulsed with each heartbeat, but it was a distant hurt. His small fist gripped the broken sword tang that still held a partial blade. A pitiful excuse for a weapon that he'd stolen from the blacksmith shop's scrap pile. Despite being pitted and rusty, it still held an edge sharp enough to cleave flesh.

The boy was trembling now from adrenaline and rage. He realized he was crying and tried to palm away the tears, only to get a fresh burst of pain from the swollen, bruised eye where they had punched and kicked him repeatedly. It only made him angry. He leaned forward and peered out the alley again.

He caught sight of the older group of boys up the street coming towards him. The ringleader, a thick-bodied brute named Mudge, had just made some joke, which had made all except one of them cackle with laughter. The butt of the joke lashed out, and the lackeys scrapped and jostled for a moment until their leader ordered it to stop. Even though he was probably only a year or two older than the young boy, Mudge was somehow a foot taller and two stone heavier. He had a bovine frame and doughy gut that made him impossible to beat in a fight by himself, let alone with his entire gang raining blows down. And as skinny and malnourished as the boy was, the fight—if it could be called that—was over almost as soon as it started.

He woke up hours later in a hog's pen, his body in agony as he'd never experienced before. That night, as he shivered under the only tattered blanket they'd left him, he made a dark vow to himself. And in the morning, when he trusted his legs to carry him again, he retrieved the homemade dagger from its hiding spot.

Now Mudge's reign of terror on the streets would end. Not just for him—the boy no longer cared what happened to himself—this was for all the other alley rats whom this bully and his gang had preyed upon. No more beatings, no more thievery from those who had nothing to begin with, and none of the other violations that left street children vacant-eyed and withdrawn. This would be righteous, terrible justice for those who had no other recourse.

He heard their voices getting louder. They were almost to him. The boy gripped the dagger tightly and hoped his aching body would hold up for just a bit longer.

Just on the other side of the corner, Mudge's pubescent voice cracked as he tried to call his group's attention to something in the road. There was cruelty in his tone. The boy knew this would be his moment. He stood, fist clenched on the blade, and—

"Say, lad, pardon. Could I ask a favor of you?"

A man's voice came from behind. The boy was so focused on Mudge, he hadn't even heard the man approach. Startled, the boy lost his footing as he spun around to see who had gotten the drop on him.

This human man was wide in the shoulders and thick in the waist. His hair and beard were black and trimmed close to his head. His face, ruddy from working in front of ovens all day. He wore a white linen shirt with the sleeves removed and a heavy white apron tied around him like a tent. His entire body was dusted with a fine layer of flour. In the thick towel in his hands, he held a dark brown loaf of bread that steamed mightily, direct from the oven. The smell of it hit him immediately—rich, toasty, and sweet. And his knees wobbled under him. The boy recognized the man as the chief baker who operated the shop in whose alley he was currently skulking.

The boy quickly slipped the broken knife behind his back to hide it. Adults could make a lot of trouble for a street kid if they suspected you were up to mischief, and this boy, covered in blood and filth, looked exactly as if he'd sworn to bring all hells and damnation on a quest for vengeance. But the baker raised an expectant eyebrow.

"I'm very displeased, lad. I'll have you know that." He said, but his face didn't look troubled. The boy looked for an escape, but Mudge and his gang were just around the corner on the street, and this large baker was blocking his only exit through the alley. His brain worked feverishly, trying to decide which direction, if any, he might be able to go. His aching ribs and fatigued muscles told him to give up now and accept his fate.

"Sir?" was all he could manage to say.

"*Well, look at this bread!*" *the baker said with displeasure, his brow creasing down. "It's a disgrace. I blame myself. Totally ruined! Why, I can't serve this to my customers! They'd toss me out of the city onto my ear. Tell me, lad. Is this loaf ruined?*"

"*I...I couldn't say,*" *the boy stammered.*

"*Well, of course not, standing way over there and just lookin' at it. You gotta taste it to know for true.*" *A playful tone crept into the baker's voice, even though he still looked angry. His large hands tore open the loaf, letting out an eruption of hot steam. The boy's mouth instantly began to water, and a low growl from his stomach seemed to echo in the alley.*

"*Well, come on!*" *The baker held a chunk of bread towards him. The boy couldn't think anymore. His caution was abandoned by his traitorous stomach. He staggered forward and grabbed off a small piece from the half loaf. It was in his mouth and swallowed before he even realized it.*

"*Aaah... That's no good. You ate it so fast, you didn't even taste it. Here, lad, you need a big piece, so you can tell me plain. Sit, lad. Sit.*"

The baker swept a hand towards a nearby crate. The boy did as he was asked, too hungry to resist. The baker placed the entire half loaf in his waiting hands, and he immediately began trying to stuff the entire thing into his mouth.

"*Slow down, boy. You gotta actually taste it. There. Now, what say you? How bad is it?*"

He forced himself to stop and just chew the large chunk that was already in his mouth. The baker raised an eyebrow expectantly.

"*It's... terrible bread. Probably the worst I've had,*" *the boy said finally and took another bite.*

"*I knew as much.*" *The baker replied in mock despair. He sat down on the crate beside the boy, which creaked under his weight. The boy was only halfway through the bread, but his shrunken stomach was already beginning to protest. He stopped and just felt the warmth in his hands. His aching ribs, swollen eye, and cut chin—he didn't feel any of it. Just a glow of contentment he'd not known since—*

"*Good thing I ran into you out here, lad,*" *the baker said, finally. "I could have made a bad mistake. One that I would sorely regret. One that would have cost me everything.*"

The boy turned to the sound of braying laughter on the street. Mudge and his gang were throwing rocks at a limping dog, chasing it down the street. He suddenly felt very foolish, even thinking of taking on the brute. He would have been killed.

"Well, I suppose you'll be wanting a bit of sweet buttermilk to wash down that horrible bread with, eh lad?"

The boy couldn't speak. He only nodded and began to cry. The big baker stood and started back towards his shop. Then he turned.

"My name's Miken, by the by. What do they call you?"

The boy looked up and managed to squeak out one word.

"Fraenk."

3

"WHERE IS OUR BACKUP, sergeant?" The partisan Lt. Doran Leafwater whined. "They should be here by now!"

"Stand to your post and close that flap!" The gruff sergeant snapped back from where he stood near the wall.

Holding a lantern high only cast a thin light into the lanes of the bazaar and sent more of it back onto Doran's fresh face. His crest of silken brown hair that poked from under his officer's cap tickled irritatingly at his brow, and he now understood why the older officers wore their hair swept back instead of the current style, which was trendy among elves his age.

Doran spotted a loose thread dangling from the sleeve of his crisp gray uniform. He plucked at it, silently cursing the cut-rate Caffery Street seamstress, who was the only one available to tailor the ill-fitting garment on short notice—which also meant at great personal expense. It was an insult compounded by the smirking Partisan quartermaster, who told Doran that it was a "standard" sized uniform. But when Doran had tried the uniform on, it hung off his narrow frame like a juggler's pavilion. It was just another of dozens of incidents and slights to him, meant to disrespect and demean him. However, if they'd intended to haze him into quitting, they would find Doran Leafwater made of sterner stuff.

Doran had taken it as a point of pride that he was both the youngest recruit and newest Partisan on the force. No amount of low grumbling from the others would make him apologize for having beat out the other arguably 'more qualified' candidates for this coveted position. And unlike many others who had it gifted to them as a privilege of their illustrious family name, his achievement was earned in a more legitimate way. In fact, it was hard won by a strategic campaign by his overbearing mother of called-in favors, generous bribes, and outright cajoling to gain him the coveted slot. What other way was there?

There came a time in nearly every elf's life when their parents suddenly developed an unreasonable attitude about allowing their children to live freely in their house and pay for all their needs. One day they'd be doing their usual complaining about untidiness or a youngling's supposed lack of life goals, then suddenly it would be a firm declaration that one should be self-sufficient. Doran had heard this speech many times, but on this occasion, his mother was actually serious enough to secure him a job. A position which he must maintain in good standing if he ever wanted to return to his life of luxury someday. Doran threw the best tantrum he could, but it was somehow ineffective. She had become immune. He finally concluded that if one must endure the indignity of labor, then he could do far worse than the enforcement of district and city-wide laws. Doran was convinced he could bide his time until his elevated rank afforded such a position where the only 'work' he had to do was extend a hand out to accept a bribe.

Doran sighed and kicked a loose stone that bounced and skittered into the darkness. His shift had barely started, and he was already counting the bells until it was over.

Why did life insist upon being so hard all the time? Doran groaned inwardly. Humans had it easy. All they had to do was go about their pathetic, meaningless lives with minimal interference or societal expectations. They worked menial, laborsome jobs and came home in the evening to their hungry, squalling brood, but their purpose was simple and unimportant.

Doran, on the other hand, carried burdens that would shatter the feeble mind of a human. He had to keep track of everything: their army's progress in the war, which apparently had been going well, to turmoil within the Sarmattian kingdom and even the salacious drama within the elven society of Arathes itself. There was a constant pressure to keep track of which family names mattered, which ones were ostracized, and the relative ranking of everyone else in between. An elf with enough status didn't have to deal with indignities such as work and certainly didn't have to take orders from any sniveling humans like this sergeant who tormented him. It was yet another buzzing resentment that Doran harbored against his no-good father that his own family name of Leafwater wasn't much closer to the top of that list. The fates of birth could sometimes be so cruel.

That didn't stop him from dreaming of one day when he would be the leader of a prominent family—maybe even breaking centuries of tradition to make Leafwater the newest member of the High Council.

"They'd have to change the name," Doran mused idly.

The 'Ten Families' as they were known each held a seat on the High Council of Arathes. They were simple enough for Doran to remember, based on the district they controlled and what each of those districts had to offer. Starting at the top of the hill in the Summer Palace was High Lord Whiteleaf, the child prince. The way he was spoken of, High Lord Whiteleaf was but a whelp, barely grown into the point of his ears. Somehow he had yet to be matched with a betrothed and was therefore without an official heir or progeny. He lived a dreamy existence within the walls of the palace, seeking whatever knowledge or pleasure he desired. It made Doran grind his teeth with envy every time he thought of it.

As for the Ten Families themselves, they were no better than the supposedly 'lesser' elven names and had certainly not achieved their lofty station by any act of heroism or virtue. They had just as many secrets, crimes, and scandals, as Doran well knew from being in the proximity of his gossipy mother and her bored, wine-soaked friends.

Without any real effort, he could immediately run through the entire reprobate list and recount what each was most notorious for. The Bellspire family was synonymous with the city's administration and laws of both the civil and magical variety. They enjoyed quietly giving preferential treatment to allies—especially those with gold. The nefarious Twinsprigs were wealthy society elves who held no discernible redeeming qualities and yet seemed to be invested in every single endeavor the city undertook, legitimate or otherwise. Apparently, the city's criminal element still referred to kickbacks to the family as "the Twinsprig tax."

The senile Graysages were as ancient as the dusty, dried-up old library and museums they managed, spending all of their day with noses buried in books. Their only importance seemed to bubble up anytime someone had an ancient territorial dispute they wanted to settle, then one could count on a well-bribed scholar to conveniently find the proper ancient supporting document. And their exact opposites, the gregarious and ostentatious Amberflax clan, who maintained the creative arts, music, sculpture, and theater districts. They were given to so many scandals—many of them happening concurrently—that it was impossible to name a most egregious one. "Overwhelm by volume" was not just their philosophy for singing, apparently.

The Hardoaks were shrewd in business and cutthroat everywhere else, even between their own kin. One had to read a contract with extra care and many times over before entering a bargain with their ilk. The Coldfrost's were tough and serious-minded elves who worked in the city's industrial sector. It was a dangerous and often deadly place, especially for those who caused them trouble. The Sweetrose family served the city's vices, such as brothels, smoke dens, and the fighting pits. They were not only first-hand witnesses to much of the respected societies' illicit behavior; they frequently held the blackmail evidence to back it up.

Of all the High Council families, the ambitious and dangerous Fernbrooks were the ones to watch. They had slipped in both wealth and status following the untimely and suspicious death of the wealthy Lady Simeras Fernbrook. She had married from a lesser house, and her husband Malgraye had already taken the unusual step of adopting her surname upon their marriage, which Lady Simeras' children hotly protested he was attempting to subsume their lineage. These protests died along with those making them shortly after the new Lord Malgraye Fernbrook took power over the district. Some complained it was an injustice, and yet was anything ever done to set it right? The High Court's inaction became tacit approval, and the Fernbrooks' new dark legacy began.

To Doran's mind, the least cunning and therefore least respected of the Ten Families was Lord Cullor Mosswater and his sewer-dwelling misfits living in the tunnels under the mountain. Their major sin, other than being uncultured and foul-smelling, was their refusal to participate in most of the honorable Elvish traditions at all. They were low, both in elevation and status, for they lived and worked alongside the dwarves, kobolds and humans who maintained the city's supposedly important hidden infrastructure functions. It was all leaky sewer pipes and greasy elevator gears to Doran, which was beneath the dignity of what it meant to be elvenkind. None coveted their district, and therefore they had nothing to worry about from other families.

And finally, there was Blackroot. It was true that they were prosperous and controlled the bulk of the Port of Arathes. But they were also near traitorous for being so closely comfortable with the humans of the city—treating them as nearly equals. This was nearly the worst breach of protocol as could be found in Arathes. Humans were sneaky and ambitious. They stole and were violent. They lacked an elf's grace, and their reflexes were slow comparatively, but there was something about them that made Doran uncomfortable to be around them by himself. The elves had worked hard to remind humans of their lower status, but here in Blackroot district, they moved with an ease and fearlessness that Doran Leafwater misliked immensely.

And now, to his deep chagrin, Blackroot was where Doran found himself stationed. Not only that, but forced to follow the orders of a human. He could not wait to secure his promotion and never come this far down into the city ever again. In this, he was resolute.

But he had to somehow convince his crusty old supervisor he was worthy of the partisan title first. His sergeant, a skarking human named Harland Hobb, who was soft about the shoulders and sported a bushy white mustache. But supposedly he had served in Blackroot district as long as young Leafwater had been alive. Despite the fact that he was just a human, Hobb was a veteran partisan and acquired a supposed wealth of insight and experience from his years of service. Leafwater was obliged to at least *pretend* to be attentive to this worthless relic, but he quietly suspected that he was being foisted upon him as some test of Doran's resolve.

And so his partisan training began. Which meant a fortnight of third shift guard duty among the lowest, vilest parts of the Blackroot district, all the while fighting to stay awake during Hobb's unbearable instruction. The grizzled old badger was very good at yelling and giving Doran a difficult time, but otherwise worthless. He had no sense of the importance of elves, nor their venerated traditions of leisure time and sumptuous foods. He was boorish and mean. But Doran consoled himself that humans didn't live for that long, and old Hobb was nearly at the end of his life anyway. Perhaps he'd do Doran the very good favor of just dying. Was that too much to ask?

Leafwater peered out into the darkness, trying to will the reinforcement partisans into existence, but the lantern light this close only made his vision swim with opaque chromatic blobs. A whole unit of Tigraen war riders could have been approaching, and he wouldn't have seen it until the very last.

The elf decided he was fine with being night blind, however. Anything preferable to looking down at the revolting body behind him.

The pathetic old human was a mountain of flesh, face-down on the stones. He had a long, ratty skirt of gray hair that ringed his bald dome, which draped over his features. Not that his identity mattered whatsoever. No human warranted this amount of fuss—especially not one who was unceremoniously ended in such a way.

There was a long dagger protruding from his back, and dark blood soaked his white tunic and pants, glossy black in the dim light. It made a wide pool out from his body, tracing the seams and cracks of the cobblestones like some unholy mortar, congealing underneath him.

It was the old man's eye that was particularly upsetting. He turned toward him with a surprised, questioning look—the same way that the foul-smelling livestock looked as they were driven from Pileusian barges into the auction pens of Arathes harbor. That eye—that single, terrible eye—peeping out from the thicket of long hair was wrong in a way Leafwater couldn't describe. Just dull pools of darkness. It made his stomach roil. He had to toe the man's hair over it with his boot to cover that horrible, accusatory gaze.

As one raised in the Elven philosophical tradition, Leafwater knew he was supposed to feel pity for the death of a lesser creature, but seeing this bloated beast up close, he could only conjure disgust. All that blood, with its coppery smell. And Leafwater was forced to stand here and endure it. What's one more dead human? He might as well be standing guard over the carcass of a dog. When he had expressed his very reasonable misgivings to the sergeant earlier, the old man's face went red, and Doran actually thought the fool was going to hit him.

A distant bell tolled five strikes, and the horizon was just starting to lighten—signs that this night might finally be over. Leafwater clenched his jaw and stole a glance over his shoulder.

"Hear that? It's been an hour, and we're left standing out here like some hoddy, round-eared valets."

Doran expected some kind of sharp reproach, but Sergeant Hobb didn't acknowledge the insult.

He was twenty paces away near the bakery, and his focus was not on the petulant lieutenant. He stood, looking like a man ready to defend himself, his scarred hands subtly gripped and re-gripped the metal baton. The sergeant's full and focused attention was on the ominous murder suspect at his feet—the *elven* suspect.

When they arrived at the scene, Hobb and Leafwater had found him right where he was now, seated with his back to the wall and tilting drunkenly. Sergeant Hobb had asked if the elf had seen what happened to the dead man, and he freely admitted to the killing. He seemed proud of it. Leafwater may have been a novice to the enforcement of law, but even he knew that there would be repercussions for such a brazen act, even for an elf.

Doran watched as the suspect stretched his legs out laconically and crossed them at the ankles. His body was lean and sinewy; it seemed to carry a dangerous air of violence. The elf was dressed in a filthy military-style gambeson that was still wet with blood. Long pointed ears protruded from the greasy silver hair that hung down between his knees. His torn breeches were soaked dark from the puddle of piss he was sitting in. He either didn't notice or didn't care.

Leafwater could hear the dark figure muttering quietly to himself in a mad polemic that slipped between the common Eastron and Elvish. He seemed to be singing snippets of a marching jody that soldiers used to keep their feet in step. It was filled with a colorful slew of invectives and graphic descriptions of prodigious genitalia. The reek that came off him could be smelled across the distance. Booze and piss—and some others smell like burning.

The entire situation sat very ill with Doran. In Arathes, especially, elves were supposed to comport themselves with ethereal grace and gentle dignity—at least where the public could see. They were called to be higher than any other species but the Lyn-Tyrians. Never given to the base desires of their lessers, like drunkenness, and especially not murder. His mother's gossip notwithstanding, Doran had been around enough elves to see a fair amount of hypocrisy in those assertions, but this was an unprecedented situation. There was indeed something eminently wrong with this elf, and it made Doran suddenly happy to be as far away from him as possible.

The elf moved suddenly to scratch his cheek, and Doran saw the sergeant flinch. It then occurred to him that this veteran sergeant was actually scared. He was doing his best to hide it, but he had wide eyes, and his knuckles were white around the cudgel's grip. This sent a slew of troubling questions through his mind. *Who really was this elf? Were they in danger? If something did happen, could this geriatric old human even do anything?* Then Doran would be left to defend himself against a murderous elf, and what would happen then? The answers to all of these were less than comforting. The only thing he could think to do was firmly establish his authority. He knew elves, and they preferred order. He was the ranking partisan, after all. He just needed to sound confident, like he was in charge.

"Watch that prisoner, sergeant," Lt. Leafwater said, lowering his voice in what he imagined was a commanding tone.

"You keep your eye on the market, ya pointy-eared git!!" The sergeant snapped. "If I hear another slossing word outta you, I'll have you standing watch on Latrine Row so long you'll never get the stink of scit out of your fancy grays!"

Doran Leafwater blanched like he'd been slapped. No human *dared* insult him like that!

A lilting giggle came from somewhere, high and sweet—perhaps pleasant in any situation but this one. Both men realized the source at the same time. The scary elf was laughing. An icy shiver raced up Doran's spine. *"You let a human talk to you that way, brother?"* The suspect challenged in High Elvish.

"Quiet you!" Sergeant Hobb pinged the wall with his club near the elf's head. The suspect didn't even flinch. Hobb turned back to Leafwater.

"Just be ready to hail the reinforcements, Lieutenant. We'll fill them in on our situation when they get here," Hobb spoke more measuredly.

"And what situation is that?"

Just then, two men in long capes suddenly melted out of the darkness of the Lower Market Bazaar. Just appeared as if from the night itself.

Lieutenant Doran Leafwater gave a startled yelp and nearly added to the list of people in the vicinity who'd recently wet themselves.

4

Preceptor Nim Stonebridge watched the young elf cycle quickly through a range of emotions. His initial terror changed to relief, perhaps when he realized that they weren't bandits or monsters. Then finally the elf's mouth began gaping open and closed, fish-like, as he recognized these incoming strangers were not the allies he'd been expecting.

Panicked, the lieutenant fumbled for the iron club on his belt, getting it comically tangled by the loop.

"You! Wait—stay there!" He shouted as he tugged.

Nim had seen his share of brawls throughout his years as a dive tavern gambler. And had even been a reluctant participant in a few as well, so he knew a dangerous man when he saw one. This reed of a lad before them, playing dress-up partisan, was only dangerous in what misery his wealthy family could wreak if their precious boy was accosted. So Nim wasn't concerned about the club the boy was struggling to put into play, nor did he want to take abuse from it either.

Stonebridge moved laterally out to a flanking position away from Fraenk. He kept his thick hands open but ready in case it did become necessary for him to intervene. He knew Fraenk could handle himself as well, and it was a sight to behold. But it was beneath the dignity of the Arch Preceptor of Blackroot to have to defend himself, especially against the likes of this green whelp who stood jerking haplessly at his tangled cudgel.

"He's like to go blind keeping that up," Nim quipped as they stepped within the radius of the lantern light, now fully visible. Their preceptor service badges were on display from the front of their cloaks.

"Powers, Neversleep! I thought you was the Grim Shade, himself!" Sergeant Hobb gasped in relief when he recognized them. He left the wall and approached where the three of them were gathered in the torchlight.

Lieutenant Leafwater had finally freed his club and was now wagging it at them threateningly.

"This is partisan business, human! Be off with you or... or earn a clout!" He blustered.

"Put that down, you damn fool!" Hobb scolded. "That's the Arch Preceptor of Blackroot. This is his district."

"So?" Doran Leafwater puffed out his chest. "Partisans enforce the laws of the city by the authority of the High Lord himself! We don't curtsy and scrape to some district window-peeper, like some fainting handmaid!"

Hobb rolled his eyes and sighed. He gave Fraenk an apologetic look.

"Leafwater, you're too young to have any good sense, but use those pointed ears to listen for once. You're gonna be on your own patrol someday, and if you don't wanna be spending all your time getting lost in blind alleys or having buttons snatched off your uniform by the alley rats, then you play nice with the local preceptors. They know the district. They can help make our job easy or vex our every step and turn it into a sweat march down to Geth's Door."

Leafwater paused to consider this. His ego at odds with his laziness.

"But you're the big scit in charge, lieutenant. Play it how you see it." The sergeant took a step back.

Nim watched the indignant Doran Leafwater lower his club to his side but size them both up with an icy glare, first to the ears then their badges. His haughty expression curdled when he realized where he really stood in the pecking order.

"Don't mind the greenling lieutenant, Fraenk. He's still wet with his mother's womb water," the sergeant added. "He don't pin on the copper twig until he lasts a moon turn under my watch. And he won't do that until he learns to show them some respect. Right, Leafwater? Weren't you just about to apologize?"

Nim watched amused as the lieutenant's face twisted with anger, then attempted to return to calm.

"I beg your pardon, Arch Preceptor, _sir_," he sneered with venomous civility.

"As you were, Lieutenant. They call me Neversleep. Welcome to the service," Fraenk extended a hand. The elf hesitated. Nim would've taken odds on whether the kid was going to shake or not. In the end, Fraenk's calm smile won out, and the lieutenant accepted the handshake.

"Lieutenant Doran Leafwater. How do you do?" he said tersely.

"Very good. Now we're all friends," Fraenk smiled. "Say, lieutenant, we could use a man at the gate to keep anyone else from walking in here."

"Yes, I'll go. I can direct the reinforcements when they finally arrive." Leafwater looked all too relieved to be out of there. He gave the sergeant a final petulant half-smile before striding away with the lantern.

With the lieutenant and his light gone, the area once again fell into darkness. Fraenk pulled out a small round glass bottle from his cloak and shook it vigorously. A brilliant, soft white light flared from it.

"What are you doing here, Fraenk?" The sergeant asked when Leafwater was out of earshot.

"We're just gonna have a look around if you don't mind, sergeant. Killings are not usually our game, but this one caught my attention."

"Well, as you can see, it's already well in hand, Neversleep. No need to trouble yourself. We got the one that did it right here. The sergeant tried to sound dismissive, but Nim could read the stress in his voice. And there was something about the figure seated in the shadows beside him that gave Nim a dread that he couldn't articulate. He realized the strange elf was watching them.

"Keep him there. We'll have some questions for him in a moment.

Sergeant Hobb faded back to his spot near the wall.

With the sergeant gone, the two preceptors looked at each other.

"Well?" Nim asked his boss, unsure of what came next.

"Now we do our job."

Fraenk took a small bottle of golden liquid from his cloak and downed a swallow of it. He replaced it and retrieved a hand-sized wooden plank with a circular notch cut in one corner. On the plank were pinned several sheets of paper that fit the area of the board and a short quill. He unstoppered a small jar of black ink and fit it into the notch on the board.

Fraenk handed the paper and board to Nim.

"Take this. Preceptors are expected to keep notes on anything you investigate and submit reports every morning," Fraenk explained. "And keep your marks clear, so I can read it later."

Nim's brows pinched, but he nodded and took up the quill in an awkward grip that looked unpracticed in writing.

"First, we examine every detail. Remember: The smallest key opens the door to the largest palace."Fraenk crouched by the body, careful not to step in the congealed blood. He inspected the hilt of the long blade that sprouted from between the man's shoulder blades.

"It's a war dagger. Most likely part of a forged set. Fine craftsmanship."

"It's got that look about it," Nim agreed.

"War dagger. Part of a set," Fraenk said again, lifting a brow in the direction of the quill and paper.

"Oh, right," Nim dipped the quill and began scribbling notes.

Fraenk leaned in and took a closer look at the pommel.

"Gold and honeywood handle with inlay tracery. Chips of emerald too. Crest of an Owl ringed with double Fern wreaths. Copy that sigil. And the blacksmith's mark on the blade."

"Oh. That's the banner of House Greenbriar. Cousins to the Fernbrooks," Nim added, happy to contribute.

"I believe they call Lord Caldox 'The Owl of Greenbriar.' But he rode out with the Arathian host against Kreeg. Last I heard, he was commended for bravery at the Battle of Blacksteel's Ruin," Fraenk added. "So what is his dagger doing here?"

"Scratching this poor sod's back?"

Fraenk shot him a stern look. This was no time for jokes.

"Sorry, sir," Nim murmured in contrition. "Maybe it was stolen? I know a few lads that would pay a fist of gold for something like that."

"Possibly. But why use it in a murder? And why leave it behind?"

"Send a message—*Caldox sends his regards.*"

Fraenk darted his eyes over to the silver-haired elf, who now looked like he'd fallen asleep where he sat.

"Every assassin I've known had an aversion to getting caught."

"Then what?" Nim said as he sketched. Fraenk crabbed around to align himself with the dagger's handle, where it jutted amidst the wide expanse of the dead man's back. The dark blood soaking through his white tunic.

"No other wounds visible. Stuck him as he was walking away... He didn't see it coming," Fraenk said evenly. "So who's our unlucky soul?" Nim pointed to the man's covered face.

As he stood, Fraenk's eyes followed up from the handle of the dagger and the position of the man's body, like some grim ley line to the old building in the corner of the Lower Market Square—the bakery.

Fraenk's body went rigid as recognition dawned. He gave Nim an odd look, like one who'd just realized their doom had been sealed already, and it was now just occurring to them. Fraenk's solemn demeanor broke as he rushed to turn the man over, sweeping the hair back from his pallid face. The terrible surprise was still frozen there.

Nim didn't understand. The man was dead already—what could be worse than that?

Fraenk's mouth moved like he was going to speak, but his voice never came. The silence grew long.

"Uh... Judging by the smock, it looks like he worked here." Nim prompted. "Fraenk, did you know him?"

Fraenk took an unsteady step back, and his heel kicked something on the ground near the baker's outstretched hand. Nim watched as he slowly bent and picked it up. It looked like a stone at first, but as he turned it over in his hands, the shape yielded in his fingers, soft and porous. It was a loaf of bread that had been torn in half.

"His name was Miken," Fraenk said, his tone heavy with emotion. "He saved my life."

Fraenk Neversleep took the bottle of amber booze from his cloak and drank until it was empty. His mind felt like it was on fire. *Why did he not recognize Miken?*

Many years had passed since they last spoke. Time had eroded the man's strong crop of black mane into a silver sweep around his ears. He'd also gone as soft and round as the balls of dough he slid into the bread oven in the back of his shop. The years had taken a toll on this man, or perhaps had been too generous, for there was little about him that Fraenk recognized.

Or perhaps Fraenk's mind saw him and refused to believe it was true, for even now a voice in his mind kept repeating, *"That's not him. That's not Miken."*

But it was. The shock and denial were giving way to an acceptance that his friend was well and truly gone.

It was sinking in that Fraenk would never get a chance to truly thank this man for all he had done. It was an ignominious and ugly end to the closest thing he had to a parent after he'd come to the city. How many times as a boy had he gone to Miken when he hadn't eaten in days? And the kind old man produced a fresh loaf of brown, ready to forebear on Frank's garbage-refined palate, assessing its flavor, texture, and even the color of his bakecraft. Never once did Miken ask for a single coin. And years later, when Miken married a jolly, moon-faced woman named Ellea and they had two rambunctious lads of his own, he never once stopped treating him much like his own son.

A wave of fury rose in him. Someone killed his friend, and this wrong would not go unanswered. Fraenk felt something warm in his fist. He looked down to see he had crushed the loaf of bread he had been holding. The bread. It was the bread that stayed his hand in the alley, those many years ago. And here it was in his hands once more, crumbling between his fingers.

Then Fraenk noticed there was a small, firm shape in the crumbled crust. He brushed the bread pieces aside and saw it was a dark pendant on a tarnished silver chain. A painfully dull-looking stone with a blue-green tinge to it—perhaps the kind a young girl would wear, but only the kind of shy, withdrawn girl who wanted no one to pay her any attention. You could buy its equivalent for a half copper from any of the market vendors.

Instinctively, Fraenk dropped it into one of his cloak pockets. Something about it bothered him, but he couldn't concentrate. Not with this body at his feet and his murderer lounging just behind him. What Fraenk wanted to do was pull the dagger and plunge it into that elf's chest. No words. Just let him make that same surprised face as he died.

But no. That's not what Miken would have wanted. Fraenk could imagine Miken's voice in his head, urging calm. Telling him to think instead. Others were watching, and an impulsive act would be worse than doing nothing.

Fraenk let his fists unclench and straightened his back. Nim looked at him, concerned.

"Sir? Are you okay? Maybe we should go."

"Nonsense. We have a job to do. Let's go meet our new friend."

Fraenk strode with a brisk pace, up to the sergeant and his captive. Nim scrambled to keep up.

As they approached, the elf lolled his head back and burped, then groaned with relief. A rancid stench wafted off him that hung in the air. Fraenk caught a whiff of some other odor, like charred meat.

"Why isn't your criminal in chains, sergeant?" Fraenk demanded.

"He—he's an elf, Fraenk," Sergeant Hobb said, confused. "He ain't going nowhere."

"So I see. Get irons on him. *Now.*"

Hobb patted around for the cuffs on his belt but seemed to make no progress on Fraenk's order.

"I'm hungry. There was a loaf of brown around here somewhere. Fetch me that bread, roundie! It's my absolute favorite." The elf demanded, rubbing his temple. His long, thin finger with a dirty nail flicked impatiently in the vague direction of the dead man. Fraenk had to fight the urge to grab and bend the digit back until it broke.

"Get him on his feet!" Fraenk growled.

Nim and Hobb hooked the elf by the armpits and hoisted him to standing. He was surprisingly tall for his kind—about the height of a human. And Fraenk could see by the effort it took to get him upright that he was perilously strong as well. But he wavered drunkenly and tilted to steady himself against the wall.

"Where are the lovely sounds of *screams, my dear...*" The suspect sang a popular song with his own improvised lyrics.

With his belly pointed forward, the large embroidered sigil of Greenbriar was clearly visible on his stained gambeson. Its crest splashed with a spray of congealing blood, like the victor of some recent battle. Once again, the voice of Miken whispered a warning to Fraenk.

Tread carefully.

Elven families made for dangerous enemies. They had long memories and longer lifetimes. Greenbriar was the original family name of Lord Malgraye Fernbrook before his auspicious marriage elevated him to district lord. It was as if the Greenbriars were lifted as well, enjoying a newfound prominence in society. A fact that they enjoyed flaunting at every opportunity. So, if this elf was actually affiliated with the Greenbriars, as his uniform suggested, then even a partisan elf would be cautious about an improper arrest that could incur a host of problems from the district lord. This situation was becoming more fraught by the moment.

Worse, Fraenk could feel his concern for Elven decorum ebbing like water from a leaky bucket. All present understood the way their society protected even the very worst of them, just as a matter of course. The elf was only further illuminating what a ridiculous pantomime this was, which made Fraenk all the more infuriated.

Nim saw it too and caught Fraenk's arm.

"He's a Greenbriar, Fraenk," Nim warned. It was his turn to look worried.

Fraenk took a slow breath and nodded. Sergeant Hobb had taken two big steps back away, literally distancing himself from the whole situation.

The intoxicated elf looked first to Fraenk, then Nim.

"Why thank you, servants," the elf said drunkenly. "I was having some trouble with my feet. They're very disobedient right now. Must have been something in my cups."

"I don't believe we've met, Greenbriar," Fraenk said coolly. "I'm Arch Preceptor of Blackroot, Fraenk Neversleep. And you appear to be in the wrong district. Did you wander away from your guard post?"

"You have the honor of addressing <u>Bas</u> of House Greenbriar. Lord Caldox is my brother."

He leaned forward and smiled, letting his redolent breath wash over Fraenk. He blinked hard to keep his eyes from watering.

"I was just resting for a moment by this wall, *Arch Preceptor*. I must have overexerted myself. But I'm feeling better, and I'll be on my way now. This place is beginning to stink like a fat, dead human."

The elf took a wild, uneven step forward as if to walk away. Fraenk's hand shot up to his chest and stopped him. Then slowly pushed him firmly until his back touched the wall again.

"Ho there, Sir Greenbriar. We're still conversing."

The elf's sigh was somewhere between fatigue and annoyance.

"*Fine.* But you'll be letting me go soon enough."

Greenbriar gave a wet burp, then smiled. For an instant, Fraenk saw tiny black worms crawling on his lips. He swallowed, and then they were gone. At the same moment, another waft of the burning smell hit Fraenk—now mixed with smoke. This foul mix made his throat tighten, and a wave of nausea rose. Fraenk had to turn his head to keep from retching.

Nim saw Fraenk pause and seamlessly stepped in.

"Your uniform's dirty, chum. Were you in the war?" Nim brushed the officer's insignia stitching on the elf's gambeson. Bas' head swung over to glare at this impertinent half-elf who was being so familiar. He snapped his shoulder away from Nim's hand.

"Keep your hands off me or I'll show you what I did in the war!"

"A soldier, eh? Then what are you doing back here in Arathes? I thought the true sons of Greenbriar didn't just abandon their forces before the army was officially disbanded. There's a catchy name for that. What was it, Fraenk? Coward? Craven?"

"*Deserter.*"

That seemed to sober the elf up some. Irritation flashed on his face.

"Fools! Bas Greenbriar is a hero!" He hissed in anger. "They'll sing songs about me in Lamentation Square. The Amberflaxes will write plays and operas of my exploits!"

"Desertion is a crime, Greenbriar. Even for an elf," Fraenk said, sensing an opening.

"I'm no *skarking* deserter! The war is over! We <u>won</u>."

Fraenk and Nim exchanged looks. News of the army's exploits had been unanimously positive, but the elves did have a knack for turning propaganda into an art form. Literally, there were operas and dramatic reenactments of heroic elven victories that could be seen on stage in the city for battles that were currently being fought. It wasn't a true picture of what was actually happening out in the field. Could the fall of a single mercenary company spell the end of an entire rebellion? And now the city would be flooded with soldiers returning home in a month? Fraenk cursed himself for not having his own informants in the ranks.

"Why are you here when you should be with Arathes' host?" Fraenk demanded.

"I was given leave from Lord Fernbrook himself. So I rode back ahead of the vanguard. The rest will be here very soon," the elf snapped.

Fraenk's mind was reeling. Ten thousand soldiers, all returning at once? The city would be in chaos for months. He had no time to raise additional security or prepare for the unexpected influx. And he couldn't concentrate with that gods-awful smell filling his head. Fraenk coughed.

Fortunately, his partner was still focused on the elf.

"Did you kill that man?" Nim asked, hooking a thumb over his shoulder. "The sergeant says you confessed."

"The law says I may defend my own walls from intruders and thieves. He was trespassing."

"It's Miken's bakery!! He's fired those ovens since I was a sprout!" Fraenk snapped, heat rising in his cheeks.

"And it's mine now. By right and by writ," he grinned maliciously, something dark moving along his teeth.

"You murdered a man in his own house!" Fraenk grabbed the elf by the throat and gripped it, surprising all of them, but the elf most. He made a high, choking wheeze. Nim stepped closer, whether to help Fraenk or hold him back he didn't know, but looked ready for either possibility.

"Wrong! It's mine!" The elf squeaked out, his face turning red as he struggled to breathe. "Gift of Lord Fernbrook for my honorable service to Sarmatti!"

"Fraenk—" Nim grabbed one of Fraenk's wrists and tried to gently intervene. Sergeant Hobb stepped forward as well, the club dancing in his fist, but he looked unsure of who he might use it on.

"The bakery's not his to give!! This is Blackroot district!" Fraenk shouted in the elf's face. Then he seemed to realize what he was doing and finally released him.

"You'll regret that, human," Greenbriar coughed and glared back between greasy locks of hair. Once his breathing had steadied, the elf's hand dug into his pocket, and Fraenk stepped back, ready for him to produce a dagger or some other weapon. But instead, what came out was a small roll of parchment.

"Your proof, Arch Preceptor," he said with all the civility of a viper.

Fraenk snatched it from the elf and read it quickly. It appeared to be some hastily scrawled transfer of ownership deed... for the bakery. The two stamped sigils at the bottom made Fraenk's heart lurch in utter disbelief: House Fernbrook and House Blackroot.

"What's this treachery?! Speak quickly, or I'll hang you for a deserter, forger, thief, and murderer!" Fraenk spat, shoving the paper back at the elf.

"I thought you Penetrators were supposed to be spies. But you don't know scit." The elf seemed to find this all wonderfully amusing. "I will enlighten you, my *lord*... This property is mine own. Earned spoils for exceptional valor in putting down the beggar warlord Kreeg. When that Tigraenian fool emptied his coffers on mercenaries, there was not enough plunder to go around between all the upper and lower lords chopping up the meager land and gold. So they found other compensation for us. Why, it was none other than your own Lady Blackroot who sold the property to us in the first place."

"She would never—!" Fraenk growled, confused. He couldn't think. The smoke and that terrible burning smell was so strong.

"Your wrinkled old Dame's been keeping secrets, my *Lord*," Bas Greenbriar purred. "Naughty girl."

Fraenk curled his fists in impotent rage.

"You're still just a wax-bellied coward who knifed a good man in the back. And I'm gonna make sure they stretch your neck for that much at least."

In the distance, two short pipes of a hawk whistle carried from across the Lower Market Bazaar.

"That's our men, Fraenk," Hobb said, hoping to bring this interrogation to its conclusion.

"I tell you what, Arch Preceptor— *I freely confess to you and all present that I killed that man. Stuck him right in the back with my own dagger.* But do you know what? Those partisans over there are just gonna let me go. Oh yes," the elf said, sounding bored and tired. "You know that no council tribunal would ever convict me of murder of that creature, more than if I'd crushed a night beetle under my boot."

An awful pit formed in Fraenk's gut. Both Nim and Sergeant Hobb looked away.

"Aww. Don't make such a fuss over a few dead vermin. It was a right *infestation,*" the elf yawned and stretched.

"What did you say?" Fraenk locked eyes with the bloodshot elves' own.

"Oh, yes... took me a while to get them all."

Miken's family—Freenk realized. His chest tightened with dawning horror.

"Hobb, Did you search the bakery?!" Fraenk's voice wavered.

"I– I... We didn't–" The sergeant stammered.

With his heart hammering, Fraenk raced over and through the doors of the bakery shop. Inside, a wave of heat and the awful smell nearly knocked him over with a wall of black smoke. He searched frantically, and what he saw made his breath catch. Blood spray on the counter and floor.

Then a body. Miken's wife, Ellea, lay slashed and stabbed beside an overturned tray of rising bun dough. Fraenk's pulse thundered, and he coughed against the haze of smoke. Anguish and rage hit him like the heat of the flames that roared and spat from the large bread oven in the back.

Be calm, Fraenk.

Miken's voice was still urging him for peace. But how could there be peace in this? The man and his wife were now dead. Their blood screamed for justice.

No... Miken pleaded. *Don't lose control... for the sake of my children.*

The boys. Fraenk's mind found clarity again. If he could only find Miken's boys, maybe he could—

Fwoosh! A fire flared in the oven as fresh air vented back into the smoke-filled room. Fraenk's eyes watered fiercely from the smoke. He raised his cloak over his face to breathe and moved closer to the enormous domed oven. Something inside was on fire and stinking horribly. Two pairs of children's legs stuck out from inside the oven's open mouth.

They burned.

Bas Greenbriar watched amused as the pathetic human emerged from the bakery in a billow of smoke. He probably fancied himself some kind of demon emerging from a hell pit. Clearly he'd discovered Bas' terrible handiwork. Unfortunately, it had to come to all that, but the baker was too stubborn. They didn't all have to die, did they?

Oh, yes. The little voices said they did. Very well then.

Bas was expecting some kind of reaction from this intemperate human, but the Arch Preceptor's face was blank. His eyes were wide and cheeks stained with soot. He wasn't screaming or weeping. He was just striding toward them and flipping his cloak back over his shoulder. Would the human try to strike him? Oh, he'd be in real trouble then. He was already going to pay for that little choking incident. But to hit an elf? That would cost him his cushy job, which he shouldn't have in the first place.

Go on, human. Do your worst. You're sealing your own doom.

Then Bas saw him reaching down for the rows of dark metal from the brace at his hip. He watched with small curiosity as Fraenk's hand came up with half a dozen dark points from his fist. They stood in clear contrast from the fire in the bakery behind.

Danger! He's coming! The little voices shouted. But Bas pounded the side of his head with his palm in a call for silence.

Then his head began to pound again like a kicked ant mound. That ward swill he was given from that sniveling, treacherous foreigner had something wrong with it, Bas realized. It was supposed to protect him, but it was making him hear voices. Bas would make him answer for that, just as soon as the partisans let him go—which would be very, very soon.

He couldn't wait to see the look on this preceptor's face then. It would be delicious.

Speaking of, the human was still coming, and now he'd drawn a hand back with one of these objects. A throwing blade by the look of it. A feint, no doubt. Meant to unman him. But Bas was well acquainted with fear. He knew how to properly create it and make someone scream for their life. But this was all pretense. A pantomime like he's about to actually <u>*throw*</u> that knife, and it was pathetic. Bas was protected. He was an elf from a powerful family, and this human would never dare.

Fraenk's hand flashed forward. And something dark moved through the space between them like a phantom.

The first blade struck Bas Greenbriar solid in the throat. He actually felt it knock into the bone in his neck. Suddenly he couldn't breathe. Something hot and red was spilling from where the knife handle was protruding out of his larynx. The wave of pain was nothing compared to the utter shock. This was unbelievable. He was an elf, and this was not supposed to—

His head jerked sideways, and his vision was gone from his left eye. The right one could see the handle of a blade sticking out. There was shouting from the two men on either side of him, but he was having trouble understanding. The little voices were all screaming.

Bas' one good eye looked up to see the preceptors' hands moving again. His face, still a mask of terrible calm. Then there was a quick succession of thump-thump-thumps that sent his head sideways. And all went black.

Part II

5

CARAX THE CUTTHROAT WAS so wide at the shoulders that he nearly brushed against the walls on either side of the narrow dungeon passage. He was being escorted in the front and back by a sweaty detail of guards, whose hands hovered nervously near the grips of their square-headed maces. Carax knew he could take on all four of them if he had the mind to. Their weapons were too awkward for the tight confines of these black tunnels, which ran along the lower levels. They were better suited for the main yard, where one could get a proper swing in. There they could do some real damage, as his body could well attest.

But even unarmed, manacled, and freshly bruised, Carax was confident he could make quick and bloody work of this quartet with just his balled fists and strong legs. These guards weren't killers. They relied too much on their weapons and armor. But they were all cowards, just like most men in a violent encounter. He could see it on their faces. That dark thought was all the reassurance he needed. Carax smiled slightly, making the crack in his lip open again.

"Keep moving!" A rough hand shoved him from behind when he lagged too far from the front guards.

"Sorry, m'lord. A thousand pardons," he demurred, trying to sound contrite. His swollen lip only throbbed with each word. Blood from a split on his brow trickled down into his right eye, and he blinked it away. Half a dozen other places on his body ached from the blows of their maces. The beating had gone on longer than he expected. But then again, for the bloody mess that he'd made of the poor bastard in the yard, it was probably deserved. He'd done it right in front of a shocked group of hardened guards as well. So he supposed that show of force from them was a reminder to all.

The funny thing was, it was a split-second decision to begin with. The other man had just looked at him—his face curious, like he might ask Carax a question or possibly smile. That was all it took for Carax to decide it would be him. Life could be so unpredictable.

The claustrophobic hallway suddenly opened into a sickeningly cavernous room where the air was cool and musty. Even with the orange light of the guard's torches, an endless pit of black stretched downward in front of them that seemed to go on forever. There was a small landing, then a curve of stairs that wrapped around the pit wall, ever downward into darkness. One side was a sheer stone wall; the other was the darkest black that Carax had ever seen. The only way forward was down.

So they descended the stairs, more stairs, and even more stairs still. His sweat cooled, and a chill prickled across his tattooed skin. This place really was like the underworld, Carax thought.

He briefly wondered about the others who had made this doomed trek. What had they experienced as their new reality set in? Were they contrite? Depressed? Ready to give up, knowing they'd never escape? Pathetic. He cursed all of them to the ones above and below. They deserved their fate. He was not one of them. Carax knew he would not die down here.

After what seemed like a very long time of stepping ever downward, the motion becoming reflexive, the next stair was flat, and he staggered off balance. Carax went to one knee briefly but caught himself. But the guard behind him was on him immediately.

"Don't try anything stupid, you gatz!" A blow from a club glanced off his shoulder without much vigor. Fezzat, the scowling, wiry guard with a crooked, improperly-set nose, grabbed him, fingers digging into the meat of Carax' neck. He leaned close to hiss in Carax's ear.

"Carve that *horrvex,* as planned, and you'll be rewarded."

Then something hard slipped into his manacled hands. Carax's large fist closed over a shaft with a sharp point at one end. He knew immediately what it was.

Cold metal, rough on the flat, but ground into an uneven but serviceable edge. A thin handle was wrapped with a hempen cord. A crude dirk. Not nearly as good as the one he had crafted and later used to bleed, disassemble, and disembowel that unfortunate soul in the yard—*with his stupid friendly smile like he was about to greet Carax and ask how his day was.* No. That weapon may have been a far cry from what you could get at a decent blacksmith, but for a prison dagger, it was an instrument he had hated to part with. This new shiv could cut flesh if he pressed hard enough. It would have to do.

Despite his seemingly dire situation, holding his new substandard shiv was a welcome feeling. He could have stabbed, slashed, and sliced into the soft parts between the leather and light chain that these guards wore. When brute force was required, you got the best brute. And that was him. He would soon be back to the dark work he did best. Not only that, but rewarded for it. Wasn't fortune fickle sometimes?

"I expect there will be no more trouble out of you, Carax," the barrel-chested lead guard with the beard said from the front of the line.

"No trouble sir," Carax promised. But if he did suddenly decide to stab this self-righteous kiv in the face a few dozen times, would they dig an even deeper hole to throw him in? The worst they could do to him now was a summary execution.

But his new friends wouldn't allow that. Not while he had a job to do.

They marched Carax down a wider hall that was lined with darkened cells. Only a few glinting pairs of eyes peered at them from behind the bars. All looked skeletal and thin with haunted expressions, like the light itself was a terror to them.

The detail stopped at the final cell on the block, and the guard, Barrel-Chest, pulled a key ring off his belt and unlocked the cell.

"Not every man knows the place where they'll die, prisoner. But now you do," he said, pulling open the door and making the hinges protest with a metallic squeal.

He lifted his lantern. The thin light cast across a dank, filthy cell. A few gaunt rats pattered away but stopped not far back. He could see the place was nearly empty, except for a filthy slop pail and a scrunched human shape curled up in the far corner against the wall.

"Oh, and look... You've got a little friend there."

A huddled figure slept on a bedroll, covered in a tatty, moth-eaten blanket. He had long, greasy hair and pale, dirty feet that stuck out the bottom. Carax didn't trust it. He'd been warned that this one was seven shades of clever. This was an obvious ruse.

"There's only one bedroll, so you might have'n to snuggle up, ya bugger," the porcine guard with the stringy mustache, whom Carax had begun to think of as 'Peccary', added, snickering at the joke he probably repeated to every prisoner who was brought down here.

"So, who is he?" Carax tried to sound concerned as Fezzat unlocked his manacles.

"You ain't heard?" The Peccary snorted. "That one murdered an _elf._ Not just that, but a brave hero of Arathes; divines keep him... recently returned home from the war. And he was just tryin' to set 'imself up with a bakery. " The fat guard tapped his heart three times and circled it. A religious gesture so old, most weren't even aware of its meaning.

"I don't like no elf-killer," Carax said darkly. The Barrel-Chest gave him a look—finally something on which they both agreed.

"Well? Get on with it," Fezzat shoved him inside the cell. "Try an' get along. Or don't. Neither of you will ever see daylight again," the Barrel-Chest said without interest as he adjusted the shutter on the lamp. Carax caught Fezzat glaring at him as the light swept by the man's face. His eyes were shooting over to the sleeping figure as if to say 'that one!'. As if this fool was expecting Carax to do the job right now in front of all of them.

Annoyance flared, and he had to fight the sudden, strong urge to put the shiv to work on Fezzat instead. _Not now_, he told himself. Because the chance for that will come again very soon.

He watched as the guards left, becoming silhouettes moving in a circle of torchlight down the hallway. In less than a minute, he was surrounded by total, unyielding darkness. Without his eyes to rely on, Carax's ears came alert.

Water dripped from everywhere. Skittering feet of rodents. The echoing sound of bodies moving in the darkness. Coughs. Sniffles. Breathing. Everything felt very close. He heard a fast movement across the room and could imagine the other man was up on his feet. He had to reason that the other man was probably armed with some makeshift blade as well. Carax gripped the shiv in his hand, quietly ready to perforate anything that came within reach.

"What's your name, big man?" A disembodied voice came echoing from nowhere.

Carax didn't reply. Giving away his position could be very unwise.

"I was wondering how long it would take to get someone down here. You certainly do impress. I suppose I should be flattered they'd send someone like you. I assume you are here to kill me."

This time, the voice sounded like it was behind him. Maybe he could find the source of the voice if it kept talking.

"I come to gift the man called Neversleep his eternal rest," Carax replied.

"Clever. I like that. But what's not clever was that you had to get sent to the black cells to do it. That's taking a big risk," the voice came again from another direction.

"Better than dying in here. An old man who can't remember what the sun looks like."

"So, just your freedom? That's all they offered you." The voice teased again, sounding low to the ground.

"A bag of gold too. Where are you hiding?" Carax said and moved into a crouch. His hands felt out the blackness. Kneading it like some grotesque shadow-dwelling cat.

"Oh, of course, the gold. Never work for free, I say. Not if you're a skilled tradesman. What else?"

"And a house and land outside the city," Carax continued.

The hidden man sucked his teeth with a sharp intake of breath.

"See, now that's where the wheels fall off the liar's cart, big man. They might pay you and let you go, but there's no way anyone's gifting you a house, I'm afraid. It's too much trouble." The voice sounded untroubled. "Sorry to tell you this, but the only land you're getting is a hole in the dirt where they'll bury you. That is if they don't just leave you down here just to rot."

"Phane take you!" Carax grunted and slashed with the blade, only clipping moist, rough-hewn granite. He was hoping for a bright spark from the metal on the stone, but the wall was so damp, it barely even threw back a sound.

"Would you care to hear my side of it?" The other one asked.

"Stand still and bleed!" Carax roared, swinging the blade blindly in wide arcs. He went the entire length of the cell and back, hitting nothing but walls and bars. This Neversleep was devilishly elusive.

Carax stopped to listen. Then he reached out again, feeling for the voice. All he needed was a body to plunge the knife into, and it would be done.

"You were paid to complete a job; I get it," the voice chided. "But we could come to an arrangement of our own."

"You think I'm a fool?! Come here, and we can settle this. You can't avoid me forever."

"Of course you're right. But one last thing before you unburden me of my precious guts... Who paid you to kill me?"

"You slayed their kin. Now they require your death to regain their honor," Carax said, finally starting to hone in on the voice's origin.

"Indeed. I think I know the elves of whom you speak."

"Then you know they will make sure it's done. Now I'm ready to be quit of this foul place, so come take your death so I can be on my way." An edge of panic began to creep into Carax' voice.

"Your candor is appreciated, sir. As the sages have written, "In truth we find freedom," the other man chided. "Not in your case, unfortunately. No. You're going to die down here."

Carax could feel the voice very close. It didn't matter what he was saying. A cornered man would say anything to keep drawing breath. Especially if it was lies or things that made him doubt the bargain he struck with his shadowy benefactors. His foot hit something close to the ground, and he realized the man was probably crouched low to avoid him. Carax reacted on pure reflex, falling on the body. The shiv pumped and stabbed the hard torso, adding fresh holes to the old blanket, and digging hard chunks of flesh from the cold body.

In a moment, Carax realized he was stabbing a dead man. One that had been dead for some time. He recoiled with a horrified gasp and clambered to his feet.

A bright light bloomed suddenly, making Carax shield his eyes. He dropped the gore-covered shiv, his hands dripping with putrescent blood. Someone was standing on the other side of the bars, holding a glowing glass orb. It was the man he was stumbling stupidly in the dark for–

The one he was supposed to kill. Somehow, the human called Neversleep was there watching him from just outside the cell.

"Neversleep?!" Carax exclaimed. "How did you—?"

"Hmm. Looks like you've done for old Jasper, there," Fraenk said. "Oh, don't worry, he died weeks ago. And honestly, he probably deserved it. He had a nasty habit of cutting up poor brothel girls."

"But—How did you get out of the cell?" Carax asked, bewildered.

"I've got my own comfortable room set up down the hall. Just there," Fraenk pointed off down another dark corridor. "Well, it's not exactly luxury, but at least I don't have the dungeon rats trying to gnaw off my toes."

"But they locked you up! I saw the partisans haul you in here!"

"And they made a big show of it too, didn't they?" Fraenk's eyes sparkled mischievously. "I arranged to get myself put in the black cells. After all, it is one of the safest places in the city, so long as they don't send a hulking killer down after you."

Carax's brow furrowed. Try as he might, his brain was better equipped at understanding simple things like where on the body to stab the most vulnerable organs. He was not good at piecing together multi-layered schemes and counter-schemes, let alone where he fit into them.

"But you killed an elf. A son of House Greenbriar," he stated, incredulous.

"And as you said, the requirements of honor demand my death. I know elves can hold a grudge for hundreds of years, but I didn't think their revenge would take *this* long," Fraenk stretched. "I don't know who should be more offended for this, me or Bas Greenbriar."

Fraenk sized the big man up appraisingly, then nodded. "I take that back. You're certainly impressive as far as paid cutthroats go. And you risked the forever darkness of the black cells just to do it. It's commendable. I'll have to let them know you did try."

"But I'm supposed to kill you," Carax sounded disappointed.

"Sorry, big fella. I really must be going. A month in the dungeon can really set you behind on one's duties." Fraenk started to turn when a bloody fist rammed through the bars. The blade of the shiv lashed wildly in the air.

"DIE!! BY THE POWERS, NEVERSLEEP. DIE!!!" Carax thrashed like a snared hellcat. His hand clawed the air in front of Fraenk, but the killer's reach was just shy from where he was standing. Fraenk tisked and shook his head sadly.

"See, now that kind of outburst was what got me in trouble. You'll wanna get control of that, or it could really get you in a bad place."

From up the hallway came the sounds of another commotion—some other man screaming and thrashing like he was being tortured. Carax withdrew back into his cell, watching to see what this was about. The torchlight coming down the hallway revealed four guards, dragging a new prisoner towards them. As they got closer, Carax recognized the broken-nosed guard, Fezzat. But instead of his leather and chain, he was stripped to a filthy set of white woolen underwear. As they dragged him, Fezzat jibbered and thrashed with incoherent terror.

"You'll be pleased to know we did get you a fresh cellmate," Fraenk said as they approached. "I figured you would have much to talk about since you both work for the Greenbriars."

The guards hauled their former coworker up and tossed him in the cell with Carax. They let the door slam shut with a clang that ran the entire length of the hall.

"See you in a month. If you're behaving yourself, I think they may be open to letting you some time in the sunshine again," Fraenk said. The big man made a noise that sounded like a whimper.

And with that, he turned and strode away, back up the stairs and back into the city that awaited him with all of its dangers. Fraenk had a nagging feeling that his troubles had only begun. This vendetta with the Greenbriars was far from over.

6

"THE VENDETTA WITH THE Greenbriars is _over_!"

Lady Arice Blackroot, matriarch of the Blackroot family, leader of District Blackroot, and sovereign member of the High Council of Elves, sat in fury on an ornate seat at the head of the council room. Her thin fist pounded the tabletop, and she looked ready to thrash anyone who defied her—and for someone who had aged well over six hundred years, this was not a trivial task. The elderly elf was dressed in elaborate arboreal-patterned silken robes that hung from her delicate frame. Her silver hair was pinned back in an angled pair of silver and starstone-studded combs that looked like swords crossed behind her head. She was resplendent in her fury.

"I have met with Lord Fernbrook and discussed the situation at great length. It is a grave concern any time an elf is killed, no matter the circumstance. And the killing of Lord Fernbrook's nephew, the brother of a sworn captain, not to mention a hero who was recently commended for bravery on the battle-field—for that, an immense price must be paid. And that cost will be _yours to bear, Neversleep._"

Fraenk stood in the center of the room with his head bowed. He looked terrible and smelled even worse. The Blackroot guards who scooped him up the moment he stepped out of Arathes Prison were insistent upon bringing him directly to see the High Lady elf. Fraenk then understood just how serious things were if the Arch Preceptor himself could neither bribe, cajole, nor threaten them into letting him wash up and put on clean clothes before he was dragged in front of the council.

All eyes in the room were upon him, which was an uncomfortable amount of attention. The entire council of Elven Acherons who managed the district's business was there flanking the room on either side. The captains of Ceremony, Coin, Building, Records, Harbor, Trade, and Defense. As the Acheron of

Secrets, the Arch Preceptor was normally their contemporary, but now they sat in icy reprimand of him from their seats. Their expressions were impassive, but there was sharp interest in their eyes. What would be the outcome of this discipline? Some of these elves were fair-weather allies at best, and others treated him with open disdain. But this was a full-blown storm, and Fraenk was at its center. All he could do was keep his head down in a suitable gesture of contrition and let the Lady's tempest run its course.

"Lord Fernbrook has asked that the perpetrator be turned over to him for a tribunal and commission of justice. Considering the trouble this has brought to the district and to me, I was inclined to accept." She let the words hang in the air, like the blade of a headman's axe.

Fraenk unpinned the silver badge of office and proffered to her in an outstretched hand.

"My Lady, I hereby resign as Arch Preceptor and accept whatever punishment you—"

"You will be silent until I give you leave to speak, Lord Neversleep!" She snapped. "Do you know what I've had to deal with while you were on your leisurely little hiatus?"

Fraenk's mouth tightened to a line. Now would not be a good time to correct her that he had spent a month in the darkest cell just to keep an assassin's blade out of his ribs. But the look she bore said she was ready to finish the job that Carax could not.

"Now, where was I? Ah, yes. The penance to Lord Fernbrook. While some of my advisors say it would be most expedient to just let his dogs gnaw your bones, Lord Evenswan has reminded me it would not be in keeping with tradition for a district Acheron to be handed over to another lord for such a punishment. It would set a bad precedent. "

Fraenk stole a glance at the Acheron of Ceremonies, Turran Evenswan. He was a prim and sour old elf who loved his rigid protocols and procedures created by thousands of years of elven tradition even more than he disliked Fraenk, which was truly quite a statement. But the elf looked very displeased to be forced to advocate on Fraenk's behalf like that. Fraenk turned his attention back to Lady Blackroot as she continued.

"Nevertheless, I could have turned you over as Lord Fernbrook demanded. But I have negotiated an alternate arrangement instead. I will not be delving into the particulars of the arrangement, but suffice it to say that it cost the district dearly. However, Lord Fernbrook has accepted terms and will command his family that the blood debt has been settled."

Gasps and loud murmurs issued from the Acherons. Even Fraenk looked up, surprised.

"Whatever deal you struck, take it back!" Fraenk shouted. "You know Lord Fernbrook, and he'd set us afire just for the light to count his coins by!"

"That's a High Lord elf, you're talking about, Neversleep!" She barked.

"I don't give a skrate's tail! You rescind that Chard's bargain, you senile old crone, or I'll go turn myself over to the Greenbriars on my own! I can deal with them. They're too cowardly to stab me in the back to my face!"

"Insolence!" Turran Evenswan shouted, his hands fluttering like surprised birds. He had apparently suffered this disrespect long enough.

"Show some respect, human!" He heard the Acheron of Coin, Olivar Arrowwisp, add in simpering solidarity.The other elves at the table grumbled in agreement.

"You will leave the Greenbiars and the Fernbrooks alone!" Lady Blackroot shot to her feet, surprising everyone. "And I warn you to keep that contemptuous tongue inside your head before I have it removed entirely!"

Then she began to creak and waver like some malevolent scarecrow. The room went completely silent. No one had seen her stand without aid in years. Her stupefied ladies-in-waiting scrambled forth to steady her.

"Touch me, and I'll have you gutting mackerel on the Fishwife's docks by nightfall," she growled, and the two young elven maids retreated.

"Now, I will say this only once and for all to hear. Fraenk— *Oh, Powers take you, Fraenk. What is your true surname?"*

"Uh... I don't have one, my lady," Fraenk stammered.

"Well, get one, damn you!" She scolded. "Fraenk, who is called Neversleep, is and will remain the Arch Preceptor of Blackroot as it pleases me and sealed by my hand, Lady Arice Blackroot. High Lord of blah, blah blah... scribes, fill in my honorarium. All of you are dismissed."

Lady Blackroot steadied herself and carefully eased back into her chair. This time she let the Elven maidens get her seated. Fraenk could see her tirade had taken its toll on her. The room filled with the grumble of conversations and bodies shifting into sluggish motion without much urgency to leave.

"Well, go on!" She snapped. "All of you out!"

This time, the room emptied more quickly of its acherons, servants, and scribes. Fraenk caught narrowed eyes from Acherons Shaleward and Hornwild, who were no doubt saying unkind things about him. He expected a poisonous glare from Evenswan, but the elf stuck his nose into the air like the prow of a ship and didn't even meet Fraenk's eyes as he sailed from the room. Let them hate him, Fraenk thought. They could despise him all they wanted, but Lady Blackroot made it clear he wasn't going anywhere and they'd still have to work with him at the council table.

The only elf headed further into the room was Acheron of Ports and Harbors, Fenduin Tallowfrond. He was the only one utterly disinterested in Fraenk's recent calamity. And in fact, he had a general difficulty understanding the social dynamics of any given situation. Now was no different, for he was undeterred by the glare she was now giving him as he approached.

"My Lady, we must discuss what is to happen about that deadbeat galleon in my dry dock! They've not paid us for the work done already, and we cannot send it home in it's current state! Every day it languishes, costing us hundreds of gold—" "Not now, my lord Tallowfrond. We can discuss it later," Lady Blackroot said wearily, rubbing her temple.

"You said that yesterday, my lady. Now, I've sent several letters to Cirrusol already demanding payment and they ignore us! " He complained.

Fraenk set a hand on his shoulder and stopped the elf's advance.

"I may have some way to get their attention, Tallowfrond. I'll meet with you later about it," Fraenk said. For whatever reason, the elf calmed around Fraenk. This answer seemed to mollify him, and he nodded.

"Uh, very well. I will expect your answer."

And with that, he exited the room with the rest, leaving only Fraenk, Lady Blackroot, and her attendants remaining.

Fraenk caught a sudden whiff of a redolent odor that made his throat tighten and his eyes water—the source of which turned out to be himself. He needed to get cleaned up, and a near-scalding rosewater and lavender oil bath was what he desired more than anything at the moment. That and a glass of amber. Fraenk turned to leave as well.

"Not you, Fraenk," she said with a voice as icy as the tomb of the frost giants of Bolar. "I require a private word with my Arch Preceptor."

Fraenk slowly turned back to face her. She waved her hand, sending her servants out as well.

When it was finally just them, Lady Blackroot fixed him with her steel-gray eyes.

"Did you really just call me a senile old crone, Fraenk?"

"Did I? I don't rightly recall."

Lady Blackroot sighed.

"After a few centuries, you stop turning the young men's heads. It is a hellish thing, growing old. But there is also a relief in it as well. My days of fighting these insipid squabbles will be over."

"I meant no offense." Fraenk started to apologize.

"Of course you did. But that's why I need you, Fraenk. You speak your mind, even when it's dangerous to you. That's exactly why I require you back in the district. We have greater troubles than some petty elvish grievances."

"You should've seen the size of the petty grievance that tried to carve out my guts."

"If people didn't want you dead, I'd say you weren't doing your job," she said with a smile.

"So, what deal did you strike with the Fernbrooks?" He asked.

"You're supposed to be the Acheron of Secrets. You'll figure it out."

"I take back the senile bit. You're too clever by half," Fraenk smiled. "I'm sure the other lord elves would see you put me back out on the streets... or far worse. I should probably thank you for leaving me my job."

"You may well curse me before this is over. But in the meantime, go out and continue to earn it. We have many enemies, as you well know, Fraenk. If that conniving scoundrel Lord Fernbrook wants you gone, I owe it to all of Blackroot to keep you right where you are."

"My life is yours, My Lady."

Fraenk clenched his fist over his chest and bowed in salute, then turned to leave. At the door, he paused.

"One thing I was pondering down during my relaxing foray in the dungeon. Did you really sell that bakery to Lord Fernbrook?" Fraenk asked.

Lady Blackroot scowled like a bitter flavor was on her tongue.

"I don't see what that has to do with—"

"That foul Greenbriar elf said the bakery was *his* property. That you sold it, in fact. Our murdered baker was dressed for work and didn't look like he knew anything about it. So I'll ask again. Did you sell Miken's place out from under him without even telling him first? Tell me true."

She paused for a long time, looking nervous and avoiding his eyes.

"You're going to call me a senile old crone again."

"Why? What did you do?"

"The High Lords have a private gathering where we meet and discuss matters of importance… and also get a respite from the piety and prying eyes that are all around us. Where we can indulge in trivialities that the rest of you get to enjoy and that we must pretend to disdain."

"You get drunk and find a handsome half-elf to nibble your pointed ears."

"Oh, grow up, Fraenk!" She looked angry and then laughed. "But yes, that does happen."

"And that night? What happened?"

"We play this game. Do you know 'Monarch's Cuckold'? There's four dice and seven cards.

"Brand's Bond! And I thought _I_ was vulgar," Fraenk exclaimed, somehow both amused and a bit scandalized. "We call it _Liar's Gambit_ in the dice dens."

"That night, I was having the best run of luck. _A Queen's Dodger. Lord's Salty Nursemaid. Healthy Squire's Tower. Twins in the Bodice._ I had all of the high elves on the back foot, and the winds of fortune were blowing at my back. And there was Lord Fernbrook, who has always had a terrible temper, just smiling and playing—losing great stacks of coin and looking like it pleased him immensely. Mind you, he never took any kind of loss with anything but cries of bottom dealing or foul enchantments. But that night, he <u>smiled</u>. And I didn't see it at first, but when I did, it gave me an ill feeling. But I was winning and a bit loose, if you know what I mean, so I kept playing. I ought to have stopped."

"Lady Fortuna slipped away," Fraenk prompted.

"But then we got to the last round. I was riding high with a _Meerie's Got Her Hands Full,_ and all he's got is a _Lonely Uncle's Hatbox._ There was one last roll of the dice. And old Malgraye goes to match the bet. Only he doesn't have enough to cover, so he puts up the East Gate."

"The East Gate as in—"

"The actual East _skarking_ Gate! All tariffs, taxes, and duties. You know how valuable that is, Fraenk."

Considering the amount of people and carts that moved through that entrance, Fraenk could indeed imagine a pile of gold nearing the size of Arathes mountain herself.

"There's no way I can lose. So the last turn came up. and by Shalokar's Own Luck, he plays a _Monarch's Cuckold._"

"He won," Fraenk clarified, making sure he understood the game.

"He destroyed me. No magic. No cheating. He'd been sitting on it the whole time," she said, still dumbfounded.

"How auspicious for our Lord Fernbrook."

"The uncanny turn from this cruk, Fraenk! It's like he's cheating somehow. But the dice and cards are blessed by a Paladin. There's no enchantment on them. I don't know how he does it."

"I don't know any Paladins who bless dice, my Lady," Fraenk replied grimly.

"They don't?" Lady Blackroot looked ill.

"So you owed him something of value. And Fernbrook asked for the bakery?"

"Not right away. He wanted his own dock in the harbor at first. But then later that night his Arch Preceptor showed up, urgently requesting the rights to that single bakery instead. Well, it was worth hardly a tenth of the value, so I—"

"You made the deal."

"What else could I do?"

"Don't keep things like that from me in the future," Fraenk said gravely. "And what of this latest arrangement? The one for my safety?"

"Fraenk. What matters is that it's all settled now. Just leave it be. The Fernbrooks have promised you'll be left alone, but you need to stay out of their district and don't cause any further trouble."

"Did they strike this latest deal with you before or after their man tried to bleed me in the black cells?"

"Enough. You've come to the limit of my patience, Neversleep. Now, go and see to my district. That is what matters now."

Fraenk left the council chambers with his mind buzzing. Bas Greenbriar was indeed the rightful owner of the property. But why was it so urgent for Lord Fernbrook to own it that night? And why did Bas kill Miken and his entire family? Surely he had no interest in making bread. The elf had some other purpose, but what?

Fraenk's mind gnawed at this puzzle. He would have no more answers until he could take a second look at the bakery. Perhaps more answers could be found inside.

7

AFTER A LONG AND luxuriating bath that left behind several weeks' worth of dirty brown scum floating in the copper tub, his skin was toasty pink and as wrinkled as an elderly kobold's neck folds. Fraenk then availed himself of a haircut and shave from the Blackroot's resident barber—a cheerful and chatty Anuras named Borpis Reedwillow. This frog-like humanoid creature warbled in a singsong voice that croaked melodically as he fretted and fussed over Fraenk's impertinent coiffure. When he was done, Fraenk looked better than he had in years.

Returning back to his tower, Fraenk found the Lady's personal tailor, Cloras, had finished hemming the set of tunics and breeches that had grown loose on his body during the month underground. He chose the set on the top of the neatly folded stack and dressed himself. Inspecting himself in the mirror, Fraenk looked like a new man.

Although he didn't feel particularly hungry at that moment, Fraenk figured he could use a proper meal, which would mean a trip down to the kitchens. It would be the first time in a while that he hadn't prepared it himself, warmed over a damp and stinking brazier. Wilted vegetables, mushrooms of every variety, or the occasional link of cured sausage were most commonly on the menu. Fraenk craved some new flavors.

Fortunately for him, the kitchens of Blackroot Estate were well regarded for both their mastery and creativity in the culinary arts. And though it was still hours from the Blackroot evening meal proper, he was sure he could coax some type of dinner from the kitchen staff. The delight would be what delicious surprise would be set before him. It made his mouth water just thinking about it.

He took stairs, then hallways, then more stairs, picking the fastest route down. Upon entering, Fraenk found a flurry of activity, bodies in motion in a cooking ballet as the lavish multi-course banquet was underway. Roast salted venison, duck braised in savory saffin root and a white pear jam, seared eel in elderflower wine on a bed of shaved turnips and gollen greens. The smells were intoxicating.

"My dear boy, Fraenk! The wayward lad returns home, eh?" The lead chef, a ruddy-faced, round man named Pollard, greeted him when Fraenk finally caught his attention.

"I've missed your skill at the skillet!" Fraenk said, gaining a chubby smile from the chef.

"Last I heard, you were eating mice and cockroaches in Arathes Prison. Did you finally escape? Or if I know the great Fraenk Neversleep, there'd be a hefty bribe involved," he chuckled, elbowing Fraenk amiably.

"Something like that," Fraenk grinned back, lifting his palm from the counter where a silver coin had materialized underneath it.

"Have a seat, my friend, I'll fix you something personally," Pollard smiled, but his eyes were moving over the various dishes currently being prepped.

Pollard smiled again, but there was hesitation in his grin. Something was off, but what it was exactly, Fraenk couldn't say.

"I will await your art with a growling belly," Fraenk tipped him a salute and moved to a seat at the side table where the servants took their meals when they weren't working. Leaning back, he pulled the flask from his cloak and sipped as he waited for his lunch to appear. The delicious smells of the foods being prepared began to awaken his hunger for real. He smiled and let his fingers trace along an old etching carved into the tabletop's wood—the word 'Fingers'.

His hunger had fully awakened by the time an old scullery maid approached holding a tray. Her gray hair was tied back under a kerchief, and she had tough, gnarled old hands that were red from soaking in scrub water all day. But her eyes were dark and youthful, strangely incongruous to the elderly body.

"Your supper, my lord," she said dryly.

The plate that clacked down before Fraenk was anything but a feast. A cold haunch of some unnamed beast, with a stale crust of bread and a cup of curdled pale green soup that turned Fraenk's appetite sour. It was hard to imagine Pollard had sent this over to him.

"The service here has really declined since I've been gone," Fraenk quipped.

The scullery maid slipped into the seat across from him. Her level gaze showed no amusement. Fraenk sawed off a chunk of meat and began to chew.

"Well, if you wanted to be a scullery maid, I could have just arranged it, Gwen." Fraenk raised an eyebrow and smiled. "Or is it *Gran* now?"

"I see the black cells didn't dampen your wit, Neversleep," she retorted. "Just in case you've not had time to read up on the reports whilst in your perfumed bath, my Lord..."

Fraenk had skimmed some of the reports from his preceptors regarding the events of the past month. Some were worth serious consideration and were hardly worth the ink to put them to paper. Nothing from Gwen's reports stood out.

"Well, go on then," Fraenk said. She gave him an irritated huff.

"While you were gone, someone tried to slip her lady a few leaves of shadewort. Fortunately, Pollard caught it while tasting the sauce. He still spent two uncomfortable days as Lord of the Latrine. You have no idea what we're spending on glamours, so I can catch this guy." The old woman rubbed her raw, inflamed hands and scowled. "My fingers are never ever going back to their normal color."

"I must have missed that. Who do you suspect?" Fraenk asked.

Her expression flashed irritation, but she took a breath and continued.

"Well, there's no one new on the kitchen staff, so I'm doubtful it was one of them. Pollard has only a few he trusts to do the actual cooking, so not them either. There's been several deliveries made around the time, but they don't get near the food. We can't know for certain until we pinch 'em in the act, so that's why I'm down here trying to—"

"Catch him red-handed?" Fraenk winked, looking down at her rosy fingers. He couldn't resist.

The murderous glare she gave him could've stopped a manticore in its tracks.

"It was so nice having you gone, Arch Preceptor," the old woman said.

"I did try to resign and hand myself over to be tortured by those sadistic Greenbriars. You would've had the top job then."

"Well, I suppose I'm happy as the Vice Arch Preceptor for now," Gwen said. "I don't imagine we could still get them to torture you."

"Who knows? I might enjoy it," he said. "So someone tried to poison Lady Blackroot. And that's why Pollard's been on edge."

Fraenk took a spoonful of soup, tasted it, and spit it back out again. "Powers, that's awful. Good thing you didn't serve her that. It definitely would have done the job."

"I'm not surprised. That plate's been sitting in the kitchen for three days. I didn't think you'd actually try to eat it," Gwen shrugged.

Fraenk's throat hitched involuntarily. He pushed the tray away and spat until nothing remained in his mouth. He took another swallow of booze just to clear his palette.

"Anything else I should know about?" He asked, trying to distract from something besides the putrid food. "The Lady seems to think the Fernbrooks are starting trouble."

"You seem to be the cause of that," she scowled.

"I did go to prison for that," Fraenk said mildly. "And apparently our Lady has brokered some kind of truce. But she's tight-lipped about the terms."

"We're doing our best out there, but you only have six preceptors, including the rookie," she sighed. "It's been chaos ever since the soldiers returned. The partisans have their hands full with drunken fights and stabbings. There's been word that remnants of Kreeg's forces have been making their way into the city—trying to infiltrate and disrupt whatever they can. Coldfrost preceptors caught a group of Kreeg loyalists trying to spike their forges. They were caught and pitched whole-body into the smelting foundry. Turned them to smoke before their screams even died away."

"They're still fighting, even with their leader gone." Fraenk mused. "That's not loyalty. It's stupidity."

"There are those who don't know when their cause is lost. They can sometimes even win in spite of it all," Gwen looked at him pointedly.

Fraenk shifted in his seat.

"This business with the elf you killed—" "That's been settled."

"Not out there, it's not," she replied hotly. "A lot of elves aren't happy about what you did, and humans are paying the price for it."

"What *I did?!* Greenbriar stabbed a man in the back! And killed his wife and kids!!" Fraenk pounded the table, making his cutlery and his companion jump. "Do they think he should have just gone free?"

"Humans don't serve justice to elves. They don't strike them. They don't even say a foul word to them. And they especially don't kill them," she replied.

Fraenk stood and grabbed his cloak.

"Let me ask you, as my Vice Arch Preceptor. Do you think I did the right thing?" Fraenk demanded.

She paused for a long moment. He could see her measuring what she would say next.

"It doesn't matter. What's done is done. All of our ashes ride the same wind."

Fraenk had a flash of the two children in the oven, burning. Their legs sticking out–

"Such a careful response," Fraenk growled and turned. "You'll have to come out of the shadows someday."

"Fraenk..." She said, stopping him before he could leave. "Your new guy... Stonebridge."

"What about him?"

"How well do you trust him?" She asked cautiously."As much as I trust anyone, I suppose," Fraenk replied, not liking where this line of questioning was headed.

"You asked me to tell you honestly on all matters, right, Fraenk?" Any hint of humor and sarcasm had left her voice. Her eyes fixed insistently on his. He nodded.

"He owed coin to half a dozen gambling dens on Dicer's Row. Dusvann the Rasp, Tia Wolfsbane. And even a grift-roller from Pileus called Silver Nik. Now he's suddenly square with all of them?"

"Sounds like he's paid off his debts," Fraenk said. "Isn't that a good thing? A man who owes money can be controlled."

"Oh, aye," she nodded. "But how's he suddenly got the gold for it? He could be selling our secrets for all you know."

Fraenk paused and appeared to be thinking. What he didn't say was that it was Fraenk himself who had paid off to clear Nim's ledger. If Nim was going to owe someone, Fraenk would rather it be himself. But that had to stay between the two of them.

"You think he's a liability?" Fraenk asked.

"I'll say this plain. You hired a criminal to be a preceptor, Neversleep," Gwen folded her arms. "I don't trust him. I don't think you should, either."

"I'll take your words under advisement," Fraenk tried not to sound dismissive. "And where is he now?"

"I sent him down to Canal Street to look in on a situation at The Languid Maiden. Something about a ruffian who was causing trouble. I thought he could handle that much at least. Anyway, he's been gone a long while. You may want to check on him," Gwen said.

Fraenk stopped and looked back over one shoulder. He arched an eyebrow.

"You sent him to a brothel. How long ago is *a while*?"

She rolled her eyes. "Longer than any woman would tolerate the likes of him."

As Gwen tottered back to her scullery duties, Fraenk decided whatever dubious entanglement that Nim may or may not be in would keep for a bit longer. Especially in light of a much more pressing matter, which was now set before him. This would require his undivided attention. It was a serving platter covered by a polished silver dome. Hand delivered and compliments of Pollard.

From inside, strange and exotic aromas spoke of unknown culinary delights. Only a thorough investigation utilizing all of his senses would reveal its delicious secrets.

"I thank you, sir. I'll be enjoying this in my own quarters."

Taking the tray, Fraenk quickly retreated to the Arch Preceptor's tower within Blackroot Estate. The room was musty when he entered and looked very much the same as the day he'd made his unexpected trip to prison. The major noticeable difference were all the reports from his preceptors, which sat in unorganized piles on his desk. Fraenk pushed back stacks of papers on his work table to clear a place to eat.

The moment he lifted the tray lid, a small face appeared at the arrow-loop window. It's large yellow, slit eyes fixed on the food. It gave a soft chitter then leaped through the window, which was perfectly sized to accommodate it's feline body. The skrate looked up at Fraenk and gave a hungry yowl.

"Punctual as ever, Keeks," Fraenk said, taking a seat. "Shall we feast?"

As always, Pollard's kitchen work remained unparalleled. There was garlic-soaked squid and tomatoes in a rich caper and herb butter, crisp fried turnips on slabs of giant's head mushrooms, drizzled with chilled corliss jelly, and a bowl of hot-spiced savory stew with large chunks of waxfish– which he picked out for the demanding skrate. And to wash it all down was a bottle of dark Astarian wine.

It was only after both man and lizard were satisfied that he noticed a warm loaf of toasty brown bread wrapped in a towel. He set it down in the middle of the empty dish, where it began to soak in the red sauce of the entree.

He looked at it and could not move. Something about its shape reminded Fraenk of a body lying on its side. His appetite was suddenly gone. Fraenk set down his cutlery and covered the tray with its silver cloche. The skrate had found a spot on the rug near the hearth to clean himself with noisy, rasping strokes of his tongue.

"You can be melancholy later," he said to the skrate.

Fraenk set the tray outside his door for the servant to collect and turned back once again to his table.

So many reports to read. If only he had kept up with them while he was in the black cells. But he had no good way to get them down to him that wouldn't attract suspicion. Food deliveries were one thing, but a daily messenger with reports would not have gone unnoticed by his enemies.

Now, he felt a heavy fatigue begin to drag at his limbs and eyelids. But if he laid down now, he had no idea how long he might be out for. And judging by the state of his table, which was scattered with bits of scribbled notes from his preceptors, there was still much to be done.

Fraenk saw that several of the pages had fallen from his desk in a fan across the floor. As Fraenk stooped to pick them up, he was struck with the notion that here was the culmination of everything which had transpired in his absence. If Fraenk had believed himself to be of importance, he had but to look at the stack of papers to know otherwise. It was all just footnotes, really. Somehow, the business of the district had commenced without him. Another Arch Preceptor could have just as easily read each one, nodding judiciously, and then drawn their own conclusions if each warranted ac-tion—which in most cases, they did not. Fraenk could feel his head getting cloudy and starting to dim from the number of drinks he had taken already. He had forgotten just how many, but his mood had turned doleful.

"Good or ill. The things we do… does any of it matter, Keeksie boy?" He asked the skrate, who was now snoring softly on the floor. Its ear twitched, but it was otherwise unmoved. He didn't normally name them, as they tended to reject outright domestication. This one was different, and Fraenk didn't know why. He watched the gentle rise and fall of the purple stripe that ran along its flank.

His answer was unspoken. It was etched into the stones and in the faces of every elf he met. Even Lady Blackroot had given away a man's entire life's work without a thought. None cared if Miken and his family were killed or why. Humans lived and humans died. Their lives were like these notes on his table. Only of consequence to someone who was interested and bothered to look.

Fraenk knew that his own life wouldn't even be worth one of these notes. He was a man of the shadows. No family or close friends. No one to mourn if he was gone. It ought to feel sad or angry, or helpless—but instead he felt nothing. Like how a steel blade must feel in a man's hand.

He was sworn to protect the interests of Lady Arice and House Blackroot, and that was his purpose. He had his duties and responsibilities, which he would carry out, even to his own hazard. And he would do it because of one elf. She could have left him to fend for himself or given him up to the Fernbrooks to appease their fury, but she hadn't.

The Lady still needs you. Fraenk told himself.

He set down his glass and splashed more booze into it. He needed fuel to keep going, and he couldn't get dragged down into melancholy. He took a drink, then got to work.

As Fraenk skimmed through the scrawled notes on the desk, he was pleased to see that most were legible, which was something he tried to instill in all his subordinates. There, in the simple words, were the shorthand summaries of Blackroot district lives lost and crimes laid bare. A sailor crushed by falling cargo on the docks; a wife and mother killed by her drunken, jealous spouse. Four separate instances of children missing. Also, a suspicious gathering of ragged outsiders inquiring about the area around the harbor.

On his work table he had a large painted map of the district and Fraenk began to organize the incidents by where they took place. Then by stacking them in order of severity of the crime. He found it was best to be organized about such things.

It also helped him better understand trouble spots within the district itself. If one area became too problematic, he could send for additional partisan patrols to that location or go himself to see if there was an individual problem that required a more creative solution. He had no compunction about having a repeat troublemaker nailed into a crate and shipped downriver to one of their neighboring port cities.

As he began to sort and stack, Fraenk could see an unsettling trend forming. Many of the incidents were occurring along their district border with the Fernbrooks. And case after case involved someone who had recently returned from the war. Sometimes the soldiers were the victims, but more often than not, they were the cause. And the intensity of the crimes themselves was worse. Death by stabbing or beatings. Someone's head stove in with a rock. Even a decapitation. The city had enjoyed a lull while these men went off to war, but now it was worse than ever. The last time Fraenk had personally witnessed this much death and bloodshed was during the Redthorn rebellion, when he was still a young man. He vowed he'd never let things get that bad again.

As he continued to set the reports out, the small stacks of paper seemed to cover every corner of the map. This was a dark portent. A sign that things were going to get much worse.

There were only a few remaining when Fraenk saw the note from Nim. It was his first real duty—the details of Miken's murder at the bakery. Fraenk snatched up the paper and scanned it quickly. It began as he remembered. Details of the blade in Miken's back, and even a half-passable illustration of the owl sigil and the name Caldox Greenbriar. How would he feel about Lord Fernbrook settling their family's blood vendetta for something other than Fraenk's life? Even with his lord's order in place, Caldox might still be inclined to seek his own justice for his slain brother.

And speaking of which, Nim had jotted down more about their suspect. Fraenk didn't realize his subordinate had continued to add to the document, even in the midst of their interrogation of the elf. Nim had sensed something was terribly amiss about Bas Greenbriar, which he had done his best to lay clear in his notes. As if somehow it might be used in a later Justice Council tribunal as evidence to possibly convict. Naive as it was, it made Fraenk smile sadly.

He thought that might have been the end of the incident, but Fraenk noticed writing on the opposite side of the page. This was far less legible and hastily scrawled.

From what he could deduce, it was a recording of events as Fraenk had been hauled away by the partisans. Nim himself had been forced to leave, which was unusual.

But the final entry was the one that stopped him completely.

Another individual had arrived shortly after Fraenk was gone. One who should not have been there, nor have any cause for their presence in Blackroot district. It was none other than Fraenk's rival counterpart, the Arch Preceptor of Fernbrook, Farathiel Gingerglade.

He was the one who had arranged the hasty exchange of the bakery in the first place and was now appearing shortly after its new owner was killed. Regardless of what he promised Lady Blackroot, the Fernbrooks were after some terrible business inside of Blackroot district. Fraenk knew he must investigate this further.

8

"**Y**ou sure you don't want an escort, Lord Neversleep?" The Guard Captain Brumgrass asked as Fraenk rode up to the gate on his huge white war destrier. The horse was a temperamental and unsubtle steed that the confounded stableman had given him to ride only after Fraenk's escalating demand. This stamping equine mountain of muscle and malice, whose given name was Jimothy, was capricious, ill-tempered, and enjoyed only two things in the world: carrots and biting people. Fraenk made sure to pack extra carrots before he climbed aboard this colossus.

"I could send Locke and Woodmire here with you," Brumbrass suggested.

The two guardsmen standing beside the captain looked like they'd both been given a death sentence for no greater crime than being in the close proximity of a madman.

"No. That won't be necessary," Fraenk said, to the guard's visible relief.

"Do you at least have one of your men standing by?" Brumgrass continued.

"It's probably best that I ride out alone." Fraenk tried patting the horse, but it gave him a dark warning look. "I think if anyone's going to take a crossbow bolt this morning, it should just be me... and also Jimothy. He's bit me twice already."

Fraenk was wearing a bright red and black doublet, a wide-brimmed black hat with a billowy red feather, and had his silver Arch Preceptor badge, freshly polished, pinned over his breast. It was an ensemble that refused any amount of subtlety. Brumgrass scratched his cheek and shook his head.

"No one's going to miss you, that's for certain. And that goes for anyone waiting out there with an arrow drawn on you either."

"If that happens, you can tell all that you warned me," Fraenk smiled.

The big horse whickered and stamped impatiently. He would not remain under Fraenk's control much longer.

"The gate, Captain, if you would. Let's not keep this possible assassin waiting," Fraenk said in what he hoped wouldn't be his final words. He quickly tried to think of something wiser, or at least somewhat profound, but all that popped into his head were lyrics to a dirty poem the street kids used to chant.

Captain Brumgrass waved a hand signal over his head to the men beside the ornate door. They pulled with some effort, and slowly the large gate doors to Blackroot Estate swung open. If the Greenbriars had another assassin coming for him, there would be no better chance than this. It would be the true test of how sturdy Lady Blackroot's truce really was. A contract such as this was only as good as both parties' ability to enforce the terms. And even the highest-minded elves who praised their own virtues of honor, chivalry, and truth could have difficulty letting go of a good old-fashioned grudge.

But more importantly, it was a chance for Fraenk to reestablish himself in the district. Show just how unafraid he was of the Fernbrooks. An Arch Preceptor who hid and skulked around his own district would quickly lose his mystique, and he needed that if he hoped to retain his authority.

The heavy gate doors stopped on their hinges with a low boom. Then there was silence. A slight breeze played with the plume on Fraenk's hat. Fraenk tried to urge the mound forward, but his voice had gone totally dry.

But without even requiring a prompt, the huge horse stepped out from the shadows of the arch. It marched resolutely into the empty plaza, seeming to challenge anyone to puncture the rider on its back. Fraenk kept the reins pulled tight, even as the horse moved faster.

He released a breath he didn't realize he was holding. There was no hit squad standing with swords drawn. In fact, the wide avenue consisted of a normal and downright uninteresting mix of foot traffic, horses, and coaches. Several passersby gave him an odd look and a wide berth, but none seemed outright hostile. The day was quiet, but for the cawing of some nearby bird.

"Not dead, Fraenk?" The captain's voice called from behind him.

"Not so far."

"I'm glad to hear it, but you just cost me two silvers."

"The day's not over, Captain. I may make you rich yet."

Then, a large, rangy-looking crow with a milky eye that had been watching the proceedings from the gatehouse tower launched itself skyward with a series of artless flaps. The bird wheeled in the breeze and then turned toward him, apparently coming for a better look at Fraenk. But at the last moment, he angled hard and launched a prodigious volley of wet droppings down the front of his doublet. Fraenk looked down, too surprised to even do anything besides watch the runny mess travel the length of his tunic. The bird began cawing noisily as it flapped away, disappearing off into the city.

A chorus of laughter erupted from the gates behind him. They had all seen the whole thing.

"Some say that's an auspicious sign, Fraenk! Fortune dumps upon you!" The captain called to another round of guffaws.

Fraenk tipped a rude two-finger salute over his shoulder, then spurred the horse to a trot. The avian assassin had completed its mission. Fraenk's dignity was entirely murdered.

After quickly stopping at one of his hidden stashes for a less flamboyant and excrement-free change of clothes, Fraenk rode down through the city on the High Street all the way to Blackroot District. Although his expression was impassive, his eyes moved quickly over the street traffic, still scanning for the first sign of a threat. If he was concerned that his transit would go unnoticed, he could rest assured that he had everyone's attention. He could feel people staring. Humans looked up from their work to watch with incurious, hard eyes. The elves and half-elves who noticed him were abuzz. Some whispered, others glared, and one old elf shook his walking stick in Fraenk's direction.

"I suppose word travels fast when you kill an elf," Fraenk said to the horse, who snorted testily through its cavernous nostrils.

The destrier did not enjoy being paraded in such a manner. Nor was he trained for a polite stroll and was quick to remind everyone of that very fact. As Fraenk tried unsuccessfully to steer him back to the middle of the street, Jimothy decided to show just how unhappy he was. The unfortunate victim was an unwary elf woman whose strutting path had strayed too close to Jimothy's massive head. In an instant, the destrier's teeth clamped down and snatched the woman's oversized floral hat from her head and thrashed it until it was a mess of fibers in his grinding jaw. She shrieked like the horse had taken a section of her head, but from what Fraenk could see, she was otherwise unharmed.

Fraenk apologized profusely for the beast, vowing to have it immediately thrown from the city via catapult. But she was unmollified and threatened some kind of response from her husband, who was apparently 'important'. Fraenk decided it was best to just give the woman her space, and he quickly spurred Jimothy on before the elf made good on her screeching calls for the partisans to haul him away.

As he rode on, several times he caught movement of someone ducking into an alley or slipping behind a wall—possible sentries reporting on his movements or ruffians avoiding the spymaster, he didn't know. Either way, his purpose was apparently successful. The Arch Preceptor of Blackroot was back—forces of darkness and booze bottles everywhere, beware!

Despite his new boldness, Fraenk avoided the route that took him through Fernbrook district. He would most certainly not be welcome there. It was one thing to live freely under the protection of the truce and quite another to test its very limits. Fraenk could imagine every person in the district were now aware of his triumphal ride and might take it upon themselves to avenge Bas Greenbriar, or at least try to curry favor with Lord Fernbrook by taking a shot at Fraenk. It was best to stay clear of that place altogether.

During the long ride down, Fraenk was getting a feeling for the mood of the city. Much could and did change in the course of a month that he was out—at least according to what Gwen had written in her reports. Now, as he rode down through the streets, he could see that Arathes was charged and manic. This early contingent of returned soldiers was like adding a heaping scoop of flame powder to a boiling pot of soup.

In the upper districts, the preceptor's report described the young elf lords, parading around in their clean, polished armor, noticeably absent of any slash or dent. They spent their days strolling the grounds of their pristine estates in retinues of beautiful young men and women. They loved quoting ancient poets and prophets on the divine calling of a righteous war—one that was blessed by the Lyn-Tyrians themselves. The young officers were in high demand at gatherings, so they could recount the elegant ballet of army formations moving on a field of battle that they had watched from afar. Their stories were already inspiring a younger generation with dreams of one day commanding whole armies of their own. Perhaps another war would happen for them as well.

The middle districts were full of handsome, brave elves, half-elves, and human unit commanders. They were the captains and junior officers who had actually led their soldiers onto the field of play. Their skin was toned and tan, bearing light scars on the flesh. They had eyes that moved quickly and a frenetic energy for life. These were ones who had seen death up close and returned to tell about it. The war had left them mostly unscathed—at least on the outside.

These soldiers freely spent their war wages on food and drink or purchasing lavish gifts for loved ones in the upscale shops and markets. Some with the extra coin for it and seeking to boost their stature in the community had commissioned songs and plays of their heroic exploits on the battlefield—with a generous amount of embellishment. Others bought property or paid the elven matchmakers for an advantageous engagement with which would advance their position in society. There was no greater opportunity to change one's fortunes than in the wake of war.

But the mood was much darker by the time Fraenk reached the lower level of the city. It was home to the working-class districts of Blackroot, Sweetrose, Coldfrost, and Fernbrook. This was where the bulk of the regular forces were now reacclimating to their former lives. They were the foot soldiers and infantry, pikemen, and archers—those who did the killing and the dying. The cost of the battle was paid in missing arms or eyes. The fathers and sons who did not return the way they had been were sometimes worse than those who didn't return at all.

Dirty, broken men hunkered in doorways and alleys; their minds couldn't let them work or go home to families. The ones who sought relief in rivers of drink or mountains of Gazean powder. They had seen terrible violence against enemies and allies alike. And worst of all, they had witnessed the being of light with the fiery sword, which was more terrifying than anything beheld in the physical world.

There was not one species that was immune, either. Although they were mostly humans, as was befitting those who fell amongst the ranks of ground troops, there were also half-elves and even full-elves whose families couldn't keep them quietly at home without fearing what they might do. These were the ones who were scooped up by the partisans from other districts and deposited down here out of the way. It would not do to have those who confused or tarnished the gleaming golden image of Arathes and her righteous war. On the streets of Blackroot district, Fraenk breathed deep the familiar pungent and distinct odors of the streets. It was truly good to be home again. Every dirty inch of this place felt like it was a part of him—an extension of his soul. A place where forgiveness was never given, nor even asked for. There were no heroes here, only varying shades of greater or lesser scoundrels. Fraenk used to be one of them, raised to the dizzying heights by a twist of fortune and the favor of Lady Blackroot. But with a single word, he could fall all the way back to these muddy streets again. Despite the years and everything he had done to secure his place, this was a hard truth that would never leave him.

As he rode by the human slums, Fraenk saw that all Gwen had written had been the truth—and even understated in the words themselves. Staring at these rows of hovels, makeshift army tents built to house the displaced, the mud and filth, that desolation of spirit was somehow a worse darkness than the black cells had been.

Fraenk's big horse moved like a ship, parting through the press of people along Blackroot's avenue of merchants. The district seemed busier than normal. He caught the eyes of several familiar faces, who nodded or smiled when they noticed him. Many more people on the streets were unfamiliar, which was typical for both a city and a district that hosted travelers and traders from all points of the compass. He noticed a lot more swords and daggers in belts. More scars and hard stares.

Fraenk saw religious pilgrims on their way to the Temples of the Powers. There were displaced families hauling all their worldly possessions on over-loaded carts, a march of soot-covered Dwarves carrying digging implements, and a sand-beaten Gazean merchant's wagon drawn by six of the large feline Shivan bondslaves. He watched a line of shaven-headed acolytes in musty brown robes trying unsuccessfully to recruit from passersby. A fleshy priest-ess was ordering the finishing touches on a tall wooden statue of their goddess Oaphaela before their annual pilgrimage out into the forest to conduct their fertility rites. One look at the elderly folds of their bodies, and Fraenk was glad the culmination of their ritual would be out of view, away from the city.

Then one figure caught his eye. He nearly missed it at first glance, but in the stream of bodies flowing along the street, this one was a stone—dark and unmoving. It appeared to be looking right at him. Fraenk could not tell if it was male or female, nor even what species, for it was completely draped in loose gray linens, which covered even its spiked headdress.

Then he realized—no. *It was not a headdress at all. It was <u>horns</u>.*

An intoxicated man with a bushy beard, wearing a studded leather jerkin, staggered into his path and was muscled aside by Fraenk's horse. Jimothy took a vicious snap at the drunk man, only missing him because his arms were wheeling to catch his balance.

"Curse ya bleedin' Hylarrscat! Watch where you're ridin'!" the offended man shouted, then, not content with a mere insult, spat a fat wad of spittle at him.

Fortunately, the drunk's aim was poor—not factoring in the wind and the forward movement of the horse—and his spittle projectile hit one of the worker dwarves in the eye. The dwarf, a sturdy one with coal dust in his blonde braids, stopped and at first was unsure of what had just happened. Fraenk and the drunk man stopped as well. *This could get interesting.*

Dwarves were not known for their forbearance and did not take insults well, even ones that weren't intended for them. Fraenk watched as the dwarf dug the liquid from his socket with a thick index finger. He squinted and fixed his good eye on it. Those in the crowd who'd seen this interaction unfold took a large step back from the intervening space.

The dwarf muttered something in the mountain tongue, and his companions now turned as well. The spitter tried to mutter something—an explanation or apology—but it didn't matter. The dwarf jabbed his spit-covered finger at the man, and then all dwarves rushed the drunk with fists raised.

"Run and get the partisans!" Fraenk shouted at a bystander as the dwarves fell upon the hapless drunk, raining blows down on him.

Fraenk urged the destrier on, trying to avoid getting drawn into the melee. When he checked the street ahead, the ominous figure in gray was gone. It made a chill run up his spine. Damn creepy, was what it was.

He turned Jimothy onto Canal Street, which was actually two streets on either side of a dark, slow-moving channel. Here was a dirtier side of the district: taverns with skrate meat soup on the menu, apothecaries that trafficked in supposed love potions, and a spice shop that was caught selling gryphon's bane venom. They were not places an upstanding citizen would spend a coin, yet they managed to persist nonetheless. As Jimothy's clopping hooves rang on the stones, a light rain began to fall, which made the streets slick and the air heavy with a humid, algae-tinged air.

Ahead on the left was the three-story building Fraenk was looking for. The hand-painted sign above the door featured the carved frieze of a buxom, naked woman reclining strategically in the folds of red silk. the door and the name of the establishment: The Languid Maiden.

As Fraenk approached, a scrawny man—naked, but for a pair of leather boots—came tumbling out the door. He quickly clambered to his feet.

"Yer thieves! The skarking lot of you!" He screeched in a craggy voice, shaking an indignant fist. Then realizing he was standing in the wide open street without modesty, he cupped his hands over his dangling parts and scrambled off down the boulevard in a bow-legged gallop. Some sarcastic clod from an open window whistled lasciviously after him.

Fraenk dismounted outside and lashed his ill-tempered white monster to the hitching post. Jimothy snuffed at this apparent disrespect and jerked his head.

"Just wait here, boy," Fraenk said. "I'll just be a moment."

In reply, the horse clacked its blocky teeth at him, annoyed to be subjected to such indignity. Fraenk returned the snappy bite—it would not be wise to show weakness at this point. Fraenk was determined not to lose his dominance to a horse... not again.

Through the soot-stained windows, he could hear a lively jig being sawed out by a fiddler and flute to the tune of the indecent tavern song, *All's Fair when the Maiden's Bare.* Inside, a chorus of men's voices cheered at a spectacle they were thoroughly enjoying. Feet stomped and fists pounded tables. They sounded drunk, and there was a malevolence to their collective voices that Fraenk could recognize well. It was the sound of predators toying with their prey.

9

Guided by past experience, Fraenk had already formed an image in his mind of what he would find before he pushed through the doors of The Languid Maiden brothel. In some respects his assumptions had been correct; in the dim interior there was a single group of sturdy men who sat together, drinking from tall flagons of ale and singing raucously along to a pair of instrumentalists. In the light of the clusters of flickering candles burning low, Fraenk could see they all appeared to be soldiers, freshly returned, for their jerkins all bore the colors of Arathes along with the same House sigil. They must have been here for a while, for their hair was lank and oily. The smell that emanated from them was of body odor, foul breath, and booze. Several had wearisome, buxom, half-naked women on their laps who feigned either enjoyment or indifference of their uncareful treatment. The men sloshed foam from mugs as they sang. All of these things were de rigueur for an establishment of this nature in this part of town.

What Fraenk did not expect to see, however, was the unusual state of the two musicians who quite literally trod the boards for these drunk ruffians.

Several tables had been pushed together to create a makeshift stage in the middle of the room. Atop them, stamping and sawing out a frenzied tune, were the two of the most unfortunate minstrels Fraenk had ever beheld.

The first was a rotund, red-faced man. He was shirtless but wearing a comical white bonnet and oversized loincloth diaper fashioned from bed sheets. His old fiddle was tucked under his fleshy chin, which he expertly played as large drops of sweat dripped on the travel-worn instrument. He swiveled his enormous, hairy torso in rhythm with the music. Fraenk noticed it was dotted with flecks of red welts, as if stricken by the goblin pox. But it became immediately apparent that it was not the dreaded sickness, as one of the ornery soldiers pelted him with another fat rougeberry, which splattered against the man-baby's gut to the cackles of the other ruffians.

The second minstrel was a little more difficult to recognize as a man at first. For as he chirped out a cheerful melody on a silver flute, he was beautifully handsome in a fancy wig of bouncy blonde curls. Adding to the effect, his torso was squeezed into a corset complete with small oranges shoved in to give him comical breasts. This costume was obviously reappropriated from one of the working women there, but it didn't look wholly wrong on the flutist.

He accompanied the baby-man fiddler, moving seamlessly from one song to another as they capered and danced on the tables. This new tune the men instantly recognized with a cheer, and they joined in, belting out the bawdy lyrics:

Old Eldric the third got a new wife, I heard.
And oh, how the farmer did plow!
She's twenty acres of woman with a massive back field,
Oh, how the farmer did plow!
He worked the rows hard, putting seed in the land.
Oh, how the farmer did plow!
Broke his old tool and had to use his hand.
Oh, how the farmer did plow!

The song went on, growing more vulgar and juvenile with every verse. The drunk men were shouting and even pantomiming the actions with whoever was closest. Fraenk could see the ladies very much not enjoying their participation in this—yet they smiled or blinked placidly, too drunk, weary, or frightened to voice a protest. All of them looked ready for the ordeal to be over.

The music finally came to a rousing crescendo, and both musicians lowered their instruments, breathing heavily. They sketched a bow together in anticipation of applause or a coin being tossed to them in appreciation. But instead, the room went eerily quiet, as if the manic frenzy of the music was the only thing keeping the darkness at bay.

It seemed to affect the ruffians worst of all, for they immediately grew agitated. And before the fiddler and flutist could take half a dozen exhausted breaths, the names of several other songs were being shouted from the tables. They gave each other the same helpless look, which seemed to ask if they were going to continue this until one or both of them were dead. And in reply, they were pelted with curses, bread crusts, the hot wax from a guttering candle, and more threats of harm until they were underway again, filling the room with music.

In all this calamity, Fraenk had scanned every dark corner and saw no sign of his wayward apprentice, Nim Stonebridge. If he were here, he certainly wouldn't have let these men carry on as they were. Fraenk felt a spike of worry. Where was he?

Just then, the swing doors to the kitchen burst open, and a woman with streaks of white in her hair came hefting a platter of steaming meat and vegetables into the room. Fraenk recognized her as the madam proprietress. She flashed a look of fatigue and annoyance before turning with a warm smile.

"Who's hungry?" She said to the cheers of the men for their arriving food.

The madam stopped beside the group, adjusting the heavy tray in her grip. She twitched an eyebrow, and by some unspoken command, the ladies all rose and stretched in feline grace, then disappeared to their rooms back up the stairs. Some of the ruffians looked annoyed about their companion's departure, but the savory meat aroma made other appetites win out.

"Well? Where do you want I should put this, lads? Just toss it in your lap?" The madam asked in a tone that was a shade lighter than an actual scolding.

A large man with broad shoulders and bull-neck stood and waved for a cease from the musicians.

"Enough! We require your stage, my sweet missy," Bull-neck commanded. And before the flutist could even figure out how to get himself down, Bull-neck wrenched him by the forearm and pulled him to the floor. He landed lightly on his feet but immediately rubbed at his offended wrist. After seeing what happened to his companion, the man-baby needed no formal invitation and jumped down on his own, landing with an impact that Fraenk could feel across the room.

Bull-neck slid the solid wood table into the center of his group and stood back for the madam to place the meal on it.

The chairs scraped forward on the floorboards as the soldiers advanced on their savory comestibles. Daggers came free from their belts as they began carving away greasy chunks of meat. Soon the room fell to only the sounds of wet smacks of chewing and satisfied grunts.

The two musicians quietly backed toward the kitchen until a mouse-faced man with a black mustache noticed and shouted across the room.

"Don't scamper off, Fabreo! You're too beautiful to leave us just yet!" He simpered to the laughter of the group.

"Every man for himself!" The maiden-clad flutist shouted and scrambled out through the kitchen. His portly companion gave a surprised gape first to his friend, then the soldiers, before barreling out the exit himself. There were dismayed shouts and commands to return. One of them even threw a boiled potato, which burst against the wall, but none rose to actually chase them down.

While they were distracted, the madam noticed Fraenk standing silently in the entrance, and her eyes went wide, but only for a moment.

"Sound the horn if you need anything, boys. I'll go see what the cook has up next," she said with smooth courtesy and melted back from the group. Instead of returning to the kitchen, the madam gracefully made a wide arch around the room, tidying as she went. She lifted an overturned chair and picked up two empty flagons from the floor. Then finally arrived at where Fraenk waited. Once her back was to them, her smile vanished.

"Hosting a private party, Teelah?"

"Tell me you have a full regiment on their way, Fraenk," she said, fear and urgency in her voice. "These goons have been here for three days. *Three skarking days.* Stopped paying after the first night, and they chased off all my regulars. I'm running out of food and drink. And the girls. The poor girls. You've got to get them out of here."

"Did you call the baton brigade?" Fraenk asked grimly.

"Twenty times at least. They either said they're too busy, or they're friends with these boys and stopped to have a drink themselves," she said low. "When I did find one to take me seriously, he said he couldn't do nothing to 'em without a whole squad to back him up. I'll never get 'em to leave."

Fraenk nodded and glanced over her shoulder at the men. "Alright. You go out through the kitchen and get the clubbies yourself—this time tell 'em Fraenk Neversleep is doing the asking and that they should come in force. I think I'll go have a little chat with our friends."

"But–" She started to protest.

"Don't worry. I won't let anything bad happen to the place or the girls. Just bring the partisans. Is Big Boy the one calling the orders?"

She nodded, tears of relief forming in her eyes.

"Thank you, Fraenk."

"Say, another question. Did you see another Blackroot preceptor show up here recently? Stocky fellow? Goes by the name Nim Stonebridge?" Fraenk asked.

She pursed her lips and seemed to run the list of patrons in her memory, then shook her head. "Just you, by Mersey's blessing. But if I see him, I'll let you know."

"Very well. Go on now." Fraenk took her hand and patted it. She blinked, and her pleasant hostess smile returned. Madam Teelah continued her circuit of the room as if nothing had happened.

Fraenk strode to the middle of the room and sat in an empty chair that faced the table. The feasting soldiers didn't notice him at first, so he slipped the bottle out of his cloak and took a drink.

"More ale!" A man with curly orange hair shouted with a belch. He held his cup out, where it remained waiting. "Hey! Old wench! More ale! Where'd you go?"

Others in the group began to look around, but the madam was nowhere in sight. What they did see, however, was Fraenk seated and watching them.

"Gods above!" The orange-haired man cried out in alarm.

"When did you sneak in, *dirty kiv*?" Mouse Face added.

"Sorry to interrupt your supper," Fraenk said evenly. "But I'll need a word with the big ugly fella there."

The sounds of cutlery and eating abruptly stopped. A ripple of drunken laughter rang from the table. The men cast expectant looks at their leader, wondering just how badly he was going to beat this fool, whoever he was.

"We're eating. Piss off," the big man rumbled and gnashed a chunk of meat with his blocky, ox-like teeth.

"You've been asked to settle up your tab and leave, I'm afraid." Fraenk pulled his cloak back to slip the bottle away. His silver Preceptor badge glinted from underneath. "It's time you do so while I'm still asking politely."

"Oh look, boys, a preceptor!" One of them mocked.

"And it's the big scit of Blackroot!" Added another.

"We fought in the war, *boy*. What did you cowards do besides stay home and plot to steal our wives and properties?" Bull Neck said between bites.

"I'm sure your wife is lovely, and you bring fresh apples to her stable every day," Fraenk replied.

"What?" He growled.

"It's nice she lets you have your leisure while I assume she's off pulling a cart somewhere," Fraenk slipped the bottle back into his cloak.

"He's havin' a jape, boys," Mouse Face cut in, trying to pick a fight. "I think the spymaster is mocking you, Lural. I think you should beat him!"

But the big man was too lazy or hungry to be baited so easily.

"Leave us alone, worm. We're celebrating. We've earned that much at least."

"And you have been for days, as I understand it," Fraenk said patiently. "The mistress of the house asked for you to bring your debt current. Perhaps if you did that, we can arrange for you to stay a bit longer."

"We don't have the coin for that," the orange-haired soldier said, drawing a dark look from the one called Lural.

"Them ain't onions hanging from your belt, sir," Fraenk pointed to a sagging coin purse on one of them. It wasn't full, but Fraenk could see that a few coins remained. It may not cover all their expenses, but something was better than nothing.

"That's all we got from the entire war! We were the ones out there, dyin', and the high lords went home with chests of Tigraen gold and plunder," Mouse Face snapped bitterly, getting a babel of agreement from his peers.

"Don't take that out on Mistress Teelah and her girls. They did you a good service. You owe them for it," Fraenk pressed. They seemed to consider this until Bull Neck stabbed his knife down into the table with a loud THUNK. He left it there, quivering in the ale-stained wood.

"They owe *us* for what we did out there! And we came here to eat and rut and celebrate! And we ain't done yet. Are we lads!? " He gave a warning look to each man at the table. They were quick to agree.

"I'm sorry to say that you've overstayed your welcome, big lad. Just settle the bill and see your way back to Coldfrost District... That's where you garrison, I presume. The Blackroots have long been your friends. Let's not turn this ugly," Fraenk said, pointing at the Coldfrost house sigils on their jerkins.

"You're gonna have to make us leave," Mouse Face growled and checked to make sure Bull Neck was ready to back him.

"It doesn't have to come to that. We're all reasonable," Fraenk began to say, still hoping he could stall for time until the partisans arrived. But there would be no more civilized conversation.

Bull Neck stood, somehow even bigger than Fraenk was expecting. But Fraenk was quick to his feet as well, ready for what was about to happen.

Even half-drunk and hungover, Lural rounded the corner of the table, charging like the angry livestock that he was. His meaty fists were balled up for a punch to send Fraenk's head over to the far side of the canal. Even the other men at the table, who had been spoiling for this fight, were caught off-guard by its suddenness.

But size had its disadvantages as well, and Fraenk was ready. He spun his own chair around in front of him and kicked it forward into Bull Neck's legs. It whacked him hard in the shins, tangling in his uncoordinated legs. The big man's reaction was slow and he tripped forward, landing face-first on the stone floor like a sack of grain. They could all hear the knock that Lural's skull made as it hit the floor. Before he could move, Fraenk closed the gap and kicked him hard in the place where his muscled shoulder connected to that thick bull neck. It was a move meant to stun Bull Neck, and it seemed to be effective—but for how long?

Fraenk did not have time to consider the threat of Lural any longer, for there were other matters to be dealt with. Five matters, specifically, as the remaining soldiers became abruptly aware that they were no longer spectators to a beating but instead compelled to replace their leader in the fight. They didn't seem happy about this.

Mouse Face was both the nearest and possibly least drunk among them, so it was only a moment before he leaped into combat, throwing a wild right-hand cross at Fraenk's face. But the swing was too slow, and Fraenk deftly leaned back out of the path. He countered with the edge of his left hand to the man's open jaw so hard, he could feel the man's teeth through his cheek. Mouse Face made a stunned *Ungh!* sound and spun with his back to Fraenk.

Fraenk grabbed the man by this thin neck like one might take hold of a chicken headed for the chopping block. With his other hand, Fraenk slipped a throwing knife from the brace at his hip and poked it up between his legs.

"What are you—ooooh!" Mouse Face screeched as he became keenly aware of the point of the blade poking into the gob between his legs. Fraenk's fingers pressed into his throat, making his cries sound like an alarmed duck.

"Stop there, lads!" Fraenk said, digging the point of the blade higher. Mouse Face went to his tiptoes to keep the blade from piercing his prize, and his voice rose in pitch along with it. He was no longer shouting, but just a high-pitched screech.

The remaining men stopped in their advance. Fraenk had positioned the wailing Mouse Face between himself and them. They looked unsure of what to do next. Fraenk saw curious faces of the women upstairs, who were now looking down through the railing at what was happening.

"What have we here, lads? A heavy pouch indeed," Fraenk smiled. "I believe you do have something these ladies want."

With a quick movement of his wrist, Fraenk's pulled the knife, then slashed a seam in the dangling coin pouch at Mouse Face's hip. A rain of copper, silver, and even a couple of gold coins spilled out onto the floor with a melodic jingle. And just as quickly, Fraenk had the knife back to its earlier spot in Mouse Face's delicates.

"You think that covers everything?" Fraenk quipped. "Or should we open *this* pouch and see what spills out?" The point of his blade jabbed for emphasis.

"It-it-its settled! The c-coins are enough!" the man cried.

The other soldiers were moving out to get around him. Fraenk could hear Bull Neck groan and start to gather himself from the floor. His momentary advantage was fading fast, and Fraenk needed a strategic retreat.

The ginger-haired man seemed not to notice nor care about his friend's precarious situation and stepped in with a mighty drunken swing. It was rare to see anything this stupid. Fraenk only had to move Mouse Face's head forward into the path instead.

"No-no-no!" Mouse Face tried to say before the man's knuckles sent teetering sideways. Fraenk shoved the oaf's body into the direction of the swing, making both men entangle with each other on the floor.

The two other men watched their friends fall, then looked back at Fraenk, a murderous glare in their eyes. Both were gripping the same daggers they had just used with their meal, which dripped with meat juices and grease.

"One moment, friends," Fraenk said, holding up a hand. "I see we are all armed with blades, and I'm worried one of us could get seriously injured. I think it would be most prudent if we all put them away before this fracas continued any further."

Fraenk straightened and slipped his throwing blade safely back into its scabbard. Then patted it for good measure.

"There! We wouldn't want this to turn deadly—oh." His smile faltered. The two men raised their greasy daggers and advanced on their now unarmed opponent. Apparently, they did not share Fraenk's offer to forego any bloodshed; they intended to carve him up much like the plate of cooling meat behind them.

"Well, that's what I get for trying to be honorable," Fraenk muttered.

The first attacker who came at him was a pox-scarred lout with a patchy black beard and rotten yellow teeth. He had an open hand up with fingers spread; the other held the blade and was cutting back and forth through the air in a swipe-swipe move. Fraenk raised his own hands in defense. Fraenk knew techniques on how to disarm attackers. Perhaps he could get the blade away from him.

"An odd fighting style, friend. Did you create it yourself?" Fraenk said. "Although if you're not careful, you could—"

The man shouted and jabbed at him. Fraenk's left hand moved viper-quick, trying to catch his wrist but only smacking his hand off course. The blade veered hard to one side and stuck into his open hand all the way to the hilt.

He looked at it in disbelief for a moment before his eyes went wide and he began to scream.

Just then, the other man shoved past him in a charge. If he'd been ready, Fraenk would have fainted to one side, but now it was all he could do to keep the man's blade out of his own belly.

Fraenk back-pedaled following the motion—it was the only way he could go with the knife coming at him so fast. Before he could plan his next move, Fraenk's back clipped off something solid in the middle of the room, making his torso twist sideways. This was what kept the dagger from piercing him all the way through and out the back. Instead, it sliced along his ribs and went through his cloak, pinning it firmly into the support beam that Fraenk had collided with. Just as fast, the man released the dagger and stepped out of Fraenk's reach before he could retaliate.

He was good, this one.

Fraenk looked into the eyes of his attacker. This man had a scar down one drooping cheek where the nerve had been severed. He was calm and moved slowly. There was precision to his steps and practiced ease to his movements. He was well-trained, and Fraenk could tell that, unlike his bumbling friends, this man was a remorseless killer.

As if to emphasize the point, he reached behind to his belt and pulled another blade. This was not the kind used for eating. It was made from black-tempered steel and had a knuckle guard with knobby spikes running the length.

The man grinned at him.

"You're Neversleep, the Lord Preceptor," he said, not a question. "You killed that elf."

Fraenk's blood went cold. This killer of men had a blade ready and now wanted to discuss Bas Greenbriar. Was he another assassin that had just lured him into a trap?

"I am. What's it to you, friend?" Fraenk said cautiously.

"I don't much like elves. Lost some good friends because some lordling got dressed up in shiny armor and wanted to play commander. Far as I'm concerned, one less elf is doing us a favor," the scarred man said, his eyes never leaving him.

"You're welcome. Why don't you and your friends be on your way, and we'll call it even?"

"You're not a real elf-killer, though. You love them. You _serve_ them, *Lord Preceptor*."

Fraenk could see him moving closer, and Fraenk's hand reflexively went to his own brace of knives, fumbling to grab one. But as he did, the other man slashed, and Fraenk had to move his arm away to keep it from getting cut to the bone.

As he did, Fraenk swung his other fist, barely clipping the man's chin, but only seemed to amuse him more than do any actual damage.

"Betray your own people so you can kiss the feet of an elf? I can't let that go," the man said, closing in now to finish Fraenk off. His companions were all recruiting themselves as well, and they would soon be back in this fight. A smart man might take this moment to run.

Fraenk tried to sidestep away from the killer, but something jerked hard at his neck. The dagger in his cloak had him pinned and collared. Fraenk was like a goat pinned to a stake, just waiting for the wolf to close in. There would be no escape.

The wolf in question looked ready to eat.

"Well, Lord Preceptor. They said you were clever, but I don't see it."

The scarred soldier shook his head in disappointment then and prepared to bury his dagger in Fraenk's chest.

"Well, maybe you can see this," Fraenk said, producing a spherical, clear object from his cloak with his other hand. The man paused in confusion. Was this some kind of weapon or a last-ditch bribe? But before he could figure it out, Fraenk hurled it hard at the floor.

Fraenk pinched his eyes shut tight and shielded himself with an arm for good measure. He had no idea if this was going to work. If it didn't, he'd be standing there like an idiot while he was stabbed to death.

But an instant later, a blinding flash of light washed the entire room in pure brilliance. Even with his eyes closed, the brightness seemed to be everywhere, going through his very flesh. There was a simultaneous wail from the other men whose eyes were unprotected. He heard a blade clatter to the floor, and several bodies fell back to the floor.

The room was dark again. But when he opened his eyes, Fraenk's vision crawled with ghost images. Fortunately, after a few blinks, he could see well enough. But that was not the case for the five Coldfrost soldiers; they all held their eyes and groaned in pain. Wispy sparkle trails still floated in the air, the fallout of Fraenk's exploding glow orb. As a rare magical item, it was something he hated to lose, but it was better than bleeding out on a brothel tavern floor.

Fraenk's gambit had worked, but it was still only a diversion. His attackers may have been blind, but they cursed at him and began feeling their way around with waving arms. The scarred man was still standing in front of him, his sightless eyes streaming tears, but his face was turning this way and that. He was listening. Fraenk waved a hand in front of him, just to make sure he couldn't see, then balled a fist and punched him square in the nose, sending him toppling back over a nearby chair.

He landed between the orange-haired man and Bull-Neck, who mistook him for Fraenk and began to beat him themselves until he could get them to stop.

The rest howled curses and staggered towards him like the awakened dead, their hands grasping in the air for him. Fraenk sidestepped their dangerous fingers as they moaned in frustration and vowed to bring him death.

Fraenk made his way to the tavern door before he spoke again.

"The lot of you are banned from all Blackroot taverns from this day forth," Fraenk pronounced. "If I catch you back in here, then there's really going to be trouble."

"Get him!" Bull Neck yelled at his companions. They lunged at where they thought he was standing. Two men grappled with each other for a moment before realizing their error.

Fraenk freed his pinned cloak and backed toward the front door of The Languid Maiden. He had to keep them following him if the girls were to be safe.

"The door is this way, lads," Fraenk said as they staggered closer.

The men blinked and rubbed their eyes. Fraenk noticed their vision was starting to come back. They squinted like men peering into bright sunlight and seemed to make out where he was standing.

"There he is, boys," the big man said, turning Mouse Face around to the proper direction.

"Yes, I can see him," Black Beard agreed.

The ones who could see grabbed the rest, and they advanced as one toward him. Fraenk let them close the gap a bit more before he shoved out the front entrance door into the street. He'd have just a few moments, but it should be enough time to mount his horse and ride off.

"Come, Jimothy! Let's be off."

Fraenk looked around. First down one direction of Canal Street, then the other. His plan of riding away wasn't the most elaborate, but it did rely on one crucial detail. It would require a horse. The only problem with this was that the large white destrier was no longer there. Neither was the hitching post he'd lashed the beast to. Instead, there was a double set of fresh holes where the posts had previously been set into the ground. They were gone, root and stem, along with Fraenk's plan.

Huh. Fraenk thought, dismayed. *Jimothy must've had some better place to be.*

The door of the tavern banged open again, followed by the sound of running footsteps. Fraenk wheeled around to see the five soldiers moving to box him in. The Bull Neck cracked his knuckles.

"We got him. Nowhere to run," he said.

"Yes. Let's see how our Lord Preceptor likes bein' blind," the scar-faced man growled with a nasty grin. And then the Coldfrost soldiers began to close in on Fraenk.

10

T HE POSITION OF ARCH Preceptor has a long and storied history in the
kingdom of Sarmatti, and unfortunately for the idly curious, most of
it is a guarded secret. It is said that these spymasters could pull the strings of
those in authority, even installing their own figureheads in leadership so they
could rule from behind the curtains. And there were a few notable examples
in Arathes, like Leawos Greenstone and Davin the Darkblade, who were not
content with staying in the shadows and eventually supplanted their elven
lords. As an interesting footnote, both elves ruled for only a short period before
meeting their own mysterious and untimely end.

Due to the dangerous nature of a preceptor's job, the use of subterfuge, deception, and even murder were seen as—perhaps not officially condoned—but
necessary practices for what allowed one to be effective. To be truly successful,
you had to be more cunning and ruthless as your adversaries, which meant
being more devious than the criminal element. Even still, the life expectancy
of a preceptor was shockingly low. The undertakings of the preceptor service
often meant being in places where one was not welcome, learning things others
did not want one to know, and strange acts of risky diplomacy that could result
in the death of one party or another. Preceptors were sometimes the last line of
defense for a district or the first soldier to fall in a shadow war.

Simply put, the preceptor's job was to make problems go away. Given such
a mandate and very little oversight, the Arch Preceptor themselves wielded a
tremendous amount of unchecked power. A single word could send scoundrels
scattering. A mere glance could stop the hardest cutthroat in his tracks. And
someone deemed too troublesome had a regular habit of coming down with a
terminal case of a missing head or an excess of new punctures to important vital
organs. However, as time went on, the very definition of who was 'troublesome'
grew perilously vague.

The Arch Preceptor's job was not only challenged by the city's criminal element and citizenry alike but was also notoriously plagued with internal corruption from his subordinates and infighting amongst the other district Acherons. When Fraenk first took over, he knew it was going to be a difficult task—to say the least. He had none of the authority and respect that an elf would command and still faced all the same perils. Many predicted that Fraenk would be killed within the first fortnight or alternately resort to committing terrible atrocities in the name of establishing himself as the first human spymaster of Blackroot.

But to everyone's surprise, Fraenk's approach was to use charm and negotiation—interpersonal skills he forged on the streets. Once he had won the hearts of the average resident of the district, criminality became much less pervasive, and a healthy stream of money began to flow back into the pockets of the elves. Human or not, his elf contemporaries had no choice but to respect him as well.

Who could have imagined that the job of the Arch Preceptor was much easier with a light touch? Information moved much more freely. Local insurgency and rebellion against authority was a thing of the past. And the critical work of keeping the High Lord informed and positioned to make the best decisions for the district was a matter of course. Fraenk's achievement—and as a result, Blackroot District's success—caused a ripple effect throughout other district's Preceptor services in Arathes.

Of course, the downside to this 'light-touch' approach was that there were still the thugs out there who only responded to a direct and intense application of violence.

Fraenk was not a violent man by nature and tried to avoid it in most situations. But he had trained with a transient monk in the combat form of Atadash, a hand-to-hand defensive style. And had also become quite adept at throwing blades, which he tried to reserve as a last resort. Some men liked to crow about their reputation for being a prolific killer, but when your business was gaining and keeping trust, that kind of thing was very counterproductive.

And so while Fraenk would have been well within his right to reach for the brace of throwing knives on his hip and drop each man where they stood, doing so would only create more problems than it would solve. He tried to figure out a way to diffuse this situation without killing and fighting them five against one was also less than ideal. They were all trained soldiers—some more formidable than others. All were a bit drunk, but they would still give him trouble facing each individually, let alone as a group. And one mustn't forget that these men were Coldfrost—who remained a strong Blackroot ally. Killing them would be very much frowned upon. Fraenk could insist they were reprimanded and punished later, but he'd need to survive long enough to do that.

"Good sirs, there's no need to continue this squabble. I scarcely even remember how it started."

"You kicked me in the neck!" The big man said angrily.

"And it hurt my foot, so maybe we're even," Fraenk suggested. They did not appear ready for an armistice. In fact, they spread out to surround Fraenk. Calling to one another to coordinate their attack.

"Grab him!" "Watch him! He's a tricky snix!" "Make sure he doesn't get by you!"

Fraenk turned to look for an escape, but he was boxed in. And to his further dismay, their shouting had attracted a curious group of onlookers. This seemed to definitively put to rest the question of if he should quickly murder these men and feed their bodies to the Mosswater carp.

Although it would not do for the Arch Preceptor to be seen publicly and embarrassingly beaten by these hooligans either. Running away would make him look like a coward. Not great, but that was increasingly becoming his very best option. Fraenk prepared himself to plow over their weakest man, which happened to be Mouse Face, and make his escape.

"He's gonna do a runner. Don't let him get away!" Bull Neck warned his friends, anticipating Fraenk's next move.

Then something unexpected happened. A tall man with a strong jaw and swept brown hair stepped into the space created by the crowd, followed by six more men. All of them soldiers, and all of them had the sigil of Blackroot on their doublets. They were dressed for reverie, not battle, but on their belts, they wore daggers instead of swords. This new faction formed up in a line behind their long-haired leader. Each raised their fists like seasoned brawlers. It was as if Fraenk's reinforcements had just arrived—and not a moment too soon.

"Ho there boys, you best be standing down." The man called, crossing his toned arms across his chest. His smile was friendly, but there was menace in his voice. The Coldfrost soldiers turned toward this new threat. Bull-Neck stepped forward to face them, but the rest of his men shrank back, their courage faltering. They could see that they were not only outnumbered but were being met by men who hadn't spent the last several days of long hours debasing themselves.

"This is a personal matter. We were just—" Mouse Face started to explain.

"From the looks of it, you were about to disrespect our Arch Preceptor," the long-haired man said. "But what you should do is head back to your district and get a little rest. You'll feel better."

The soldiers exchanged furtive glances with each other and the contingent of Blackroot men, who looked ready and eager to beat them all bloody. Then, as bullies who suddenly find themselves outmatched, shrank like dungeon slugs in a bucket of salt water. Even Bull-Neck could see his men wavering and lost his own manly vigor.

"I notice that you're still standing here. I guess that means we stomp you," the Blackroot man said and tipped two fingers in their direction. Blackroot soldiers stepped in like they were advancing on the enemy. The Coldfrost men broke ranks and immediately scattered, shoving through the crowd and off down the street.

"Blackroot!" The long-haired man shouted to the cheers of the crowd.

Fraenk tried to straighten and felt a sharp pain across his ribs. He could see an opening through his tunic where there was a long but superficial cut that leaked blood.

"That's the second shirt today," Fraenk muttered, dismayed.

The long-haired soldier approached with a broad smile. Up close, his features could have been that of a handsome man, but somehow their assemblage and proportions made him somewhat of an acquired taste. Fraenk was glad to see him nonetheless.

"Leos Muninger, I suppose I owe you a drink for that one," Fraenk said, picking up his cloak. "The boys too."

"What that? Nah. It was nothing. I was doin' *them* a favor. Powers help the man that crosses Fraenk Neversleep," Leos clapped Fraenk warmly on the shoulder. "Besides, we can't let those unruly sons of skarks in here, upsetting the general folk. Gets 'em thinking they own the place and can do whatever they want."

"It would seem these men came home and forgot how we do things in the districts—even the ones that grew up here," Fraenk replied levelly. He removed a tiny jar about the size of his thumb from another pouch inside his cloak. He winced as he smeared white cream from the jar on his cut.

"That's true enough..." his friend conceded. "Many of us found out the hard way that the lovely war ain't like what the singers tell us in their songs, neither—promising we'd each come home with a fat chest of gold and the hand of a pure maiden to greet us. But it's not half the glory and double the sorrow."

Then Leos' smile faltered.

"It does appear like most come home with some misaligned expectations. Like they still got some warring to do," Fraenk pressed a clean piece of linen against his wound to stop the bleeding.

"Aw, just give 'em time to settle back in, Fraenk. They're not bad men. They just need to keep their hands busy. You might think about adding on a few extra guards to help keep the Lady's peace in the meantime," Leos suggested.

"More guards," Fraenk repeated.

"More preceptors, too," this time he heard an inquiry in Leos' tone.

In his mind, Fraenk had a picture of that bent-nosed prison guard, the one who slipped the shiv to the assassin Carax, now with a preceptor's badge pinned to his cloak. A single infiltrator breaching the preceptor service could be damaging, but several could be catastrophic to the entire district. And there was the *other* matter as well. He and Leos might be friends now, but the past was a thorny place. The scars made there might fade, but they never went away entirely.

Before Fraenk could reply, his attention was turned to the pound of approaching footsteps. Nim Stonebridge was coming up the street, pushing through the dispersing crowd.

"Well, well. My auxiliary finally arrives, just in time. Fraenk said sarcastically. Nim stopped in front of them, red-faced and out of breath. It took him several seconds before he was able to speak.

"Do you need to lie down first, Nim?" Fraenk quipped.

"Sorry, Fraenk... I came as soon as... I heard the trouble..." Nim wheezed.

"I think we got it under control now," Fraenk saw Nim give a questioning look at the other man. "Nim Stonebridge... Meet Leos Muninger. He's an old friend. Nim works for me when the opportunity suits him."

The two men shook hands. Nim turned back to Fraenk.

"Well?" Fraenk asked.

"You see, I was on my way here and got tipped that members of the Palewood Brethren were poking around the docks. Rumor goes they're looking for a place to summon some god from the underrealm called Bultzoaan. So I followed these acolytes—"

"Backwoods Tigranean cultists *here*?!" Leos' laugh was big and echoed off the window panes on the street. Fraenk looked dubious as well. "From the reports I've read, the Interrogers questioned the very last one of them cultists until all his fingernails came off," Fraenk said, tapping his lip.

"I thought they'd already summoned one because of the helltouched they were with," Nim replied.

"*Helltouched?*" Fraenk was suddenly curious. "I think I've seen him too. Where is he now?"

"I was by the Lower Market when I saw them conversing."

"Hmm. Should we go have a look just to make sure there's no cultists over there now buying affordable trousers from the merchants of Selucis?" Fraenk winked mischievously. Nim was unamused.

Fraenk swept on his cloak and tied it about his neck. Then he pulled out his note board and quill.

"And while we're there, I need to look into something that's been troubling me about that bakery," Fraenk ruminated as he scratched out a quick note to himself. "Oh yes. I suppose I should probably inspect what foul deal Lady Blackroot has wrought in the market as well. Did you know she made some absurd bargain with the Fernbrooks on my behalf, Nim?"

Nim's eyes widened with apprehension.

"Uh, sir... I believe everyone knows, unfortunately. Did she tell you specifically what she arranged?" Nim asked, but Fraenk was turning back to the large soldier.

"Leos, I still owe you that drink." Fraenk warmly gripped the man's hand. "But it will have to be later. Duty calls. Excuse us."

"Alright, Fraenk. I'll find you later. We have much to discuss!" Leos Muninger said with a toothy smile and waved as Fraenk strode away.

"Sir, I'm serious. Did no one tell you about the market?" A panicked Nim scrambled to keep up.

"What in the Bright Book of Brand is going on here?!" Fraenk roared, standing at the entrance gate of the Lower Market Bazaar. Large green banners bearing the Fernbrook sigil fluttered in the gentle breeze on either side of the gates. Under them, a row of Fernbrook guards in shiny gold armor and tall spears stood glowering at everyone who entered.

"I tried to tell you, sir," Nim breathed heavily, still trying to keep pace.

"That dotty old bat traded away the entire bazaar? For me?!"

"It appears so, sir," Nim looked down.

"Does she know how much gold this place brings in?!" Fraenk growled, getting even more heated.

"I'm sure the Acheron of Coin has made her abundantly aware of it." Nim wouldn't meet his gaze.

"Then why did she do it?!" Fraenk snapped.

"I'm loathe to hazard a guess, sir. You're certainly not worth it."

"I KNOW THAT!" Fraenk shouted, drawing a look from several of the Fernbrook spearmen. They fixed him with narrowed eyes then exchanged an animated whisper with their leader, a half-elf with gold-trimmed epaulets. He, too, threw a pinched glare at Fraenk, then marched directly toward them.

"Arch Preceptor Neversleep!" The captain barked as he approached. It was as much a challenge as an address of rank. Tanned and toned, the captain was easily recognizable as one of the recently returned soldiers. One who probably commanded an entire unit in the army and was now somehow reduced to a simple guard duty position.

"That's right." Fraenk's temper boiled at the surface and he was in no mood for foolishness.

"Oh, look, sir. Someone else who doesn't like you," Nim said under his breath.

The captain halted and clacked his heels together with military precision.

"It is my duty to inform you that Lower Market Bazaar is now under the protection and purview of Fernbrook District."

"I can see that," Fraenk hissed, then added. "All they had to do was murder a baker and his family, and now they've got the whole market all to yourselves."

The captain flashed irritation for a moment but refused to be baited. "Furthermore, by order of his lordship, Malgraye Fernbrook, you and the members of your preceptor service are henceforth and forever banned from the grounds of the bazaar," the captain said with a slight curl of satisfaction on his face.

"Banned?" Fraenk's eyes narrowed. "As in...?"

"As in, if you are caught inside, I have been authorized to use whatever force necessary to remove you." That nasty curl of a smile again.

"What if I want some bread from my favorite bakery?" Fraenk asked, watching his reaction. The captain's almost-smile fell away.

"There's no longer a bakery in the market, I'm afraid," the captain said, not sounding sorry at all. "After the fire, it was a complete ruin. Lord Fernbrook has declared a guard station will be built there in its place."

Fraenk clenched his fist for a moment, then released it.

"Alright, Captain. Your message is received. You won't catch me inside the bazaar," Fraenk said levelly.

The captain tipped his head slightly, the barest courtesy, then performed a crisp about-face and strode back to his men. They had been gawping and now straightened again with their leader's approach.

Fraenk pulled Nim by the arm and marched him away from the gates.

"This entire situation is the darkest manner of foul," Fraenk growled once they were well out of earshot.

"I know, sir. That was the best bread in the district."

"Not that, ya ground slug!! Miken's murder! This bent deal with the Fernbrooks! Not only is there a complete sanction for preceptors from entering the market, but they're covering it over with a guard post. It can only mean one thing."

"They hate you specifically for killing their kin and have found creative ways to retaliate." Nim suggested.

"Well, yes. Fine. It can mean several things, but it means there's a bigger plan at play here," Fraenk tapped his lip, thinking.

"Sir, I think you may have had a little too much time alone in that moldy dungeon," Nim said gently. "Bas Greenbriar was a lunatic. He killed a human family, and you gave him what he deserved. I'd be willing to call that justice and let the whole thing be."

Fraenk looked over at Nim, surprised. "You agree I did the right thing?"

"I think we should try to find these Palewood Brethren lads."

"That's too easy," Fraenk snapped his fingers and began to pace. "The Fernbrooks made a last-minute deal for that bakery, giving up a more valuable piece of territory, which Fernbrooks *never* do. Why is that bakery so important?"

"Perhaps they wanted control of the Lower Market all along. Everyone knows how important Miken was to the entire bazaar. No one set up shop there, save by his blessing."

"I thought about that too. Then why kill him? They already owned his shop," Fraenk replied.

"He wouldn't play nice. Or they wanted their own man for the job. I've seen that happen plenty, you know," Nim recalled with a grim expression.

Fraenk nodded, but he wasn't content to let the matter go.

"There's something else. You remember Greenbriar's war dagger?"

"Left it stuck right in the baker's back..." Nim shuddered.

"Exactly. That means he must've killed his wife and children first before he spoke to Miken. We just assumed it was the other way around."

Nim looked shocked. "Why would he do that?"

"Why indeed?" Frank pulled out his bottle and took a quick drink. He handed it to Nim, who nearly drained it.

"One more thing... while I was enjoying my leisurely vacation in the black cells, I sent out a few inquiries and uncovered one more piece of the puzzle. Our psychotic little elvish friend was no war hero like they're claiming him to be; he was an interrogator. His job was to break teeth and cut off tongues to find enemy gold and valuables. They don't give out property to torturers, and they definitely don't make midnight deals that lose them valuable territory just to give him one cozy little bakery as a war prize."

"Miken must have had something of value. Or knew something..." Nim rubbed the point of his ear.

"The answers must be inside that bakery. But I <u>need</u> to get in there before they turn it into a skarking guard post!"

They both cast a glance back over their shoulders at the downright excessive amount of Fernbrook soldiers posted there. Several men still had eyes on Fraenk and Nim across the distance.

"Even without the army out front, it wouldn't be easy, sir. That's one thing the skriffs always complained about. There's bars on the sewer holes and between buildings. Spikes on the fence and any flat surface above. One way in and out."

"Exactly. Who do you think worked to seal up all those weak points?" Fraenk said with a grim smile. "A minimal guard rotation with half a brain could protect it. Only a fool would attempt to venture inside."

"We have that much at least," Nim nodded.

"What I really need is a distraction."

"Why didn't you say so, sir?" Nim smiled. "I can help with that."

Part III

11

KYLA GRACEFIRE MIGHT HAVE been asleep when it happened. She had been sitting by the window that overlooked the Lower Market and had a long but unobstructed angle on the charred husk that was formerly a bakery. For days that stretched into weeks, she sat and watched and waited. Since the baker had died—been killed, more accurately—it was all she could do. Watch and wait. Wait and watch. If the baker had been the only one who knew, he could not give up his secrets now—they had made sure of that. Powers damn them. She hoped the other one was somewhere safe, lying low.

"Please be alive." Her whispered mantra whenever she thought about him, which was often.

Sometimes the most unpredictable and therefore dangerous part of her job was the clients. They were often rude, unreliable, petty, greedy, and occasionally prone to aggravating acts of shortsighted betrayal far more often than one would believe. Wasn't it simpler to just pay for the item you hired her to steal? If they weren't smart enough to pinch it themselves, why did they think they could outwit the ones that did it professionally?

Of course, Kyla knew this was the hazard of her particular line of work. And it was why they had such elaborate systems in place to try to prevent such catastrophic breakdowns. For some reason, it was usually the clients who were particularly wealthy and powerful who attempted such double crosses and also believed they could get away with it. Most often, they refused to pay, sometimes trying to have her crew arrested. It was a staggeringly foolish thing to attempt on someone who professionally stole valuable things and breached locked rooms. That was a good way to find the valuable in question missing, along with additional items equal to twice the original agreed-upon fees. The offending client couldn't be surprised by this because they were always clear about this contingency before any job began.

She didn't even want to think about the string of failures that led to her current predicament, but that was all she could do: sit in this small second-story room, wait for the other one to return, and think. Oh, and also recover from being stabbed and shot with an arrow.

There was that.

What was most troubling was how fast and efficiently the mad elf had dismantled her team here in the city. They had called themselves The Circle, and they were nothing so ostentatious as The Thieves' Guild, which was a top-heavy organization that spent more time stealing from its rank-and-file members than it did pulling actual thievery jobs. Kyla's group was instead a loose and efficient association of professionals who each were experts at their given discipline, but with enough separation so that any point of failure wouldn't jeopardize the entire group. That was the theory anyway, and one that apparently didn't survive contact with a psychotic elf with a blade.

He went for the Broker first, obviously. She was mid-aged, short, and had a gregarious charm that was infectious. If she didn't know everyone who was anyone in Arathes, she definitely knew someone who did. The Broker's public job had something to do with actors in the theater district, for she always had a revolving stable of handsome young men around that she rented out as performers for this play or that opera—and, if rumors were to be believed, male companionship to some unnamed high society clientele. These "stallions" as she called them—not to mention her position in society—should have shielded her from any harm. After all, she was just the Broker. Just a dealmaker and go-between. She didn't handle the money or the goods. But she was the trailhead for this macabre odyssey. The partisans found her dead, bound up with her eyes outside of her head, two bleeding boys by her side still alive but with tendons slashed and would never walk again. They heard her finally give up the name of the Pickup.

The Pickup's job was to collect the fee from the client and keep it secure until it was time to divvy up. In the case of Kyla's Circle, their Pickup was actually a pair of muscular twin brothers. Their forte was evasion techniques—wearing identical clothing and carrying identical bags, which they swapped, stashed, retrieved, and exchanged several times in the course of their mission. This made it nearly impossible for someone to waylay them on their journey back, laden with coins. While they could fight, their most effective defense was to reveal to a potential mugger that their bag was actually filled with rocks and the real target was now long gone. The sadist elf had used their close bond against them, however. Torturing one while the other watched. They must have known more about the others than she realized, because by then the mad elf knew them all.

Had Kyla herself been the third—technically, fourth—target? Or did the killer find the other one too? She only remembered flashes of the attack. The smell of him. And his stained mouth—horrible and crawling with tiny black worms. Then the blade through her side. He was fast, but something was wrong with him. She did somehow manage to escape by climbing instead of going down the alley. If she had, the arrow would have found a lethal mark instead of grazing her calf muscle. She scolded herself that she still had time to warn the baker, but she was bleeding badly and probably would have just ended up dying at the hands of the elf along with the old man and his family. She shuddered, remembering how they carried the small, charred bodies out of the ashen ruins.

She had grieved for all of them. They were as close to family as she had. They were all gone except for possibly the last one. The one she didn't dare even picture in her mind or say his name until she knew they were both safe. She vowed if the bad ones ever caught her, she'd never give him up, no matter what. They'd just have to kill her.

In the weeks that she'd been up here recuperating, training to regain her strength, and watching the bakery, Kyla tried to only sleep during the day. There was no reason to expect he would try to reconnect in daylight anyway. The place was constantly defended by too many guards. First by the ones in black and more recently by the ones in green who betrayed them. It was even more dangerous now that they had apparently taken over the entire district. Would the others dare come back now? Perhaps he already tried while she was still lying up in bed and fighting a fever. Maybe he thought she was dead like the rest and moved on. She chased that thought away. No. He must still be alive. And if he was, he probably had the item.

The dreams that plagued her over the course of the month were as vivid and terrifying as she'd ever experienced. She could barely remember them upon waking, but they always left her in a cold sweat and a dangerous foreboding. As if a giant malevolent eye had its sights on the city. A constellation of hateful yellow stars that became the eyes of some great black beast wading through the blood-soaked streets while everything burned. An elven king splashed with blood, whose laughter sounded like the squeal of a pig. She saw a beautiful and terrible winged man with a sword of flames, one blow turning a field of men and horses into cinders. Then a cackling demon deep in an ancient tomb whose body was trapped between worlds. Primordial dragons battling giants over a frozen land. A great tree and high in its branches... it was *him*.

He looked confused to see her, but then held his cupped hands out like she should take what he was holding. She wanted to. She tried to hold out her own hands, but somehow she knew what he had was terrible, and she pulled back, afraid.

That's when Kyla opened her eyes. And for a moment, she thought she was still dreaming, for there was a giant maiden gliding down the road. Her hands were outstretched in benevolent welcome, her ample chest bare, and her skirts were in flames.

The Elven guards saw her approaching as well and began to shout and scatter. Kyla saw the giant woman made of wood and rolling along on wheels—in a cart, to be precise—which was accelerating as it rumbled by perpendicular to the Lower Market gate entrance. The elven guards tried to stop this burning colossus even as it collided with the corner of a building and sent a pillar of orange cinders skyward, like a rapture of fireflies.

That was when she noticed something else at the gate. A crouched figure in black slipped through the unguarded entrance. Her heart immediately began to hammer. She leaped up, ignoring the lingering ghost of pain in her side.

This was it. *He had come back.*

As far as distractions were concerned, a twenty-foot, flaming, bare-breasted woman rolling down the street in a cart was not quite what Fraenk had been expecting. But it did achieve the desired effect. Fraenk nodded in spite of himself, grudgingly impressed with Nim's resourcefulness on short notice. But he supposed he'd owe the followers of Oaphaela a sincere apology and a generous tithe for this misappropriation and immolation of their deity's carved likeness. But that would be a problem for tomorrow's Fraenk.

Right now, he had an open path to the market and perhaps his only opportunity to get some answers. Fraenk crouched low and slipped inside before any of the guards could spot him.

The Lower Market Bazaar was already a much different place than he had left it a month ago. Several of the smaller stalls stood completely vacant. And even a few of the larger ones were in the process of being dismantled. Was this a voluntary departure of merchants who were unhappy with the new management or a purge of those who might still be loyal to Blackroot? Fraenk didn't know without asking and would probably never get the chance.

Fraenk moved quickly down the row and toward his target. The former bakery was just a blackened husk now. The soot-blacked windows like empty eyes staring at him. He stepped around the spot on the stones where his friend had bled out. A dark stain still haunted the stones here like a spirit.

Inside the building, he crept low and kept to the walls. All the tables, chairs, and really anything that wasn't part of the building itself had been cleared out. The entire place had been swept as well—from crown to corners, as the old saying went. And by the looks of it, brushed more methodically than he'd seen some Elven lord's personal chambers. The place was spotless. He searched all the way to the back of the place. Nothing. He even forced himself to look inside the ovens. They, too, were swept down. Someone had been over every inch of it.

Thorough... was the word for it. If there had been any clue to be found here, it went out in the dustpans.

"Hells..." Fraenk whispered in dismay.

Then he heard a faint scuff of boot on stone. Someone else was here. Fraenk froze and listened. Whoever was there was very quiet—so not one of the Fernbrook guards. *Assassin!* Fraenk's paranoid brain screamed. Having a big dustup in this well-dusted bakery would drop a fat, squawking crowbird on his attempt to investigate and slip out unnoticed. But there was a narrow chance that whoever this was didn't see him enter. If he could hide somewhere, maybe he could just wait for them to leave.

Finding a place to hide would be his next insurmountable obstacle. Aside from the immovable ovens, the place was empty.

"The ovens it is," Fraenk thought and crouched as quietly as he could. Anyone doing even a basic search would find him immediately, but it was too late now. He heard the soft scuff again—this time further in. This one was being very stealthy. Fraenk didn't like it. Just then there was a sound that seemed loud against the ocean of silence. It was a melodic three-note whistle through clenched teeth. Like the song of a woodlark.

Go away, little bird. Fraenk urged with his thoughts.

And then again. It was a signal of some sort. Someone knew he was here.

"*Posuu?*" A woman's voice whispered. It was a word he didn't recognize. Maybe it was a passphrase. She would expect the proper reply. Whatever that could be, he had no idea.

"Hey. Whoever you are, I saw you enter. I know you're there. Come out right now!" Her tone changed, dark and decidedly unfriendly. Fraenk heard the familiar creak of a bowstring being drawn back tight. The woman was armed. This was not ideal.

"Madam, if I may," Fraenk slowly raised his hands into view, showing they were empty. He heard her feet move quickly and the bowstring tense again. If she hadn't been aiming at him before, she definitely was now.

"Stand up!" She hissed low, so her voice didn't carry.

"Alright. Just ease back on that draw a bit. I'm not your enemy."

"I will judge if you are or not. Now show me your eyes," she ordered.

There was a pause, which Fraenk imagined was the time for this mystery woman to lower the bow. He then took a deep breath, hoping it was not his last.

"Here I come. And I'd prefer to remain arrow-free, madam."

Fraenk stood and was disappointed but not surprised to see she still had an arrow drawn and pointed at his chest. The woman was slender and neither tall nor short. She was wearing an all-black ensemble of some lightweight fabric that was loose around the hips and shoulders but gathered tight on her forearms, lower legs, and waist. She had a tight black hood around her face that only showed her eyes, which were framed by a sliver of reflected light.

And when he saw her eyes, Fraenk couldn't help but be pulled in like a magnetic draw. There was something powerful but also puzzling about them. They were large, with long lashes and deep pools of blue that made his scalp prickle the longer he stared. But gazing at them was like hearing a fascinating tale spun by a master storyteller and one had to stay fixed in place to hear its conclusion. Fraenk's body became light, and his hands began to lower slowly to his sides. He felt like he was being pulled across the floor toward her. He had to tell her something that would win her favor. Maybe that he loved her... that he'd ALWAYS loved—

Fraenk shook his head hard, snapping back to reality. The cloudy feeling dissipated. The woman must have had some kind of mesmerizing enchantment on her. Fraenk set his will against the charm. He would not let himself be so easily played.

"Who are you? What did you do with him?" She demanded.

"They call me Fraenk Neversleep. And can you lower the bow, please? Your arm is just going to get tired, and that'll throw your accuracy way off. You may even hit me." "Just tell me now, or you're no good to me alive," the woman growled.

"I'm happy to help if I can. Which 'him' are you referring to?"

"If you're snooping around in here, then you know who I'm talking about."

"The baker, Miken?" Fraenk asked. "He's dead."

"You all saw to that, didn't you?!" She hissed. "I should kill you where you stand!"

Fraenk could see her fingers were starting to strain.

"The man was my friend." Fraenk's voice was calm and sonorous. "I'm here trying to find out why he was murdered. Please, if you could lower the bow—"

"Liar!" She grunted. Her arm was shaking.

Fraenk could see beads of softly glistening sweat forming on her radiant skin. He suddenly felt a strong desire to hold her.

"Damn my eyes!" He gasped, battling the intoxicating feeling from his mind. She was doing it again somehow. Perhaps she had no control over it.

The distant shout from guards came from somewhere back in the market. Nim's distraction must have run its course.

"Those guys with the spears are going to be back patrolling this place soon. I don't know about you, lady, but it wouldn't go too well if they caught me in here. We should–"Fraenk saw her hand spasm a half a second before her fingers lost their grip on the bow string. It's probably what saved his life. He had just enough time to drop straight down out of the path of the arrow. It sheered just over his head, caroming off the empty oven's dome. The sound produced was one of the most unique Fraenk had ever heard, like skipping a flat stone off a hollow cistern.

Unfortunately, it was also one of the loudest as well. Tolling like the brass death bell, they gonged at the shrines for the sailors from distant Sho—the ones who drowned on the crossing.

"Skit! Sorry!" The woman exclaimed, covering her mouth. "Did I hit you?"

"Very subtle. You think the guards heard that?"

Half a second later, shouts and whistles sounded from the end of the market. The alarm went up. Soon the place would be crawling with overzealous soldiers who would not be happy to see him in here.

Fraenk sat up in time to see the woman stride to the center of the room.

"There's no way out of here. If we surrender, I think I can—" Fraenk began to say. She stomped a foot down on an off-colored stone block in the floor. A ridge of stones was lifted by some unseen pivot raised nearby. The woman in black stooped, gripped the ridge, and opened the trap door that was cleverly hidden in the bakery floor. A hidden room?

"Now, how long has THAT been here?" Fraenk asked, astounded.

"Don't follow me!" She shot him a warning look, looped the bow around her shoulder, and jumped into the hole that was set in the floor.

Fraenk could hear shouts and footsteps approaching. They would arrive in moments.

"I'll take my chances with the succubus," Fraenk said. He scrambled into the hole after her. He pulled the trap door shut just as the first guards came pattering into the now-empty bakery. He held his breath, waiting.

For long seconds all he could hear were perplexed, muffled voices. The heavy thumb of boots crossed the floor several times.

Fraenk could hear them mutter angrily, and one of them said the word "arrow" loud enough for him to hear it clearly. They'd obviously found the shaft, which had nearly killed him. But that was the only clue anyone had been in here. After several more tense moments, the footsteps moved off.

"I think they're gone," Fraenk said, turning to the mystery woman. There was only darkness.

"Hello?" Fraenk called. He could hear a faint echo that bounced off the walls. A slight current of air brushed his cheek.

"And you're gone as well."

He reached out and found the walls on either side of him. In front was empty darkness that continued on in front of him. This wasn't a hidden room buried in the floor of Miken's bakery. It was a secret tunnel.

Fraenk could leave and take his chances with the guards in the market, but that was hardly a good option. Especially not with this mystery beginning to unfold with the arrival of the woman in black. She had some part to play in this, and Fraenk had to learn more.

All that remained was to follow the empty passage, which led back into the darkness.

12

A S HIS EYES ADJUSTED to the black of the secret tunnel, Fraenk realized what he was actually seeing was the luminescent worms and roots in the tunnel walls, which were giving off a faint visible glow. It was the absence that suggested the shape of the dark passage ahead. Instinctively, he reached for the glow orb in his cloak, which of course wasn't there. He had destroyed it in the encounter earlier that day, when someone else had been trying to kill him. Why didn't he just let himself get stabbed just a bit? Then he'd at least be able to use his handy light-giving implement right now. Well, no point in lamenting it now. What's done is done. One thing he had to grudgingly admit that Lady Blackroot was right about the frequency and regularity of attempts on his life.

Unbidden, a story came to mind Fraenk had heard of a kindly and gentle farmer who had been plowing his field when he uncovered an old box. Inside was an ornate gold ring, which, unbeknownst to him, was cursed. It had a malicious charm, which caused nearly everyone around him to become easily incensed by the very sight of him. Everything he said or did was cause for offense, and the smallest disagreement quickly came to blows. Unfortunately for the farmer, he then spent the next several difficult months in a state of near-daily scrapes with various personages of his town—the same people he had once called neighbors and friends. This combative crucible resulted in turning a once sweet and peace-loving man into the village's premiere fistfighter. Unfortunately, this also led to his arrest and subsequent jailing for brawling. No one in town came to his defense at the tribunal, for they all were annoyed by his pleas of innocence. It was only when the jailer took away the cursed ring that cured their antipathy toward him. No one felt much like fighting him anymore and had forgotten why he'd bothered them so much in the first place. But by then the damage had been done. In an odd way, being the Arch Preceptor was like wearing that cursed ring.

With his hands extended out in front, Fraenk felt his way down the long, dark tunnel for a distance that was difficult to judge without visual landmarks. Mercifully, it was straight, and when his searching hands found the rungs of a ladder, he climbed. Fraenk reached the top and pushed out another one of the hidden stone trap doors.

He emerged in an alleyway not far from the Lower Market but outside the high fence. This must have been a smuggler's tunnel. Arathes was a twist of various false doors to hidden passages, tunnels, wormways, and sewer ducts. Not even he knew where they all were. In Mosswater district alone, there was an entire underground waterway for delivering goods on barges that left the elves with an unspoiled view of the lake. Not to mention the immense cargo elevator constructed, maintained, and operated by the dwarves. The city was truly a maze. The existence of this passageway should not have been a great surprise, except for the fact that Miken had never mentioned it to Fraenk.

Not for the first time, Fraenk was struck by the sense that the old baker had parts of his life that were hidden from him. For a man who was suspicious of all and completely trusted almost no one, Fraenk was caught surprisingly flat-footed by this revelation. Miken was not just the kindly old friend who helped him through some of the most difficult years of his life. He had secrets. Ones that Fraenk hadn't even considered were possible. Whatever intrigue the old baker was a part of, now had a hidden smuggler's tunnel attached to it, as well as a mysterious woman in black.

She was a reckless interloper who... had the most oddly beautiful, beguiling blue eyes. Fraenk shook his head again. If anyone had answers, it would be the woman. Now all he had to do was find her again. That should be easy enough, right?

Fraenk checked the alley in both directions. There was no sign of her. Fortunately, Fraenk knew this whole area better than even some of the alley rats. Anticipating that she would try to avoid the main avenues and especially the entrance to the market where the Fernbrook guards were on high alert, her escape route would take her up the hill and into the heart of the city. She would be forced to weave through the narrow passages behind buildings and up a steep, crumbling stairway, which would be slow-going for even the most nimble body.

What she wouldn't know was the shortcut through Twelvespire Lane. If he moved fast, he might just make it in time. Without another moment of hesitation, Faenk sprinted out the alley and up onto the High Street. She would not get away so easily.

A feminine-shaped shadow dropped silently onto the cobblestones just between the butcher shop and Gorthan's Apothecary, who was notorious for their use of Gazean White powder mixed into the tinctures to give their clients a temporary boost followed by an insatiable craving for more. This seemed appropriate given the certain quality about this woman that had the same properties as the drug—a dizzying euphoria, followed by a simultaneous letdown and the urgent, annoying need to recapture the feeling. She straightened and looked around. Then, in the cover of the shadows, she began to strip out her dark clothes.

Fraenk watched all this from his hidden vantage in a nearby door stoop. As she peeled out of her top layer, his mouth went dry, and his hand unconsciously searched for the bottle in his cloak. He should say something, but his throat was much too dry. A moment later, when she stepped out into the light dressed in nondescript commoner's robes, Fraenk finally understood why she had this charmed effect.

She was Lynblood. One of the heavens blessed.

Fraenk could see immediately in her delicate features, somehow more proportionate and exaggerated in a way that evoked some inarticulate but commonly agreed upon aesthetic ideal; she was, for lack of more eloquent terms, _beautiful._ And in that, beautiful in such a way that the ancient elven poet Aristane would say 'typified the way that all creatures found enjoyable to look upon'. She was like some type of immutable law of reality.

They were a highly favored species, the Lynblood. Many lived quite comfortably upon no other merit than the dice toss of their birth. Good things naturally happened for the Lynblood. Fortune seemed to always smile at them. And yet, here was this one—a thief, and... _What? A terrible archer? Someone who knew Miken?_

Fraenk lowered the bottle from his lips. How did that get there? He hadn't intended to even take a drink in the first place—and now it was totally empty. Some fool had drunk it all. His head, however, was swimming in a delicious haze that dulled her hypnotic effect.

He watched the woman, seeing her entire face now. She had made a commendable yet unsuccessful attempt to appear ordinary in a patchy brown cloak and matching rough-spun dress—somehow elevating the commoner's garments rather than the opposite. Her golden and wavy hair was unperturbed by being wrapped up in a hood. It fell in golden ringlets, which framed her face in a lovely way.

Fraenk decided no good would come from further describing her beauty, so he stopped.

The Lynblood woman cautiously scanned the streets, making sure no one was watching. And, certain that she was in the clear, she stepped casually into the moonlight of the open boulevard.

"I must say, I'm impressed! You're faster than I expected," Fraenk said, also stepping out into the light so she could see him. She leaped in surprise, hands grasping for the bow, which she had so recently bundled with her infiltration garments. It was woefully tangled, and she gave up when she recognized who was speaking.

"You!? I told you not to follow me," the woman said, then had another thought. "Wait. How *did* you find me?"

"I know this city," Fraenk said.

"How can anyone know this city? It's worse than a tangle of giant's beard," the woman countered.

"I realized I couldn't let you go until I got your name."

"You chased me down for that?" She scoffed.

"It's a promising start," Fraenk said, stepping closer. His hands raised in a gesture of peace. Her eyes narrowed, then seemed to relent.

"Kyla," she said.

"A pleasure. My name is Fraenk."

"Neversleep. Yes, I remember. The one who dodges arrows."

"Well, you're no master archer," Fraenk quipped. "But you are looking for something. What is it?"

"How do I know you're not working for the Fernbrooks?" She questioned

Fernbrooks? Fraenk paused. This was interesting.

"The only thing they'd hire me for is to be a full-time corpse. They're still a little sore about me putting down that mad dog elf who murdered my friend Miken and his entire family. Does that sway you in any direction?"

She stopped, considering.

"You don't look like a thief. Are you in a tragedy?"

"I don't think my life's _that_ bad."

"And what of the _Ynne es Tylubourne_?" She arched an eyebrow. "I never miss an opportunity. So... _relaxing?_" Fraenk smiled, wondering if his improvisations were working at all. Anything to keep her here and keep her talking.

"You're an idiot," she said flatly.

"You're not the first person to tell me that... today," Fraenk replied. "At least you didn't call my life a tragedy again. You could have easily hurt my feelings, if I had any."

"No, a 'tragedy' is what they call a theater troupe in Drialadon—you know what? Nevermind."

Kyla seemed to regard him for a long time before she cracked a smile. Fraenk couldn't help but smile as well.

"So, what about the dog? Is he with you?"

"Oh, they don't allow pets where I live, I'm afraid," Fraenk said. "Plus, I'm more of a 'skrate' person."

"Are you sure that's not yours? It looks like he knows you."

On her face, Fraenk saw concern quickly turn to fear. An echoing low growl came from behind him. Fraenk froze. That wasn't the sound of an ordinary dog.

Fraenk spun, expecting to see one of the mangy street mongrels that wandered the alleys of Arathes, although he knew somewhere in the dark recesses of his mind that would not be what he discovered. Instead, he saw... nothing.

Well, not exactly nothing. A thin shape was moving toward them at a trot. It was darker than the night around it. Not a dog, but the absence of one. The void in space where a dog should be.

As it moved, it seemed ethereal. In fact, Fraenk could see entirely through its body. Then, as it passed through a shaft of moonlight, the creature turned briefly solid. It stopped and stared at them with hateful yellow eyes. Its lips peeled back to reveal gleaming white teeth that didn't need the moonlight to appear solid—and deadly.

"Are you sure that's a dog?" Fraenk asked.

"Far worse. It's a blackhound," Kyla breathed. "Summoned by dark magic."

"That can't be. Magical creatures aren't allowed in the city," Fraenk said incredulously.

"I don't think it cares."

The blackhound growled, smoking black tendrils rising from its back. It whined and contorted, its body clenching in a spasm. Then it split into two smoking beasts.

"I think you're right," Fraenk said, astounded. "How'd they get past the Paladins? No matter. I'll sort these two out presently."

Fraenk stepped forward, brushing back the cloak and exposing the brace of throwing knives. In one deft movement, he slid two of the blades and drew back.

"Wait! That's not going to—" Kyla began to say.

He flung the blades at the blackhounds. Each knife flew through the air together and took its intended target with a satisfying, hollow crunch. The dogs recoiled backward into the shadows. The moment they left the light, their bodies roiled into vaporous smoke. Fraenk's knives clinked and clattered on the cobblestones.

"Yeah. I was trying to tell you that wasn't going to work," she said.

The blackhounds reformed, undamaged, and now angry. Their yellow eyes flared.

"Huh," Fraenk muttered.

"Run!" Kyla shouted and took off down the street.

The blackhounds made a keening snarl and charged.

Fraenk, too, saw the wisdom of beating a hasty exit and ran after her. She was fast, but no one could outrun these creatures.

"This way!" Fraenk shouted, turning sharply into an alley where a wide shaft of moonlight was shining. She followed, ducking just in time as Fraenk toppled a stack of wooden crates back toward the mouth of the alley. The falling boxes caught the blackhounds just as they rounded the corner. The dogs, now solid in the light, hit the wood in a splintering crash. Fraenk knew they weren't down for good, but it did buy them some time.

He raced to catch Kyla, who was already at the far end of the alley. Instead of waiting for Fraenk, she chose a direction and ran. He caught up to where she was a moment later.

"That way's a dead end," Fraenk was starting to say, but then he saw her get to the end of the alley and continue straight up the wall. She took three steps against the vertical stones as if they were stairs and then grabbed on to the flat wall like it was rungs on a ladder. Barely slowing, she scaled the wall like a skrate and launched herself over the top. She stood a moment later, looking back down at him.

"How did you do that?" Fraenk wondered aloud and apparently to himself because Kyla tipped a two-finger salute off her brow and started running again.

"Oh, well, don't worry about me. I'll take care of these murderous shadow dogs, myself," he shouted.

Fraenk heard wood smash behind him and that keening cry of the blackhounds. They were free of the boxes now. And once again, it was time for him to run for his life. He made a brief mental note to research what other careers involved more sitting and fewer attempts on his life. He bet old Acheron Turran Evenswan never had anyone try to kill him while he was preparing the Solstice of Prayer.

As Fraenk ran, he noticed the blackhounds weren't as fast as they had been initially. Stealing a glance over his shoulder, he saw one of them had just a single glowing eye and the other was limping from an injured back leg. He might have felt a twinge of pity for them, if not for the fact that they were both still very much set on tearing him to bloody ribbons. They would not give up. Fraenk had to stop them once and for all. But how could he do that if they continued to turn into formless black smoke?

They weren't always formless, though. They became solid in the moonlight. That was it—he needed *light*!

Fraenk dug inside his cloak, again lamenting the glow orb he no longer had. No use complaining about that now. Perhaps if only he'd thrown his trusty bottle of booze at the Coldfrost soldier instead. But knowing his luck, the whole building would have caught fire, and he'd be in worse trouble than ever.

Then an idea struck him—fire. Perhaps these ill-tempered canines might have a weakness for immolation.

Unfortunately, all the delicious, flammable liquid from his bottle was sitting happily in his belly. It was where it needed to be. But he did have a backup supply stashed near the Blessed Waters of Kyleria fountain. Its sacred flow was said to heal dysfunctions of the mind if one would drink from it while gazing into the flames atop its ever-burning plinth. The acolytes of their order kept a flaming oil lamp always lit. If he lured these two beasts there, he could soak them in his booze stash and burn them back to the smoke they seemed to be anyway.

All Fraenk had to do was make it there alive. It was worth a try.

As he ran, Fraenk could hear the dogs behind him. Their claws clicking the stone and breath panting. They were gaining. In fact, they seemed to be drawing strength back from the night. The longer they were in darkness, the more they seemed to recover. His odds of making it to the fountain before the dogs caught him were quickly dwindling.

Then he saw a floating light just ahead and nearly cried out for joy. Someone with a lantern was coming down the street toward him in the opposite direction. Fraenk couldn't make out who was holding it, but whoever it was, they were about to save his life.

"H-halt!" A startled, yet familiar, voice rang out as Fraenk approached on the run. "Partisan patrol! Stop where you are or I'll–!"

There was no time to stop and explain why he was being pursued by magical dog monsters, and so Fraenk opted to continue without.

Whoever this partisan was, he must have thought he was under attack, for his lantern began to shake in panic and alarm. Closing the gap, Fraenk heard the distinctive metallic hiss of an iron cudgel scraping from its loop. As he reached the light, Fraenk dropped his shoulder, placing his hand on the stone street, and tumbled in a tight roll. He felt, as much as he heard, the *woosh* of the long and weighty club pass just over him. His evasive maneuver complete, Fraenk uncurled and stood, deftly pulling two more knives from his brace.

Finding his targets, Fraenk flung the blades. The lantern light solidified the dogs, just as the blades caught them. Both blackhounds tumbled backward. They yelped painfully with throwing blades stuck in their bodies.

Fraenk glanced at the man with the lantern. It was in fact the very person he suspected.

"Lieutenant Leafwater, well met, sir," Fraenk said, breathless. The lieutenant, still recovering from his miss with the club, tried to catch him on the back swing. Fraenk was well out of striking distance, however. But Leafwater's other hand, holding the lantern, swung wildly, throwing light and shadows everywhere. The moment the beam left them, the blackhounds became formless again, and Fraenk's blades started to fall from their bodies.

Fraenk caught Doran's lantern hand and steadied the beam on the dogs. They both solidified again, this time with the throwing knives embedded somewhere inside their bodies. They writhed and howled.

"Neversleep?!" Lt. Leafwater cried when he realized who was holding him. "Unhand me, by the Powers!"

"Just keep that light on the dogs!" Fraenk ordered. Then he released Doran and took off up the street. But if Fraenk was expecting any kind of common sense from the elf, he was immediately disappointed because, as he ran, Doran spun to follow Fraenk with the lantern beam.

Fraenk heard his blades clink against the stones and the howl of the hounds again coming after him. The fool lieutenant hadn't bought him as much time as he had hoped, but it might be just enough. He rounded the corner into the plaza and saw the fountain was not far ahead. It was a mad, lung-burning sprint, but somehow he closed the distance. The blackhounds had closed the distance and were right on his heels.

He didn't know what kind of divine trouble he might be inviting by defiling a holy fountain with his wretched body, but it was his only option.

"Forgive me, Kyleria," Fraenk gasped and dove for the fountain just as vicious teeth clamped onto his ankle.

13

FOR THE DEVOTED OF Sarmatti, the Lyn-Tyrian powers were divine beings who were worshiped for their governance over various aspects of the world. The one called Kyleria stood as a protector of the waves and the seas. Her celebrants brought her offerings with the birth of every child and at the death of a loved one. It is believed that her very servant Geth guards the door to the underworld. She is widely understood to be tempestuous and fickle. And the thing she despises more than anything is the undead and dark creatures from the underrealm. These tenets of faith are things widely taught to all children in Arathes—at least in the homes that were not claim to other foreign religions. But this doctrine was not something that a malign magical evil such as a Blackhound would be privy to.

And yet, somehow, whether by pure instinct or bloodthirsty enthusiasm, the terrible creatures were determined to not let Fraenk reach the sanctuary of Kyleria's fountain.

Just as he reached the zenith of his arc, Fraenk felt the bite of the blackhound's powerful jaws close on his lower leg. The pain that coursed through him was only the first part of his troubles, however. The light from the fountain's lamp, which bathed the entire plaza in a warm orange glow, now gave the shadowhound's bodies actual substance. They now had weight. The reverse momentum with additional drag caused his headlong leap to now run short by a significant margin.

Fraenk slammed the rim of the fountain with enough force to propel him back onto the stone street. With the wind blasted from his lungs, Fraenk lay gasping and coughing as the second blackhound circled around to get between him and his goal. It saw Fraenk's exposed appendage as a prime target and latched onto his mid-forearm. He cried out as he felt the bones inflect with the force of the bite.

Their claws dug into the stones as they jerked their entire frame into a full-body sawing that attempted to pull Fraenk apart.

Fraenk would have screamed if he had not been still gasping for air. Then a strange sensation came over him, like he wasn't a part of his physical form anymore. Like he was floating.

Something about being in sight of a holy place and getting mauled to death by these decidedly unholy beasts filled Fraenk with a weariness that bordered on exhaustion. How fitting that the Exalts would sit idly by and watch disinterested as an average guy was killed by a pair of magical beasts. They either didn't exist or seemed to take fiendish joy in ignoring the plight of a lowly man such as Fraenk.

The Blackhounds themselves were not even supposed to be here. How did these creatures even get into the city in the first place? They must have been conjured by someone, but doing so should have triggered all kinds of wards. If he survived this, there'd be a few Arcane Lords and negligent Paladins that Fraenk would like to give a piece of his mind. But judging by the way he was currently being mauled, there was not likely to be any part of his mind left.

This last thought was particularly troubling. Not for himself, but that he would have failed old Miken and his family. They had died at the hands of that deranged elf—and for what? The title to a bakery and a broken crust of bread? Fraenk had an image of the half loaf he had picked up from beside Miken's body. Still soft. Then another memory of that night came. The strange pendant was stuffed inside the crust. Like it was hidden there. *Something Miken didn't want Bas Greenbriar to find.*

The piece of some puzzle locked in place. That pendant was important somehow. Fraenk had to know what.

Then the anger he had always felt bottled up inside, ever since he was a little boy living on the streets, boiled up as the dogs thrashed viciously at him. He had survived much worse. It was going to take something far worse than a couple of smoke mutts to be the end of Fraenk Neversleep.

Returning to his body, the pain intensified, but he could also feel his other limbs—the ones free of blackhound teeth. Fraenk kicked out with his right foot, scoring a direct strike to the dog's muzzle. It whined in pain, releasing its grip momentarily. That gave Fraenk just the opportunity he needed.

He pushed up with his feet, surging forward toward the other dog. With his free hand, Fraenk caught the other dog under its belly and scooped it into the air.

"Time for a bath!" Fraenk said and dumped over the rim of the fountain with the writhing creature. They hit the water with a splash. Immediately, the water seemed to boil. The blackhound released him, thrashing and screaming in pain. The water was somehow *burning* it—eating through it and turning the dog into a white steam. The blackhound thrashed free of Fraenk's grip and scrambled for the edge.

"Not so fast, boy! You're not clean yet," he said, pulling the shadow dog back into the fountain. It only took a few more seconds until the blackhound dissolved completely.

The other dog barked and snarled, making a short lunge, then jumping back.

"Come on and get me!" Fraenk called, waving his arms. He tried goading it into attacking, but it had learned already that the water was lethal. It growled and circled, keeping it's hateful yellow eyes fixed on him. It would not be baited in, nor was it leaving. They were at a standoff.

Fraenk tried splashing water out of the fountain at it. The droplets sizzled away against the dog's fur, which the creature didn't enjoy but wasn't doing much beyond that.

"Am I going to have to come out and get you?" Fraenk asked the creature. He didn't know if that plan would go the way he hoped. Knowing his fortune as of late, probably not.

As Fraenk considered how to lure the other dog into the water, something odd began to happen. The fire at the top of the fountain's pediment began to first turn a sickly green hue, then gutter. *What fresh hell was this?*

Fraenk looked up and saw that, even in spite of the lamp being supplied by a basin of oil, the fire was going out. Something unnatural was choking the flames. The plaza was dimming back into darkness.

The blackhound began to pace and change directions, this time in anticipation. Its teeth popping and snapping its jaws.

"You just stay right there. This water is very dangerous!" Fraenk splashed, this time defensively. The shadowhound stopped, letting the water pass completely through it to drench the stones of the plaza. Its shiny white teeth bared in a murderous smile beneath malevolent yellow eyes. The rest of the shadowhound was shifting black smoke.

Fraenk didn't need to look up to know that the lamp had hissed out entirely. The fountain's water could no longer touch the dog. He might still be safe inside the fountain.

The shadowhound trotted forward, then deftly leapt up onto the rim.

"Be careful, boy. You might–"

The shadowhound stepped out onto the surface of the water. Not touching it, but somehow stepping just above the water surface.

"Hells," Fraenk muttered.

He launched himself out of the far side of the fountain, the shadow dog pursuing a moment later. Fraenk sprinted across the courtyard, trailing a spray of water behind him like a sodden scarecrow in a downpour. He saw the blackhound pitching and trying to keep its footing on the churning water, but it would only be delayed a moment longer.

Approaching the side of the garment shop across from the fountain, Fraenk kicked a leg out in front of him and slid. He caught a loose stone in the side of the shop and pulled. Inside was the glorious sight of several bottles of the amber liquor that he favored.

The shadowhound cleared the fountain and was now stalking towards him. It seemed to be enjoying this, which Fraenk didn't particularly like.

"Sorry to have to do this, old friends," Fraenk said, and he tossed the bottles out. They sailed, landing in a spray of liquid and shattering glass at the feet of the blackhound. It snarled, unperturbed by this flagrant waste of booze.

"Taste hot death, hell beast!" Fraenk shouted, pulling a craggy chunk of flint from his cloak. With his other hand, he drew a throwing blade and scraped it across the rock.

Typically, striking a flint would result in a shower of sparks, which in turn would ignite the alcohol and burn the dog. However, Fraenk's recent foray into the fountain left his flint quite soaked and therefore not much good for creating the aforementioned sparks.

"Well, that's not fair," Fraenk muttered and straightened as the blackhound snarled again, this time ready to tear out his throat.

"Need a light?" A voice called from somewhere above. A woman's voice. Familiar and somehow annoying. Fraenk and the blackhound looked up to see Kyla standing on a nearby balcony, beside an iron cresset that cast flickering light. She had skewered a luminescent orange coal from the torch's bowl on the point of the arrow, which was drawn back into her bow.

She released with a twang, and the arrow flew. The flying coal glowed bright orange and then ignited right at the shadow dog. It struck the ground, igniting the pool of alcohol at the blackhound's feet. Light and flame exploded up. The beast was engulfed. It screeched in a very undoglike way, thrashing violently for a moment before turning to pale smoke.

"Thank the Powers," Fraenk sighed and tipped sideways against the wall. Pain and exhaustion flooded him all at once.

"You alright?" Kyla called from across the courtyard.

"I'm fine. I could have handled that, you know," Fraenk shouted back.

"You're welcome," she replied. "Now this time, I mean it... Don't follow me!"

"Be on your way. I think I've had enough fun for one night." Fraenk groaned and raised the hand that wasn't bleeding. She paused for a moment and waved back. Then she slung the bow across her body and disappeared back across the rooftops into the night.

Fraenk could hear the shrill alarm whistle of the partisans now and the clomp of boots on stone. He slipped into unconsciousness.

It felt like hours before Fraenk was allowed to leave the plaza of Kyleria's fountain. Perhaps that was her punishment for his intrusion. First, he went through a carefully edited version of the events with the contingent of partisans who showed up in the immediate aftermath, summoned by the intrepid Lt. Doran Leafwater. Then again, while he was being seen by the healers at the nearby temple of Mersey.

As he was being bandaged, Fraenk was approached by a pair of big-headed and incredulous Arcane Lords, who took his narrowly escaped death by magical creatures as a personal affront. They insisted it wasn't possible. They blustered through an exhaustive list of the wards, spells, and excuses why Fraenk could not have been assailed by any variety of unholy beast in the first place. But their tone became much more curious when they heard Fraenk recount how he had actually defeated the blackhounds. When he finished his story, they seemed grudgingly impressed.

"Well, you did it the hard way. But I guess it could work."

The first one, Stannris, was a large, jowly man with stringy black hair drawn up with a ribbon at the back into a horsetail.

"So what you do is you'd want to cast a petrify, turn 'em to stone, and then hit them with a shatter. Collect all the shards and purify them in a basin of rectitude," added Timulot, his equally jowly partner with a tight, curly blonde beard.

"Uh, not the exact way I'd do it, but yeah. Technically, it would do," Stannris replied.

"But don't use magic," Timulot wagged a chubby finger at Fraenk.

"That's true; there is no magic use permitted within the city by order of the high council."

"We can use magic because we have a special dispensation," Timulot interjected.

"That's what I was saying, Tim. Only those with special dispensation may use magic. But not average citizens like him."

"Well... He could do spell, potion, or charm at the novice level, Stan. With proper supervision."

"Those spells are basically worthless, Tim. Illumination? Evaporate? Basic frost ward?" Stannris scoffed.

"I mastered the novice level when I was a childling," Timulot retorted.

"I *highly doubt* you mastered novice spellcraft as a childling. How old?"

"I think I get it, lads," Fraenk said, watching them like they were two large boars contesting a dropped sweet roll.

"Just don't use magic, or you'll be hearing from the Arcane Lords," Timulot said and smoothed his curly beard.

"Yeah, let us deal with anything like this in the future, got it? We will handle it. You didn't have to get everyone else involved." Stannris waved his hands with an irritable flap, then cinched the loosening belt on his robes again.

Fraenk tried to imagine either of them running for anything but to be first in line at the feast hall. They both looked sweaty just from the conversation they were having.

"You got it, boys. Thanks again," Fraenk said. "You just keep working on that charisma. You'll be ready to appear out in public in no time."

They gave him a confused look, then waddled off back to whatever dark basement they spent most of their days haughtily criticizing each other with deeply sarcastic correspondence. While Fraenk was grateful to have the Arcane Lords around for large magical emergencies, he found the least amount of time spent around them, the better.

The sky was painted an indulgent pink and orange when Fraenk stepped out of the temple at the final gong of the dawn bell. The pain in his wrist, ankle, and side was all but a distant throb from whatever the healers had applied, which was supplemented by a generous quaff of his own liquid painkiller. He hoped he could make it back to his room in Blackroot Manor before exhaustion overwhelmed him completely. The healers had done all they could, which was a lot, but they also exhorted him that only a solid rest would help him heal completely.

"Fraenk Neversleep."

A familiar, deep, and elderly voice came from behind him the moment he stepped from the healer's temple. Fraenk turned to look, perhaps too quickly, and stutter-stepped to catch himself as a sudden wave of dizziness came over him. Fraenk realized he might have overdone it a bit with the self-medication.

A grizzled elf with short-cropped hair, wearing a long dark cloak that covered his uniform, stepped up beside him. Under his cloak, the elf's uniform robe was a pristine slate gray with a high collar and was closed with gold frog buttons down one side and a gold braid hung from his epaulets. This was no common elf.

"Well, if it isn't the Arch Partisan himself," Fraenk mused aloud. "This truly is an auspicious start to my day. How's the view from the top of the city, sir? Can you see all the criminals from that far up?"

Arch Partisan Olwynn Brightrock had a spiderweb of scars that extended from the corner of his mouth up the side of his face. It succeeded in affixing a permanent ferocious scowling grimace. One which he would have even without the disfigurement.

"I don't like coming down to Blackroot district—it stinks. And I especially don't like hearing the name Fraenk Neversleep whispered in my ear as many times as I have for any other context than an *in memoriam.*"

"We'll see if we can do something about that smell, at least," Fraenk replied.

Olwynn made a sound that was halfway between a chuckle and a growl.

"Looks like someone worked you over, Neversleep."

"Sir. I appreciate your concern, but I'd just like to make it home before anyone else tries to kill me," Fraenk added wearily.

"You do have that effect on people," Brightrock agreed and scratched at his ear—or rather the ragged edge where most elf's ears come to a sharp point.

"My Lady would agree with you on that point."

"You humans are a pestering annoyance in my city," the Arch Partisan said finally. "A great deal of the trouble the partisans deal with on a daily basis is from humans. Petty squabbles, fights, drunkenness. All of it is much worse now as the army returns. There are some elves who propose that anyone without elf blood should be expelled from the city entirely."

"You'd have no one to empty the chamber pots or wash your stockings," Fraenk said.

Brightrock nodded.

"I don't hate humans like some do. In fact, I prefer them to the insufferable politics of the elves. It is their endless games. The infighting. Their hunger for territory and power... That will be the downfall of Arathes. Our lives may be long, but our memories are tragically short."

The Arch Partisan sighed and let a long pause hang in the air.

"I have to ask something of you... as much as it churns my stomach to do so."

"You did do me a good turn by sending me to prison," Fraenk smiled.

"*Hmpf.* You saw it as a favor. I was pleased to have one less preceptor making my life difficult. Would that I could lock the entire lot of you up?"

He turned to look Fraenk in the eye.

"Whatever business remains between you and the Fernbrooks, I'll have an end to it."

"It is over. Lady Blackroot brokered a truce—" Fraenk began to explain.

"No, she did not! Otherwise, there would not have been a burning statue outside the Lower Market and a troublesome Arch Preceptor in the nearby vicinity fighting shadow cats!"

"They were dogs."

Olwynn Brightrock squinted and gave Fraenk a hard glare. Air whistled through the open scar of the elf's mouth.

"I was in my own district, doing my job. I'm assuming that's still allowed," Fraenk shot back.

"All you have to do is stop going after them. Let it lie."

"You mean we're supposed to belly over so the Fernbrooks can gut us?"

"You killed an <u>elf</u>. And a member of their family, Fraenk! And I backed you up. Did you ever ask yourself why I did such a stupid thing?"

"Certainly not for the sake of your job," Fraenk spat. "Or an overabiding sense that justice be done, especially for those annoying humans. If I didn't kill that elf, he'd be walking free today."

"That's not how justice is done in Arathes. Half of the high council was ready to see you hanged, just to set an example. I didn't like it, but I was ready to carry it out, too. But something changed my mind."

"Perhaps Lady Blackroot bribed you with the other half of her district?"

Brightrock ignored that comment.

"One of the soul stewards who was present as they were preparing the elf's body for the funeral pyre, they saw it when they were removing your blades."

"What?" Fraenk asked.

"Bas Greenbriar had a head full of black worms," the Arch Partisan said low enough that only Fraenk could hear him.

"He had *what?*" Fraenk asked, suddenly growing queasy.

"You couldn't tell from the outside. But they were eating up his brain. I remembered you saying something about worms in his teeth after the incident. There was something foul brewing in that elf's head, which explains his actions. But you can rest assured that whatever those things were that ailed him, also burned up with him. "

"Did you have a temple healer or an Arcane Lord examine them?" Fraenk asked, feeling another wave of nausea.

"I didn't find out about it until after he was gone."

"Malgraye Fernbrook put him on the pyre before anyone could verify. You don't find that suspicious?"

"I told you this to satisfy your curiosity, not pique it further, Neversleep."

"Sounds more like Fernbrook's got you barking while he holds the leash."

"That's enough!" Brightrock snapped. "I am tasked with keeping the law and peace in Arathes, and if you're going to be an obstruction to that, I can get you back in that cozy little corner of the black cells. That, or you can take your chances outside the city. Either way, I will have no more news of you entangled in the doings of the Fernbrooks."

Fraenk keeled over and retched at his feet. Brightrock stepped back in disgust.

"I'll take it from here, Arch Partisan, sir."

Fraenk heard the familiar voice, then felt the strong arms of Nim catch him before he pitched forward into his own sick.

The Arch Partisan sidestepped the colorful procession of liquid that Fraenk was divesting himself of.

"Go easy, Fraenk. Or you'll be your own undoing," Olwynn Brightrock said and gave him a sad, pitiful look. There was something unexpectedly tender about it. Perhaps his stony heart had a tiny bit of warmth after all.

"Come on, sir. Let's get you home," Nim said encouragingly, moving him toward the street. "Look, sir. I found your horse!"

The large white destrier was standing in the street, making people cross the avenue to avoid it. It turned its immense head and blew a hot puff of breath from cavernous nostrils. Its face bent and twisted as everything began to swirl around him.

"Oh no... Not Jimothy..." Fraenk said, and slipped into a dull, semi-conscious twilight.

14

Fraenk blinked awake, staring into the face of a dark-eyed servant girl who looked to be about seventeen.

"He lives still," she said flatly, more than a hint of disappointment in her tone. "Pity that."

"Oh, Gwen. How could I torment you if I were dead?" Fraenk rasped through cracked lips.

"A clever one like you would find a way," servant girl Gwen replied, then handed him a bowl of steaming amber-colored soup. "You should eat something, though. If you died, then I'd be the one everyone would be trying to kill. Better if it's you."

Fraenk took the bowl, then gave Gwen and the soup a leery look.

"Oh, it's fine. I just brought it up fresh from the kitchen."

Fraenk eased himself to a seated position and saw he was in his own quarters. He was also pleased to notice that all of his injuries did not seem to be bothering him at the moment. The healer's work was indeed miraculous. Fraenk scooped a large spoonful and swallowed. It was some kind of savory broth with chunks of vegetables. Perhaps it was his hunger, but he had difficulty remembering anything so delicious.

"It's good," Fraenk said, scooping up more.

"Excellent. You don't taste any Shadewort?" Gwen said. "I'll let Pollard know the soup is safe to serve."

"*What?!*"

"I'm jesting," Gwen said, her face not suggesting that she even possessed a sense of humor. "Anyway, we caught the culprit two days ago. A Tigraenian dissident, gone mad about his farm and fields being burned by our forces. He was slipping Shadewort leaves with the gollen greens in our regular delivery."

"That's horrible. So, our army burned him out of house and land?" Fraenk asked.

"Don't worry. He was tried and hanged in the square this morning."

Fraenk set the soup aside, his appetite gone.

"I wish someone would consult me about these decisions," Fraenk said bitterly.

"Well, the mythic Lord Neversleep was dead to the world. You can thank Nim for getting you back here before your reputation was shattered entirely. Neversleep, indeed," she said, taking a seat in Fraenk's padded chair.

"Wait. How long was I out?" Fraenk asked, suddenly alarmed.

"Two and a half days."

"That's madness!" Fraenk swung his legs out of the bed onto the cold stone floor. A wave of vertigo hit him.

"I-I want a full report," he groaned against the pounding in his temples.

"I can only do half of one. We're still awaiting word from some of the preceptors," Gwen said. "But it's the usual district morass now with a steaming shovel-full of Fernbrook skit thrown in."

"What's this about the Fernbrooks?"

"Apart from them being a pustulant boil on our backside? Whoever was responsible for giving them a foothold in the heart of our district should be flogged in the neck with a headsman's axe. They've been harassing businesses around the market and generally being a nuisance in the district. It's taking all of our guys to keep things under our control. We need the Fernbrooks out of here, Fraenk."

"I know."

"Get them out or they're going to take over our entire district, and you know where that would leave us," Gwen said directly.

"I will. I just need time to think."

Gwen collected the bowl of soup and turned to leave.

"Oh, and one more thing. That scary-looking helltouched you were asking about was spotted twice more in the district."

"I never said it was scary."

"Oh, but he is," Gwen said. "You know, I've heard that people like to hire the helltouched as assassins because the last thing you see before you die is the face of a demon."

"How is that helpful?" Fraenk narrowed his eyes.

"I don't know. Sounds like the kind of vindictive thing that the Greenbriars would do."

"They're not allowed to come after me."

"Yes. _They're_ not," she said, looking at him directly.

"Do you know where this supposed helltouched assassin is?"

"No," Gwen shrugged. "He's very clever about giving the slip to anyone who tails him. One might even suggest... _magically_ so."

"I'm wondering why you bothered saying anything at all. I require only good news from now on," Fraenk grumbled. He started to rise, and it suddenly occurred to him that he was naked. He clapped the blankets over himself.

"Allow me to leave before I spy something that makes me regret most if not all of my recent decisions. Oh, my delicate young eyes... Gwen smirked.

"Speaking of. What's with this latest glamor?" Fraenk said, gesturing to her younger appearance.

Gwen sighed wearily.

"Our Lady Blackroot is now convinced one of the serving girls is stealing her jewelry."

Fraenk suppressed a smile. Servant girl Gwen curtsied and flipped a stray lock of hair from her shoulder.

"_Iff'en it please, me Lady, can I fetch ye 'ary an 'ot tottle fer yearkin' corn 'yins?_" Gwen intoned in a savage parody of servant girl patois. "Ugh. If one more of these aberrant lord's wandering pincers so much as considers a quest toward my delicate backside, I'll flatten 'em clean. How do the lady younglings even put up with this base treatment?"

"Well, if you do catch our light-fingered maiden, try not to hang her immediately, for Gromm's sake," Fraenk replied.

When Gwen had taken her leave, Fraenk dressed and first checked all the trips he had set for any spies infiltrating his quarters. They were subtle indicators to show if an unseen agent had been about his effects while Fraenk was not there. Several of the standard ones had shown signs of disturbance, including one hidden compartment on his desk. He suspected that was the work of Gwen while he'd been unconscious. And there was nothing contained therein that she shouldn't know about. Most of it was intelligence gathered on the friends, false friends, and foes of Blackroot, as well as plans, either theoretical or in progress, to nullify any adverse effect they could have on Lady Arice's interests. In fact, Fraenk was heartened that she was putting her preceptor craft to work. She would make a good Arch Preceptor of Blackroot someday when Fraenk's short but tumultuous tenure was brought to an end.

He was more relieved to see that his most secure stashes remained all untouched.

Fraenk slid the heavy bookcase, then triggered the catch that released a false stone in the wall. He opened the small iron door with a key and peered into the dark space where he kept his most forbidden items. His fingers searched past the amethyst dagger of Xaldoria, a half-eaten jar of Yellow Honeyjack preserves (which wasn't magical, but Fraenk didn't like to share), and a rare copy of Beveran's Tome of Unwholesome Body Contortions, which was kept as evidence in a crime and for no other reason. He finally found the item he was looking for.

Fraenk lifted the pendant to eye level and watched it pendulum before him.

The neck chain was a dull, tarnished metal that refused to be either iron or copper. And the stone set in it could have been the broken chip of a cornerstone for a taxation office. Dull, unremarkable, and downright bland. It was as if someone had gone to great lengths to make this particular item unappealing. He felt bored even looking at it. Something odd occurred to him as he forced himself to examine it further.Most jewelry was designed to catch the light and dazzle the eye. A sparkle or a flare that sprang from every delicate facet. But the opposite effect seemed to be happening for this one. It had no glint or spark. Nothing to attract attention. It had the effect of refusing the gaze of the viewer and creating a general disinterest in it entirely.

It did not want to be seen.

"Huh," Fraenk exclaimed, dangling the necklace in the candlelight. His eye wanted to look at something else—anything else. It was starting to take real effort to continue his examination. That was interesting, Fraenk thought.

Put it away. His inner voice urged. *Put it back in the wall and lock the door. Forget about it.*

Fraenk couldn't tell if this desire was echoing the words of the Arch Partisan, wanting him to abandon this case and forget this clue. It would be easy and expedient to do so. He had much bigger problems, which were fast approaching and bearing the sigil of Fernbrook. But he owed something to Miken. And this Fernbrook business did have something to do with his death. Why did he suddenly want to give it up? He needed answers and

Fraenk realized he was now just staring at the stone wall, the necklace laying on the floor. When he picked it up again, he felt that deep malaise return again.

"Oh!" Fraenk said, a realization dawning. "You are a naughty one."

This pendant had some kind of enchantment on it.

From what he'd been told about cursed objects, they all wanted to be worn so they could wreak their havoc on the wearer or those around them. But this one actually repelled attention and didn't want to be put on. Why make a necklace that doesn't want to be worn? Fraenk knew it was likely a very bad idea, but he needed to find out. For all he knew, it could transform him into a lupine man monster and send him on a murderous rampage across the city until he was finally beheaded by a Paladin's holy sword. Or make him speak an endless stream of gibberish until his vocal cords ruptured, and he drowned in his own blood. Those were just a couple of colorful possibilities. But something suggested the true answer would be much darker.

Its resistance to attention did explain why Fraenk had dropped it in his safe box and forgotten about it. But now that he knew the jewelry's secret, Fraenk wondered if it might contain answers to so many other questions that were swirling around this mystery. *Why had Miken hidden it in the bread? Was it the reason why he was killed? What was its purpose and why would the old man even have such a thing in the first place?*

The intellectual part of his mind said he had to try on. That was how he would know. But this turned out to be easier in the saying than the doing, though.The moment he made the decision, Fraenk felt his hands go cold and clammy. Ashe opened the chain loop, his dull sense of boredom quickly became a whole-body fatigue. The closer he drew to it, that feeling became boiling disgust. Fraenk strained and pushed past the sensation. Then his effort to wear the necklace became a repellant loathing.

Whatever he did,Fraenk could not bring himself to get the loop around his neck. Finally, he dropped his trembling hands. A sheen of sweat on his brow.

"Oh.So, that's how you play," Fraenk smiled. "You are a very naughty girl, aren't you?"

A soft, almost imperceptible tapping came from his chamber door.

"'Tis some visitor," Fraenk whispered, cupping the pendant secretively in his palm.

"Fraenk?" Nim's voice filtered through. "I heard you was awake. I wasn't listening, or nothin', but it sounds like you've got a... friend. I mean, I'll come back later when you're ready to—when you're back on the job, I mean."

"I'll be right out," Fraenk chuckled.

Fraenk quickly returned the room to its former condition. He slipped the pendant into an inner pocket on his cloak.

Then Fraenk cracked the door, still red-faced and sweaty from his skirmish with the necklace. Nim took a look at him, then a curious glance over Fraenk's shoulder into the room.

"Who was... there with you?" he asked finally.

"I don't know what you're talking about," Fraenk said. "Well, what's your report?"

"Well, sir, it's definitely the Palewood Brethren, I think," Nim spoke in a conspiratorial tone.

"Nim–"

"I've been quietly following them, just like you showed me. They've been down at the port and the shipyard. They were even poking around the canals of Mosswater district until the dwarves run them off. I'm telling you they're up to something." Nim's expression was of earnest concern.

"Did they break any laws?" Fraenk asked. "Anything we can have the partisans arrest them for?"

"Well, not in the strictest sense. But–"

"So you spent two days following a bunch of shaved-head gawpers with an interest in boats?"

"When you put it that way, you make it sound like an idiotic waste of time," Nim replied, crossing his arms defensively.

"That's good because I wasn't sure if I was being too subtle," Fraenk smiled.

"It's a hurtful thing to say to someone who is just trying to do his job. At least I wasn't holed up in my tower doing who-knows-what with a hidden ghost woman."

"Guard that tongue around my ghost woman." Fraenk let Nim stew in distress for a moment before he could contain his laughter any longer.

"No one likes a deceitful spymaster, sir," Nim said sulkily.

"Come on. I need you to track down some information for me. Find out if anyone else was murdered the same night Miken was killed. The partisans should have a record."

"Where are you going?" Nim asked.

"The last place I'm supposed to be. Fernbrook district."

"Didn't the Arch Partisan <u>and</u> Lady Blackroot both tell you not to have further contact with them?" Nim asked.

"They did."

"And you're deliberately disobeying them," Nim said.

"I have to."

Fraenk started to walk away.

"Sir?" Nim called, making him pause. "I have something very important to ask you, and I feel like this may be my last opportunity."

"Very well. What is it?"

Nim gave him a grave look.

"If something happens to you and you don't come back... Where do you hide all your coin?"

Deep beyond the backalleys of Fernbrook district, there was a secret shop. It was nowhere that an average person would stumble into looking for a chop of meat or a cut of exotic fabric. In fact, it was set up in a place most sane folks avoided at all costs—the back of a plague house.

The proprietor of this ominous boutique was a colorful and unscrupulous man who served a unique niche within the greater community of Arathes, especially for those looking for highly specific information. For this man was a buyer, seller, and trader of the magically charmed and the arcanely cursed. While his business was not strictly legal within Arathes and most of the items he traded in would be enough to see him thrown into that special prison for wizards, his presence was tolerated and even protected by those who valued his unique function.

While the Arcane Lords and temple paladins were powerful magic users themselves, their dogmatic prohibition on its use for anyone else created an uncomfortable tension for those occasions when a little magic might be particularly advantageous. Or if, for example, one were to discover a mysterious magical trinket that needed to be identified for its function and side effects, asking an Arcane Lord would be the quickest way to see it confiscated and not receive any helpful answers in return. It was their own fault for making such a place necessary, really.

So although Fraenk kept on friendly terms with the man, he knew this character was not at all to be trusted. He had a bad habit of bragging to Fraenk about all the other clients he brilliantly deceived about their dealings, while assuring Fraenk himself that he was speaking with complete candor. His only truth was the confession as to being a liar.

But with no better place to turn for answers, Fraenk found himself heading in the direction of Fernbrook district. It was somehow fitting the man would choose it of all places to operate. The elves there seemed to tolerate far more dubious activity than even the lowly Mosswater district, which was home to slums, gambling dens,and the city prison itself. Lord Fernbrook probably had no idea that it even existed. Greedy fool that he was would probably try to exploit it for his own gain. Fraenk took a small joy in knowing this man was operating right under Fernbrook's nose.

Fraenk took his time on a meandering, circuitous patrol route to arrive at the far side of the district. Several times he had the distinct feeling that he was being followed,but if by an individual or group, he caught no obvious tails. Fraenk did, however,notice a black raven watching him along various points of his walk, but it was too distant to tell if it was the same one who be spoiled his doublet.

Yes, Fraenk, a bird is out to get you. He silently mocked himself, then continued on.

Within three blocks of Fernbrook district, Fraenk quickly ducked into a members-only bathhouse that seemed to cater exclusively to the round-bellied and hairy variety of men. Fraenk waited to see if anyone followed. Then he changed into a soap-stained laundress' disguise and used a servant's entrance to deposit him out of a nearby boiling house into the drying yard, where clean, elvish laundry hung to dry. Steamed billowed out in white clouds that smelled of lye soap. Blending in with some bundle-toting washerwomen heading toward Fernbrook textile dyers, Fraenk twice more switched disguises and used alternate building exits before emerging back on the street near the district border. To his own estimation, Fraenk had vanished into the role of a poor but fervent monk whose holy service was to witness to the sick and dying. It was both a job and type of individual that most others avoided so as to not catch a horrible disease—or, arguably worse, part of a sermon.

The poor monk that was formerly Fraenk ventured forth, crossing into the Fernbrook district. If this disguise failed or anyone recognized him, Fraenk would be in serious danger. But so far, everyone he encountered quickly avoided eye contact or moved out of his path. He had a good feeling this was going to work.

Then, as he rounded the first corner, Fraenk nearly collided with two of the Fernbrook guards. They were both elves, and they stepped back to look at him; their faces were young but bore a cruelty that reflected how they treated all their citizenry. For several heart-pounding moments, Fraenk lowered his head, hoping they didn't recognize him or his little adventure would be over before it started.

"Watch where you're walking, dirty fool!" the taller guard barked.

"I'm sorry, sir. Powers keep you." Monk Fraenk bowed low, turning the piety up as far as it would go. "I'm just on my way to tend to the plague-stricken and the dying. For as the blessed words of Saint Candlewax says in the Tome of—"

"Ugh! Silence your braying! Be off with you!" He shouted and raised his gauntleted hand to clout Fraenk, then lowered it again in disgust, not wanting to dirty his polished armor with any part of him. Fraenk bowed a few more times and then scurried off.

After twenty minutes of walking and keeping to the less busy streets, a gentle breeze picked up and cooled him in the itchy woolen robes. Fraenk was starting to feel more confident. Maybe this plan was going to work after all. Most passers-by either ignored him or avoided eye contact entirely. Along the way, he saw other Fernbrook guards shaking down an elderly shoemaker for protection money and a woman getting robbed of the jar of milk she was carrying, only for the thieves to dump it out on the street still in sight of her. This was no way to run a district, but he could not intervene and maintain his disguise.

And so Fraenk proceeded on into the most squalid quarter of the district. Here he would find none wearing the sigil of house Fernbrook, only rags and hard stares. This journey had been a lot less dangerous before he made an enemy of one of the city's most powerful families. Fraenk wondered if he'd ever again be able to raise a pint in the legendary tavern, The King's Brigand—a notorious haunt where rugged adventurers from all parts of the land mixed with desperate people carrying a sack of coins, looking for a hero to solve their problem. Surely, following any one of these quests would result in quite the epic tale. If only an enterprising scribe would follow along and write down the events. It could make for a thrilling read by candlelight before bed.

Fraenk dismissed the idea. Leave that to someone with a more adventurous life.

Keeping his pace steady, Fraenk's mind began to go back over the details of the case. What did he know? Lord Fernbrook insisted on taking the bakery. Then, in the wake of the fire, having it swept entirely clean. The body of Bas Greenbriar quickly burned up as well, along with his head full of worms. This mysterious Lynblood woman, Kyla, was searching for something there too—what word had she said? And finally, the unwearable necklace. How did his new trinket fit into the overall puzzle?

He was almost to the street corner that led down to the plague house, still trying to piece it all together, when some annoying bird started up with such a racket, it almost seemed like Fraenk was about to step on its nest. He saw it perched in an open window across the street, carrying on with a pesky cawing noise and ruffling its body feathers. Birds were strangely territorial sometimes and weren't shy about chasing off much bigger creatures.

"There's plenty of street for the both of us," Fraenk said, walking on.

He could feel the answer to the puzzle was there if he could only concentrate. But the bird flapped around again and moved closer. Its maddening squawks louder. Fraenk sped up. Maybe around the corner, the bird would leave him to think. But it only launched itself up and dropped onto the road behind him.

"Stupid crow!" Fraenk growled. Then stopped in his tracks. Fraenk spun around to confirm his suspicion. The bird had a cloudy-white eye and tattered plumage. It was <u>the</u> crow. The one who'd addressed him earlier.

"You!" Fraenk exclaimed.

It blinked the other good eye and bobbed its head as if to agree.

"What do you want?" Fraenk asked, unsure if he expected the bird to answer or not.

The bird slowly spread its wings. With the missing feathers, it looked like the gap-tooth smile of an old hermit. It opened its beak and gave Fraenk a slow, ominous hiss. Then, with several jaunty bounces, he hopped into a nearby darkened alcove of a derelict house. It came back out, hissed again, then returned into the darkness.

Was the old bird trying to lead him somewhere? It was too odd to ignore. Fraenk wasn't given to spirit guides or omens, but there was something about this bird's insistence that was worth a look at least.

"He leads you into that building where you get jumped by a group of thugs," Fraenk said aloud.

This time, the bird flew out of the alcove and grabbed his woolen robes with its claws and flapped in the direction of the door. It was literally trying to pull him inside. Fraenk had to laugh.

"Very well, then dark guide. What do you have to show me?"

And so, with bemused skepticism, Fraenk proceeded after the crow.

The moment Fraenk was out of view in the shadow of the alcove, a terrifying figure rounded the corner. He was tall, with dark red skin, cruel orange eyes under a slanting brow, and a large set of spiraling horns.

The figure was of the Cursed Ones. The *helltouched.*

And he was coming their way.

15

The moment he saw the nightmarish helltouched, Fraenk was grateful that this rangy old crow had diverted him. Had that been its plan all along? That was probably giving this old crusty bird too much credit.

Peering out from his hiding place, Fraenk could see the helltouched man was tall, slender, and had a malevolent air about him. His black hair was oily and hung to his shoulders in uneven trusses. He was wearing the same light gray overcloak Fraenk had seen him with days ago on the street. Under was a much older set of robes; black, worn fabric with arcane lettering stitched down the front. It reminded Fraenk of something he'd seen somewhere—in an old tome or a scroll—but in this tense moment, he could not remember.

Fraenk pressed back against the stone wall, hoping the hard shadows of the sunny day concealed him. The entrance where he found himself was to a roofless building that had been abandoned some time ago. There were several others like it in this part of the district. If he had to hazard a guess why, Fraenk would have surmised that its proximity to the plague house or possibly the Fernbrook's fickle taxation schemes caused the owner to leave. For whatever reason, Fraenk was all alone out here, with just an old crow at his side.

It suddenly occurred to Fraenk that this noisy menace had, as of very recently, been sounding an entire cacophony of squawks and other bird noise. One more of those would give away his location entirely. And yet, it stood as austere as a statue, just tilting its little head and blinking with its one good eye, nearly invisible in the shadows.

I should really wear more black, Fraenk thought.

The helltouched man moved at a brisk pace that seemed to suggest he had a destination in mind and not much time to get there. Fraenk knew this was good. He would probably not be wandering off for a sightseeing tour of the local derelict ruins. If Fraenk and his ancient avian accomplice could keep inaudible and avoid alerting their assumed assailant, they'd altogether avert an accosting. They waited, breath held as the man moved past them on his course, not noticing his onlookers. Fraenk was almost ready to move when something strange happened.

The helltouched recoiled as if someone behind him loudly shouted his name. His hand flew up to his neck, and he turned. Fraenk saw he was gripping an ornate metal collar with a brilliant emerald jewel inset that rippled the air around it. The helltouched man swiveled his head, scanning the ruined buildings with his hateful orange eyes. He didn't seem to see Fraenk yet, but something was nudging him ever closer.

Fraenk froze; maybe he could still stay hidden and hope that the demon-blood moved on. The helltouched raised both hands in a fluid motion, his fingers tracing and articulating a specific order of gestures. His mouth moved, uttering some arcane ecclesiastic. Then dark purple energy gathered at his hands. He was casting a spell—and not the harmless kind that the Arcane Lords say was lawfully permitted in Arathes.

The last thing Fraenk wanted was to fight this out. But his options were quickly diminishing. Taking on a magic user was a tremendously bad idea, but he might be able to catch this fiend off-guard if he hit him with a face full of throwing knives before he could react. This was a tactic his combat instructor called a Haan pre-emptive offensive. "Strike first, fight dirty, and live" seemed a much better maxim.

Knights and Paladins may pledge to fight with honor on an open field of battle, but preceptors were bound by no such codes. Their job was to achieve their aims by whatever means necessary. Let the honorable dead heroes have their ballads of remembrance written about them. What good is a song if you won't be alive to hear it?

Fraenk's hand slowly lowered to his brace of throwing knives. But found, to his vexation, that he was still dressed like an unarmed lowly monk and had virtually none of his typical Arch Preceptor's accouterments. The only weapon he carried was a short dagger strapped to his leg, which he couldn't easily reach. For all of the hearty back-patting he was doing earlier about his perfect disguise, Fraenk now discovered its major drawback. Next time, he vowed to pose as an armored crossbowman, maybe a guard captain with a contingent of heavy knights and a battle mage—if there even was a next time.

Fraenk had the giddy, ridiculous thought that they could perhaps just talk through their differences instead. If he was being paid by the Fernbrooks, then

Fraenk could find an amount to supersede their offer. Helltouched were just people after all—albeit with an excessive amount of demon blood, which gave them a higher predilection towards evil. At least that's what his research in Arathes' Great Library had said.

The helltouched man was steadily and cautiously advancing in his direction. Dangerous energy crackled from the spell on his fingers. He was ready for something to jump out. There was no escape, and he couldn't hide much longer. Fraenk decided he might as well reveal himself before this situation escalated.

Just as Fraenk shifted his foot, the crow burst into flight in a commotion of feathers and squawks. The bird shot right for him like a black dart. Instinctively, the helltouched crossed his hands at the wrists, sending a blazing dome of energy over him in a brilliant flare of interlocking symbols. When the crow hit the barrier, a sound like a thunderclap echoed through the area. It sent a faint *woosh* of air that wobbled loose stones in their masonry, releasing cascades of thin granules and dust.

The bird vectored in a new angle off the shield, flapping furiously to correct its course. And already, the helltouched man was turning to follow its path with his gaze. He was chanting in some guttural tongue, very different from the earlier spell he cast. The helltouched man pulled a leather pouch off his belt and began pouring out what looked like black sand onto the street in a fist-sized circle. The crow was still fluttering away fast, getting smaller in the sky, as the man pulled an acid-etched dagger from his belt and drew it across the back of his arm. Immediately, a line of dark blood runneled out from the cut. He moved his arm over the drawn circle, letting his blood soak the black sand. His utterances grew louder and something strange began to happen within the radius.

The helltouched man's sand and blood mixture first boiled and then burst into polychromatic flames. A tainted blast of air erupted skyward from within. Fraenk could see something inexplicable happening in the area above the flames. It was as if reality itself became thin and translucent, and behind it, another realm came into view. But if our world was sunshine and blue skies, this other place was its dark opposite. Even the air that sucked through the hole seemed rank and poisonous. Fraenk wondered what kind of magic could do such a thing, or to what hellish purpose it might serve.

Then he watched as something terrible crawled through the opening.

Fraenk could see it was black and hairy. It moved awkwardly, trying to reorient itself in its new world. Then it spread leathery bat wings, but this was no bat. It had a bulbous green eye on a swiveling stem. Under its body were dozens of whip-like appendages that lashed and writhed continuously. The effect was unpleasant, to say the least.

This must have been how the blackhounds got into the city, Fraenk realized.

Immediately after it was through, the helltouched man kicked the blood circle with his boot, destroying the effect, and the portal immediately vanished. What was left behind was the hellish cyclopean bat-like thing from the chaos realm. A *chaosbat* seemed like the most appropriate thing to call it.

The chaosbat opened a triangular mouth that had a double row of curving teeth. It locked the hateful green eye first on the helltouched man and uttered an unholy *SKREEE!* Then clearly showing no allegiance to the one who called it forth, it flung itself at him in a flapping attack of claws and teeth. The helltouched man was ready for such a sudden-but-inevitable betrayal, however, and bounced it off a hastily cast shield spell. The chaosbat seemed neither injured nor perturbed by this and took off in a new course—toward the escaping crow.

As the other man's attention was diverted, Fraenk realized this distraction might be his only opportunity to escape. And so while his back remained to him, Fraenk quickly and silently ducked out of the alcove and around the corner where the helltouched man had just come.

Fraenk slipped the dagger from his boot and waited. He strained his ears, listening for any approaching footsteps. Then, after a moment, the ones he heard were of someone heading further away. Fraenk allowed himself a soft exhalation. The bird had saved him.

He distantly hoped the crow would be alright. But whatever its fate, it was beyond anything Fraenk could do for it at this point. He reminded himself to alert the local Arcane Lord about that loose chaosbat who was now flapping around the district.

As for this magic-wielding helltouched, Fraenk vowed to deal with him personally.

Venantius Dextur was born into a prominent Pileusian family of Cirrusol. His father was a brilliant government operator who wrote searing, incisive edicts and powerful proclamations that were the pride of his fellow statesmen and the envy of political enemies. He had an entire cadre of apprentices who studied under him, spending each day under his tutelage, waiting for a morsel of his brilliant thoughts. His mother was a singular beauty, a romantic conquest as desirable and unattainable as the tallest mount in the Runsir Peaks. This didn't stop the endless stream of potential suitors from calling. In the end, it was his future father whom she had chosen herself.

As the story goes, the man had been giving a speech on the topic of what defines beauty while he was in the forum, and he had been partway through a carefully reasoned and epistemologically justified discourse that would define exactly what beauty was when she caught his eye. Then, upon seeing her, the man threw down his notes and fell totally silent. He called this woman to the center of the forum and presented her as his final proof—to the thunderous applause of all present.

Shortly thereafter, they were married and produced a son, whom they named Dextur, which meant "favored one". He was the ultimate blend of them both—beauty and brains combined into a single human. He was their pride and joy. They frequently opined that this child—their perfect son—was possibly their greatest feat and contribution to the grand Pileusian Empire.

Then five years later, and to their mild annoyance, their second son, Dandrikan, was born. His name translated roughly to *"drunken mistake"*. And from the moment he was thrust forth, squalling into the uncaring world, Venantius Dandrikan had to struggle for all he had.

His father and mother had not wanted a second child for differing reasons. She was still upset by the toll that childbearing had taken upon her body, leaving it with unsightly pale marks on her skin and a new, more generous waistline. Her popularity and desirability were already in decline amongst the various handsome gentleman callers who would show up at their estate unannounced while his father was busy lecturing or otherwise distracted with his academic pursuits. And his father had already invested his energy and professional reputation in the superiority of the older son, Dextur. He chose to redouble his interest in the first boy instead of carving out more of his personal time for another child.

But with a spare child on hand, the man had the unique opportunity to instead treat the younger boy as the subject of one of his most controversial thought experiments. It was one that he'd been unable to attempt prior, as the local orphanages refused to oblige him with one of their charges, deming it to be 'unethical' and 'unnecessarily cruel'. But as a parent, one was free to raise their child however they chose.

Sir Venantius posited amongst his learned peers that a child who was raised without any of the advantages of an elite station—education, money, or even parental affection—any privilege whatsoever could still become a productive member within society provided they were quirted with the proper whip. His detractors called it a recipe to create a monster.

Yet to the unexpected delight of all observers of this dubious experiment, Dandrikan actually exceeded all expectations. His desire to please unapproving parents and strict instructors made him work all the harder, and soon he surpassed his charmed older brother in all areas of education, elocution, and even arms training. Unfortunately, this was a great blow to his father's test—not for Dandrikan's personal achievements contradicting the hypothesis, but because the lad was overshadowing his clearly superior brother Dextur. Meanwhile, the elder boy was proving to be distastefully entitled, unambitious, and a bit of a dull wit. This was *not* acceptable and downright embarrassing to the father.

Dandrikan soon found himself shipped off to apprentice at the Wizard Academy in Sarmatti. It was a notoriously dangerous and highly selective school that turned out the most elite wielders of magic anywhere in the land. What he didn't know before he arrived was that most students had been training since they were old enough to speak.

This disadvantage proved insurmountable, however. Despite his best efforts, Dandrikan could not catch up to even the most mediocre apprentices. He found himself in constant trouble with the teachers and given excessive menial duties, which only made him fall further behind. Eventually, Dandrikan was removed from classes and sent down to the storehouse, where they kept the mildly cursed and arcane objects. This assignment offered him unique access and deep knowledge for any item imbued with magic. He would remain there for years before deciding one day to boldly strike out on his own and share his unique gift with the world. As a parting gift, Dandrikan also took more than a few of the choicest items with him when he left.

Standing now in this very same dealer's illicit backroom trinket shop, Fraenk waited patiently for Dandrikan to finish the telling of his difficult and somehow triumphant personal history. *How much of it was true?* Fraenk guessed very little. It was the third such tale he had heard from the man, and very few of the details overlapped. One theme that did seem to emerge in all of them was about how Dandrikan himself was an unsung hero, misunderstood genius, and destined for future greatness. This was in stark contrast to his public perception of being a sad, bitter, lonely man who was forced to sell his cursed wares in a reeking plague-ridden house of the dying. "Pathetic" was often the word added to any mention of his name.

Fraenk had fortified himself with a couple of quaffs from his trusty bottle before entering. This helped him tolerate the man, if not the smell. To his credit, though, Dandrikan was a gracious host from the moment Fraenk entered. He lit several sticks of incense and propped open the ventilation windows, which allowed a refreshing cross breeze to carry the redolent scent of sick out the other end of the building.

"Neversleep! It's been ages!" Dandrikan beamed when Fraenk had entered. He then launched into a monologue, which covered not only the tale of his impressive pedigree but also a brief account of his recent travels to Tigraen for a pick-up of some pilfered Interroger confiscations, which he'd purchased at a bargain price. Stolen, more likely, Fraenk guessed.

"They are industrious, those dirty interrogers," Dandrikan continued in a sly tone. "Torture you just the same as look at you. And those doey-eyed locals just let 'em do it to them, too. Line right up with a proud smile on their dumb faces. Ooh! Me next, sir! I'll prove I'm a loyal servant of the Tyrant!"

"Some people don't understand loyalty," Fraenk said dryly.

"Exactly!" Dandrikan agreed. "I'll give 'em this much at least. The interrogers do end up with some wicked little trinkets."

As the dealer went on to describe his latest acquisitions in great detail, Fraenk watched the man himself with quiet interest. He supposed that Dandrikan could have been of Pileusian blood, as he'd claimed. His face was still youthful, possibly even handsome, if he'd bothered to bathe and visit a tailor. With the right grooming, he would've looked at home in the upper market district, where the fancy elf lordlings spent their day shopping, drinking expensive vintages, and quoting poetry to one another. But Dandrikan seemed oddly content where he was, if a bit starved for attention. Fraenk supposed there was something inside the man that kept him from finding a place among the common folk.

Dandrikan's contrarian views on the war and specifically the warlord Kreeg were another reason he had difficulty fitting in with the average citizen. Half the things he said would've earned him a beating from any loyal man in Arathes. Fraenk was too busy to care about most elf business in the kingdom, nor did he care to hear Dandrikan's repugnant views on it either. And yet somehow he'd managed to turn the discussion in that direction anyway.

"Not all of 'em are weak, mind you," Dandrikan was saying as he was puttering over an iron teapot. He poured out two steaming cups with a scattering of dry leaves. Dandrikan's ring-adorned fingers clinked cheerfully against the porcelain as he handed the cup to Fraenk.

"Some's got true strength, if you know what I mean. Power goes to the ones who can take it," he went on.

Even though it was still very hot, Fraenk sipped his tea to keep from saying something that would upset this man. He'd have to wait to do that until after he got Dandrikan's help.

Fraenk hated the endless bickering from folks whose opinions mattered not at all and did his best to avoid the arguments that popped up like random grass fires. He wasn't interested in discussing politics for his own city, let alone another kingdom. Tigraen's controversial leader, The Tyrant, as he had taken to calling himself, was an endless source of discussion in Arathes and parts beyond. Some thought his strong leadership style was what that divine-forsaken land needed to purge the evil from the cursed Tigranean soil. Others argued that Sarmattian forces shouldn't be sent out to die for some despot, even if he was battling another warlord. In some darker sectors still, they quietly believed that the elves should be supporting the upstart Kreeg, who had a legitimate right to conquest, but those extremists had all but gone silent after news of his defeat came back to the city.

Dandrikan either didn't get the news about Kreeg or was continuing to support him in spite of everything. Either way, Fraenk was tired of hearing this man go on.

"Speaking of rallying undercover forces..." Fraenk said, pretending to remember something he secreted in his monk robes. He pulled out a small bottle and held it up.

"I picked this up from a trader the other day. Care to make your tea Tigranean style?" Fraenk whispered a little of the amber liquid into his cup. Dandrikan's eyes lit up.

"Oh gods, Fraenk! You always come bearing the good stuff." Dandrikan made room in his cup and emptied the remainder of Fraenk's booze into it. He sipped and smiled happily.

"You like it? I bought a crate of them. I'll have a bottle sent over to you," Fraenk smiled.

"You'd do that for me?" Dandrikan looked surprised and thrilled. A coy smile played at the corner of his mouth. "You're a good one, Fraenk. If there's anything I can ever do for you—"

"Nah. I wouldn't press on your kindness, Dan. I value your expertise. The way you helped me figure out that it wasn't a cursed corset causing Lord Fairtwin's daughter to, uh...

"-mount half the squires in his Lordship's retinue like they were palfreys?" Dandrikan waggled his eyebrows suggestively.

"That's a matter he still appreciates your discretion on. At least until he can find her a good match and marry her off."

"Well, if he ain't too choosy, I'd propose myself. I do enjoy a randy maiden."

"I'll be sure and let him know," Fraenk promised, knowing he would do no such thing. "I'm actually here for information on another matter, however. One I'm pleased to pay for."

"Ah, another case! Very good." Dandrikan gulped the dregs of his cup and set it aside. He stood and walked behind the wooden counter where he liked to conduct his appraisals. Dandrikan pulled a stained cloth apron he had hanging from a hook on the wall and slipped it on, covering a very old leather belt adorned with strange symbols that looked like clouds. He deftly tied the apron strings behind his back, then unfurled an oddly pristine rectangle of dark blue crushed velvet on top of the counter—his field of battle was ready.

"What do you have for me, Fraenkie?"

"Well, it's a little appraisal, if you would."

Fraenk stood to join him on the other side. As he reached into the hidden pouch in his belt, Fraenk's fingers slipped through the chain loop of the strange pendant. He felt a wave of something ran up his arm, and a bad feeling came over him suddenly. Like it was not only a terrible idea for Fraenk to be here, it was worse that he brought the necklace with him. The jewelry itself was fighting him. It did not want to be seen or known. Bad enough that Fraenk was focused on it, but now another?

He felt a chill crawl up his fingers and hand, which was actually rather painful. It gave him a pause. Maybe this was more than the effect of the necklace, or maybe this necklace was going to fight him at every turn. Would it actually go so far as to hurt Fraenk, or worse? Perhaps it was too risky to take this matter any further.

But Fraenk had made it this far already, both figuratively and literally. He'd made it through the worst parts of Fernbrook district, where plenty of elves would love to see him dead. He had also slipped by that terrible helltouched with the help of the roughest-looking crow he'd ever seen. Now he was just moments from having some kind of answer as to why this pendant was important. And knowing that might tell him something about why Miken was killed.

This was the moment of truth.

Fraenk was fully prepared for Dandrikan trying to cheat him in some way. He knew it was magic, but the unscrupulous dealer would likely try to tell him it wasn't. Or that it was junk. In fact, the more Dandrikan tried to downplay its worth, Fraenk knew the more value it possessed. What he really wanted to know was what its true purpose was—why was it made? What could someone do with it if they could actually put it on? Could Dandrikan even tell him? There was only one way to find out.

Fraenk pulled the pendant out and let it dangle in the light, ready for Dandrikan's depreciative assessment of it as a worthless trinket. Instead, they were both surprised to see that Fraenk's hand was covered in a delicate layer of frost crystals. They both stared in wide-eyed amazement.

For a long moment that seemed to stretch on, the trinket dealer said nothing. He looked to Fraenk and then back at the jewelry.

"Well, what do you think?" Fraenk asked, waiting for him to deny or deflect what they were both seeing.

"Oh, that's a very cursed necklace right there," Dandrikan gulped.

16

“**Y**ou're wrong! This necklace is cursed! " Fraenk exclaimed. "Oh wait. That's what you said."

They both watched as the frost quickly turned to beads of moisture on Fraenk's hand in the afternoon heat. There was something in Dandrikan's reaction that Fraenk had not expected—a sort of awe. And for someone who had a wild confabulation for not only himself but every wondrous trinket in his shop, this was quite unusual. He was not sure what to make of the dealer's response, but hopefully it was a positive development. They could at least dispense with the jousting over whether the necklace was magical or not.

"How... did you come across this?" Dandrikan asked carefully.

"My questions first," Fraenk replied.

"Of course, Fraenkie. Happy to provide my expertise." There was something odd and nervous in Dandrikan's voice.

"Well? Do you recognize it? What is it?" Fraenk thrust the pendant forward, and Dandrikan immediately stepped back from the counter. He looked scared to touch it. Fraenk immediately wondered if it was safe for himself to be handling it, but it was too late for caution now.

"It's–" Dandrikan was in awe. He shook his head as if to clear it. "It's very cursed, is what it is."

Fraenk laid it out on the blue velvet cloth. Just sitting there, it looked flat and boring, but Fraenk knew that was part of its magic.

"I've got that much at least," Fraenk said impatiently. "I mean, have you ever seen anything like it before? Who made it? What does it do?"

Dandrikan looked flustered by all the questions.

"I don't know Fraenk. It's... not like anything I've ever encountered." He turned and rummaged below the counter. A moment later, he produced a huge, dusty leather-bound tome with iron locking straps across it. He thumped it down and unlocked it with a key he had around his neck.

"The Arcanum Maledictum may have it cataloged. Let's see here..." Dandrikan flipped through page after page of assorted items that appeared innocent enough but were apparently inflicted by insidious dark magic. Fraenk had not seen this book in his previous visits, and now he wanted more than anything to have a copy of his own to study at his leisure.

"A chair that eats whoever sits in it? And a spoon that makes its user ever hungrier? These are dastardly," Fraenk whispered. Dandrikan flashed an annoyed glare at his professional secrets being divulged. He flipped faster so Fraenk would have trouble prying.

Dandrikan stopped suddenly at a dog-eared page, and there it was. The page bore an ink and watercolor illustration that seemed to struggle to capture the dark jewelry's true likeness. Understandable, Fraenk supposed, since the item's charm probably prevented someone from faithfully recalling any detail with which to render it. Large lettering at the top identified the item.

"The Headsman's Mistress," Dandrikan read aloud. "Ooh, this is a real nasty one you got here, Fraenk."

"Go on then," Fraenk urged, and Dandrikan continued down the page.

"Let's see... Origin. Commissioned by Lord Nichwane Magjor the Green. The necklace was originally intended to be a gift to his favorite concubine, but upon discovering her infidelity to him, he had it cursed to—"

Dandrikan paused for dramatic effect. Fraenk knew this was part of the theatrics. Whatever had flustered the dealer earlier was now gone, and he was back in smooth sales broker mode.

"What? What does it say?" Fraenk urged, playing his own part.

"Slice the head from the shoulders of its wearer with a single command." Dandrikan looked up at him. "You haven't tried it on, have you?"

"No..." Fraenk said, touching his neck, visibly relieved. "So? Did he use it on her?"

"Mercifully, she never wore it. Lord Magjor's scheme was discovered by a heroic Paladin..." Dandrikan paused to make a sour face, indicating his feelings toward this particular hero or his profession in general. "... and the evil Lord was summarily executed. But! It says that he went to his grave, never revealing the secret command that would trigger the wearer's beheading."

Dandrikan screwed up his face in a pantomime of empathy.

"Oh, it goes on to say the necklace did change hands many times over the years and unfortunately did have several other unintended victims as these poor, unsuspecting women wore it out in public. The secret command would be accidentally spoken in conversation by someone in the crowd—and woosh! Off with her head. Which is how this loathsome charm earned its name. How awful!" Dandrikan was doing a poor job masking his delight in the sordid details.

"And no one remembers the specific command?" Fraenk ventured.

"Tragically, no. It ends by saying The Headsman's Mistress was finally turned over to the Arcane Lords in Corron. It is supposed to still be under their watch, but obviously, someone else got their hands on it." Dandrikan narrowed his eyes suspiciously. "So how did *you* get this gem, Fraenk?"

"Found it on a headless body near the docks," Fraenk replied evenly. "But we had no suspects, so..."

"Ah. Of course." Dandrikan's tone and expression said he didn't believe Fraenk but didn't call him on the lie either.

"Does the book say anything else about it? Secondary effects?" Fraenk asked. Dandrikan made an exaggerated show of re-reading the page. He shook his head.

"No, there's nothing."

"What about the frost?" Fraenk countered.

"—other than the chill frost that precedes an activation," Dandrikan added quickly.

"Lucky me. I almost lost a couple of fingers," Fraenk mused. "So no other enchanted effects? I just want to make sure it hides no other surprises."

"Misfortune follows the longer anyone possesses it. That's everything it says in the book, Fraenk," Dandrikan said, folding it back shut again, as if to conclude that the matter itself was closed. Fraenk noticed sunlight flicker off the gem in the gold ring on Dandrikan's pinky finger. It was one of several jeweled ornaments the man wore. Dandrikan seemed the type to keep his most magical and valued items on his person. How many of these trinkets had little tricks of their own?

"So. How much?" Fraenk asked. "You buy this kind of unholy dross, right?"

"What?! I–I don't want it," he replied defensively. "Sorry, Fraenk. It's dangerous. And if the Arcane Lords don't know it's missing already, they'll eventually come looking for it."

"That's everything you sell, Dandrikan! You're already wearing enough contraband that they'd send you to that special prison for warlocks."

Dandrikan stepped backward, clasping his hands in front of the belt with the cloud patterns on it. Then he smiled. "Well, in Tigraen, they'd just try to hang me. Anyway, I'm not interested."

"Alright. So the necklace isn't worth anything? What if I gave it to you?" Fraenk pressed. "What if I *paid* you to get rid of it?"

"I can't help with this, Fraenk. But I'm warning you not to hang onto it, either. It's a heavy anchor on your neck, and you're running out of chain. You have to pass it off to someone else. That's the only way." For maybe the first time in their conversation, Dandrikan looked genuine and concerned.

Fraenk nodded. Then quickly picked up the necklace and slid it back into his inner pocket. As he did, Dandrikan busied himself with refolding the blue cloth and deliberately not watching where Fraenk put the necklace.

"Alright. Thanks for your help. I'll be going now," Fraenk said and clacked several silver coins down on the counter. "For your trouble. And your learned expertise."

He turned to the door and was just about to push outside when it finally came—the final step in the brokering dance. It had to come at the very end. One remote possibility for an offer too hard to resist.

"Fraenk, wait," Dandrikan called out, like he suddenly had a bolt of inspiration. "I can't guarantee it, but I think I know someone who might buy the necklace."

"You do?" Fraenk turned back, showing hope on his face.

"There's a certain collector. I need to speak with him first. But he's into all kinds of twisted arcana. This might be something he would want."

"You'll speak to him? And get word back to me?" Fraenk tried to keep his tone inclined but not eager.

"Yes. But, Fraenk, I have to warn you. He's very private about his collection, given his place in society. He buys through me exclusively. He wouldn't be interested if another dealer approached with the same item."

"I get it. You want to keep this between as few parties as possible," Fraenk said.

"I knew you'd understand. Just come back with it the day after tomorrow. I'll get him here so he can see it with his own eyes." Dandriank tapped his lip. "Now that I think on it, if he is interested—and I'm not promising he will be—but if he is, we might be able to take a nice stack of gold from him in the exchange."

Ah, yes. Fraenk thought. *Here was the old familiar Dandrikan that he knew and nobody else loved...*

The moment he was around the corner from Dandrikan's plague house, Fraenk ran.

He fully expected the unscrupulous dealer to lie to him about the trinket, which he did. The necklace illustrated and described in the book was not the same as the one in Fraenk's possession. Its appearance and effects were all different, and there was no mention of its aversion to attention. In fact, Dandrikan appeared to be ready for such an inquiry; the dog-eared page of the Arcanum Maledictum was marked beforehand as a likely misdirection. Its select purpose, Fraenk reasoned, was to make it undesirable and of little value to him—not to mention scaring Fraenk from attempting to try it on.

He also anticipated Dandrikan would try to contrive a way for Fraenk to rid himself of the cursed item and make himself the reluctant recipient. Dandrikan skillfully added the hint of jingling coins to appeal to greed or recoupment of any money Fraenk spent on the necklace's acquisition. This, too, came as no surprise. He also didn't want Fraenk showing the trinket to anyone else either, lest it change hands to someone else.

What caught Fraenk off guard was the man's clumsy attempt at a trap. Dandrikan's final invitation to come back alone with the necklace in hand, expecting to return home with a fat coin purse, was indeed laughable. The twisted fool must have forgotten the time he elaborated on this very scheme. Dandrikan had hired some local goons to waylay a greedy mark who thought he was coming to sell an enchanted painting that made all its viewers think fondly of their mother. He must really want the necklace if he would resort to such desperate measures. And considering who Fraenk was and what he was capable of, he had to imagine that this unfortunate encounter would necessitate Fraenk's untimely death as a result, lest he seek retribution. Dandrikan would insist upon not having any loose ends.

Of course, all that was a series of leaps on the slippery stones in the river of logic. Dandrikan had always treated him warmly as a sort of friend. It was possible that Fraenk was being extremely paranoid—an understandable reaction given his job and recent misadventures. Perhaps Dandrikan had earned enough goodwill over the years to receive the benefit of the doubt? After all, he could have just taken it when Fraenk offered the necklace to him in his shop, and yet he refused.

But there was one last thing that kept Fraenk from dismissing this incident as a distrustful misunderstanding. When Fraenk had picked up the necklace for the second time to put it away, he could swear that he could—for lack of a better expression—*feel* Dandrikans overwhelming avarice and desire to take the necklace. Just grab it right out of Fraenk's hand. There was also a secondary, more rational drive in the man's mind that kept the first one in check. Dandrikan's yearning for the necklace was the same as Fraenk felt when he spent two days without a drink.

It was an urge almost unbearable. Something a man would do nearly anything to quiet—including betray a friend. He was done with Dandrikan.

As he made his way back across the Fernbrook District, Fraenk noticed something odd. The soldiers who were previously absent on his way to the plague house now seemed to be out in full force. Fraenk did not want to conflate every disadvantageous event, explained or not, directed at himself personally. But this did seem unusual.

Initially, Fraenk was worried that somehow Dandrikan raced to the Fernbrook guards and alerted them to his presence, triggering a district-wide manhunt for their sworn enemy. But logic failed for that explanation for several reasons. The unscrupulous dealer avoided the Fernbrooks, and he certainly wouldn't want them to take Fraenk into custody while he had the necklace in possession.

Another possibility was that they were looking for the ill-tempered, helltouched man, but somehow he doubted that was the case. The demon blood seemed to have an uncanny knack of avoiding detection when it suited him.

But then, what other explanation remained? Some other incident that didn't involve him at all? Not likely.

Fraenk spotted a cluster of guards standing around ahead, blocking his most direct exit. He veered onto a side street—there were other routes. He found three other avenues with a contingent of guards or armsmen bearing Greenbriar sigils. Fraenk was running out of clear paths out. He was close to the border though, just a little further.

When he had to double back from his second to last way due to the sudden appearance of a guard post right on the district border. His suspicions seemed confirmed.

For safe measure, Fraenk stole drying laundry from an unwatched backyard and updated his disguise to look more like a rather unremarkable workman. He quickly wove through a thinning crowd. There was one last crossing that ran beneath the wide oxcart bridge that spanned the industrial sectors of Blackroot and Fernbrook. It was never guarded because the local vagrants who lived down there would run any authority figure off, starting with thrown insults and moving quickly to projectiles of a more intestinal production.

As he made his way ever closer to being home free, Fraenk was definitely convinced something foul was going on in Fernbrook district. But how could this be about him? No one else knew he was even here.

No one except Nim.

No. It couldn't be...

Fraenk had just stepped into the shadow of the bridge when five figures emerged from behind the pylons. They were all wearing silver chainmail and had tall spears, with the distinctive circle sigil of Fernbrook on their chest.

All of them except the elf in the middle, who wore a long dark green cloak and the silver pin of the Arch Preceptor.

"Hello, Arch Preceptor Neversleep," he said, a smile curling like the savage grin of a fox staring at a helpless chicken. It had all been a trap, and Fraenk had stepped right into it.

17

"WELL, IF IT ISN'T my favorite counterpart in the Fernbrook district," Fraenk said, taking a casual stance. "How's whispers, Fart?"

"That's Arch Preceptor Farathiel Gingerglade to you!" an indignant guard with thick arms spat. His surcoat bore the emblem of Greenbriar, and his head and body were encased in silvery chain. Fraenk guessed this one was kin to the elf he had killed.

"Relax, Sir Edwyrd. Let us speak," Farathiel said, raising his hands and motioning for all of them to stand down. The armored guard set the butts of their spears on the stone but still looked very much ready to run Fraenk through at the slightest provocation.

"I just want a word, Neversleep," Farathiel approached Fraenk with his hands spread.

"That's a lot of steel for just speaking a word," Fraenk said wryly. "Is there a military demonstration following?"

"Don't mind them. They insisted on coming along. Somehow they got the idea that you'd do something unpredictable."

"Like kill an elf?" Fraenk asked. "Turns out that's more trouble than it's worth. I don't recommend it."

The Greenbriar man gripped the shaft of his spear so tight, Fraenk could hear the wood creak in protest.

"Indeed. So how's whispers in Blackroot, Neversleep?" Gingerglade asked without interest.

"Been quite busy, I must say. Lots of new friends in the neighborhood. Some of them are having trouble fitting in," Fraenk replied.

"I'm sure you're extending the hospitality that Blackroot is famous for," Farathiel said.

"Alright, Fart. Do you feel like we've exchanged enough pleasantries, and we can get to the crux of this visit?"

"Got somewhere to be?" Gingerglade arched a brow.

Fraenk saw the guard contingent standing relaxed, but their eyes were all still locked on him.

"Well, if we're talking about hospitality, you've brought a lot of steel just to say 'hello'. Why don't you and the boys join me back on my side of the river? I know a place where we can get the best—"

"I didn't come here to beat you up like some common thug, Neversleep. My Lord says that the matter is settled, and I agree. I helped broker the truce, even. There is something else I needed to speak with you about, off the rolls."

"Some under-the-bridge diplomacy, just like the old days," Fraenk smiled. "What is it?"

"Well..." Farathiel paused. "I need some help tracking down someone whom we believe is in your district."

"That's a good one, Fart. You think I'll help you bag a Blackroot district citizen? You really do have rocks in your head."

"Oh no, Fraenk. Nothing so base as kidnapping. We wouldn't even ask about that," Farathiel laughed.

Yeah, you'd just do it. Fraenk thought but kept it to himself.

"One of our senior house servants has gone missing. He is a favorite of Lord Fernbrooks and an absolute wonder. He knows how the Lord likes his meals served and has the Lord's pipe ready on the stroke of the night bell. He is <u>dearly</u> missed."

"I suppose he brings the Lord's chamber pot back smelling like rosewater, too," Fraenk said dryly.

"Yes exactly," Farathiel agreed, missing the barb.

"I don't suppose you could train another servant to replace this one. I hear that's a thing you proper elves do."

"Oh no. Lord Fernbrook likes him in particular. And besides. He's under bond."

"Ah. Bought and paid for," Fraenk said. "I was having trouble imagining anything Fernbrook loved that wasn't gold-colored and clinked when you dropped it."

"Just so," The other Arch Preceptor's laugh was a bit too forced. "Nevertheless, he does want the servant back. As you suggest, coin is coin. Even the one that falls between the stones."

"Why do you think he's in my district?"

"You have the only hovel of kobolds in Arathes." Farathiel looked directly at him. He seemed to be gauging Fraenk's reaction.

"Your missing servant is a *kobold*?" This genuinely caught Fraenk by surprise, and he made no attempt to hide it. Kobolds were half the size of a man and looked as if a tiny dragon had decided one day to start walking around in human clothes. They were coarse and unhygienic. They could barely be considered civilized, for they started fights at the smallest provocation and caused no end of trouble for everyone they encountered. One could hardly suggest they were intelligent, and they were barely suited for the dangerous work of climbing between the massive gear teeth of Arathe's great elevator. They certainly were not a creature you'd want serving drinks on a crystal tray in a lord's manor. It was the reason why they were relegated to their own slums in the far corner outside the city walls.

"Oh yes. They're all the rage in society right now. And it's so hard to find a well-trained one," Farathiel returned to fidgeting with his pale piglet leather gloves.

"Right. So you want me to poke my head in and see if he's hiding out there? Because if he spied one of your oafs coming, he'd disappear forever."

"I knew you'd get it. They *trust* you."

"They don't trust anyone, and my answer is no," Fraenk replied. "But I wish you Shalokar's own luck in finding him."

Gingerglade seemed to expect this response. He sniffed and waved off a fly that was buzzing around his face.

"Don't you want to hear the offer?"

"I doubt you have anything that I want," Fraenk said. "Unless your lord wants to give back the Lower Market. Then I'd bag that kobold myself."

Farathiel laughed high and clear. It was a grating sound.

"Sorry, Neversleep. That's not on the table," he said. "But I bet I do have something you want. Three *something's*, to be exact."

Fraenk did not like the way the Arch Preceptor of Fernbrook was now smiling at him. It was the same look he'd had when they first met. His mind raced as to what this devious elf could have that Fraenk might value so much that he'd do the dirty work of a Fernbrook. Then it hit him like a war hammer to the chest.

The three preceptors who didn't check in.

"You've got my men?!" Fraenk shouted. His fists clenched.

Farathiel Gingerglade stamped a foot, and all his guards snapped their spears down to point right at Fraenk. One more step, and they were ready to create a lot of new openings in Fraenk's body.

"They are <u>guests</u> of ours, of course. And free to leave as soon as you return our house servant. Don't play clever, Neversleep. It fits you poorly. I know that's why you were poking around our district. You won't find them."

Fraenk slipped his hands in his pockets and stepped backward. He didn't want one of these overeager guards to decide now was a good time to settle the score.

"All you want is the kobold?" Fraenk asked.

"That's all. Delivered by around this time tomorrow, and you'll even get your guys back alive. You have my word."

Fraenk's fists tightened in his pocket, anything to keep them from smashing this elf's smug, perfect face to a bloody ruin. He felt the loop of metal in his fingers go icy-cold.

"What can you tell me about this kobold then?" Fraenk growled.

"His name is Posuu Faljaon. And he's..."

Then something odd happened. Fraenk heard the Arch Preceptor continue to speak, but his voice became faint and distant. Instead, Fraenk was battered by another voice, loud and disembodied, which also belonged to the elf. "THIEF! SCUM! STOLE FROM THE MASTER!" There were also flashes of images; they appeared to be from inside Gingerglade's perspective.

Lord Fernbrook, in a rage, threw a chest of gems across the room. Walking behind a line of servants, sifting through white dust. Then a view of Fraenk's three preceptors standing in the street, unaware that they're being watched. A malicious feeling, like intent on capturing them, as half dozen Fernbrook men starting towards them...

Fraenk stood blinking. He realized that Farathiel had finished speaking and was just staring at him, confused. But at the same time, Fraenk *felt* the elf's confusion in his own head.

"Neversleep? You look a little green. Are you ill?" The Arch Preceptor said with false concern.

"A hearty drink will set me right," Fraenk covered quickly and wiped his brow. He noticed on his hand the last few crystals of frost melting to water.

"We'll see you tomorrow then? With the kobold in hand."

"You treat my boys well. If I find out you've harmed them... you're going to have something a little sharper than a chest of gems thrown at your head."

Farathiel Gingerglade's eyes narrowed and color warmed in his cheeks—as if he were embarrassed that Fraenk somehow knew about Lord Fernbrook's tantrum.

This was interesting, Fraenk thought, reading the other's reaction.

With a swish of his cape, the Arch Preceptor of Fernbrook irritably motioned to his guards to follow. Cautious, Fraenk stepped back to avoid being shouldered off the walkway by the spiteful guards.

"Oh... I almost neglected one final thing. I did say I wasn't here to rough you up. But you were trespassing in our district without my leave. And I'm a stickler for district rules. I'm sure you understand..." Farathiel, along with five of the six guards, strode by, giving Fraenk devilish smirks before proceeding up the stairs that lead back into their district.

"Let me guess who volunteered to give me a reminder," Fraenk said. He turned to see Sir Edwyrd advancing with fists up and already swinging.

There are those men who enjoyed a good scrape. A dust-up. A pugilistic repartee. The exchange of knuckles. For what could someone know about themselves without having one's face bashed and giving back in kind?

The lesson Fraenk had learned from being in many fights was that it was indeed preferable to be on the winning side of them—and the more one-sided, the better.

Fraenk was not winning this fight. It wasn't even close.

The burly thug was clearly a conditioned warrior. He had Fraenk in weight by a full three stone. His reach was five inches further, and he was thick with muscle. He also happened to be wearing a shirt of chainmail, which didn't seem to affect his speed at all. But it certainly did hurt when Fraenk tried to get in a return shot on Sir Edwyrd's body. Fraenk was no slouching in scuffle, but all of his tactics and training were confoundingly ineffective against this beast.

And so, as his own body was receiving brutal new impacts, Fraenk soon began to wonder about time. How long had this beating been going on? When would it stop? If the very nature of time itself was somehow not constant but could expand and contract relative to the person experiencing it. This last one seemed far less important at the moment.

His vision was starting to dim when the tempo and ferocity of the punches diminished. This was good because Fraenk's body was definitely ready to give out. He couldn't be sure he wasn't hallucinating, but it appeared that a figure had just crept out of the shadows of the pier behind Sir Edwyrd.

"Alright," Fraenk spit blood from a broken lip. "I think we've both had enough, don't you?"

Sir Edwyrd breathed and panted, stepping a few paces back. The hood of his mail shirt had slipped down, exposing his sweat-soaked hair and ears that were round, not pointed, neither half nor full.

"A human?" Fraenk also gasped, more out of pain from aching ribs. "They got us fighting each other."

"I wouldn't call what you're doing 'fighting'," Sir Edwyrd replied.

"Still. You're human. You go against your own kind." Fraenk knew that appealing to their common species was a gambit. Tensions between humans and elves had been higher recently and he knew odds were good that the Greenbriars didn't treat this man well. He might be able to turn him against his sworn house.

"I loyally serve House Greenbriar. Whatever is required of me."

So that idea was out, Fraenk thought.

"But they're not your house, are they?" Fraenk said. "You're nothing but a human, not elf kin. Your devotion is but sloss to them."

This seemed to give the guard pause. The dark figure behind him crept closer.

"House Greenbriar is honorable!" He shot back defensively. "House Greenbriar is—"

"That could've been *you* that Bas Greenbriar killed. And no one would have fought to avenge your death. They wouldn't even care about another dead human."

Fraenk saw the man's eyes dart rapidly, like he'd triggered some memory.

"You... you saw it, didn't you? What he did?" Fraenk asked.

"No!" Sir Edwyrd waved a hand as if to bat away Fraenk's words.

"Your honorable house killed a man. His wife. His two boys... and you _serve_ them!"

"And you're just some jumped-up round-ear who doesn't know his place!" Sir Edwyrd roared, red-faced and raising his fists.

"I tried to reason with you. Then you say hurtful things like that," Fraenk shrugged apologetically.

"What are you going to do?" Sir Edwyrd laughed.

"I'm just the one distracting you. I think that guy looks like he's going to put you out." Fraenk said, pointing at the man who had just picked up the guard's spear. Sir Edwyrd turned just as the man swung the weapon shaft in a level arc. It splintered into shards as it broke on the side of the guard's head. Sir Edwyrd dropped, boneless in the shallow stream of water.

Fraenk tried to stand, but a wave of dizziness hit him, and he began to tilt. A strong hand caught his arm and pulled him back upright. Fraenk found himself again looking at a familiar face.

"Leos?"

"That's the second time I've had to save you, Fraenk," his old acquaintance, Leos Muninger, said, smiling.

"From him?" Fraenk painfully turned around. The battle rush of the fight was wearing off, and now he just felt completely spent. "He was just giving me directions... back to Blackroot."

Fraenk bent over and turned Sir Edwyrd's head so he wasn't lying face down in the water that ran in the canal below the bridge. Whatever their differences, Fraenk didn't want the big guy to drown while unconscious.

Leos watched and continued to smile placidly. He made no move to help Fraenk.

"How about that drink now? We have much to catch up on," he suggested.

"I have to... I... need..." Fraenk wobbled, uncoordinated.

"Come on now, Fraenk. All of that spy stuff will keep for a few hours. You're not fit to do anything but fall on your head," Leos slung one of Fraenk's arms over his shoulder.

Fraenk let the big man support his weight as they made their way up the far side of the canal and back into Blackroot District.

"Thanks, Mudge," Fraenk smiled. "You're a good friend.

18

I T WAS WELL INTO the supper hour when they reached The Three Arrows, a tavern with decent food, strong drinks, and most importantly, open seats. Leos urged that they continue all the way to The Sapphire Slash, but brothel food was notoriously substandard, and Fraenk was in no mood for that kind of atmosphere. Fortunately, there were plenty of ladies from the district in The Three Arrows enjoying food and ale, so his friend couldn't complain too much about being denied some kind of opportunity.

It had taken them a while to finally arrive, and they were both ravenous. Fraenk had to first retrieve his Preceptor's cloak and clothing from the bath-house, then visit the healer to have his injuries seen again. The nurse there instantly recognized him and gave Fraenk quite an earful as they reset cracked ribs, a swollen eye socket, and various other cuts and bruises. He was again ordered directly home to rest, which Fraenk swore to do as soon as he was able. Only then did they make their way to the tavern, where they now sat at a table near the side wall, away from the untalented troubadour who was struggling at the lute.

Neither man spoke much as they devoured two plates piled high with beef haunch roasted in butter with chunks of onions and saffin root. Leos accompanied his supper with three foamy pints of a dark Isten Brown beer. Wanting to keep his wits, Fraenk kept himself to only one and drunk it slowly. When they had finished, Fraenk leaned back in his chair, his belly starting to protest uncomfortably from the rich food. Leos waved the barmaid over to refill their tankards.

"That's all for me," Fraenk said, pulling his cup back from the robust woman who had a red cluster of prominent sores at the corner of her mouth. She topped Leos' tankard off and gave him a wink before waddling away into the crowd.

"I saw her first, you dog," he said and took a long drink.

"She's all yours, my friend," Fraenk said and burped. The pain in his belly abated some.

Leos Muninger curled his lip and unleashed a belch that sounded much like an unhappy Shivan getting his tail stepped on. It was answered by two others like it from different spots in the tavern. The energy in the tavern was celebratory, and Fraenk saw several women wearing wreaths of lavender on their heads. It must have been one of the holy or feast days, but he couldn't recall which one.

"I like this place, Fraenk," Leos laughed and gulped down more beer.

After another hour, the lutist took mercy on their ears and packed up his instrument for the night. Fraenk noticed they had stayed long enough for the tavern to empty out and was starting to fidget. He had much to do. But it would be very bad form to twice abandon the man who saved his life. Fraenk had to wait until his friend felt justly rewarded before taking his leave. If that meant buying the last pitcher of beer in this place, then that's what must be done.

Leos' smile faded, and he got a distant look.

"I'm worried about you, Fraenk."

"Is that why you were following me?" Fraenk asked.

"*I wasn't-*" Leos smiled again broadly. "Ah, very well—our second meeting wasn't as accidental as it appeared."

"I didn't think so."

"So?" Leos said with a drunken smile. "What do you think?"

"What do I think about what?"

"Me being a preceptor. I think I've proved myself."

Fraenk arched an eyebrow. This conversation just took an uncomfortable turn. His friend seemed to be waiting to spring this moment on him for a while. Now his courage floated on a river of beer.

"I'm smart. And I can fight. I know the district, good as you. I can help you, Fraenk," Leos said. "And Powers know you need it, too. Every time we meet, someone's trying to kill you."

"I'm around many different people while someone's trying to kill me. It's a dangerous job."

"Well? I can help. You know me."

Fraenk could still feel the hot swelling around his eye and knew that his friend was right—about all of it. He was a mess, and he did need every man he could get, especially with three of his other preceptors now kidnapped. But something stopped Fraenk. He couldn't take Leos Muninger into his service now—and maybe not ever.

His friend read Fraenk's hesitation and darkened.

"I know we have a past, Fraenk," Leos said.

"What do you mean? We're friends."

"We've known each other since we was kids. But we wasn't always friends," Leos sighed heavily, then looked up. "You called me 'Mudge' today."

"I did?" Fraenk asked. "Must've been from getting hit in the head a few dozen times."

"Look, I know you didn't mean nothin' by it. But you said it. You still don't trust me."

There it was, Fraenk realized. *That was the reason.* There had been too much history. Too many beatings as a kid. Too many exhausted days running down the street from the gang. Too many nights spent scared that they would find him while he slept. This man was, and maybe always would be, his bully. And the bully of every street kid he knew growing up.

But hadn't Fraenk forgiven him yet? They had made peace at some point as adults. It wasn't some mushy child's fable, like they preached in the cathedrals, either. How foolish to believe in some profound moment of repentance and forgiveness, a wrongdoer reformed in a shaft of holy light?

No. Instead, they both grew up and found jobs, tipped back a few tankards in the off hours, and became actual friends. And nothing bad from their childhood was supposed to matter anymore, so they didn't ever talk about it. And even though Fraenk decided he would forget the past, he realized he still carried it. That weight. The history. It was all still there, buried down and festering right back up.

"Leos, I'm sorry," Fraenk said. "I've just got too much happening right now to take you on. I've already got an apprentice as well. When things calm down a bit—"

"I saved your life twice!!" Leos snapped. Several startled patrons looked over, then quickly away. "You think a few drinks are going to cover that?"

"And I'm grateful, Leos. I am. I owe you something for all you've done, but I can't make you a preceptor. I have to do what's best for Lady Blackroot. Everything I do is in service of the family. There's a process—"

"Black Blood of Zanod!" Leos' curse cut him off. Several nearby patrons gave him a startled look.

Fraenk could see the glossy shine in his friend's eyes. He was very drunk, but that didn't mean he was lying. Probably the opposite. Leos began to tear up then. Fat dribbles spilled down his cheeks onto the craggy wood tabletop. His gaze went up like he was looking at something far away. Not just distant in miles, but years as well.

"You don't understand. I need this, Fraenk," Leos began softly. He took a shuddering breath. "I was there on the field that day with the army. It wasn't a miracle; it was death writ large. And we were <u>all</u> guilty and deserving of that fiery sword. The winged man's gaze *showed* us that. Saw into our souls. Our deeds. It burned us too. We only survived because of which side we were standing on; that's it. And do you want to know the worst part? The part that won't leave my head?"

"What?" Fraenk's voice was barely a murmur.

"I saw the Black Door open for me, Fraenk. They were calling my name. They said I'm coming there soon. The hells were readying a spot just for me."

Fraenk sat in stunned silence.

"I know I can't atone for all of it, Fraenk. All the other kids we run with are dead. Got sick, or hanged for stealing, or the wrong end of a knife. But you. You're the last alive. Maybe the ones above will forgive me if I make it right with you."

"Hey, it's alright. Don't worry about that now. You've saved my life twice now. Don't you think you've atoned?" Fraenk tried to reassure his sobbing friend. He knew he should say the words aloud that he forgave Leos right there, but something small and dark and hard inside him wouldn't let him. So he let old Mudge spill out his remorse for the sins of the past.

After his friend's crying had gone on long enough to dampen the entire mood of the tavern, Fraenk paid for the meals and the drinks, then secured Leos a room upstairs. Curious patrons watched him maneuver his large drunk friend up the staircase and into a small room with a stale, musty mattress.

"I won't be there next time to save you," Leos vowed darkly as Fraenk pulled his boots off.

"You don't have to. Maybe I don't deserve it," Fraenk replied and draped an old blanket over him. Leos was snoring loudly by the time Fraenk closed the door behind him and left.

It was dark when Fraenk emerged from The Three Arrows. The healer's medicine and good meal had done wonders, chasing many of his body's complaints away. Well, he could walk at least. And his head was much clearer—which was good because he needed to think and he didn't have much time.

The torches and braziers had been lit along the High Street, casting warm flickering light for the travelers and patrons still out on business after sunset. Fraenk's first instinct was to get back to Blackroot Estate as quickly as possible. Gwen needed to know about the kidnapped preceptors, and he also wanted to stash the cursed necklace away in his room until he could really have a chance to figure it out.

It would take too much valuable time to go all the way back up, however. To pass along the message, Fraenk opted for the next best thing—or possibly the worst.

In a nearby alley, Fraenk used some dried fish to coax out one of his many conditioned skrates. It would be a gross exaggeration to call them 'trained' for they listened about as well as a dead mackerel. He scribbled off a coded message, loaded it into the pouch on the lizard cat's neck, and gave it a whiff of a small square of fabric that carried Gwen's scent. Fraenk wondered if the skrate could still find her if she was wearing a glamor, but the animal was already scrambling away. Too late to do anything about it now.

Fraenk's message about the missing preceptors might be entrusted to a semi-feral, bite-happy feline reptile, but this magical necklace that could perhaps peer into minds however could not. Nor would he let it out of his possession without putting it someplace that was completely secure. An object that could read someone's thoughts was a dangerous item, if that truly was the necklace's function.

Had he imagined seeing the thoughts of Arch Preceptor Gingerglade? Fraenk wondered. He had taken quite a few punches to the head. Perhaps his addled brain had made it up. That had to be the reason.

But, no, that wasn't it. Fraenk was clear-headed when it happened. He heard Farathiel's voice. He was calling someone a thief. He saw Lord Fernbrook throwing a tantrum over his missing kobold. And his own missing preceptors, who were apparently kidnapped and soon dead if he didn't move quickly. The pendant had shown him glimpses of all those things.

"What are you?" Fraenk pulled the necklace out to examine it in his palm. The dull stone looked flat and unappealing. He could feel its magic, wanting him to lose interest in it, but Fraenk was more intrigued than ever. How does it actually work? Fraenk had somehow triggered it accidentally when he was talking to the Arch Preceptor, but could he do it again?

The streets had mostly quieted at this late hour, but maybe there was someone he could try it on. The ethics of using an untested magical item on an unsuspecting individual were dubious at best. Fortunately for Fraenk, his job duties allowed him to waiver any moral quandary in the name of district security. He tried not to abuse this privilege. And additional recompense, Lady Blackroot would make a good faith offering at the temples for any serious violations Fraenk perpetrated in the name of the family.

Now, to find someone whose mind he could gaze into. To his right, a tavern door banged open and a soused group of mismatched travelers stumbled out. They looked to be in the midst of some quest, or perhaps they'd completed it, given their celebratory mood. Fraenk clutched the pendant and moved closer. Then the large, burly man with fur-lined armor doubled over and vomited on the stones.

"Giant nauseous drunk? Hmm, no. That was a bad idea," Fraenk said to himself.

A man with stringy brown hair stood with his back to Fraenk on the street further down. He seemed all right. Fraenk crept closer, gripping the pendant.

"Hells fire! Two cats in a pot. My teeth know when it's raining!" The man screamed aloud and twitched.

"A big 'nay' to the madman as well." Fraenk pivoted quickly across the street.

As he got to the corner that led to the docks, Fraenk saw a scrum of the shaved-headed hayseeds in their dark roughspun frocks. They were clustered around their elderman, a fat, bearded blowhard with a shiny domed head.

"Turn from your wickedness and join the brotherhood, city of devils, city of demons! We will call forth the Under One to cleanse this place. The blood star will be the sign. Lament and wail..." He boomed, his voice carrying like thunder down the street. The other members surrounding him yooped and gibbered in ecstatic agreement.

Ah, here was Nim's supposed Palewood Bretheren, Fraenk guessed. For being a dangerous cult of self-mutilating demon summoners, it sure looked like they had fallen on hard times. They were all stringy and sunken-eyed—with the exception of their leader. Fraenk guessed the big man who was round-bellied and ruddy-cheeked. It was clear he kept his flock in thrall with religious fervor so he could live the good life.

In any case, Fraenk wanted no part of any of their cultish minds. He also made a mental note to have them run out of town at the earliest opportunity.

This was not going well. Perhaps it was time to move on.

Then he spotted the perfect candidate ahead. An old woman was in the process of taking down her fruit stand that she had operated every day from that location for many years. Fraenk had purchased many a ripe, crisp apple from her that always seemed free of worms. Elise, her name was, or Elsie—Freenk couldn't recall exactly.

She had just picked up a woven bushel basket half full of the apples, which didn't sell that day. Elsie recognized Fraenk immediately as he approached and smiled.

"Good evenstar to you, Arch Neversleep." She said cheerfully in her old, craggy voice.

Fraenk stopped in front of her, holding the pendant loosely. She looked at him, an expectant curiosity on her wrinkled face. He would certainly find nothing terrible in this woman's thoughts. Perhaps a mild annoyance for apple worms or a kind prayer for her beloved grandchildren. Fraenk clenched his teeth and took a breath, fingers ready to close around the necklace. He needed to test the necklace. There was no better opportunity.

"Would you like an apple?" She asked sweetly.

"I–" Fraenk stopped.

"Oh, please, Arch Neversleep, you'd be doing me a favor. Lighten this old woman's burden by just a bit." She set the basket back on the ground and selected the nicest fruit she could find. She held it out for Fraenk to take.

Fraenk looked at the red apple, then the woman's gray eyes. A tight smile pulled his lips and his hands closed around the necklace.

Fraenk took a large, crunchy bite from the apple that Elsie *(or was it Elise?)* had given him. His attempt to try out the cursed pendant was a bust. Ethical carte blanche aside, he couldn't bring himself to use it on that sweet old lady.

He took another annoyed chomp. The sugary juice was spraying as he stomped down the street. The first lawless goon he encountered, Fraenk, vowed to burn a hole in his brain with that necklace. But for now, he slipped it back into an inner pouch. He had to move on to the other pressing matters, and Fraenk was running out of time.

His priority now was to recover his missing men. And to do that, he needed the full strength of his preceptor service. Unfortunately, this made it rather inconvenient since three of them were the same ones being held hostage. Fraenk finished his apple and lobbed the core over the fence into the Lower Market Bazaar as he passed it.

"What am I supposed to do? Go snare this kobold and deliver him to the Fernbrooks, myself? That's just giving them exactly what they want," he growled to the air. Fraenk refused to just play right into their scheme, whatever it was with this kobold.

But then another thought occurred to him. Giving them what they wanted was *exactly* the answer. If the Fernbrooks went through the risk to capture three of Fraenk's preceptors, they must really want the filthy scamp. That meant he could be used as leverage. Perhaps Fraenk could work out some scheme with him to rescue his men and keep the creature out of the Fernbrook's hands—assuming the dim little toe-chewer wasn't a complete pickle like the majority of his ilk.

What was his name? Potsoup? Potoo? *Posuu?*

Posuu Faljaon.

That was it. That was the name Farathiel had said before all his rotten thoughts dumped into Fraenk's head. The name sounded familiar somehow. Hopefully, the thick-headed kobolds would recognize it and give him some good information as to the little guy's whereabouts. Fraenk grimaced at just the thought of trying to explain himself to a clan of greedy, bunk-eyed filth eaters.

As Fraenk was figuring out how best to proceed, the clatter of horseshoes turned his attention. Someone was riding up fast.

"If one more person tries to kill me today, I swear to Gromm..." Fraenk grumbled, then was actually relieved to see the rider was Nim Stonebridge.

Nim reigned up the horse awkwardly and nearly fell from the saddle as he dismounted.

"Fraenk! Thank Mersey I found you. Someone saw you walking this way," Nim said.

"And where have you been?" Fraenk asked.

"Tracking down the other murders, like you asked me." Nim replied. And Fraenk recalled the mission he had sent the junior preceptor on. He had a suspicion from what the beautiful Lynblood woman had said that Miken wasn't the only one killed that night.

"Right. Sorry, Nim. Other murders? What did you find out?"

"It, uh, took me a while, on account that the partisans were not exactly talkative with someone who's run afoul of them in the ancient past." Nim scratched his head sheepishly. "I had to promise the Arch Preceptor of Blackroot would owe a few favors to get some answers."

"Oh, did you now—?" Fraenk frowned. An owed favor to a partisan could get costly. "What did my generosity buy me then?"

"Well, there were three murders that night that stood out. All of 'em were tortured first," Nim said, checking the notes on his jotter.

Fraenk perked up.

"Fair to say that's the work of our maniac elf. Who were they?"

"Two brothers, twins. Ehric and Dahric Thorbin. They worked in a tannery. One of them got it real bad; it took a long time to die. The other just got a blade to the throat."

"So, not just torture. He wanted information." Fraenk reasoned aloud. "Once he got it... What about the last one?"

"Arika Broadwaters, she was a—"

"—theater district stud broker. I've heard of her," Fraenk said. "Rumor was she got her ears sharpened so she'd pass for half-elf."

"Studs weren't all she brokered, apparently," Nim continued. "The partisan I talked to said she had a secret compartment under the floorboards. But it was all opened when they found her body. Had one of those forbidden paintings and some kind of Gazean magic fertility talisman. *Heh.* The poor sap who picked it up ran straight home and put a set of triplets in his wife's belly that night!"

Nim's laugh died when he saw Fraenk's grim expression.

"That's some pricey wares to just leave behind. The elf was looking for something specific," Fraenk said. "He was willing to torture and kill to get it."

"This was worse than torture, sir. She held out for a long time, watching her boys bleeding on the stones. Then apparently he plucks the right eye clean out of her head and sets it out for her to look at with the 'tother 'un," Nim added. "This was pure evil."

A long silence followed. The melody from a children's deadsong began to play in Fraenk's mind. Kids sang it to one another at night to elicit chills, a summons for the recently dead to come back for one more to join them.

"The broker. The brothers. The baker..." Fraenk intoned eerily, like the most gruesome bedtime poem. *"...went to meet the Maker..."*

"Stop that, Fraenk," Nim said nervously. "I don't like it."

"... with worms in teeth. And worms in head..."

"Please! Stop it!"

"... give me what I want, or you'll... be..." Fraenk trailed off.

Fraenk had an image of the bread loaf on the ground near Miken's hand. His hands crumbling it, and hidden inside was a hard, dark shape.

And then Fraenk knew what Bas Greenbriar was after—the necklace. The one he now had in his pocket. But why was it worth this much carnage? As far as Fraenk could tell, a trinket that gave images of someone's thoughts was a cantrip at best. A silly trick. Something a wealthy elf lord would gift a spoiled daughter, who would then use it twice before abandoning it in one of her many overstuffed jewelry boxes.

Certainly not worth dying for, let alone holding out from torture. And why were these victims a part of all this? What was the connection between them? It didn't make sense. There were pieces yet missing from all of this.

"What now, sir?" Nim asked, seeing Fraenk's intense expression.

"Do you still have friends in Rounderville?"

"Well, yeah, but..." Nim suddenly realized what Fraenk was asking. "No. No! Fraenk. We can't go down there. I'm not one of them no more. They certainly don't like you."

"That's why you're coming with me." Fraenk said. "You're going to make sure no one bothers me while I look for a kobold."

19

R OUND EAR VILLAGE, ALSO known as The Rounds, The Pit, Human Hollow, Rabbit Town, or as its most common epithet, Rounderville, was in fact just a designation for the slums just outside the city walls. Its population makeup matched the demographics of the city itself, except for a lack of anyone with Elven blood. Elves may be the lords of Arathes, but this was one place where they were specifically not welcome. The name itself came from a pejorative joke that elves sometimes made to one another that goes something to the effect of:

Human lives are round like their ears... short, dull, and pointless.

Inane elven humor aside, the village itself was intended by the high-minded elites to be fair and humane accommodations for the thousands of non-elves who worked in the city doing backbreaking and often dangerous labor but made poverty-level wages. The Elvish bureaucrats and security officials, citing concerns about defense and environmental impact, required that the village be limited to only semi-permanent structures. Buildings could not be higher than one story and be built with nothing stronger than wood. In the event of an enemy attack, they could disassemble or burn the village and leave the area open for city defenses.

The end result was a sprawling, muddy slum filled with crime and violence, run by human gangs that even Fraenk avoided. It made perfect sense that the kobold would hide out here. There's no way Arch Preceptor Farathiel Gingerglade or any of his posh goons could even get close to him down here. They'd be met by an angry mob that would tear them to pieces and leave nothing behind but the points of their ears and the tips of their boots. Which is precisely why the conniving knave needed a foolhardy mercenary to go into the shantytown for him.

"Arch Neversleep, sir... I can say with all certainty that this is a bad idea. And Brand knows, I've held my tongue on plenty of ones previous to this. But I just gotta say it." Nim trailed Fraenk by a pace as they clomped along the slightly raised planks that kept all the foot traffic out of the mud. A light drizzle began to fall, sending many of the residents indoors. Fresh rains or no, the streets in Rounderville always seemed like a mire, rutted by tracks of cart wheels and heavy hooves of oxen. Vile brown water stood in every runel, pock, and divot.

They were both dressed in local garb, as near as Fraenk could estimate. Mud brown trousers, mud brown shirt, slop hats slung low on their brows, and cracked leather boots with holes worn through on the bottom. When Nim complained that they still stood out, Fraenk said he could roll in the mud if he liked to complete his disguise—which succeeded in shutting him up for a little while at least.

"Well, if it's a kobold you want, I could get you one. I could get you *two* even," Nim whispered after him.

"I'm looking for just this one in particular. The fancy lad belonging to Lord Fernbrook."

"We could just dress one up in the fluff and finery. Old Ferny would never know the difference."

"He'd figure it out soon enough when the little blagger *eats* the man's slippers instead of fetching them. Then what?"

"We'd be long gone. Safely back in Blackroot district, raising a hearty pint with the boys," Nim said with reckless confidence.

"No. More like we're in the midst of a trade and the little skit can't carry a tray. Or tries to nibble one of the elven maidens in the bumps. Or drops a huge smelly scat on the floor like a dog! We're not putting our lives in the hands of a kobold!" Fraenk snapped, leaping across where the planks were too far to step. Nim went quiet for a bit, and Fraenk could tell he was planning his next riposte.

The light rain and time of night made Rounderville much more sedate than usual. There were still plenty of lights burning inside of the shacks and a few watering holes that had a lively drunk crowd inside, but for the most part, the mud streets had few people out on the boards. Fraenk caught some glances from the residents, but none seemed to care or make any effort to hinder their progress. They could still hear the occasional shout or curse carrying in the air, but the chaos was at a safe remove.They passed an old man seated in a chair outside his shack, puffing a cloud of aromatic white smoke from a long-stemmed pipe. He nodded to Fraenk as they passed and squirted a black jet of tobacco spit into the mud. They stood aside to allow a chattering foul-mouthed group of workmen, probably headed into the city for their shift. Fraenk made sure to duck his head in case they might recognize him. Then carefully stepped around a drunk man who had passed out across the plank itself.

Further down, a pair of naked toddlers burst out between them from the open door of a house and spilled, squealing, into the muddy streets like a couple of happy piglets. Momma Sow emerged from the doorway after them, shouting and threatening to switch their hides raw— but to little effect. The children seemed to know she wouldn't follow, and they giggled all the louder.

Soon, they reached the end of what Fraenk hadn't even realized were 'the nice houses' and moved into a grimier quarter of the slums. Here there were no planks to keep boots out of the mud. And the shanties could barely even be called that. They were loose boards hammered into rough rectangles, with large open holes everywhere that did very little to shelter from the elements. Fraenk could recognize by the stench that this was Koboldtown.

"See Fraenk? We got all the way down here, and you didn't even need me," Nim complained.

"Just stay close and keep your eyes sharp. We haven't bagged the little dragon-fart yet."

They got reproachful looks from the kobolds as they made their way down the muddy street, but none challenged their presence. Ahead, they approached a gathering of kobolds who were standing around a large cookfire where a pot-bellied cauldron encrusted with the soot of countless flames contained a simmering of stewed meat and dark tubers that were completely inedible to human digestion, all bubbling in a rich aromatic broth. A quartet of the creatures played a rough but melodic jig, two with crude homemade stringed instruments and one tapping out a rhythm with sticks on pitched boards cut to differing lengths, and the last blew a jaunty base note across the opening of an empty jug. This was some sort of communal evening meal. He knew he shouldn't be surprised, but Fraenk found himself in a quiet state of wonder.

"Is this what they do?" Fraenk asked, immediately realizing it was a dumb question.

"When the humans and elves aren't working 'em to death, yeah," Nim said, giving the musicians an appreciative nod. Their improvised tune wasn't half bad.

A group of the walking lizards passed them, all clad in mud-stained castoff rags that were in too poor of a condition for even the poorest humans.

"I can't tell which is the one we're supposed to be looking for," Fraenk realized to his dismay. *Why did he ever think this might be even a little bit easy?*

"I'll keep a sharp eye for the proper little fellow in the fancy servant's uniform," Nim replied.

"Everyone, listen to me!" Fraenk waved his arms and shouted over the din. "We're looking for a kobold. One of you. He's a servant." The music stopped, as did their conversations. No one answered. He only got sour looks from every face he saw. The wind seemed to shift, and an acrid odor bit at their nostrils.

"No one's going to speak with us, Fraenk. They have a hierarchy," Nim whispered.

"Very well. Where is your... *leader*? *Chief?*" Fraenk couldn't remember what they called their guy in charge.

"Fraenk, he's called 'the long tooth'. It's like–" Nim made an odd guttural phonetic combination that Fraenk nearly confused with a clearing of the throat. "Something like that. My Dragontongue is pretty rusty."

Fraenk tried again, asking and doing his best to approximate Nim's translation. All they got back were angry murmurs and a few curses, which were in a language they understood. One even spat at them.

"I don't think I'm saying it right," Fraenk shrugged.

"You not belong here, human!" An elderly voice croaked at them. "Can't you smell? Don't want you here! Go away!"

They turned to behold, quite possibly the oldest kobold that Fraenk had ever seen. He had deep-set, slitted eyes and was encased in folds of wrinkled, scaly skin. One of his horns was broken off, and the other was worn down to almost the same level. It made Fraenk immediately curious how old kobolds could get—if allowed to do so naturally and not, as so often the case, met with an early, violent end. That was their fault, though. Nasty creatures, always fighting and stealing and causing trouble.

"We will leave. But answer our questions first," Fraenk said, taking control of the exchange. He was not about to start taking commands from a dirt-eater. The old kobold sucked at his gums sourly, only a few rotted yellow teeth still fixed in his mouth. When he sighed in exasperation, two thin wisps of smoke jetted out of his nostrils.

"Well, go on, go on," he grumbled. "We is busy. Go, your questions."

"What's your name, big man?" Nim asked just as Fraenk was drawing a breath to begin his inquiry.

"Ah, so they do have the manners." The old kobold crossed bony arms across a narrow chest. He nodded appreciatively at Nim. "I see's you, the big man. You call me—" The old kobold made a noise that sounded like, "Krak Bone Thack-en-swick". Nim tried to imitate the sound but only made the old kobold wince painfully at the butchery of his sobriquet. "...just say Kevin, like other humans."

"*Kevin??* What a dumb name," Fraenk whispered out of the side of his mouth. Nim almost burst out laughing, but quickly shushed Fraenk. The old kobold gave them both a dark look.

"Is only name that dumb human can say," Kevin smirked. *This one was half clever*, Fraenk realized.

"Very well, Kevin. We're looking for a fancy kobold. His name is Posuu Faljaon."

The old kobold didn't react. Just continued to wheeze breath, puffing delicate gray clouds from his wrinkled nostrils.

"We need his help. We can pay him," Nim tried.

"We can pay *you* if you tell us where he's hiding," Fraenk cut in.

"No," Kevin replied. "Can't say."

Fraenk noticed the other kobolds had quietly started to move closer, seemingly curious what this exchange was about. Despite their silent approach, the kobold's ripe, odorous bodies growing more offensive to Fraenk's nostrils gave them up.

"You can't say?" Fraenk pressed. "Or you *won't?*"

"Don't know Posuu. He's not one of us."

"Not one of you? He's a kobold."

"Far away kobold. Not *Ar-ha-Thees* kobold. Not from *Sah-hara-matti*." The way Kevin pronounced their kingdom took Fraenk a moment to understand. The kobold Posuu Faljaon wasn't from their tribe. They didn't know him, and he probably didn't know them.

"You think all kobolds know each other? Dumb human." Kevin clicked his tongue—a chastising sound that apparently transcended all languages and cultures. It said, Shame on you.

"Well, hells..." Fraenk muttered, trying to think of what he would do now.

"Sir?" Nim said, urgency in his voice.

"I know, Nim. We wasted a trip down here. You don't have to say it."

"The other one ask same question," Kevin said, his tone growing darker.

"What? What other one?" Fraenk looked up, curious.

The old kobold raised the hand that was tucked into his armpit. It was missing a pinky from the mid-knuckle. The scar was ruddy and already beginning to show the regrowth of a new digit.

"Sir!" Nim said urgently. Fraenk looked around. All the kobolds had crept in, quiet as cats, and were surrounding them. The creatures were armed with shards of metal, whittled wooden spears, and clubs fitted with broken bits of glass.

"The black mouth elf ask bad questions." Kevin rubbed his hand.

"Black mouth elf?" Fraenk asked. "You mean Bas Greenbriar? He was here? He asked about Posuu?"

The old kobold sneered viciously. "We say 'not again'."

"I think we should go now, sir," Nim exclaimed.

"Kevin, wait–" Fraenk pleaded, grabbing for a pouch on his belt.

The old kobold uttered a keening cry that was taken up by the rest of the group.

"We can pay you for your troub—"

Just as Fraenk was raising the fat pouch of coins he had tied to his belt, the kobold just behind him stabbed with a jagged strip of sharpened metal. It sank deep into Fraenk's shoulder. The surprise and shock of it instantly made him cry out and lose his grip on the pouch.

It tumbled end over end through the air, its drawstring loosening and spilling a galaxy spiral of iron, copper, and silver in the air. For one brief moment, the sky shimmered with wealth. Then a rain of metal clattered off wooden roofs, stones, and kobold heads, ringing with the unmistakable chime of the mint.

The kobold's coordinated attack was thrown into immediate chaos. Half scrambled to collect the scattered money that was even now being lost in the mud. The others still tried to jab their adversaries but were being knocked and buffeted by the first group. Some of the kobolds rallied to give chase, but the delighted cheers of the treasure seekers finding prizes quickly turned them back to scour for whatever coin remained.

"Go!" Fraenk yelled, shoving Nim back the way they'd come. They plowed past a trio of snarling kobolds, two of them scoring small punctures on Nim and Fraenk. The preceptors ran on, legs pumping to keep from getting stuck in the mud.

They could hear their leader, Old Kevin, calling out to his clan in their language, a keening roar, reminiscent of their dragon cousins. It was a call to arms, verbally lashing them back into pursuit. Several of the bigger ones took up their blades and gave chase.

"Sir, they're still after us!" Nim said, stealing a glance over his shoulder.

"They'll give up, right?" Fraenk panted, hoping that was true. They ran on, moving faster now that they were back into the human quarter, but the angry kobolds did not give up pursuit and were actually gaining on them.

"I guess they're not giving up," Fraenk wheezed in dismay.

"Sir, I can't believe you did that," Nim puffed as they pounded along the planks. "Throwing coins at those poor kobolds. That's just insulting."

"*Well, I beg thee pardon, M'lord!* I was trying not to die!" Fraenk said. He was holding the cut on his shoulder, trying to staunch the bleeding. All the running was beginning to tire him and awaken his bodily complaints. Nim—who had only minor injuries from a jab with a splintered stick—was out front of Fraenk.

"Well, some knowledge for the future..." Nim continued, again checking to see that the kobold mob was closer still. "Next time, any gift of coin, you hand to the elder. And he distributes it... based on his own... kobold criteria," Nim scolded. "It shows respect that he's in charge." "Next time, I'll do that," Fraenk growled. "And maybe next time, you—"

Nim suddenly stopped in his tracks on the boards. Fraenk tried to stop in time but skidded right into him. They both nearly toppled into the mud.

The half-elf wore a terrified expression, lit by yellow flickering torchlight. He was staring at something ahead of them on the path. The light grew brighter.

On the planks ahead was a mob. Dozens of humans with lit torches, carrying shovels, axes, meat cleavers, and even a few pitchforks—what *mob would be complete without a few of those?* They were coming up the street in a wave, blocking Fraenk and Nim's only exit.

"Look, sir, it's a mob," Nim stated the obvious.

"Really?! Where?" Fraenk shot back, annoyed.

The pursuing kobolds saw the mob too and skidded to a halt. They, too, did not like the looks of this wall of torch-bearing humans. Fraenk and Nim saw they were cut off now in both directions. They might try to take their chances with the half dozen large kobolds with rusty metal shard knives and would most likely die, but there was no way they were getting through a mob.

The crowd moved closer until their apparent leader, a serious-looking man with an ornate bandana across his brow, long beaded braids, and a silver arrow-point chinbeard, raised a fist and his torch over his head. The crowd came to a staggering halt.

Fraenk could make out the constituents of this mob much better now and did not like what he saw. It seemed to be composed of members of all the various gangs that haunted Rounderville. Their various factions were delineated by vaguely coordinated colors and styles. Offhandedly, Fraenk wondered if the matching outfits were planned or occurred naturally by virtue of a proximal fraternity. Or, it was more like a military uniform—no different than the elves peacocking around in their surcoats and sigils.

A few moments later, the old kobold came riding up on the shoulders of two more stout kobolds and was followed by the remainder of his able-bodied kin, like some mockery of a great war general.

"What now?" Nim whispered out of the corner of his mouth.

"Perhaps this doesn't involve us," Fraenk suggested.

"These humans are our prisoners now!" The arrow-pointed beard man announced to the kobold leader. "Return to your homes or there will be battle!"

The mob beat their weapons together and shouted, making a loud clamor.

"Humans OURS! Give us humans!" Old Kevin shrieked, and his army hissed and screeched in reply.

"You were saying..." Nim arched a sardonic eyebrow.

Fraenk Neversleep had been in situations where the odds were against him. But he'd never had this many individuals all trying to kill him at the same time.

"You know, I've not been this far out of Arathes in many, many years," Fraenk said. "That just occurred to me. I should have traveled more."

Part IV

20

"*S*TAND DOWN, VILLAINOUS RABBLE, *or my armies shall crush you!"
Fraenk yelled, holding aloft the carved wooden figure of Sir Bryant of
Aubleshaent, setting him boldly at the vanguard of his army of twigs and broken
sticks laid out in neat rows before him.*

*"Surrender, Sir Bryant of Wobble Shanks! We're here to eat all your pies and
steal your virgins," Fraenk answered in a high-pitched screech of the sneering
enemy army commander.*

"Very well then, rebel scum! I shall put you all to the fork!"

*The small boy jumped the wooden knight figure forth upon the opposing army
battalion of rocks, pretending to eat the enemy with exaggerated chomping noises.
As far as military campaigns went, it was a total rout. Fraenk mimicked a
satisfied belch.*

*"Well, that was breakfast. When do we sup?" He mocked the knight's husky
tone.*

*"Fraenk! Don't let father hear you mock our sworn knight or he'll tan your
backside with the belt!" His sister Flora shouted at him as she strode by carrying a
basket full of chicken eggs. She was four years his senior at age eleven and already
beginning to show signs of the shift to womanhood. From Fraenk's perspective,
Flora had gotten taller, meaner, and didn't like to play in the dirt with him as
much anymore. She spent much more time inside with mother, learning how to
do all of the womanly duties that she would be expected to know.*

*The boy stuck his tongue out at her defiantly, knowing she would not interrupt
her chores to pound him, then continued his play chatter, setting up the two armies
for another battle. He was thin, but healthy, with a messy tangle of straight blonde
hair that hung in his eyes. His breeches had an eternal set of matching holes in the
knees, no matter how many times his mother sewed new patches over them. Young
Fraenk was a cheerful boy, helpful with chores but also easily distracted.*

He had just set up his army again, when an enormous foot swept the battlefield, decimating both armies.

"An ice giant attacks!!" Flora shouted, giggling. Snapped from his reverie, Fraenk looked up in wide-eyed shock for a moment, then registered the playful gleam on his sister's face. He grabbed up the carved knight and held it in front of him.

"Finally, a decent portion to stave my appetite!" Fraenk made the knight say. Flora uttered a mock scream and took off running with Fraenk and the hungry knight close on her heels.

"BOY!!" An angry voice shouted, stunning both children. Two guardsmen were standing on the path and glaring at them. On their stained, padded gambesons, they bore the sigil of the local protector, Sir Bryant of Aubleshaent, and Fraenk gaped at the heavy billhooks they had in hand. The children both stood straight as posts, and Fraenk tried hard to remember if he had said anything mocking about the knight that these two may have overheard.

"The butcher—" The guard with the black mustache waxed into curls began.

"Father's not here, sir. He's at—" Flora blurted nervously.

"Shut your mouth when a man is speaking, ninny!!" The guard roared, making her gasp. She covered her mouth, and Fraenk could feel her start to tremble beside him. The mustachioed guard shifted his weight and started again.

"Your knight protector requires the butcher to supply another hog for tonight's banquet. You are to bring him your fattest, most succulent one immediately."

For a distressingly long moment, Fraenk was stunned, frozen in silence. He had long been taught to heed the words of adults—especially those in power—but the words this man was speaking to him were so incongruous that his young mind just locked up.

"Boy! Are you daft?!" The guard grew red-faced, knuckles tightening on his weapon handle.

"Good men, how goes your patrols this day?" The familiar and comforting sound of his mother's voice sent waves of relief through Fraenk. He nearly loosed his bladder. He then felt her hand, warm on his shoulder. Her other one to Flora's, who had been weeping soundlessly beside him.

The guard rolled his eyes in exasperation—the effort of having to repeat his order again being nearly unbearable. Fraenk was young, but he could definitely tell this one had a particular distaste for answering questions from women.

"Fetch your best hog to the butchers <u>now</u>. Your knight protector demands it!" The guard, Mustache Turd—Fraenk quietly decided this was his name now because

he had a mustache and looked like dog droppings—barked at his mother. He felt her fingernails dig softly into him, then release.

"I am sorry, good men. We have none. Our Henrietta just farrowed last moon, and none of her piglets are ready for the shop yet." Fraenk's mother gestured toward the hog pen, where the enormous sow lay on her side and the ten little pink bodies grunted and drank heartily from her swollen teats.

Fraenk loved the piglets. And he especially liked chasing them good-heartedly around the pen until he caught one, hoisting it up until it squealed in protest. Then he would turn it loose again, unharmed.

That sound. The sound he would soon never want to hear again.

He stole a nervous glance up at his mother. He knew what a trip to his father's butcher shop meant for a pig. It was a one-way journey. Fraenk did not want to see one of the adorable baby pigs get the bleeding knife.

"Then take the big one!" The guard said as if he were the only person in the whole countryside with any wits.

"She's our breeder, sir. And the little 'uns aren't weaned yet." Fraenk's mother replied.

"So?!" This commonplace agrarian logic did not seem to sink in for Mustache Turd. The other guard—or Dumb Face, as Fraenk cleverly named him for his weak chin and fat, ruddy cheeks—who had been silent until this time then decided he would try to calm the waters with a kinder voice.

"Madam. Our stores are empty at the holdfast, and we're hosting a feast for—" Dumb Face explained.

"Quiet, Dorlik! We don't explain ourselves to peasants," Mustache Turd snapped.

Door lick?! Young Fraenk forced himself to suppress a laugh, imagining Dumb Face lapping his fat tongue against a wooden door. He didn't know why, but some sad, naive part of his brain actually thought his mother was winning this argument. She had always done so with their father, who capitulated to her with either a stern look or gentle touch. Mother was powerful, and all feared her.

"You know... we could do some chickens instead. Fraenk, go fetch us four of the fattest chickens."

Although her voice was even and friendly, Fraenk could tell something was wrong. He felt his mother's hand trembling before she shoved Fraenk off in the direction of their chicken yard.

"No chickens!" Mustache Turd shrieked. "Are you a complete fool!? We were sent for proper meat for a feast!"

"*Friends, please, we just served up our prize boar last week to good Sir Bryant.*" *A tone that sounded like pleading crept into his mother's voice.* "*And we'll have more meat in a few moon turns... but we need this one. Henrietta's always given big litters. Even in these lean times. Just let us keep her... so there's more pigs to send up in days to come. Maybe even a few choice cuts for you. Please.*"

"*I don't give a swing from Skylae's sweet tits, woman!*" *He sneered dangerously under that detestable mustache.* "*Now do as you're ordered, or I'll stroke that skarking hog with my billhook, and you can <u>drag</u> 'em there dead!*"

When no one moved for a moment, Mustache Turd started toward the sow's pen.

"*No! No, we'll bring her. We'll bring her!*" *Fraenk's mother yelled, raising her hands out to block his way.*

He watched hatefully as they slung a rope around the huge pig's neck and quirted her with a switch until she rose grunting ponderously from the mud, like some dark porcine god. Fraenk was surprised to find himself holding the lead rope. And then his mother, with tear-filled eyes, instructed him to lead Henrietta off to father's shop.

Convinced the task was well in hand, the two guards returned to the path. Mustache Turd turned around for one last warning.

"*If there's not roast pork on our plates tonight, I'll personally come back here and kill every last animal I find,*" *he threatened ominously. Whether he meant just the animals themselves or something more was dangerously open-ended.*

Fraenk followed the path to town, where his father's butcher shop was. Along the way, he had many thoughts. He considered running away with Henrietta, but she was fat and slow, plus she ate a lot, which were not attributes that made for a good fugitive.

Perhaps he'd meet a wandering wizard who could turn Henrietta into a fearsome dragon, like in his stories. Then instead of fat Sir Bryant eating her, she could dine on roasted knight.

Or another, better and more noble knight would come by and hear Fraek's tale of woe. It would pique his sense of honor and justice, and he would duel the slovenly Sir Bryant in single combat. This heroic knight would simply ride down his opponent after Sir Bryant crushed his own horse by sitting on it. Then slash open his fat belly and let all the eels that wriggled inside him spill out on the ground. And Fraenk and Flora would be there to point and laugh and be grossed out by the slimy eels. Fraenk actually smiled at this thought.

Of course, none of those things happened, and he found himself standing at his father's shop door before he even realized it.

Wordless, his father came out the door, crimson to the elbows in blood. His apron too, a study in red. He took the rope to lead away Henrietta for the last time. Fraenk didn't love the huge sow, but something made him want to hug her or kiss her—give some kind of inexpressible apology for a day that began so perfectly ordinary but would end in horror.

He looked up at his father, hopeful to receive, perhaps just this once, some kind of comfort. The man had always been distant, which Fraenk only understood at that age as not very talkative, playful, or affectionate with his children. When the man had been in his cups at an increasingly greater frequency in the past few months, Fraenk's father alternated between simmering hairtrigger anger and just staring bleary-eyed at the fireplace. Fraenk could see, even now at work, his father had been drinking.

"Father?" Fraenk said, at first not sure what he wanted to ask.

His father turned to fix him with watery, red-rimmed eyes.

"Are... are you well, father?" the boy asked.

"I curse them, Fraenk," his father slurred. "Sir Bryant and his lot of villains. They've taken everything from us. We're going to starve while they feast and grow fat! They're a curse on these lands. And no one will save us."

"We can pray at the shrine of Skylae or Tolwyn... they come to the aid of mortals," Fraenk said, trying to block out the nasty words Mustache Turd had said about the fair Celestial of Justice.

"No. They ignore men's cries." His father tried to crouch but came down hard on one knee. Then he leaned in close, and Fraenk could smell the hot, sweet bite of corn liquor on his breath.

"There are the other ones, though. <u>They</u> listen," he whispered, close. Fraenk felt a wild chill run the length of his back. Whatever this was, Fraenk knew it was dangerous.

"They will help me. I just have to pay their price."

"Father, no."

"Go home and lock the door," he said, standing.

"Father?!"

The man pulled the rope around Henrietta until she was fully inside the shop. He gave Fraenk one last wild-eyed look, then slammed the door tight.

⁂ 90 ⁂

Later, with Sir Bryant's holdfast in flames that brightened the night sky and distant wails echoing, they heard the sound—the inhuman squealing. Terrified, Fraenk, Flora, and their mother barricaded the door as best they could and tried to stay quiet. But the squeals only got louder. Their mother stroked their hair, and Fraenk breathed in her scent like he might never smell it again—because somewhere inside, he knew he wouldn't.

The infernal squealing was louder still, and Fraenk instinctively knew there was a monster outside their door. But it was not the one they imagined.

A loud SLAM rocked the very beams of the house. They all screamed. Something wanted inside. Another KRACK. The wood of the door splintered, jutting inward. The squealing grew louder. One more hit, and the thing would be inside.

Their mother pulled them suddenly to their feet. With a chair, she smashed out the glass of their window. Flora and Fraenk were both crying.

"Go! You have to get away!" She sobbed, kissing each of them on the forehead. "Run far and don't stop! I love you."

A huge CRASH sent the door flying apart in broken bits of wood. The monster stepped through the threshold. Fraenk was frozen in incomprehensible horror at the sight of it. The thing—because it could not truly be called a man anymore—had fused to its shoulders where a man's head should be, was instead the severed head of their sow, dripping gore down its front. And it had on the same butcher's smock like his father wore—that too was caked in blood and chunks of flesh. Gripped in its hands were the tools of its slaughterous trade—the meat cleaver and the bleeding knife. It opened that horrible pig mouth and squealed again.

SQUEEEEEE! Its eyes glowing a hateful red.

Fraenk felt his mother lift and then throw him through the open window. He was weightless. Then he hit the ground, feeling glass dig into his skin. To his later overwhelming shame, he never looked back. Never thought to wait for his mother or sister.

He ran. Terrified and sobbing, he ran. And behind him were the screams of his mother and the unholy squeal of that pig.

Fraenk would never sleep well again after that night. In his nightmares, it would be that sound. The squeals of the Mad Boar... and its footsteps growing louder. Ever closer.

Coming for him.

21

T HE TWO DE FACTO armies of Rounderville that had assembled on either side of Fraenk and Nim stood at a standstill. To the south, a snarling assemblage of offended kobolds, commanded by the decrepit elder, Old Kevin. And to the north, blocking Fraenk's way back into the safety of the city, was a conglomerate of the human slum's notorious gangs, whose spokesman looked like he considered piracy not something that should be limited to boats. Somehow rallying every nose-breaker from the slums into putting aside their differences in what could have been a real step forward toward peace in Rounderville—that is, if they hadn't all been carrying a full armament of mob-style weaponry and torches.

This was about to get violent.

Fraenk briefly wondered if the pendant had some kind of bad luck charm attached to it along with its other unusual and mostly unhelpful other ability. It certainly hadn't brought him anything but trouble from the moment he found it. Perhaps he would be well rid of it. Sell it to Dandrikan for whatever he could get—assuming there even was a legitimate buyer for it. The shady trinket dealer would probably keep it for himself and use it to read brothel girl's minds, cheat at cards, or get people to reveal where they hid their coins, selling the information to the local thieves' guild.

Fraenk wondered if perhaps he could hire a skiff and throw the cursed chain out into the heart of Lake Ewyn. Knowing his foul fortune, however, it would be swallowed by a fish, which would in turn be caught and served to him at dinner the next day. Fraenk would lift his fork and find the pendant dangling from the tines.

He was broken from his thoughts when the apparent spokesman for the human mob stepped forward and called out to the old kobold.

"Give up your claim on these humans. They belong to us," the man with the arrow-point beard called.

"They offend us! Disrespect our ways!" Kevin the kobold called back in his craggy voice.

"What did they do, exactly?"

The old kobold seemed to falter in his fervor.

"They... ask many questions. And then throw coin at us," Old Kevin said back.

"That's it?! They asked you questions and gave you money?" Arrow-point smiled and looked at the men around him. "Well, give me the life of a kobold where someone tossing you some coin is a bad thing!"

The mob laughed with Arrow Point. He caught Fraenk's eye and gave him a quick wink. Fraenk's eyebrows shot up in surprise.

"No! It not like that... They are bad!" Kevin tried to keep the energy of his gang up, but they were already starting to lower weapons. "They bring the bad elf. He do this!" Again, the old kobold displayed his missing finger, shaking the hand at them accusingly.

"You'll grow it back," Arrow Point waved dismissively. "And besides, they didn't bring the bad elf. These are the ones what *killed* 'im. This here's Lord Neversleep. You shouldn't be trying to hurt him; you should be thanking him."

A confused murmur ripped through the kobold ranks. The two kobolds holding Old Kevin dropped him roughly off their shoulders. There was a lot of angry chatter, and many among them turned to head back to Koboldtown.

"In fact, you should return his coin!" Arrow Point went on.

"No! We keep the money. Is *ours* now!" Kevin shouted back defiantly and scrambled to catch up with the remainder of his retreating forces.

Fraenk and Nim turned back to the mob and their speaker. There were still dozens of armed, dangerous gang members there—now all staring at them intently. A long, uncomfortable silence filled the chilly night air. They obviously knew very well who Fraenk was, and they didn't come out to just drive off a crowd of grumpy kobolds. Fraenk felt a finger poke him in the back.

"You should say something," Nim whispered.

Fraenk cleared his throat, and his mind went completely blank.

"Uh, I thank you for that," he began shakily. "If you don't intend to bludgeon or imprison us, we'd be well pleased to leave and bid you a pleasant evening."

"Nonsense, Lord Neversleep," Arrow Point smiled. "You can't leave now! You are the hero of humans and our honored guest!!"

A loud cheer went up from the mob. Again, Fraenk's eyebrows went up so high, they nearly fell off the back of his head.

"I'm *what?!*"

Fraenk had been to parties before. He had worn fancy regalia at soirées for the High Lord elves and fallen down drunk in the gutter with lowlifes who should have been in prison. He had been to celebrations, reunions, weddings, funereal mourning, fairs, rituals, rites, and festivals. Fraenk had experienced many a gathering where the expressed purpose was to test the limits of intoxication.

But nothing was quite like the reception he received from the people of Rounderville. His cup remained at capacity the entire night—and by that, he barely had a chance to set it down after taking a drink before more was being added to it.

Unbeknownst to him, Fraenk had become something of a folk hero out in the shanties. The baker, Miken, was much beloved for his breads and pastries—not to mention his generous spirit for those in need. News of his murder hit the community hard, but at the same time, word of the avenging angel, Fraenk Neversleep, was spoken in reverence right alongside. He was the human who did the unthinkable—killed an elf in the name of justice for humans.

Fraenk had never shaken so many hands, nor had he been asked so many times to repeat the story of his glorious victory over Bas Greenbriar. The men demanded each moment be rendered in gory detail. And the bleary-eyed children who were awakened from their beds received a much more story-tale version of the elf's untimely demise. Either way, it drew an interested crowd every time. No one seemed to care that Fraenk had been in a fugue of blind rage or that Greenbriar was completely incapacitated and had not even tried to defend himself.

Fraenk was sure to omit certain details of the story, which were still part of his ongoing intrigue, like the black worms and the pendant. He knew it was well enough to keep that to himself.

At some point in the proceedings, Nim, caught in the wake of Fraenk's popularity, was swept up, poured full, and then carried off by some very robust-looking women who would not be easily dissuaded by Nim's half-hearted protests.

But Fraenk was getting tired and too drunk to function. He still had that voice in the back of his mind that the hour was counting down for him to find this missing kobold. Three of his preceptors' lives hung in the balance. He could not have it hanging on his conscience that he was off imbibing and being hailed as a hero while letting his own men die by the hands of the sadistic Fernbrooks. He had to find that missing kobold somehow.

"Lord Neversleep—" began the arrow-point bearded man, who introduced himself later as Joeth the Shantylord and had been Fraenk's ubiquitous host throughout the events. The man had never left his side and masterfully deflected anyone who became too cloying or obnoxious.

"Please call me Fraenk."

"Ah, that wouldn't do, calling you such a familiar name, like we're long friends," Joeth smiled. There was something both charming and devious in that man's smile. Like being his ally meant a fierce kind of loyalty, but an enemy would receive wrath that one would not soon forget.

"Then just Neversleep is fine," Fraenk said.

Joeth nodded and went about the business of packing one of the long stem pipes that the humans of this quarter seemed to favor. He packed it full of a rich, aromatic tobacco and used a splinter of wood, lit by the low candle on their table, to kindle the smoke. His friends also lounged in seating around the room, drinking or nimbly manipulating knives in a weaving dance between their scarred fingers.

They were seated at Joeth's personal table in the watering hole he owned, which was one of several in the village. He was not only an entrepreneur but the head of a local social club for the rough-and-tumble guardians of a particular territory; the term 'gang' attracted the wrong attention from the overzealous partisans and busybody civil servants, who enjoyed finding excuses to send baton brigades into their controlled domain.

"Time was an elf-pet coming down here, being disruptive, picking fights with the kobolds... And by the way, they're not so bad once you get to know 'em. They just get ornery every so often, so we gotta show 'em we're not about to tolerate it."

"Sure. Kobolds are just like us," Fraenk smirked, still feeling the throb in his shoulder where he'd been stabbed.

"But time was, the elf-pets that come down here to make trouble would get a quick dagger to the lung and be buried in the mud flat." Joeth puffed quickly, getting the pipe stoked. He handed it to Fraenk, who tried to politely demure.

"Come on, it'll clear your mind from all the drink."

Reluctantly, Fraenk took the pipe and drew in the rich smoke. He was no stranger to a pipe, but whatever burned in this one was like flaming acid in his lungs. Fraenk shot upright in his chair and coughed violently, smoke jetting from his nose and mouth.

"Whoa, Dragonborn! You gotta puff easy on your first go," Joeth said, chuckling. This was obviously the same initiation he'd done to countless others before. Strangely, though, the effect it had began to work with surprising speed. The alcoholic muzziness in his head began to stitch back together. Double vision merging into one.

"What is that?" Fraenk asked when his lungs had finished spasming.

"I call it 'The Trumpet of Fire'. It's a blend of tobacco and a mix of a few other plants and powders that are not local to these parts. You don't want to use it too often though or you'll start coughing up blood," Joeth said ominously.

Fraenk made a mental note to uncover the recipe nonetheless.

"Neversleep, I'm pleased to be wrong about you," Joeth continued. Fraenk almost returned the underhanded compliment but stopped.

"In what way? We've never met," Fraenk said evenly.   "Yes, but *I know you*. The Neversleep. The only human Arch Preceptor. You think we don't hear about that?"

"Aye," Fraenk conceded.

"And how does a human become something only elves get to be? We wonder."

"A tale for another time," he replied, a hint of warning in his voice. "Let's just say it wasn't easy. Nor has it been easy ever since. If I only knew what trouble it would bring..."

"You rose up in Arathes!" Joeth beamed. "That is a greater feat than most humans can claim. Just ask Ozreus of Tigraen. Oh no, you can't. Because *he's* lying beneath the mountain, filled with the shafts of elven arrows." Fraenk had a sudden vision of the carved wall in Blackroot's garden. Elven archers and dead humans.

"But sometimes when fledgling birds fly, they forget where their nest is," Joeth continued. He puffed out a ball of smoke that rose up towards the hazy ceiling.

"You think I've forgotten who I am?! You don't think the elves remind me at every opportunity?" Fraenk leaned forward, glaring at Joeth. A few of the men within earshot turned heads, attentive to the raised voice.

"Easy, easy, Neversleep," Joeth patted the air, as much to calm his men as Fraenk. "I'm only saying you don't *want* to remember. At least, that was what we thought—"

"—until I killed the elf."

"A hero arises!" Joeth clapped his hands. "You ARE one of us."

There was a weird, manic energy about Joeth that made him charming at first, but now, as Fraenk had spent time with him, it was concerning. This man had plans within plans, swirling and moving like the gears of a clockwork.

"You showed us something new, Neversleep," Joeth continued.

"And what would that be?" Fraenk had a sinking feeling about where this conversation was going.

"That we could ask questions like, Why aren't there more of us at the top? Why do so few elves decide what happens to so many humans? Why is there no justice when an elf kills a man, but if a man kills an elf...?"

"No," Fraenk cut in. "Whatever you're thinking. You need to stop."

"Did you know what happened after you gave that elf to the dirt, Neversleep? Maybe not—I heard you were sent to prison." Joeth rekindled the pipe as he spoke. "For us, the city became a very bad place for anyone who wasn't elf. Very bad. Those in charge came looking for retribution... to hurt us because they couldn't get to you. And they did. Any excuse—you're not working hard enough, human! *Wham!* You pick a fight, round ear! *Bam!* Look at me wrong, Hardback! *Wham! Wham! Wham!!* We suffered for <u>you</u>."

The words hit Fraenk hard. The true cost of his rash decision continued to ripple. But this was also a gambit, he knew. Joeth was playing toward something. And he needed Fraenk to feel indebted.

"Blackroot has always been a sanctuary to every kind," Fraenk replied. "The Lady herself would not allow that kind of foul treatment in her district."

"Aye, true," Joeth admitted. "Blackroot was better than most. But that's one district. The city itself is poisoned, Neversleep. And you are the antidote. You're a champion to many. You can inspire them."

"Only martyrs inspire people," Fraenk retorted dryly. "I'll stick with being an Arch Preceptor. It's slightly less deadly."

"We'll rally behind you. This is your chance to end the oppression of your brothers and sisters. I know you care about that." Joeth said carefully.

"Is this some "Eleventh District" nonsense?" Fraenk asked, already knowing it was not. For many years, the humans and other non-elves had tried to form their own district in Arathes, led by one of their own, with the goal of representing their interests. It was an idealistic and foolhardy notion, to say the least. The elves would never allow a human to have equal power to them, so any district leader would be a figurehead at best. The point was moot anyway, because humans could never agree on a single person to lead them.

Joeth's speech was taking on a much more seditious tone. But if there was a conspiracy that affected Blackroot, Fraenk needed to hear him say it.

"How would you like to lead the Blackroot district? Sit a council seat instead of trodding in cold kobold skit in the middle of the night? We outnumber them, five-to-one. They need us, *not* the other way around."

Fraenk Neversleep took a long moment before answering.

"You've been a good host, Joeth, so I'll say this politely," Fraenk began, any warmth in his tone was gone. "I want NO part of this. And as a courtesy, I will forget all said hence. We'll just call it the hazard of too much drink."

Fraenk set his hands flat on the table and looked Joeth directly in the eyes.

"But you will speak no more of this <u>ever</u>—because if anyone up there catches wind of what you're suggesting—it's treason and open rebellion. They'll use every stick of wood in Rounderville to build a gallows big enough to hang you all at the same time. Do you want to be responsible for that?"

Fraenk paused. Joeth gave no indication if his words were getting through.

"Then I urge—no, *implore* you to stop. Live your life and don't give the elves further cause to treat you foul."

"That is disappointing," Joeth leaned back, blowing smoke from his nostrils. "But I should have expected as much. You're still an elf-pet, Neversleep. Still keeping them in power."

"You'll have to talk tougher than that to hurt my feelings," Fraenk said, leaning back.

"The suffering of your fellow humans means nothing to you?"

"Well, you'll have to take 'human suffering' up with the divines." Fraenk slipped his bottle out and took a drink. "I came here looking for a kobold. If I don't find him, three good men of mine are going to die."

"I'd say you found some kobolds," Joeth replied. "They weren't too happy about that."

"I need one in particular."

"Tell me. Maybe I can help. We know a lot of kobolds," Joeth said, leaning back in his chair and stretching his arms out wide. "Maybe we can help each other."

"I thought we've walked this path already," Fraenk said.

"You may yet come around on that, but there are other ways to help, Fraenk. You're looking for that runaway, yes?"

Fraenk perked up. Joeth had tilted his cards for just a peek.

"You'll have to be specific. I'd want to make sure we're talking about the same one," Fraenk countered.

"The servant from Fernbrook, then. Everyone knows they're out trying to hunt him down. First the elf, now it looks like they've got you on it." Joeth puffed a smoke ring, then another. "You seem to rather *enjoy* helping elves, Neversleep."

"And what if that was the one? Where could I find him?" Fraenk asked.

"Well, since you say you have no interest in leading our cause, let's talk about how the Arch Preceptor of Blackroot might be useful to helping humans outside the walls make a better life for themselves."

"And just how would I do that?" Fraenk replied, already not liking the answer.

"The sewer tunnels from Mosswater, which lead into the old Breakflint Warehouses. There used to be a way we could get food and clothing—medicine even—out to our people without the elves' heavy tariffs. But now they're all sealed up."

"The Seventh Gate," Fraenk said evenly, doing his best to keep his face from reacting. Here it finally was—the true purpose behind Joeth's entire evening. It was all leading up to this.

For years, the sewer tunnels beneath the district had been a smuggler's paradise. A highway of illegal goods and shady individuals gaining access to Blackroot and the city beyond. They were uniquely valuable not only because of their utility for moving anything in or out of Arathes, avoiding the guards and customs officers who exacted a toll on goods being sold in the city. It was the only 'unofficial' access point that allowed for transport on a large scale. There were other tunnels in, of course, but no other could accommodate a two-yoke ox team pulling a fully loaded cart. Any one person or gang in control of this would quickly control all the illicit goods moving into the city, making them tremendously rich and powerful. Which is why one of Fraenk's first tasks when he became Arch Preceptor was to have the tunnels closed and sealed for good.

Fraenk briefly weighed giving immeasurable power to Joeth, whom he liked well enough but didn't trust, versus the lives of three of his preceptors. It suddenly occurred to Fraenk that in his haste to recover them, he didn't even know which three were missing, and a deep shame washed over him.

At that moment, Fraenk decided that it didn't matter. He would not be giving anything to this man who was unwittingly gambling with their lives. Fraenk subtly thrust his hand into his pocket—a casual move that he hoped would not attract suspicion. He smiled as he let his finger slide through the chain of the pendant and slowly closed his fist around it.

"I'd be happy to consider it," Fraenk said, looking interested. "I'd need to be sure you know the exact location of the kobold, though."

Joeth looked up and met Fraenk's gaze. "Ah. Smart man. I knew you were reasonable. And please know that you have my assurance..." Joeth began to speak, then his voice faded to somewhere far away.

Fraenk felt his hand go icy cold. Then images suddenly flashed in his mind. A tall, decrepit stone tower, crawling with vines. And at the top, he saw a glowing light. The voice of Joeth whispered in his mind: *"The light in the Wizard's Tower"*.

Fraenk gasped—it *was working!* Joeth seemed to notice Fraenk's change and made a face. *"What's wrong with him?"* Fraenk could hear the man ask himself. He realized he had to keep Joeth's thoughts on the location of the kobold.

"Alright. I believe you. But who's going to lead me down the path to our little friend?" Fraenk asked, hoping to get Joeth to picture how to get where the kobold was. The prompt worked better than he expected.

In his mind, Joeth recalled the exact visual journey. Fraenk could see him moving in snippets down a darkened path outside the city. Through a splashing river. The stone path was wet from the spray. Then, onto a stone where the solitary tower stood. The cold in his hand had become painful.

"I'll send Jesyn with you. He knows the way," Joeth replied. Fraenk could feel the other man's caution turning more hopeful— jubilant, almost—like his plan was working and he would soon have what he wanted. Joeth nodded to his man of mention, who cracked his knuckles and tipped a friendly two-finger salute. There was one last piece he needed to find the place, though: the point of origin.

"Exiting from which gate?" Fraenk pressed. The excruciating cold in his hand had become numbness—which was not a good sign. Fraenk surged into Joeth's mind and could begin to feel the man's emotions. But as an image of the gate began to coalesce, a countermand fought against it. Somehow, Joeth was fighting back, trying to resist giving up this final valuable piece.

"I–I don't..." Joeth said, his brow furrowing.

But the chain felt powerful in Fraenk's hand. It was an unfathomable undercurrent, like he was swimming in Lake Ewyn, whose depths were somewhere dark and far below. All he had to do was reach for it, and it would answer. Joeth shifted in his seat. Small beads of sweat were forming on his brow. He looked uncomfortable, but the pain in him was everywhere.

Tell me now! Fraenk urged with his mind. *Give me your secret!*

Fraenk pushed his will and found that Joeth's defiance was but a thin membrane. One that he could slice open with what could only be described as a mind knife. Joeth's inner being, the constituents of his mind burst open, spilling forth like the abdomen of a butchered hog under the knife, loosing its guts onto the ground. And Fraenk found himself awash in the man's anger. Then fear. And panic—

Joeth's eyes suddenly rolled up until only the whites were visible. He pitched backwards in his seat and began to convulse violently.

Fraenk was slammed by a wave of sensation. Light, noise, and feeling all hitting in an overwhelming wave. Fraenk tried to release the pendant, but his hand was completely numb. Then he too began to convulse. If he didn't let go of the pendant soon, both of their brains would destroy each other. Awash in pure sensation, Fraenk felt the world begin to close in around him.

A feeling like falling came over him, and Fraenk distantly wondered if this was finally his end.

22

FRAENK WAS FALLING.

Not in a poetic, spiritual, or metaphorical way. He was actually thrown backward in his chair by the men who barreled past him in a headlong effort to help their boss. The impact of hitting the floor did have one major positive effect on Fraenk's immediate wellbeing—his hand was jarred loose of its grip upon the pendant, and its magical effects immediately stopped.

Fraenk heard shouting as he lay dazed on the floor. His hand had a thin layer of ice surrounding it, and his head was throbbing with quite possibly the worst headache he had ever experienced. He lay there for a time, letting his senses slowly return to normal, before he dared himself to get up again.

Joeth was not as fortunate. For several long minutes, he convulsed, foaming from the mouth, then finally lay still. He was breathing but unconscious, and no amount of his men's shouting or tapping his face brought him around again.

Fraenk rose slowly and joined the scrum of people helplessly looking in on Joeth. One of the men had already been sent to fetch their local healer. Fraenk knew things were much more serious than that, and some two-copper medicine man would probably only make it worse.

"He's had a fit. You have to take him into the city—Mersey's temple—right now!" Fraenk ordered the man with beaded braids and tattooed shoulders, whose name he thought was Tyesen.

"You did this to him!" Tyesen shouted, fear and anger on his face. He pushed Fraenk back hard in the chest. Several of the other men turned too. All of them were looking for someone to help or for someone to blame. Fraenk had to take charge or this would turn ugly.

"Hey, I was on the floor too!" Fraenk shouted back. "It's that smoke! Whatever he mixed in that tobacco. I'm lucky I only had a little bit!"

Fraenk knew it was a lie, but if they found out this was his doing, Fraenk and Nim would both get their throats cut and be buried in the mud flats. Tyesen glared for a few tense moments, then his face crumpled in a frown.

"We kept warning him that stuff was bad!" He whimpered.

"Listen, you have no time to waste. Get him to a temple healer as fast as you can, understand? The ones in Blackroot are his best chance. And the sooner he gets there, the better his chances are of not dying."

He could tell by the man's reaction that the gravity of this situation finally sank in. Fraenk pulled a tabletop sideways beside them.

"Here—set him on this and each take a corner. Use it as a litter to carry him that way."

Tyesen nodded, and the other men quickly and carefully set Joeth on the tabletop. They carried him out the door of the bar and off into the night, bickering and cursing each other the entire time. Fraenk soon found himself standing with one crying barmaid. He turned to her and pressed one of the emergency coins he carried on an inside pouch strapped across his chest into her hands.

"Please tell my friend Nim that I had to leave. He should head back to the district whenever he's capable of walking again. You'll do that?"

The woman nodded and wiped her eyes.

"How did that happen to Joeth?" She asked as Fraenk was about to leave.

"I'm not really sure," Fraenk said, his fingers clutching the cold and shifting chained mass through the fabric of his pocket. It seemed to be silently scolding him.

I warned you not to toy with me.

Fraenk took an alternate route back into the city so he could avoid running into the litter-bearing crew that was carrying Joeth. He had no idea if the healer would be able to do anything for him, but it was his best chance. A phantom pang of guilt tried to creep in. Joeth had been a generous host right up to the point where he tried to extort Fraenk and become the gang lord of Rounderville, but he didn't really deserve what happened to him. Then again, how could Fraenk have even known what the necklace was fully capable of?

"Looks like you got to test the necklace after all," Fraenk said to himself.

As Fraenk ran along outside the city wall, he touched his pocket to make sure the pendant was still there. This thing was definitely dangerous. He had no magical training nor natural inclination at all; imagine what someone who knew how to use it and was trained in magic could do—like a wizard. He definitely needed to find a safe place to stash this thing, like a vault or in one of the bottomless holes under Arathes Mountain. Someplace it would not fall into the wrong hands.

Fraenk thought about having his own safe commissioned and infused with protection spells and wards. A place where he could keep all these items, which seemed to accumulate with the job. He was already running out of space in his hiding stash behind the bookshelf. It wasn't the most secure place to store things anyway. Any reasonable thief who knew where to look could break in and steal his stuff.

Fraenk had the disconcerting image of Kyla in his room at this very moment, going through his cache of valuables. He pushed both the thought of the beautiful thief and the notion of a built-in safe for his chambers out of his mind. He needed something more secure.

Perhaps he could commission the construction of an entire vault somewhere in the lost tunnels beneath the city. But that opened up a whole slew of new problems—from who would build it to how it would remain secret to who would have to guard it.

No... that wouldn't work either.

Fraenk considered just turning the cursed pendant over to the Arcane Lords and being done with it. This was probably the most reasonable action—but Dandrikan's tale of how he came to Arathes in possession of so many cursed items stolen from the Arcane Lords had given Fraenk doubts about how secure the wizards kept their storerooms.

The necklace was so dull to look at anyway and even contained some kind of spell, which made viewers even more disinterested. He could probably leave it out on a pedestal somewhere, and no one would even give it a second glance.

Then a strange idea came to him—the Royal Museum! Arathes had one of the most impressive museums in Sarmatti and possibly the world. A collection of artifacts, art, armor, and the spoils of wars fought centuries ago. The elves loved their own history as much as they did the natural world. Perhaps it was ego or possibly nostalgia—maybe just the curse of their own long lives without the memory to go along with it. Elves could live an entire age, then later forget all the deeds they've done in that time. The Great Library and the Royal Museum seemed to be the only salve for it—an official record and history of themselves.

It was guarded, of course, but not so well that Fraenk wouldn't be able to sneak the necklace into an exhibit and possibly recover it again if the urgent need arose. The best part was that no one would be searching for it there. It would be just another necklace among thousands. And one that actively made viewers bored and disinterested—which were the feelings that many visitors to the museum were already experiencing. Fraenk made up his mind that he would stash the necklace in the museum at his earliest possibility.

Right now, however, he was running out of time to find the kobold and save his men. The sun had just begun to rise, casting brilliant beams of light across the upper part of the city.

The tower he saw in Joeth's mind was like nothing he recognized anywhere in the city or its outlying vicinity. Nor did the path leading to it look familiar. Was this hiding place somewhere far out in the hinterlands? The idea made a cold chill run across his skin. Fraenk tried to focus on the last image that Joeth had in his mind before it all went foul: the city gate.

If he knew where to start, he could find the destination, since no other landmark presented itself within the recollection. But what he saw in Joeth's mind was just a brief flash of the gate with the doors shut and the portcullis down. Even the design of the gate itself wasn't familiar. This was not helping. It was as if it wasn't a memory of something witnessed at all.

Fraenk stopped in his tracks. The gate wasn't anywhere in the city *because it wasn't real*. If it was, the details would have been sharper, accompanied by other senses—this was just an image because it was *imagined*. And if that was the case, Fraenk could guess that the other things he saw in Joeth's mind were also imagined. Had the bastard been lying about what he knew? Fraenk felt a cold weight drop in the pit of his stomach. The heights of hope being dashed upon the rock of despair.

No. That couldn't be all just imagined, Fraenk realized. Joeth had specific ideas that came to him immediately, but the images were just of imagined places. Which meant he knew the kobold was in an actual place, but just not one he'd personally seen. So his mind just made up what it looked like. What were the words he'd heard—"Wizard's *Tower*"? As far as he knew, that wasn't the name of a tavern or brothel. It was the actual dwelling of a wizard.

Fraenk smiled; hope daring to emerge again. There were ways to find a wizard if you knew where to look.

Eager to act and perhaps still a bit unsteady from the night's gaiety, Fraenk turned too quickly, stumbling over some tree roots that were sticking up near the roadside. He managed to catch himself, but just barely, and after a lot of acrobatic arm waving and rebalancing. The motion made his head swim fiercely in a way that his stomach was very much displeased with. Then a full riot began from his throat, going down into his abdomen. And in a redolent and unholy geyser, it all came up.

Two steps off the roadway, Fraenk emptied his stomach dry, then continued to heave a few more times for good measure. After several miserable minutes, he wiped his mouth and tried to settle his breathing. His heart hammered and his stomach muscles ached from the exertion.

"You can't keep doing this to yourself, Fraenk." He heard the voice of the old baker saying to him.

"What do you know? You're dead." Fraenk grumbled.

"Fraenk?" A voice called out from the pre-dawn shadows.

Fraenk turned to see the tree roots suddenly move. They weren't roots at all but a man's legs. The top half of him sat up, wrapped in a blanket.

"What are you doing out here?" The man asked him. The voice was familiar, but he couldn't place it.

"I-I had some business, but it's all sorted now," Fraenk replied, trying to whip his mind into placing who this man is. A cold prickle shot through him as the man pulled off the blanket and stood. He approached, and finally Fraenk could see his face. It was Leos Muninger.

"Leos? What are you doing out here?" Fraenk asked, straightening.

"Oh. Well, you know. Ever since I was in the war, sometimes it's hard to sleep inside the city. Safer for me and everybody else..." Leos chuckled, but Fraenk was anything but amused.

"I didn't know that."

Leos smiled his large, cheerful grin. How many times had Fraenk seen that expression? It was a mask, he realized.

"You look like you're off on another mission," Leos said. His breath was still vaporous from his own boozy odyssey. "Hold up, and I'll go with you."

Leos turned and began packing up his tiny encampment with a soldier's efficiency. Curling up his bedroll, folding away the blanket and stuffing it all into the pack that was issued to the foot soldiers in his battalion.

"Actually, Leos, I appreciate it, but I need to keep moving. I have an urgent matter to attend to." Fraenk felt his throat starting to prickle and wanted more than anything for a cup of water to rinse out the bile.

"I'm near ready!" Leos said, stuffing the last of his effects into the bag. "Go on and start if you need to. I'll catch up on the trot."

"Nonsense! You rest, my friend," Fraenk waved him off. "How's about if we meet up later this afternoon? I know another good place we can go that makes the best fish soup."

"Why are you talking about taverns? You need my help right now," Leos bore a confused expression as he paced over with his packed gear.

It suddenly occurred to Fraenk that this was the third time in recent memory that he was refusing help from the ex-soldier. He wasn't sure why. Something instinctively told Fraenk he needed to move unencumbered, and having Leos there would be a liability more than a help. Plus, Fraenk was running out of time, and he had no patience to play nursemaid to a man who simply refused to listen.

"Leos, I thought we settled this matter," Fraenk said, irritation edging into his tone. "I can't take you on as a preceptor. I'm sure I can talk to the captain of the guards at Blackroot."

"You think this is about the job?!" Leos' smile was gone in an instant. "I'm offering my arms as a friend, and you don't want that?"

"I'm on official duty. And besides, you can't get in where I'm headed. It's an elven hall in the upper district."

Leos crossed his big arms over his chest and glared.

"So, you stumble over to kick me awake and retch near my bed. And I'm supposed to just lie back down in it?"

"I could get you a room at the—"

"Hells with your money, Fraenk!!" Leos shouted. "All I wanted was a friend."

Fraenk didn't know how to respond. There was nothing he could say, short of an apology. Even that seemed trite at this moment. He owed Leos something better. Somehow he'd do that, but he couldn't right now.

"Well, you've got somewhere to be. Go on then. Don't let me delay you, Lord Neversleep!" Leos turned and stalked away.

Fraenk watched him depart, turning from a man back into another shadow in the darkness.

From its earliest days, the Elvish High Lords of Arathes all agreed that magic and its usage should not be permitted within the city proper. There were too many cautionary tales of the ills that befell a city where powerful spells can be cast at random. Wanton death and destruction came from those using magic for evil. Dark forces summoned could run amok. Entire cities being held hostage by the mad whimsy of a foul enchanter. Or worse, communities battered to a stalemate between multiple wizards.

The problem they faced was how to enforce a complete ban on magic use. Their answer was naturally to use magic—and, apparently, irony. The Bureau for the Management and Registration of Magic, or as it was now commonly referred to, *The Registry*, was formed to regulate not only how and what magic should be used in Arathes but, more importantly, *who* could use it. This body of learned wizard bureaucrats was able to heavily regulate and restrict any who wanted to toss a spell greater than a 'light room' or 'spark fire'. Anyone, elf or human, who did not comply with the rules would face severe punishment depending on the type of spell and its resulting effects. Those permitted to use magic had to pass a licensing exam and competency test before the Registry elders and pay a small fortune in fees for the various permits, documentation, and certificates. Not only did you have to be a capable magic user, but also have a deep coin purse to go with it.

In the early days, the Registry's enforcement arm, who were called the Arcane Lords, were obsessive about keeping unauthorized magic users and magical creatures out of the city. They had detection spells cast strategically throughout Arathes and were ready to respond on a moment's notice. And respond they did, with a vicious fanaticism.

There were many setbacks in those first centuries, but through merciless enforcement, the city's spell-free reputation took hold and even became the norm for other areas in the region. Eventually, the active combat work of the Arcane Lords became more infrequent and less severe. Their mighty enforcers moved on to the good work of magical scholarship instead, and the battles of arcane superiority became more conceptual.

This fighting (if it could still be called that) now took place in dank rooms below ground as the Arcane Lords spent their time pouring over dusty ancient tomes in order to prove oneself superior through a caustic exchange of sharply worded correspondence between rival colleagues.

Nowadays, it was reasonable to assume that there were no unlicensed wizards in Arathes. Even dressing too much like one was a good way to be reported and brought in for questioning. Those who were authorized and with permits would tell you it was hardly worth the trouble, for The Registry required a magic user to maintain updated personal information on file with them and could drop in on them unannounced at any time. This was quite annoying for anyone who wanted to keep their spellwork private.

But such information was tremendously handy for someone who, for example, was just now looking for a registered wizard who resided in a tower, somewhere in Arathes. All Fraenk had to do was slightly misuse his authority as the Arch Preceptor and sweet-talk the shy receptionist, who just so happened to be smitten with Fraenk.

"I'm sorry, Fraenk, we have no record of such a wizard." Glynnaeh, the curvy elf at The Registry, said after checking the ledger three times. She looked up at him with dark eyes and fluttering lashes.

"He's gotta be here somewhere," Fraenk said to himself. "What if he didn't register? Or was in hiding?"

"Even using a small charm or being in possession of a magical item can trigger an alarm. And most casters don't go a full day without spelling on something," she added. "Once a wizard, always a wizard, as we say."

Fraenk had to believe her. Wizards trained lifetimes to learn their craft, which was something they were immensely proud of. It was not something they would soon give up, even if it meant the indignity and expense of registering.

And Fraenk supposed that running afoul of the Arcane Lords wasn't the risky proposition that it once was. Could there be one such man out there, evading both detection and capture? Only another wizard could manage that.

Fraenk paced the cavernous lobby, which was the only part of the Magic Registry that was open to people not employed there. He began to wonder if perhaps his headlong rush all the way up here was not a huge waste of time. If anyone should know about a wizard in town, it would be The Registry—and yet, they didn't. Why not?

Fraenk let his eyes drift over the room as he thought. The building was exquisitely crafted, as most elven architecture was. High arching ceilings and everything with beautiful curved lines. Large, majestic carvings of the city's most famous magical pedigree. Quidriun the Sage, Belrustia the Learned. Zidrowaen of Adjudicator. For those commemorated, there certainly seemed to be a heavy emphasis on being wise. And yet, they still lacked the answers he was looking for.

He turned to gaze out at the open windows, which gave a vista of the harbor. He could see the port full of ships, their tall masts bare. The flare of the lighthouse light passing around its continuous circuit of the lake. Seabirds wheeled and turned in the air currents, chased by some dark flapping bat-like creature. Something prickled at his mind, like a task he was supposed to remember to do, but then just as quickly slipped away.

Fraenk turned back to Glynnaeh, who was now standing at the front of her desk and following Fraenk with her eyes. A curl of her hair had come loose and dangled against her nose. Glynnaeh blew at it and gave Fraenk a playful smile. He could tell she genuinely was trying to be helpful, but his query was indeed a vexing one.

Fraenk went over what he knew so far. No registered wizards lived outside the city, not in towers, houses, hovels, or caves. The place he was looking for apparently didn't exist.

"What if he quit?" Fraenk asked suddenly.

"Quit what?" She blinked, not comprehending.

"Using magic."

The smile she gave him was one of sadness and pity. Like watching a puppy try to operate a crossbow. But Fraenk knew he was onto something with this.

"I'm serious. What if he gave it up entirely? Or was cursed. Something so that he could never cast another spell or be near anything magical," Fraenk reasoned. "Then he's no different than a regular citizen. And The Registry only tracks magic users." Glynnaeh sat on the table and crossed her legs.

"And we'll never find him," Fraenk said, continuing to pace.

He was annoyed and keenly aware of the time slipping by. Each minute he wasn't closing in on the kobold, was a minute closer to his men dying at the hands of the Fernbrooks. Glynnaeh watched him, her dark eyes following him across the room and back. Something appeared to be on her mind as well, but it wasn't this missing wizard.

In desperation, Fraenk thought about the partisans. His friendship with Arch Partisan Brightrock might be worth calling in for an unannounced raid on Lord Fernbrook's properties in order to find his men. Of course, that was more than an ask. That was more than a simple favor—even for someone who owed you a big one. There was no easy nor fast way for the partisans to assemble a raid on a member of the High Council. The mere suggestion would be dead in the water before Fraenk could even say it.

"Fraenk?" Glynnaeh called out. When he turned, she motioned him closer.

"I hate to even mention it, but we do have a little something we use here at the Registry that you could try. It's against the rules, but there's a spell that can detect something with magical *potential*. You could find that wizard with it," she whispered conspiratorially. "But you'd have to be real close, like *this*."

She stepped forward so that her full bosoms were against his chest.

"Well, thanks, but I don't use magic." Fraenk replied.

"Not at all?"

"I suppose I just have to get by on wits and charm." Glynnaeh bit her lip.

"It's real easy. Here, just go like this—" She waved her fingertips in a spell-casting manner. Fraenk knew immediately that he would not be able to emulate whatever she was doing. A thin wisp of color and light trailed from her fingertips and began feeling their way through the air—and down toward the front of his trousers. It stopped at the very place where he was keeping the pendant. The whole front area of his breeches began to glow. Glynnaeh's eyes went wide.

"Oh my! Are you sure you're not magic, Fraenkie?" She grinned, her fingers dancing down the front of his shirt.

Fraenk quickly took her hands in his. *Why did he remember her as being shy?* "Well, I've never had any complaints before. Excuse me—" He gave her a wink and backed away.

Fraenk looked down and was relieved to see that whatever was happening with his pants, at least they weren't glowing anymore. Carrying this necklace around was becoming a big problem. He'd have to find some place safe to stash it, and soon.

Something flashed in the distance and caught his eye. Fraenk looked out at the harbor. Several large ships under sail were making their way towards the city. Then a few moments later, the beam of the lighthouse swept by.

Why couldn't he figure this out? He tried to remember the images from Joeth. The stone path. The river. Water. Moving out to the tower. And in the window at the top...

A light. Fraenk saw the sweep of the lighthouse pass again. The light in the wizard's tower.

The revelation hit him so hard, he almost fell backwards. "Fraenkie? Are you alright?" Glynnaeh asked. "I know where to find the wizard," Fraenk smiled.

23

F RAENK WAS NOT NOW, nor would he ever, be that interested in the nautical trade. He made sure he knew enough to do his job. Blackroot district was home to the Port of Arathes, which was technically property of the High Lord but was managed by the Blackroots. This was merely another detail in the many things he might need to concern himself with on any given day. Boats, ships, barges, and really anything to do with the traversal of aquatic byways were best left in the very capable hands of Fenduin Tallowfrond, their experienced, if eccentric, Acheron of Ports and Harbors.

Tallowfrond had sailed the entire world in his youth before ending up in Arathes and pledging his service to Blackroot. And for what he lacked in social decorum, he more than made up for with his talent in mathematics and obsession with the transport of cargo. Lady Blackroot's trust in the elf's abilities to manage the port was near total, for he also seemed to lack the instincts for any kind of graft or duplicity.

Fraenk regularly crossed paths with the Acheron while he was dealing with thieves and smugglers or in their district meetings with Her Lady, where Tallowfrond never failed to bemoan about the massive deadbeat Pileusian Galleon, which remained perpetually squatting in their dry dock, costing them gold. Of all the elves that Fraenk knew, Tallowfrond exemplified their high-minded ideals better than most.

When he arrived at the busy port, Fraenk felt an instant sense of being out of place. Part of it had to do with the fact he was mounted on the huge, bitey destrier, Jimothy, who drew startled glances and stares as they clomped past.

Fraenk watched as the port moved like a buzzing beehive. Workers were busy loading and unloading cargo from the tall three-masted ships that arrived in the night, using enormous cranes that had counterweights to balance out the loads. Smaller vessels carrying passengers, trade goods, or livestock disembarked right on the harborside road, where they could easily transport their wares up to the market, and also in a place where they wouldn't get in the way of the bigger cargo. Further beyond that, the night fishermen were hauling in their catch into the cleaning houses, where workers cleaned and gutted the fish, packed them in ice, and loaded them into carts going to every part of the city.

Horse-drawn carts rumbled by with full loads. Gawking tourists and religious pilgrims stopped to marvel skyward at the gleaming heights of the upper city. White and gray seabirds who were not filling themselves on fish guts from the cleaning houses circled and called overhead in lazy circuits of the blue sky, looking for an opportunistic meal from an unguarded basket. A wind was blowing in off the lake, making the morning air almost chilly.

They were temporarily delayed when Jimothy found an open crate of apples and began to help himself. Fraenk jerked at the reins, but the destrier only swiveled its massive head and fixed him with a glossy black-eyed glare, warning him not to do that again or there would be incisor-related consequences. Acquiescing, Fraenk released his grip and moved as far back in the saddle as he could. The horse held his ground against a whole squad of dockworkers, driving them back with bites and kicks. Only after he had eaten nearly the entire box did he discharge a steaming pile of green turds on the dock boards, then allowed himself to be led away.

Fraenk offered to reimburse the workers, but only if they shipped the nasty horse off to be fed to the Kraken of Caladel. For some reason, none of the men took him up on it.

With any luck, Fraenk could get to the tower, find the kobold and make the trade before that sadist Farathiel killed his men. He was already crafting some kind of retribution for the rival Arch Preceptor's actions. It was one thing to use manipulation and extortion to achieve your district's goals, but kidnapping and killing their preceptors was a whole different story.

You're already at war, Miken's voice told him in his mind. *And if you have to fight, then <u>win</u>.*

Whether it was the crisp wind off the lake, the plaintive cries of the gulls, or just remembering his old friend's voice, a wave of grief hit Fraenk unexpectedly. His eyes welled with tears. Fraenk was tired, hungry, and aching in more places than he could count. And everything was dumping out of him at the same time.

"I'm trying, Miken. I won't let you down," Fraenk said to the air. Perhaps the wind would carry his message on to his friend, wherever he may be.

As Fraenk moved down the docks, something odd began to happen. A kind of collective lull rippled through the area. The people who were working slowed and stopped what they were doing, then turned to look off in the distance. Their gaze was all fixed on the same thing—something was happening at the lighthouse.

From his high vantage on horseback, Fraenk could see above the heads of the gathered crowd that, sure enough, a force of gray-uniformed men were running out on the jetty and forming up around the lighthouse. They were followed by several others on horseback. It was a contingent of partisans.

"Hells!" Fraenk snarled and dug his heels into the horse's sides. Jimothy seemed to sense aggression and shot forward, clopping so loudly on the wooden dock planks that Fraenk began to worry they'd go crashing through. People who saw him coming jumped out of the way to keep from being smashed aside by the snorting beast.

Heavy hooves thundered on the dock boards. Fraenk caught a fleeting glimpse of a stalk-eyed bat creature feasting on a gull carcass. An instant later, Jimothy's hoof dashed it into a spray of black viscera.

In less than a minute, they were riding out onto the jetty and up to where Arch Partisan Olwynn Brightrock and two of his Vice Arch Partisans were surveying the area like military commanders.

"What is going on here?!" Fraenk demanded as he reigned up the huge destrier before it flattened a squad of partisans. The two other elves beside the Arch Partisan shot Fraenk a scathing look, but Brightrock put up a hand before they could speak.

"See to this. I'll have a word with Neversleep... since this is his district." The Arch Partisan commanded his underlings. He turned and nudged his horse up alongside Fraenk's. It looked like a pony in comparison.

"What is this?"

"We got a tip that two dangerous fugitives are hiding out here. One was just spotted heading inside. We're here to arrest them," Brightrock said plainly. "Do we have your leave for that? Yes? Good. Thank you, Neversleep."

"Hold on. I got a whisper that the bite I'm looking for is in there as well," Fraenk growled. "So who tipped you off to this?"

"The bounty hunter. That's him right there."

Fraenk followed Olywnn Brightrock's nod behind him. Coming down the jetty, between the two pudgy Arcane Lords Fraenk had met after the blackhound incident, was the helltouched man with the emerald gem collar. Fraenk snapped around so hard, he almost fell out of his saddle.

"That one?!" Fraenk exclaimed. The helltouched man seemed to innately sense that Fraenk was watching, and he looked up to match the stare with his own orange eyes.

"Sorzon Brimblade... said his name was. A rather eccentric sobriquet if you ask me."

"He's no hunter! He's a foul wizard or something. They should be clapping him in irons!" Fraenk said vehemently.

"And just how do you know that, Neversleep?" Brightrock arched an eyebrow.

"Well, it's my job to know, isn't it?"

Brightrock either smirked or made the same face he always did with the ruinous scar at the side of his mouth—it was really hard to tell the difference.

"The story he told us is that he's working for the Fernbrooks to find their missing kobold servant. The little skriff lit off with some kind of family treasure. He tracked his accomplice here and is pretty sure they're both inside."

Fraenk's mind was racing. How could one man have such foul luck? He almost had the kobold in hand, and now everything was falling apart. He cursed himself for not thinking that the Fernbrooks would certainly find other means to getting the kobold back. Everything was happening too fast. There was nothing he could do now but watch.

"The Arcane Lords are here. We're ready to go in, sir." The shorter partisan Lieutenant with wavy brown hair announced. Fraenk and Olwynn turned their horses to face the lighthouse.

The two Arcane Lords had a debate amongst themselves over who would take the lead—which was ultimately decided by a quick round of the children's hand gesture game Wizard-Soldier-Dragon. The winner and the one with the honor of leading the operation fell to Stannris and his oily black ponytail.

Stannris strode forward among the lean and athletic partisans, looking about as out-of-place as Akkadian Griffin scat on the white sands of The Monarch's Beach. He stepped in front of the formation and made wide dramatic movements with his hands, while bellowing in an affected tone the words of his powerful spell.

The wizard's melodrama only made Fraenk more annoyed. This whole scene with the Arch Partisan and a full battalion of his men standing ready to capture a kobold and whoever his accomplice was? It was a mockery of puppet theater.

A very loud and public show to capture a supposed dangerous criminal. Fraenk stole a glance at the Arch Partisan—his steely eyes were fixed on the tower. Was this his idea, or were his strings being pulled by another from the shadows?

Then a loud CRACK and fizzle sent a brilliant shower of sparks skyward and a blast of hot air back through the ranks. When the dust cleared, Stannris was seated flat on his backside and the effects of his spell were still trailing off his hands.

"By the Powers!" He exclaimed in a high-pitched whine. He rose with some difficulty, trying to not appear injured and only looking doubly so. The other Arcane Lord Timulot was already pushing through the lines of partisans to join his colleague.

"Stann! That didn't work!"

"I know that, Tim!"

Fraenk caught just a snippet of the angry wizard's bickering before it was carried off in the breeze. They proceeded to argue and gesticulate for longer than Brightrock had the patience for.

"My lords, just try again!" He hissed through gritted teeth.

Stannris repeated his spell, drawing it out longer and punctuating each move with a sharp staccato rhythm. The energy of the spell swirled in around him, and he shot his hands forward, sending the powerful spell toward the lighthouse door.

BOOOOM! A sound like thunder buffeted everyone there. Stannris had planted his feet this time so he wasn't thrown to the ground, but the shockwave did slide him back a foot. Fraenk watched the sparks rise into the sky again. Up almost to where a small black dot was soaring above them.

The lighthouse door was undamaged.

"Is there a problem?" Arch Partisan Brightrock called out, annoyance in his tone.

"It's protected by some kind of spell!" The Arcane Lord called back. For what he lacked in proficiency of magic, Stannris did display a complete mastery of the obvious.

"Well, then I suggest you keep trying until you're in!" Brightrock smiled—or possibly sneered (again, it was so hard to be sure). Then uttered a low 'skarking *morons*' that only Fraenk could hear.

Fraenk couldn't help himself by wondering why all this trouble for just one kobold? He wasn't some wanted fugitive or escaped bandit king. His name wasn't written on wanted posters across the city. Posuu was just some filthy pet that they taught to carry a tray and light a pipe. Surely the expense and headache of all this far outweighed anything that Lord Fernbrook paid for him—even if he was specially trained and imported from faraway lands. What in Galhadria could possibly be worth all this?

"Sir, did you say the kobold *stole* something? A valuable possession of some sort? That's what all this is about?" Fraenk asked.

"That's what I'm told," Brightrock replied, still watching as both Arcane Lords again prepared the spell together.

"Seems a bit much if you ask me."

"You've got a more powerful spell up your sleeve, Neversleep? You want to take a crack at it?"

"No, sir. I'm talking about all of it. The bounty hunter, full brigade of partisans. Two Arcane Lords.""I only wanted one, but the other insisted on joining," Olwynn Brightrock growled.

"It's still a lot of rah for just a single kobold fork-swiper," Fraenk scratched his chin.

"They're thieves. They're part of an upper-city larceny ring. Ripping off wealthy elves and moving the goods out of the city. And these are the last two."

"What exactly was stolen?" Fraenk pressed. His Arch Preceptor instincts were telling him that whatever Brightrock knew was important. The sound of the spell forming was a low drone.

Brightrock breathed in, about to say something, then stopped.

"Sir, you have to tell me what they took. They might have hit us too. Lady Blackroot has some missing jewels," Fraenk said, just trying to keep the old elf talking but then realized it was actually true. His second in command, Gwen, was posing as a servant girl trying to track a thief. Fraenk didn't believe for a moment that Lady Blackroot's supposed missing jewels were even missing, but it was a reason for him to remain close to this operation.

"Sir, it sounds like we're both after the same cruk. What did he take?"

Seeing Fraenk as a victim and not just another preceptor hunting for information softened Olwynn Brightrock finally.

"They took valuables that powerful elves weren't too keen on reporting stolen. Cursed trinkets. A forbidden painting. Some kind of fertility doll."

Fraenk's eyes went wide, and he was hit by the shockwave. Not just the magical one cast by the two bumbling Arcane Lords, but an impact of realization on how the kobold fit in with the other murder victims. The stolen items matched everything that was stashed in the Broker's house. That meant the kobold, the broker, the brothers, even Miken. *They were all a team of thieves.*

The Arcane Lords immediately began arguing with each other as to who bore more of the blame for their apparent failure. Brightrock growled, pinching the bridge of his nose.

"Did anyone just try the skarking door?!" He shouted, silencing both wizards.

The Arcane Lords exchanged a glance, as if to see which one of them would field such an inane question. *Of course,* someone tried the door. *How stupid did he think they were?*

Then a flicker of doubt. *They did try the door, right?* Stannris gave a derisive scoff and waddled over to it. He was just drawing a breath to vindicate himself when his thumb pressed the latch and the door lazily swung open.

Brightrock's face turned two shades darker.

"Don't just stand there!" Brightrock spat. "Go get him."

Three teams from the partisan battalion raced forward into the breach, clubs raised.

Fraenk's mind was still reeling. Bas Greenbriar was looking for Fernbrook's kobold servant and found out Miken was part of their ring of thieves. Maybe the old baker was hiding the kobold. Buying him time so he could slip out the secret tunnel beneath the bakery. And that's why the woman—

Another revelation hit Fraenk like a lightning bolt. The mysterious woman, Kyla. The Lynblood. The first thing she had said when she found Fraenk in the bakery was– POSUU. She was looking for the <u>kobold</u>. He was supposed to meet her at the bakery that night.

If Fraenk had any more surprises in this moment, he thought his head might explode.

He wasn't sure how much time had passed, but soon the elite partisan guards were coming back out of the lighthouse. Four of them had slung between them the manacled figure of a woman. She had a black hood slipped over her head. She was sobbing a wail of true anguish.

The partisan in charge strode directly over to the three partisan commanders.

"It's her, sir. Came without too much of a fight."

"What about the other one? The kobold?"

The guard paused. "He's dead. Looks like he has been for some time."

"Dead?!" Fraenk interjected. "What? How'd he die?"One of the Vice Arch Partisans started to say something to Fraenk, but Brightrock raised a hand for silence.

"Alright Neversleep. We're done here. We'll be on our way," Brightrock turned back to his man. "Take the woman to the cells. And the kobold... give him over to his kind so they can bury him or do whatever is their custom."

"Actually, Arch Partisan, that kobold belongs to Lord Fernbrook," A familiar voice came from behind Fraenk. He turned to see Farathiel Gingerglade smiling viciously. "And our lord would very much like his property back."

Fraenk turned to glare at his nemesis.

"Oh, and Fraenk? I no longer require your help in that other matter. Consider our deal... *dead.*" Farathiel smirked wickedly.

Whether it was exhaustion, frustration, or the simple fact that he probably deserved it, Fraenk pulled the reins to turn the big white destrier toward Farathiel. The smug elf looked amused, like there was nothing that Fraenk could do or say to stop him.He was wrong about one thing, however. There was something Fraenk could say.

"Jimothy," Fraenk growled low. "*—bite!*"

The horse's instincts were sharp, and so were its teeth. Gingerglade got an arm up just in time to keep Jimothy from taking a chunk out of his face. But the horse caught his forearm and lifted the elf screaming from the ground. Farathiel was like a child's rag doll, being thrashed in the air.

Then, chaos erupted as it was Fraenk's turn to grin like a madman.

Part V

24

K YLA GRACEFIRE JOLTED AWAKE, sweaty and gasping—afflicted by another one of those dreams. There were no dragons or giants in this one, however. No beast emerged from the pit. Just strange, shifting visions showing things that were happening or could still happen. Of course, they were never direct or straightforward. The mystic dreams always seemed to be coded in symbols and visual allegory.

For years as a girl, Kyla had been forced to write them down—everything seen, heard, and felt. She filled tomes with long passages that read like the storybook of a madman. Her caretaker's intent had been to one day find a seer who could read and interpret them. None could with any accuracy, but that did not stop the endless line of pretenders. Sages and charlatans alike—there was no difference in Kyla's mind—poured over the volumes, making predictions and portents from her words. The accuracy of their forecast was far less important than their conviction that it would come to pass. Occasionally, there were interpretations which could be seen as correct; most others were wrong a great majority of the time. Her dreams were like a precious ore that just lacked the right process of refinement. But eventually, just like a gold mine that failed to yield, her caregivers abandoned her dreams, hoping she would follow suit.

As she grew into her teens, Kyla had a new resource that could be exploited for gain—for her body was just starting to ripen into womanhood. She ran away not long after that. Her line may be special, but she was no brood mare to be sold off to some wealthy elf lord who wanted the essence of the divine in his progeny. Despite the curated nature of her life, Kyla immediately saw through their transparent attempts to see her productive. Handsome elf-kind spending hours doting on her with their cloying sweet demeanor, like a whole jar of honey poured down the throat. And then there were the others who were more... *direct* with their intentions. Those, too, got rebuffed with a reciprocal enthusiasm, which made them disinclined for amorous adventures—at least until the swelling subsided.

Kyla would be scolded and ordered to behave, which was a concept she understood meant subservient. This was something she had neither the inclination nor the capacity to do. It could have been the dreams speaking to her, but somehow she knew her value, and it was not to make wealthy a room full of sanctimonious hypocrites who claimed to be servants of the divine.

The caregivers had given up on her mind and therefore underestimated it. It was something they would lament after she orchestrated her elaborate escape. In their fury, however, they did not tire of trying to find such a valuable creature. Kyla became a woman without a home and in constant danger, but she was liberated. There was no better feeling. Kyla would have liked to see those men's anguished faces when they finally realized she would never be returning to them. And perhaps she did, once, in a dream.

As much as she would have liked to ignore it, the dream Kyla had just awakened from was heavy with portents. There was something urgent in the message. Like a friend shouting a warning from the other side of the room through a closed door. She reached for parchment and quill instinctively and was about to write it all down. But she stopped herself. Why was she doing this?

Kyla told herself that there was nothing to be gained from it. Just another scribbled page in a jester's tome, colorful but lacking meaning. She looked down to see her handwriting on its own accord. Transcribing the visions she had seen.

A darkened room, and in it a table with a service of silver plates, each set with their own item. And then, from above, blood poured down over them. There was a fetish doll with oversized breasts, two identical candles, a loaf of brown bread steaming fresh from the oven, and finally a crystalline tray with a pipe—all trickled with rich sanguine doom. She ran from the table before the blood found her next.

Then Kyla saw a dark prison cell with stone walls and iron bars blocking all the exits. But from far down came a flickering light and a hand emerging from the sonorous gloom.

A circle of men raising their arms in ululation around an orbit of flames. Their leader was someone familiar, but he wore a subtle, beautiful mask.

Then Kyla dreamed of the great tree again. The one she had seen before in previous night visions. And _he_ was up there. She saw his sad face. The kobold—the one she loved in all the world. He put out his hand to her, but as hard as she tried, she could not reach it. Then a mighty phoenix rose up and beat its flaming wings of cinder and sparks until all that was left of the tree was the tall white trunk and brilliant light coming out of the top.

A sinking feeling like she was dying gripped Kyla, followed by intense vertigo looking down from a great height, but at something terrible and hungry. She heard a voice yelling, "Pull! Pull!" But she had nothing to grip. Her hands only felt air.

Smashed from her thoughts, Kyla looked at the parchment and her scribblings. It was worse than a page full of gibberish. It was warnings she could not heed and hope she could not believe in. She almost crumpled the page and tossed it to the floor. The one part she held onto, though, was of him. He was still reaching for her. She had to find him. If he was still out there somewhere, she could not give up.

Kyla swung her feet to the floor, and the sensation of the cool stone grounded her. The little adventure she had with that mysterious man in the bakery had taken its toll on her body. She thought she was ready, but the exertion and running away from arcane shadow dogs had proved too much, too early. Kyla was forced to spend several more days in bed to recuperate.

In those hours, Kyla had time to think. About everything that had transpired and what it meant. Specifically this dark specter, whom she initially mistook as Posuu. Who was this, Fraenk Neversleep? From what she could tell, he was reckless, persistent, annoying, and... what else? Stupid. Yes, quite a verified fool, this one.

He also had other qualities that she had to admit weren't completely terrible. He did help her escape the blackhounds by letting them chew on him instead. Another strike in the 'stupid' tally. He couldn't climb walls, which... wasn't entirely his fault—Kyla had acquired special enchanted gloves and boots that helped her with scaling difficult inclines. He wasn't mean or cruel; she could tell by his demeanor. Not bad. And there was a sort of annoying charm about him. His smile was acceptable and pleasant to look at. By certain standards, some might even say he was quite handsome—but not Kyla, of course—she was just trying to objectively weigh his merits.

"So, he's a handsome, annoying idiot that I'm certainly not attracted to." Kyla said aloud to the empty room. "Okaaaay, Kyla. Time to get up."

Kyla rose and walked around the room. Despite the downtime, her legs were unexpectedly steady, and the pain in her side was nearly entirely gone. She enlisted the help of the innkeeper's gawky son to procure healing tinctures from the temple, which he was all too eager to do once he had gazed upon the splendor of her face. It was unethical to use her innate ability in that way, she knew, but Kyla needed all the help she could get. Without the potion's healing effects, her recovery would have been much longer and much more difficult. She had lost so much time already and couldn't bear any further moments lying in bed.

Whether she felt ready or not, she had to get some answers. Their job had gone wrong. Well, 'wrong' was an understatement akin to calling the Pale not a very safe place to build a house or saying that the Gazean dragon priests smelled a bit like grilled meat. Since that sadistic elf monster had assassinated the other members of her team and they had no contingency for such a disaster, where was her friend likely to turn?

If he were even alive... She started to think, then pushed it away.

Their client had used an intermediary, but she nevertheless figured out his identity nonetheless. It was part of what she did, and it was supposed to keep them from taking jobs, which would get them in trouble. The reputation of Lord Malgraye Fernbrook had suggested from the start that he might betray them.

First was the mere fact that he was an elf—and a wealthy, entitled one at that. Elves were no more honest than the average human, despite their supposed reputation for being honorable. Kyla had come to know that men with power held in lower regard those who were beneath them. They wouldn't even see it as wicked to take advantage of someone; it was merely the privilege of their station.

Second, Lord Fernbrook himself was said to be quite shrewd in business, which was a diplomatic way of saying that he had a nasty reputation for underhanded dealmaking to his own benefit. He left a swath of unpaid tradesmen for various goods and services over the years. And any that complained too loudly or would often turn up dead in an alley somewhere. According to some whispers, the Hardoak elves refused to do any kind of deal with him whatsoever. Those two reasons alone should have been enough to call off the job.

The final warning sign was that their cloying Arch Preceptor had been investigating them in turn. He was excessively interested in how they were going to go about securing the item in question. He had insisted upon meeting members of their team before he engaged their services; they'd instead presented him with a group of itinerant mercenaries. He asked about their process and how each part would go. The Broker had deflected, charmed, and lied where she could in order to secure the job, but something felt wrong about the way the elf probed into them. He had reminded Kyla of a young elfling suitor she knew who said he enjoyed cutting open live animals because he said he wanted to "see how they worked."

In Kyla's experience, those who wanted to know too much were either past victims of a deal gone wrong or looking for an opportunity to exploit the plan—either way, it should have been the final weight that tipped the decision scales into abandoning this caper.

But Kyla's objections were ultimately overruled by the others. They were more desperate and downplayed the risk. The Broker had received half the money before the job even started, and the payoff was too good to be ignored. And even if things did go awry, her failsafes should have protected them. There was no way she could have predicted just how badly this whole situation would get. It didn't stop the guilt she felt, however.

The Fernbrooks obviously didn't know where Posuu or the item was. If they did, they wouldn't be making such a clumsy attempt to recover it. Buying the entire Lower Market Bazaar just to sweep out the bakery? Ridiculous. And their Arch Preceptor with his brutish attempts to locate both her and the kobold, was easily avoided.

What she could not figure out was where Posuu Faljaon went. If he couldn't reach Kyla or any other member of the team, where would he turn? He didn't know anyone else in the city. The uneducated might assume he'd turn to the other kobolds who lived here. But kobolds were mistrustful by nature—even towards others of their species who were not part of their clan. No, Posuu would have gone to an ally. Someone they all knew and who knew the city. Someone they might be able to trust. Then, Kyla had a strong inclination of who that might be.

When she finally tracked him down, Kyla found Dandrikan seated on a wooden stool at The Royal Consort, a grimy tavern just on this side of the border of Blackroot district. Kyla noted how the conflated name of a place was often directly opposite to how nice of a place it was. This filthy watering hole exemplified that rule completely. Nearly every surface was tacky with some kind of unknown greasy substance—including the regulars, who silently nursed pint after pint of ale in a slow march toward whatever merciful darkness would claim them.

A disguise was typically required for her to be out and attract no attention. The natural allure that she seemed to radiate was like the bright phosphorescent glow of a cave mushroom in the otherwise pitch darkness. Her need to stay incognito was also compounded by the unsurprising fact that no other ladies seemed to patronize this place. More the wiser, them. This place made a dung heap seem like a preferable location to sit with an ale.

Using the skills of her tradecraft, Kyla dressed in an ensemble that gave off a look of 'out-of-work-fishmonger' with a touch of 'might be infected with the skin scales'. In the end, the result worked a little too well, and she had to wait half an hour to finally be served. This, too, was fine. She wasn't there to drink, just to give that appearance.

Kyla had followed Dandrikan to this place at a safe distance. He walked with the unhurried meandering of someone too oblivious to even realize they should be paranoid. Not once had he checked behind him, changed directions suddenly, or even done anything to throw off a pursuer. Over-confidence was the domain of men who believed their deeds would never catch up with them. Perhaps he truly did not have a care in the world.

Once he had found a seat in the tavern, which put him at the focus of the space, Dandrikan started into a conversation—but not with her. Whoever this large, brooding figure was that Dandrikan was talking to, Kyla didn't know and decided it was best to find out before she made her next move.

"I feel like I know you from somewhere, sir," Dandrikan started cheer-fully. Kyla had noticed the big man seated there when she entered, and his whole being made her feel unsafe. His shoulders were broad, and he had long, greasy hair that hung in his face. When spoken to, the large man uttered a bear-like growl to scare this annoyance away. But Dandrikan was oblivious and undeterred.

"A hero of the war, perhaps?" Dandrikan continued. "Although why a champion of Arathes would be drinking alone, I know not."

Dandrikan made an exaggerated effort to peer into the man's cup. As he did, he slid into the chair beside him.

"And your tankard is dry. Well, I won't have it!" Dandrikan tapped a coin on the bartop twice and laid it flat. The slow-eyed barkeep waddled over and refilled the soldier's cup. Instead of thanking him, the soldier took a long drink and then gave Dandrikan a scowl.

"You're wasting your coin, fool," the soldier grumbled. "Whatever your wares, I'm not buying."

"You wound me, sir. As you can see, *I'm* the one buying. And I've got coin, aplenty."

Kyla signaled for a drink from the barkeep as well, just so it wouldn't look like she was there to eavesdrop. What was Dandrikan up to? He was definitely a talker and more than a little lonely, hiding out in his plague house all day. Was this brutish man his idea of good company? Something told her there was more to this than what was on the surface.

The soldier raised his cup and drained it—his throat ratcheting to swallow the dark, bitter spirits. He belched and wiped his mouth with the back of his hand.

"A mighty thirst!" Dandrikan seemed delighted and quickly beckoned for another pour. "I am called Dandrikan, if you wish to know the name of your refreshing benefactor."

The soldier belched again, even louder, then smirked. "Did I say it right?"

"Very droll, sir. Very droll!" Dandrikan barked with laughter.

"If you like that, I can do one that sounds exactly like a Shivan when you trod on their tail."

Who was this guy? Kyla decided she didn't like this soldier much either.

"What do they call you, sir?" Dandrikan pressed after the man's cup was finally refilled.

"Leos Muninger," the soldier replied, his mood turning brighter with each drink.

"Very pleased, indeed." Dandrikan shook his hand before Leos could offer it. "Say, why are you alone here in such a place... at such an hour?"

There was a thin dig in the question, Kyla could hear. The big man didn't seem bothered, however.

"No work. No coin. What else am I to do?" Leos said bitterly. "I almost had a job, but an old friend backed out on me. Foul cruk."

"Oh, that is a shame," Dandrikan cooed. "Who was this brigand who wronged you?"

"The great Lord Neversleep! The Golden Man of Blackroot," Leos spit the words with heavy disdain. "He was raised in the streets, you know? Just like me. Forgets where he came from."

Neversleep? Kyla's ears perked up even more. Why were they now talking about this man? Was there anywhere in this city she could go to be away from him?

"More's the loss for him." A playfulness came back into Dandrikan's voice. "Well, I should think that an able man such as yourself would have no trouble in the rough and ready trades."

"Yeah. Me and every other swinging *kiv* out there. Not enough work to go around," Leos said and took another big drink.

"Nonsense!" The young man pounded the bar with his fist. The sudden loud noise drew sideways looks from the regulars. Dandrikan grabbed Leos by the shoulder, then leaned in close. If the place had been busier or noisier, Kyla would have missed what was said next.

"I happen to be looking to retain such a ready figure. My line of work sometimes requires a guard."

Muninger leaned back on his stool to get a full measure of this man. Dandrikan in his faded robes, which were meant to give the impression he was some type of wizard. His smell distantly carried the essence of the plague house. And yet, despite a bevy of indicators that would warn caution, Dandrikan seemed to charm anyway. It was how Kyla and her crew were taken in as well.

"I pay well, and you'll never go thirsty. Plus, I offer something else that I'm not at liberty to say around this mangy lot," Dandrikan said and cast suspiciously about the room. For one heart-stopping moment, his eyes fixed right on Kyla. She was certain that somehow he recognized her. But then Leos spoke, drawing his attention back. "I could use the coin, I guess," Leos shrugged and drank more ale.

"Excellent, sir. Leos? May I call you that? I'm certain we will become fast friends." Dandrikan clapped the big man on the back. "Come by my place on the morrow—Fernbrook Plague House, around back. I've got a very important task for you to do."

What illicit dealings was this? Was Dandrikan worried about his security? Kyla smirked to herself. He probably should be, considering how she had tracked him down and was now waiting for her chance to confront him. But there was something about this exchange that seemed very off to her. What was his plan, and would it go poorly for this unwary man, Leos? Probably it would, given what traumatic events she just survived.

Kyla had to fight the sudden urge to jump up and caution the soldier against any and all dealings with this man. She wasn't sure to what purpose, but Dandrikan was a schemer—others *had to see it, didn't they?*

Instead, she chose to keep silent. She would soon have her moment with Dandrikan, and she wanted it to be a private one. Kyla would have answers, one way or another.

Some time later, Dandrikan hobbled out of the bar. To Kyla, he looked tipsy but not completely drunk like the other man had been when they finally parted company. She followed quietly, watching as he oriented himself on the street and turned in the direction of his home. After walking nearly a block, the call of nature apparently grew urgent, and he turned into an alleyway. Dandrikan muttered to himself and fiddled clumsily with the drawstrings on his trousers before turning his pizzle out and firing a hot stream of urine against the stone. Dandrikan tipped his head back and sighed deeply with satisfaction.

That was the moment when Kyla pressed her blade against his throat.

25

"WHOA, WHOA! FRAENK, I can explain—" Dandrikan stammered, his piss spraying wildly.

"I'm short on patience, so unless you want me to drain you further, you'll answer me plain and speak quick," Kyla growled in his ear. Her dagger was a cold edge against the underside of his jaw.

"Yes, of course, my lady—if you'll pardon. You caught me at an inopportune moment." Dandrikan began to quickly fumble to get his trousers tied.

"Did the kobold come to you after the job? Answer false, and you'll speak next through a new hole in your neck."

"Lynblood? Is that you?! I'm so glad you're alive! I was worried—" His voice cut off abruptly as the blade dug into the fleshy part of his neck. Any more pressure, and it would slice him open.

"Answer me!!" She snapped. "And—?!"

"He said he needed a place to hide. But my shop wasn't safe either. Greenbriar was coming for me next. And probably would have too if he didn't get a face full of knives first."

"Then where is he? Where is Posuu?!"

"I told him to hide in the only place I could think of where the elf wouldn't get to him—the Tower of the Wizard."

"You sent him to a *wizard*?!" Kyla grabbed a fistful of Dandrikan's curly hair. "Were you trying to get him killed?"

"It's the lighthouse on the jetty. It's deserted. The wizard hasn't been seen for months. But there are warding spells all over the place there. It's safe. As far as I know, the little guy is still there... waiting for you."

Hope was a fluttering bird inside Kyla's chest. She couldn't let that distract her from what she had to do. This guy might say anything to get out of a red smile.

"And you just left him, injured? I should kill you," she said, fingers tightening on the dagger.

"I thought I was the last one," he said quietly.

"What?"

"When none of your crew came back, I assumed the elf got to you all."

Dandrikan's words stung. Her mind flashed to her days spent lying in bed with a fever, then later watching for him out the window at the market. All that time, this man knew where Posuu was. Why didn't she go to him sooner?

Dandrikan seemed to sense the tension change in her. He continued on.

"I couldn't get over there myself; the Fernbrook spies were watching me. So I hired some hard-backs from Rounderville to go check on him. But on their way, they got attacked by a helltouched warlock. They couldn't get close. We had to back off and wait."

Talking seemed to ease Dandrkan, even with a knife at his throat. The question was whether or not she could trust his words, and the better part of her wanted to. That foolish optimism, which seemed woven into the very blood of exalts, was the only thing that now stopped her from sawing his bastard head off of its shoulders.

"But I think you could get to him, though," Dandrikan suggested. "Everyone thinks you died. They won't be looking for you."

This man was trying to get rid of her. And she wanted nothing more than to be gone. Kyla had been ready to run to the kobold the moment she found out where he was. But that would be foolish. The Fernbrooks had tried to kill them all for one stolen item—and that was still unaccounted for.

"Did he have it when you saw him?"

"Have what?"

Dandrikan was playing dumb, and she was sick of it. Kyla jerked the curly blonde hair, wrenching his head back. He yelped in pain.

"Ow! No! No! He—I was ready to pay him, but he—he said he didn't have it! He stashed it in a safe place."

"How do I know you didn't kill him and take it?"

"B-because everyone is still looking for it! All the Fernbrook men. I'm even looking myself—my client is still very interested. He'll pay top coin."

That felt like a lie, but it didn't matter. Her business was done with this man. They could find different buyers in another city. If the item was worth this much carnage, it must be very valuable indeed.

"I never want to see you or that cursed thing again. You can find it and keep it for all I care! I just want my partner," Kyla said, her tone convincingly worried.

"Very well then. Go get your kobold, dear Lynblood," he urged. "I bandaged him as best I could, but I'm no healer. Kobolds are tough, but he can't stay in that tower forever."

There was a long pause. Kyla's knife poised, unmoving, ready with anticipation. Dandrikan closed his eyes and waited.

"If you've betrayed me, I'll find you again, and only the knife will speak."

The blade rasped stubble as it moved away from his throat. Her fingers released his hair. Dandrikan waited a long moment before he raised a hand to rub the spot where it had been. A thin tinge of red stained his fingertips. When he turned, the woman was gone. The start of a smile crept into the corners of his mouth.

Kyla tried to outrun the feeling of panic, but it was tenacious as a blackhound. It surged with each breath, each heartbeat. She knew it was foolish to run headlong through the city and did her best to take whatever shortcut she had learned in her time living here, but Arathes would always be an infuriating maze to her. Twice she had to double back when she found the street she thought she wanted to be on began to curve away from her destination.

It was on one of those sudden changes of direction that she caught sight of the hell-touched man. Of all the various types of people within the city, the helltouched were about as uncommon as her own kind. Perhaps there was a type of cosmic balance at play here, but to see a rare sighting of one was the kind of thing that should stand out in a person's mind—at least it would have if she had not been so hurried. It might have made her use more caution, and she could have avoided the terrible events to come.

Instead, she had only one goal in her mind, and that was to find Posuu. And now she knew where to go. Nothing else mattered. If only she could get there in time.

The third time she veered onto the wrong street, Kyla was done with this elvish labyrinth. She could see the harbor, not far off to the right. But a row of close-set houses stood between her and the next lane. Kyla checked in either direction—every other person she saw on the streets was busy with their own lives. No one was looking directly at her. She decided to abandon caution entirely.

Sprinting forward toward the candle shop, Kyla launched herself off of the lip of a large potted fern out front. Catching the ledge of the rooftop, she planted her feet on the side of the building. The enchantment in her boots caught traction, and she pushed off again, straight upward, the force propelling her onto the roof. Kyla rolled and was on her feet, using the momentum to gain speed.

An open courtyard stood ahead and below her that would be too slow to climb down and too far to jump across. Instinctively, her mind drew a path to the next rooftop. Kyla raced toward the flat wall that abutted the side of the courtyard. Without slowing, she angled her body and stepped against the vertical surface. Again, her boot gripped tight, and with a few long strides, she leapt down from the wall onto the opposite rooftop.

Then, springing off a post, she again ascended onto the support beams of a leafy trellis. Balanced cat-like, she ran on. Launching herself recklessly across a narrow street and onto a balcony. This time she leapt back and forth between two narrow buildings; then, catching onto a smooth tree trunk, she slid until her feet touched ground.

Ahead of her was an open street to the docks. At the far side was the jetty, and at its very end, with wind and waves crashing against the rocky shoreline, was the lighthouse.

"Almost there," she said between breaths. "Just hang on, Posuu."

Kyla was familiar with the lighthouse, so knowing where to find it wasn't a problem. In fact, it was the first place that she and her team had identified as a potential target when they began to work together in the city. It was probably not a coincidence that it was Dandrikan himself who brought it to their attention. It had been something the man had been salivating for, like a hungry dog watching a butcher carve up a ham bone—deliciously tempting and just out of reach.

The story was that a reclusive wizard had taken up residence inside. And the very few who had seen it said the place was full of magical items and powerful objects of an arcane nature. A veritable treasure trove for someone who traded in such things; sure to yield a fortune if sold.

The younger generations of elves were the perfect customers for such things. Too lazy to learn magic for themselves and obscenely wealthy enough to pay boxes of gold to own enchanted items that required little effort to produce magic. From what she knew of Dandrikan, however, he never had the kinds of enchanted objects that were popular amongst the young elves. They didn't want nasty things set with curses or could only do hurtful tricks. So stealing some high-quality magical goods could be a real change of fortune for the dealer.

The job turned out to be insanely dangerous and was unanimously voted down by all except Dandrikan—whose vote didn't count. No matter how much gold the man could promise them, it was not worth invoking the wrath of a wizard. After that, things began to turn sour between them and the dealer. They never ended up taking any of the commissioned work he proposed—at least before this last one. Dandrikan's jobs were either poorly conceived or reckless, or he was casually flippant about a member of Kyla's team getting caught or killed. They were like pieces on a game board to him, and he was incensed that they would not comply with his demands.

Dandrikan was a good fence for them, and they tried to keep him happy. They seemed to smooth things back over again by selling him any unexpectedly cursed or otherwise unwanted goods from other jobs. A man like him was an unfortunate necessity in her line of work.

Dandrikan's callousness prickled in her mind as she approached the lighthouse. Kyla wondered how wise it had been to send her friend here. If the wizard returned suddenly, how would he react to finding a kobold inside? Or her, for that matter? The lighthouse itself had magical protections on it, but they discovered that the front door remained unlocked. A person could simply stroll right in, easy as you please. Whether this was a fiendishly wicked psychological tactic meant to beg, just BEG some black-hearted idiot into attempting to steal something and get their bones turned to acid, brain eaten by carnivorous ants, or something even more terrible than that which only a maniacal wizard could concoct. Or, on the other hand, perhaps the old guy just didn't like locking his door. Both options were equally possible. This is why you _never_ steal from wizards.

Nearing the far end of the jetty, Kyla tried to look casual—like just any ordinary Arathenean out for a solitary stroll near the magical tower of an unknown and possibly dangerous wizard. But after running across half the city in the hot afternoon sun, she was a sweaty mess. The moment she entered the shadow of the lighthouse, however, an icy chill ran through her. There was a primal energy that seemed to corrupt this place. It made the faint exalt markings along her skin twinge with discomfort.

The lighthouse itself had a squat stone building at its base. Their reconnaissance had revealed this was the wizard's home and apparently some kind of metallurgical workshop. Every other wizard Kyla had known—and there had been a few—was deeply invested in the study of magic. They filled their homes, castles, or dungeons with books on magic and the arcane. They practiced spells and invented new ones. It was all they were interested in or ever wanted to talk about. But this one was different. He liked things that moved by mechanical force. Gears and pulleys. Switches and levers. His books were about how to create things from wood, metal, rope, and glass. Even though everything she had seen was spied through the strangely unflawed windows, Kyla didn't have to step inside to recognize an obsessive when she saw one. This man had <u>ideas</u>. And that could be both wondrous and catastrophic.

A light flared above her, and Kyla looked up in time to watch as the broad sweep of its beam passed over her and out onto the water. Then something in the position where she stood in relation to the building was somehow entirely familiar. It was a memory of this place, this view. And then she understood it immediately, like a native tongue spoken in a foreign land. A literacy with the very fabric of symbols, portents, and signs of all matter to have existed or might sometime come into being. The tower looked exactly like the tree in her dream—or rather the tree as an immutable emblem, a fixed point in the order of time. This place and time and her. All meeting together gently and unavoidably. The dream was merely an echo, but one that came before the voice could shout. Not one for others to interpret and ponder over, but her dream to live out, if she chose it so.

Kyla understood that this was the place where she was always meant to pause briefly before moving onto the other points ahead or behind. Time moved in circles if you stood still and in tunnels if you moved forward. She could then see this is where the mighty phoenix lashed the tree and destroyed its branches—then it was always a tower with light at the top. This lighthouse.

She almost ran at that moment. Forgetting everything that came before or what could happen after. The cascading sensation of fear and impending doom closed in, trying to shake her from where she stood. Like there was some kind of force that opposed destiny itself. An "anti-fate" attempting to break this destined convergence.

The sound of hoofbeats in full gallop snapped Kyla out of her transcendental reverie. She turned to see a man riding down the jetty towards her. A moment later, she recognized it was the helltouched she had spied earlier. Kyla instantly realized he was coming for her, and he was bringing destruction with him.

The hell-touched dropped the reins and began to wave his arms. Trails of flared energy rose around him as he called some spell into being. Pure instinct took over, and Kyla sprinted in the opposite direction, toward the lighthouse. Her years of living on the wrong side of the law taught her that a target moving at random vectors was much more difficult to shoot. She hoped the same principle applied to spell work.

Just as Kyla pivoted sharply on a new trajectory, a blast of blue light blazed past her, missing by inches. She could feel the ice crystals form in the humid lakefront air. He was trying to freeze her.

The thunder of hooves was getting closer. The helltouched would not miss at this distance, no matter her evasion. Kyla had one option left.

She hit the front door of the lighthouse and punched down the latch. By some mercy, it was still unlocked, and she dove inside. She kicked shut the wooden door just as another spell hit. A deafening boom hit the building, but oddly, only the terrifying sound found its way inside. An electric and altogether quite satisfying crackle rippled through the building and dissipated out the other side. Kyla paused. The wards this wizard had created were indeed strong. She stood, suddenly feeling confident.

"Just try an' come for me. See what befalls you, dirty phalet!" She yelled, knowing the helltouched would hear her.

For a moment, he looked ready to call her bluff and try to enter. But after more taunts and cursing, her venomous posturing seemed to give him pause. Kyla stood by an elevated window and watched as he cast about in an angry tantrum, then mounted his horse and thundered off back toward the docks.

Kyla slumped in relief on the lighthouse stairs for a moment. The ecstasy of not being killed abruptly switched to concern as she realized where she was—inside the wizard's house. But if a trap had been laid for intruders, surely she would have been its victim by now. And maybe Posuu had discovered all of them already and had disarmed them, as his talent had always been. Posuu. Her brother. Her friend. The one who had saved her. He was so close now. All she had to do was climb the stairs.

The strength of hope moved in her legs, and she found herself rising. Stair by stair, footstep by footstep, she pushed herself on. She could see his face and his smile. A charm that was most overlooked when all they saw was a kobold. He was smart and clever... and cute, if one could have the eyes to see it.

He had been her first friend when she had fled the caregivers. The first one to see her as a person and not just an exalted—someone to be exploited for gain. Not only did the kobold know how to use the parts of cities that most avoided, he was kind and thoughtful. Somehow, through every terrible thing he had experienced, Posuu chose to rise above it. And to give, even when he had none. Protect one who could be so easily exploited. From then on, Kyla pledged to love and trust him above all else.

And the beauty of it was, no one would imagine a more unlikely duo. One could not find a more overlooked creature than a kobold nor a more attractive figure than a beautiful Lynblood woman. What could be better for a team of thieves than the ability to control the attention in one way and go unnoticed in another?

The tower seemed to rise around her. And as Kyla got closer to the top, she began to call out for him.

"Posuu! It's me! Posuu!" Kyla called upwards, hoping her words would find his ears. Give him strength. Whatever he needed to carry on.

She got to a heavy door that opened into the lantern room. She shouldered it open and stepped through just under the large, sweeping light beam.

"I got here as soon as I could—"

Aside from the constant rumble of gears, it was eerily still. Kyla looked in every corner—if a round room had such a thing—but her head moved too fast, and her eyes resisted focusing enough to actually see anything. She forced herself to slow down. An awful cramp was pulling a knot in her stomach.

She closed her eyes and took a breath. Warm streaks of sweat ran down her cheeks. Then Kyla opened them again. She looked and finally saw.

Her gaze locked on something formless and incomprehensible. Kyla blinked away a blur that kept filling her vision until finally she made sense of what it was she was seeing.

A body.

Dehydrated, pale blue-gray scaly skin stretched over a frame of bones. Too large to be a child and skeletal formations too distinctive to be anything but a kobold. He had expired on his side, holding a wound. A cracked and peeling mat of dried blood pooled out around him.

Some kobold died up here; how odd. Kyla thought distantly. Its face was a rictus grin of sharp dragon teeth and shriveled eyes in large hollow sockets. The points of horns jutting from the back of its head.

Another kobold? How could this one be up here? It didn't make sense. Posuu would have helped him. Posuu wouldn't let someone die...

Kyla wanted to scream, but she couldn't. Why couldn't she? Mercifully, another woman was already screaming, and it was right. But then she had to breathe and realized it was her.

This wasn't real. It was all she could think. Somehow the wizard's tower had tricked her. Made her believe her beloved was gone. Just a desiccated husk. The real kobold was on the other side of a membrane, reaching out to her. His hand extended like in the dream. Then, looking sad, knowing she could never reach him... not anymore. Kyla collapsed. She cradled his body against hers. Even when the phoenix beat its wings against the tower, she held him. And it wasn't until the hard men in gray uniforms pried her fingers apart and slid the bag over her head, making all go dark, that she lost him again and knew she would see him no more.

26

JIMOTHY THE DESTRIER DID not have coherent thoughts like the sentient creatures around him. He was a horse, after all.

While the minds of animals were assumed to be much more basic and unsophisticated, their inner workings were still somehow an unknowable thing. They had no reference for esoteric concepts like death, beauty, or justice, nor even such a notion as petty revenge against an insufferable rival. What Jimothy did have in his darkly horse-shaped mind were pure instincts, desires, the only remaining knowledge of the secret location of Lord Honeyforge's missing fortune, and years of the finest military training a warhorse could receive.

Thus, when commanded, in this case, to bite a certain elf with an arrogant demeanor and obnoxiously loud perfume, it was not merely Jimothy's pleasure to do so; it was his duty. A duty which he enjoyed immensely and would happily carry out, even if he wasn't ordered to do so. There was no malice or deeper thought behind it—biting was what Jimothy did, and he did it better than anyone.

And since Fraenk was not on the receiving side of it this time, he finally understood its appeal. He watched with satisfaction from Jimothy's back as the horse first grabbed, lifted, and then throttled Farathiel Gingerglade like a child's sawdust doll. The power and ease with which the warhorse could toss this reprehensible elf around was godlike, akin to witnessing a miracle. Indeed, nearly everyone there—the partisans, Olwynn Brightrock, even the helltouched man— gaped in reverent wonder.

And in this moment of sublime bliss, Fraenk had temporarily forgotten why he had even ordered such a thing. But hearing Farathiel's anguished screams brought it back. These grasping Fernbrooks, the kidnapping of his preceptors, the wild search for the kobold, and now this final act of betrayal and cruelty at the lighthouse. The elf deserved every sharp incisor, but Fraenk knew if he didn't stop Jimothy soon, he would make everything far worse. And not just for himself.

In what seemed like minutes but was actually only moments, chaos erupted on the jetty as partisans grabbed for the horse, the yowling elf, and Neversleep at the same time.

"Jimothy, cease. Bad horse. No biting," Fraenk tepidly scolded before he was pulled to the ground. Fortunately, the horse either lost interest or obeyed, and his jaw opened. Farathiel Gingerglade fell from the height of Jimothy's open mouth and landed on the stones. He clutched his already swelling limb.

"*Aaagh!* He broke my arm!" Gingerglade howled and kept repeating calls of "Arrest him!"

While Fraenk was hauled roughly to the center of the scrum, only a few of them moved to help the injured elf, who screeched and howled the moment anyone tried to see to his arm.

One of the partisan lieutenants tried to offer a healing tincture to Farathiel, but he was caterwauling too much to drink it. Finally, Stannris of the Arcane Lords stepped forth, eager to test out a new healing spell he'd learned. On his second casting, he managed to passably mend the fractures in the elf's bones and left it with only a slight bend.

Farathiel shot Fraenk a murderous glare. Now it was Fraenk's chance to return a nasty grin. He decided that whatever they may do to him, this moment made it all worthwhile.

"I want this man arrested for assaulting an elf! I seek a full justice tribunal!" Farathiel Gingerglade snapped at Brightrock. The Arch Partisan's eyebrows raised slowly. He was not accustomed to being told what to do, least of all by the likes of Gingerglade. But whatever distaste he had was overridden by his sworn duty.

Arch Partisan Brightrock nodded, and the burly partisan nearest to him seemed to magically manifest a pair of manacles that would soon be on Fraenk's wrists. Only then did it occur to him that he could be in some serious trouble. He had to think of something quickly.

"Sir, Gingerglade's kidnapped three elves from my district! He's going to kill them," Fraenk blurted.

Many eyes shot in Farathiel's direction. Fraenk didn't want to resort to this option, but he had little choice left. Crimes against an elf were very serious, and he knew that Brightrock wouldn't overlook it. If his preceptors were still alive, Fraenk hoped he could convince the partisans to do a thorough search of Fernbrook estate to find them.

And if they were dead already, then Farathiel would have some punishable crimes to answer for. Fraenk felt a tug at his elbow, like one of the partisans was trying to pull him out of the crowd.

"I don't know what you're talking about," Farathiel said, sipping at the potion and making disgusted faces. "Besides, <u>he's</u> the one who should be clapped in irons. Look what this beast did to me!"

Then the elf gingerly raised the arm cradled in front of him, showing off the torn shirt sleeve for all to see. When he was convinced the crowd had enough time to witness, Farathiel winced dramatically and lowered it again.

"Yesterday, he ordered his men to kidnap three of my preceptors. Then he told me he was holding them for ransom in return for finding that kobold," Fraenk went on.

"Preposterous!" Farathiel scoffed out a derisive laugh.

"You'll find them within Fernbrook Manor," Fraenk continued. "You'll need to search the place top to bottom."

Fraenk saw a look of worry on Farathiel's face. Perhaps he knew that if the partisans moved quickly on this, they would have no time to hide the kidnapped elves. Or he was thinking about the abuse he'd receive from Lord Fernbrook after allowing a full partisan raid on the estate, uncovering all manner of illicit activities.

"*Neversleep, stop!*" That small voice again hissed. Someone familiar. Higher register, but male. He was like a buzzing fly in his ear. Then he felt someone press a fold of paper into his hand.

Meanwhile, Arch Partisan Brightrock had gone from looking annoyed for having to pry apart a street boy squabble to the serious accusations and an investigation of murdered elves. He fixed his steely gray eyes on Farathiel Gingerglade.

"Well? What of these men?" Brightrock demanded of him.

Farathiel squirmed.

"I-I haven't a clue what my good Arch Neversleep is talking about. He's clearly been under difficulty and strain. Just look at the state of him!"

"What kind of elf values a kobold over the lives of his own kind?!" Fraenk went on, feeling someone stepping down uncomfortably on the toe of his boot. *Who was this irritation?*

Just then, Jimothy suddenly wrenched free of the two partisans who were desperately trying to keep him under control. The horse reared back, front hooves slashing dangerously in the air. Men on all sides jumped back to avoid being struck.

In the chaos, Fraenk felt a sharp ridge hand hit him directly in the kidney. The pain was immediate and intense. It was a move he taught his preceptors as a method of stunning an unwary foe in a crowd of people. He contorted and twisted around to see who had done it. Fraenk came face-to-face with a young partisan with a sweep of brown hair. His features were delicate, but he had very familiar brown eyes.

"*Gwen?* Gods, that hurt…" Fraenk gasped, recognizing his vice arch preceptor, this time wearing the glamor of a city partisan.

"Our men are safe. Read the skarking note, you fool!" The young partisan with Gwen's voice growled, then abruptly turned and disappeared into the throng of soldiers.

Beside him, Jimothy came down hard, then took off at a gallop. Several men dove out of the way to keep from being trampled. Olwynn Brightrock took a casual side-step, just enough for the horse to miss him by a hair's breadth. They all watched as the great white beast went clattering back up the jetty and off to terrorize other parts of the city.

During the distraction, Fraenk unfolded the paper. Gwen's handwriting was both neat and angry.

It read: *Preceptors Maches, Dremore, and Spythe received a tip of contraband Gazean White. Moved to intercept. Led on chase. Day's ride out of Arathes. Found it was Fernbrook decoy. No powder. All preceptors accounted for at Blackroot Manor.*

Fraenk's cheeks flushed crimson at the final underlined words. _Not kidnapped, idiot._

A mix of giddy relief and embarrassment flooded him. Although Gingerglade had played him exquisitely— making him believe his men were taken. And like a fool, Fraenk rushed headlong into doing the elf's dirty work. Fraenk always believed he was too smart to be manipulated so easily, but this was evidence to the contrary.

He'd certainly dug himself into a sloss pit with this situation. Maybe Fraenk *was* an idiot.

Fortunately, being an idiot did have its advantages, and Fraenk knew exactly how he was going to extricate himself from this situation. Of course, it would involve more buffoonery.

He watched for a few more seconds. Just as Gingerglade was really beginning to sweat under the partisan's questions. As much as Fraenk would like to see his enemy taken off to jail while partisans crawled over every inch of Fernbrook district, he knew they would likely find all manner of other crimes and contraband, but no kidnapped elves. It was not yet the time to take his retribution on the Fernbrooks. For now, Fraenk had to stop this from going any further.

"WAIT!" Fraenk shouted above the din. "My lord, I must apologize. I was mistaken!"All eyes were on him once again. Fraenk sighed.

"What's this about, Neversleep?" There was an edge of warning in Brightrock's voice.

"I've just received word that my men are free." Fraenk said. "In fact, they're here with us now. Boys? Boys, come on out."

Fraenk pantomimed looking around the crowd while drawing up one of his hands behind his back.

"Oh, here they come!" Fraenk drew out his hand and raised the three-fingered hand gesture generally considered so offensively rude that even some dockworkers and prisoners were squeamish about employing it. Fraenk gave Gingerglade an eyeful. A scandalized and bemused astonishment ran through the ranks of the partisans. To Farathiel's credit, he took the insult without flying into a rage or renewing calls for a tribunal. Fraenk could only assume this wasn't the first, nor hundredth, time that Gingerglade received such disrespect.

"Are you quite finished, Neversleep?" Olwynn Brightrock asked, growing irritated.

"It's what he deserves for wasting my time and resources that could be better served in my district!" Fraenk snapped. "In fact, you're no longer welcome in Blackroot, Arch Preceptor. See your way out before I have a few of my own men show you what we do with trespassers!"

"Enough!" The Arch Partisan Brightrock snapped. "I'm tired of playing nursemaid to you two. Neversleep, control your anger, or I *will* have you arrested. And you, Arch Preceptor Gingerglade, see to your business and be gone. And before you object to being nibbled by a pony, I will tell you that you have no idea what a proper injury looks like."

He paused to glare. His breath moving through the ragged corner of his mouth.

Mustering his dignity, Gingerglade straightened his robes, either having forgotten about his supposedly injured arm or the healing drink having done its job and he was no longer feeling pain.

"Very well, I'll just take my lord's property, and we'll go." Farathiel's tone turned genteel and exuded reasonableness. Whatever his purpose for taking the kobold, Fraenk couldn't let this Fernbrook stooge gain anything that he had come all this way just to get.

"Sounds like he kept this kobold as a *slave*," Fraenk remarked loud for everyone to hear.

"Ridiculous!" Farathiel sniffed, whether from some nasal irritation or mock emotion. "The kobold was actually a beloved servant of my Lord Fernbrook. He's been missing for many days, and we'd like him to be returned to us. It's true he owed us a significant debt when he died, but with no other kin, his ledger is clear."

"Couldn't find anyone else to pay for it, more like," the voice of partisan Gwen came from somewhere amongst their ranks. This drew a few chuckles.

"Then pray tell, why do you require his body?" Fraenk pointed his question at the elf. "Are you going to sell it? Maybe have him stuffed, and he can sit on the fireplace beside your master's favorite pipe."

The subject of ownership of other intelligent species was a hot topic of discussion amongst the high-minded elven elite. They all, of course, held entire armies of servants in poverty wages, working long hours that left little time for their own lives. But at the same time, the notion of outright slavery was abhorrent to elves. All life was precious, after all. How did they justify this paradox? By publicly condemning slavers outside the elite—including ones they themselves had patronized—and by crushing any suggestion of their own complicity in the ongoing problem. It required immediate and vehement denial.

"What? No! This kobold was a cherished and well-cared-for servant of our great High Lord. He was a favorite, in fact, and treated with the utmost respect!" Farathiel blustered.

"If you loved him so much, then why did you send a bounty hunter and myself after him for stealing?" Fraenk countered.

"Well, we... were very concerned for his safety, obviously. And too late, I might add!" Farathiel countered. "He is a member of our household, after all. We must see to the funeral rites."

"As it shall be," Arch Partisan Brightrock said, his patience obviously at an end. "Send the kobold on with the Arch Partisan of Fernbrook, that he may have rites and honors in accordance with kobold custom."

Farathiel gave a victorious sneer. Fraenk watched the small wrapped body being moved along to the Fernbrook men.

He knew his goodwill with the Arch Partisan was all but used up; Fraenk could not let them take the kobold. He had one final dice to roll.

"Of course you are right, sir... but shouldn't he be checked first? For bugs... *or worms*." Fraenk intoned. Brightrock met his gaze, and an understanding passed between them. The old elf flashed a look of concern.

"Wait. He's right. The body must go to the city physicians first for a medical inspection," Brightrock said. "There's been an outbreak of plague in kobold town. I'd hate for your Lord Fernbrook to get infected with the blight by his beloved servant."

Farathiel sputtered then went silent. Brightrock's word had always been unimpeachable, which is why it was so jarring for Fraenk to hear him lie like this. In an odd way, this might have been the most unsettling thing he had experienced in recent memory.

Nevertheless, Fraenk felt a quiet relief as the kobold's body was taken back and loaded onto a partisan cart.

"Well, if we can't take the kobold, what about our stolen property?" Farathiel chimed in with his reedy voice. "Lord Fernbrook should be able to recover his own rightful property from the little bugger, right? Have you even searched for him?"

"Very well," Brightrock answered. "What was taken?"

A cold chill shot up Fraenk's spine. He knew before Gingerglade began to speak.

"A trifle, really. But it reminds his Lordship fondly of his dearly departed wife. The article is a simple pendant with a plain stone on a silver chain. Imbued with a slight charm."

Farathiel was downplaying it as much as possible, but he was talking about the cold lump of dark magic in Fraenk's pocket— he was after the cursed pendant. They could search the dead kobold all they wanted. As long as Fraenk kept calm, they wouldn't discover it was actually in *his* possession.

"We wouldn't even need to touch the little skiffer. We can locate it by detecting its magic," Farathiel mused. "Sir Brimblade, you know the spell, correct?"

Fraenk felt his bladder clench. He looked over at the two Arcane Lords to see if they were going to intervene in this use of magic, but they too were eager spectators.

This situation had taken a sudden turn into bad territory. Fraenk wondered if there was a way he could slip out of the crowd unnoticed. Or save that, leap onto Jimothy's back, and go thundering away, but of course the horse prudently had already left.

The crowd of partisans moved aside as the hell-touched man stepped forward, predatory and dangerous. They seemed to instinctively withdraw from his hateful presence. Brimblade's seething orange eyes burned into Fraenk. He met the scary man's gaze and returned it with similar intensity.

Despite his bravado, there was something that would soon be revealed that would cast a very dim light on Fraenk and would force him to answer some uncomfortable questions. Like, why did he have stolen Fernbrook property on him, and was Fraenk possibly working with this group of thieves?

Of course, a smarter man may have opted to stash it someplace—anyplace, really, that would keep it from falling into the hands of his sworn enemies. But considering how his fortune had been recently, Fraenk should have known better and taken more precautions.

Was it really that unreasonable to expect to arrive at the lighthouse alone and find the kobold alive? Instead, the worst of all possibilities happened. And now his effort to protect the strange magical jewelry had turned to its greatest hazard. Fraenk cursed himself for not just hiding the damned thing in the Royal Museum when he had the chance. Now it would fall right into the hands of—

He stopped. Fraenk suddenly had an idea. It was risky, but there was a chance it might work. If only the Lynblood woman would help him. And why wouldn't she? Especially after finding out Fraenk had been hired to hunt down her dead kobold. And that he had the necklace as well. Oh, this was a dubious plan...

The moment the hell-touched Brimblade began to curl his fingers, invoking a spell to detect magical items, Fraenk stepped forward. There was a saying in the business of secrets and whispers: If you can't control the facts, at least control how everyone *understands* the facts.

"No need for that, good sirs. I have the item in question with me," Fraenk spoke loudly and stuck out his closed fist. He turned it over, and there in his palm it sat. Dull and lifeless. Almost difficult to observe for any amount of time.

It made the mind grow bored and wander the longer one tried to look— like a squirrel bounding amongst the branches of a tree.

Yes, squirrels. They were jolly, weren't they? Living carefree lives of—

Fraenk snapped himself out of his reverie. He had been staring off into the distance for a time. And so had all observers, it seemed. A quiet hush fell over the cluster of people around him; they were all looking away from the necklace, lost in thought. He closed his hand around it, and all eyes seemed to refocus on him again.

"This is the article in question, yes? I recovered it at the scene of a murder." Fraenk shot a pointed look at Farathiel. He could see hunger and greed in the elf's gaze. *So the Fernbrooks had seen this before,* Fraenk realized. That was interesting. And this— all of this— from the killing of his friend to the farcical standoff at the wizard's lighthouse... it had all been for the necklace.

"Our Lord Fernbrook is grateful to Arch Neversleep for the safe return of our property," the other Preceptor preened.

"I am happy to return it to its rightful owner. But it's not Lord Fernbrook," Fraenk grinned back and extended his hand towards Olwynn Brightrock. "See that this makes its way back to the Royal Museum of Arathes."

Farathiel Gingerglade's triumphant smile curdled.

"What! No. I just told you Lord Fernbrook is its owner," Farathiel protested and reached for the necklace.

"It's stolen *museum* property," Fraenk said.

Arch Partisan Olwynn Brightrock's fist closed around it like a vault door slamming— and was just as secure. At that moment, Fraenk could not have been more grateful for that grizzled old battle-hammer of an incorruptible, law-abiding elf. Unlike so many of the ruling class who spoke epic poems about character and virtue, this was one who actually lived it. Which was maddening at times, but here and now, it was glorious.

"I'll require you to explain yourself, Neversleep. But be brief and to the point," Brightrock said. The surrounding partisans were riveted— this drama was better than anything at the Royal Opera. Even the men who were holding the woman with the black bag on her head had paused to listen.

"I'm willing to grant that Lord Fernbrook might have possessed it for a short time, but he's not its original owner. It was stolen first from the Royal Museum before he acquired it. Then later stolen from him by the kobold." Fraenk went on.

"Lies! Filthy lies and slander against a High Lord of Arathes!" Farathiel's voice pitched in a vehement fit of pique.

"I'm not accusing a High Lord of thievery, nor that he paid others to steal on his behalf," Fraenk purred and shot Farathiel a knowing look. "Perhaps he purchased it afterward, innocent of the knowledge of the necklace's sordid path to him. Either way, it's not his rightful possession. It belongs back in the museum."

"I still insist that it is rightfully and fairly the property of Lord Fernbrook. So it becomes a question of whom you will believe, Arch Partisan. The word of a *human*—" Farathiel spat the last word out like a rotten bite from a bitter stone apple. "—or the word of an elf."

"Perhaps you'd be persuaded by the word of a human <u>and</u> a Lynblood," Fraenk countered.

A murmur rippled through the crowd. Lynbloods were a rare kind of creature who held a charmed place, somehow above even elves. The irony was, of course, that Fraenk was relying on her virtue whilst simultaneously impugning her character. She might dash his pick-stick army with one swipe of her foot. He could only hope her vitriol for the Fernbrooks would outweigh all else.

"Go on and ask her," Fraenk urged.

"Bring the woman forward," Olwynn Brightrock hissed through the broken side of his mouth.

Moments later, a trembling figure was set in their midst. With a single motion, the black hood was swooped off her head, and a breathless inhale came from several in the crowd. Even though she had been crying for who knows how long, her face was still beautiful. Perhaps even more so in her heartbreak. Fraenk, too, found himself drawn in, feeling her pain, radiant and pure.

Her red-rimmed eyes twitched open, and she cast about wildly at all those present until they finally found his. The look she gave was akin to the illustration he had once seen of the hateful glowing glare of a mummified Vigabrockan ice panther, ready to kill. He almost jumped back.

"Curses upon you, Neversleep! May every foul beast in this world and the next tear the flesh from your bones!" She spat in fury. A manful *"Ooo!"* rose from the jocular partisans— they were enthralled by this hellcat of a woman and in particular her loathing of Fraenk.

Arch Partisan Brightrock raised his hand yet again for silence, then fixed her with a look that demanded honesty.

"Speak true, woman— the punishment for lying will be quite severe. Are you and the others part of a thievery cabal that is responsible for stealing valuables around Arathes?" Arch Partisan Brightrock asked. Fraenk's stomach tightened—if she denied this now with a reasonable alibi, she may go free and his entire plan for keeping the necklace out of the Fernbrook's hands would blow away like ash. Most were inclined to believe that the Lynbloods were instinctively drawn to be right and good anyway. It was much more of a stretch to see them as someone who flouted the laws. But as the expression went, the arrow had left the bowstring— all Fraenk could do now was hope it hit the target.

"Careful how you answer, miss," Farathiel interjected as if to counsel her. "He's asking you to confess to criminal acts. You'll end up in prison."

"So?! What of it? You think'n I'm a-scared?" She growled. "I freely confess that we's the best there is at thievin'. Nothing we can't lift."

There was something surprising about the way she spoke, Fraenk observed quietly. It wasn't like their first encounter. She had picked up some street lingo and seemed to be affecting a passable, but not great, Tigranean accent. From the faces of those around him, Fraenk could see that none seemed to notice. They were all the more drawn in by the luridness of this fallen Lynblood, with her tear-stained cheeks and mucousy nostrils. Grief threatened to bubble forth, but she forced it back with an angry snarl.

Arch Partisan Brightrock motioned for quiet to the chatter and posed his next question.

"And where was this stolen from?" He held out his fist and let the stone of the pendant dangle in the air.

Her eyes locked onto it, then back to Fraenk— a look of hurt and betrayal passed over her face. *You had this and didn't tell me? How could you?* Fraenk felt a rare pang of guilt. She had only been trouble for him and was even now the central figure in this drama and the cause of his having to give up the dangerous necklace. But she did save his life from the blackhound. And there was some deep, inner, lonely part of him that saw something in her— but what?

"From the Fernbrooks, of course... My partner swiped it right from their strongbox," she leveled a malicious glare at Fraenk again. *Oh, this was bad,* Fraenk thought. She's serving the necklace right into the hands of Farathiel and Lord Fernbrook. Maybe there was some deep malice she felt towards him. Somehow it outweighed even her disdain for the elves. Fraenk felt hope slip away as Arch Brightrock gathered the necklace in his hands again, ready to hand it to a jubilant Farathiel Gingerglade.

"—But that was *after* they refused to pay us for stealing it in the first place!" A wicked grin curled on her face.

"That—that's a brazen lie!" Farathiel sputtered.

"It's the Brand's honest. They was swore to pay us five thousand gold for stealing it from the Royal Museum. A display of Queen Faylen Carsys, I do believe. I didn't look too close on account of us nipping it and getting out."

All eyes shifted to Lord Fernbrook's uncomfortable emissary— all eyes except Fraenk and the Lynblood woman's. He could only gape open-mouthed in amazement at her masterful play. She met his gaze, and he caught a faint smile curl at the corner of his mouth. Then she winked.

The Lynblood woman—*Kyla,* Fraenk now remembered her name—turned her vitriol back to Farathiel.

"They cheated us! And so we took it back! Now they sent their dirty goons to kill us!"

"No!" Farathiel screamed and launched himself forward, grasping for the jewelry. Arch Partisan Olwynn Brightrock gripped the necklace back and mounted his horse as the partisans grabbed and subdued the enraged preceptor. Fraenk could see that was the moment his judgment had been rendered.

"Take the woman into our most secure cells to keep her safe until the tribunal. And I will speak with the curators at the Royal Museum about their missing article," the elf pronounced, wheeling his stately horse back from the scrum.

In a matter of minutes, the Arch and Vice Arch Partisans rode back down the jetty, carrying the necklace, Kyla, and the body of the kobold, Posuu Faljaon. It was a Naduumian victory, to be sure; neither side won, and both left burned. But at least his enemies had not ended up with the necklace. Fraenk found himself left alone with a seething Arch Preceptor Farathiel Gingerglade and the hell-touched bounty hunter, Sorzon Brimblade. Even Fraenk's disguised secondary, Gwen followed in line with her apparent cohort. There was no one to back Fraenk up now. But nevertheless, he felt charged and ready to face a dragon.

Then, a sort of standoff ensued in the blowing spray of air off the lake.

"I trust you'll see yourselves out of my district now. Before something un-fortunate befalls you, good sirs. Our district is home to all types of unsavory characters as of recently, and I most certainly cannot vouchsafe your health here."

Fraenk took a swig from the bottle in his cloak. He could hear the seabirds circling overhead and the sound of wind flapping at the men's robes.

For a moment, it looked like violence might erupt. Farathiel looked mad enough to murder him, but Fraenk was confident he could best the elf in a straight-up fight. The hell-touched, on the other hand, was cut from a tougher hide. Fortunately, there were still too many partisans in the near vicinity to keep the Fernbrook goons from trying anything.

"Your troubles have just started, Neversleep. Let's go." Farathiel spat and turned with the whip of his robes. The hell-touched narrowed orange hateful eyes at Fraenk as if to warn of an impending fatal calamity destined forthwith. Fraenk returned the look, vowing an equal preemptive action.

"Goodbye, Fart. And don't come back without my say-so. Neither of you," Fraenk pointed at them in turn. He knew there would be devious and devastating repercussions from the Fernbrooks for this— the brokered truce was now null and void—but right now Fraenk wanted to revel victorious in this moment. He stood, sipping from his bottle and watching the two Fernbrook enemies slink away. Fraenk hardly noticed as a ratty-looking crow flopped down to land on a wood post nearby.

"Well played, Neversleep," an avian voice—if there was such a thing—cawed from beside him. Fraenk turned, and no other person was there. Just a large, gangly black bird.

"Excuse me?" Fraenk asked.

"We need to talk," the crow said to him, then took off in the direction of the lighthouse.

27

"I CAN'T BELIEVE YOU can talk. And that you *shat* on me," Fraenk said in a sort of astonished vexation to the bird. The crow blinked its one good eye and bobbed its head in a bird-like nod.

"I was trying to get your attention," the crow replied.

"That was a nice doublet you ruined," Fraenk muttered and took another long drink.

"Let's talk inside before you get too uncoordinated."

The bird launched into the air with an ungainly series of flaps. It glided low up to the front door of the lighthouse and landed with a set of hops on the front stoop.

"Come on, Neversleep! This is getting annoying."

"What now?" Fraenk grumbled and restowed the bottle in his cloak. He followed the bird to the lighthouse.

Once he had unlatched the door and let the creature inside, the crow set out on a sort of methodical chaos-storm of flights across the workshop. He clearly had some kind of goal, but to what end, Fraenk had no idea.

Fraenk's attention was immediately overwhelmed, drawn around to nearly everything inside this place, all at once. It was an absolute trove of gear work, gizmos, and gadgetry. While the items all had a familiar look, Fraenk recognized almost nothing. It was like an apothecary shop for brass work, with each thing having a function but requiring an expert to say exactly what.

Perusing a shelf, Fraenk reached out to touch an object with a series of brass pipes attached to bottles holding various colored liquids. He poked it with a finger.

"Don't touch that unless you want to incinerate yourself," the crow squawked, flapping by with a small vial of green liquid in its claws. It deftly popped open the lid and poured it into a pungent mixture that it had been conglomerating in a small cast iron pot.

"Well, incineration isn't on my list of priorities today," Fraenk said, pulling his hand back. "Fetch us a light for this, would you?" The bird said, perching on the pot hook holding the cauldron over a stack of wood in the fireplace.

"Why not?" Fraenk shrugged. "The bird is hungry for a stew, apparently."

He reached inside for his knife and flint. He bent at the kindling and was about to scrape sparks into the tinder when the bird pecked his hand. He dropped the flint.

"Ow!" Fraenk rubbed his thumb where the crow had struck him. "I'm trying to do what you asked!"

"Not that way. Too slow. Look on the bench. Get my kindler," the bird pointed with its beak.

"A bird is better at sparking a flame than I am, I guess," Fraenk quipped. He strode to the workbench that the crow had been indicating. An array of tools and devices was scattered everywhere. The crow was apparently quite the scavenger.

"It's right there, Neversleep! The—it's the little brass square near your hand," it harked impatiently. "Hurry, I grow tired of this form."

Fraenk found the item in question. It was a small rectangle of brass with rounded sides and was beautifully etched on its face and back. He could see it was built in two pieces that fit together on the upper third of its height.

"Go on. Open and press the lever."

Fraenk fumbled at it, uncertain what the bird was even referring to. He pushed, twisted, and finally pulled, which popped a section of the brass encasement back on a hinge. Fraenk turned it over.

"Come on now. A child could figure this out faster than you. Stop toying around!"

When he turned it, the device suddenly fit perfectly in the palm of his hand. Right at his thumb was a metal tab, which seemed to be the lever that the bird was referring to. He pushed it down. A small column of flame burst forth from an opening near his thumb.

It was so surprising that he cursed aloud and dropped the device. It clinked noisily on the stone floor.

"Hells, Neversleep. Be careful with that! It's of very precise construction."

"Sorry. I've never seen a... fire-maker-box-thing before," Fraenk said, picking up the gadget again.

"Oh. Yes, that. I call it a kindler. But please, light the fire, if you would." The bird blinked and bobbed. Fraenk aimed the aperture of the device at the wood and pressed the button. Nothing happened.

"Blast it all. You broke it.""No, I didn't!" Fraenk retorted, knowing full well he probably did. "It just needs another—"

"Don't tell me what my own inventions need, sir," the blackbird shook its ruffled feathers at him. Fraenk pushed the button again, and *WOOSH!* A jet of fire blasted out, igniting the dry wood in the hearth.

The crow flapped away to avoid being consumed by the subsequent fireball that burst forth in the flue.

"Powers, Neversleep! You always manage to *SQUAWK* things up," the crow scolded, hopping from one surface to the next, trailing a thin wisp of smoke from its wings.

"Well, I beg your pardon. Wizard gadgets are new to me. Here's your apparatus back," Fraenk offered the kindler to the bird, who ruffled its feathers again.

"You might as well keep it," the bird said. "Call it a gift for your help. It's all out of whack, anyway. I'd fix it, but you know, there's only so much you can do with a beak and claws."

The old crow then scooped up a wooden spoon in its beak and began to stir the simmering mixture in the iron cauldron. Fraenk found a chair and toyed with his new device. He couldn't make it produce a flame with every press, but it was consistent enough that overall, he deemed it still a tremendous boon over scraping sparks from a flint.

When the arcane stew had reached a rolling boil, the bird jumped off the pot hook and dug an empty glass jar from a crate full of them. "Pour the solution in here," the crow instructed. Which Fraenk did, curious where this whole intrigue was headed. The contents of the cauldron were thick and syrupy—and seemed to pulse softly with a dark red glow. The entire mixture gave off a rank smell that Fraenk had to turn his head to avoid smelling. After it had congealed in the glass jar for a few minutes, the bird hopped up beside it.

"Hopefully it's cool enough. Dump a bit of that on me."

"Are you sure?" Fraenk asked, skeptical. He didn't want a bird's self-demanded scalding on his conscience, either.

"Go on! Before I lose my nerve," the crow said, ruffling its tatty feathers. It squatted low as Fraenk poured. A fat glob hit the bird in its mid-back, and steam hissed. A rank odor of boiled poultry filled the room. The crow gave off a curdling screech.

For a moment, Fraenk was worried that the bird had fulfilled an elaborate plan to destroy itself. But soon an odd thing happened. The crow's wings began to shake and its feathers all fell out onto the table, leaving it with thin, pale limbs on either side of its body. Ripples traveled down the length of its obscene, bare pinions as they cracked and jerked. Then tiny sprouts emerged, which became fingers. And then a hand. To his awe, Fraenk saw that the crow's wings had transformed into small, human-like arms—like some living oddity one would find floating in a jar of a traveling minstrel cart of freaks.

The crow shook them out and wriggled its fingertips. It seemed pleased by this result.

"Yes! This is good," the bird with human arms said with relief.

"You can start charging people a couple of coppers just to see you," Fraenk mused.

Now unable to fly, the bird stepped over to the edge of the table and looked down. "Set me on the floor, please. Last request," the crow prompted Fraenk. He did as asked.

The bird began to move and gesture its human arms in a way that Fraenk recognized as spellcasting. A swirling energy vortexed around the creature, building in intensity. Then—*FWOOSH!* A soft cloud of cold blew through the room.

When it cleared, in place of the bird, Fraenk found himself staring at a stern-looking naked elf with thick gray hair.

"Maybe that's enough drink for one day." Fraenk replaced the bottle he had taken out back in his cloak.

"Robes. I could use my robes," the elf said, casting about for clothing. Fraenk tossed him a heavy cloth that had been draped over the back of his chair. The elf wrapped it around himself.

"Incredible. You don't know how good it feels to get out of that form," the elf sighed, stretching his back. "Neversleep. Thank you. I'm—"

"You're the wizard who lives in the lighthouse," Fraenk said with a smirk.

"Ex-wizard. I don't do magic anymore... unless I have to," the elf said. "Call me Valthor."

"No family name?" Fraenk asked. "Heh. None that you'd recognize. They've disowned me two centuries ago. Of course, they're all dead now," Valthor chuckled, then noticed Fraenk's reaction. "*What?!* I didn't kill them. I just didn't want to be a party with their ilk, either. Horrible, the whole lot of them."

Valthor found a set of dusty robes and slipped them on. He still moved sort of bird-like, as if some vestige of his past form was still attached to him.

"Well, I'm sure you'd like a better accounting for the Ynne es Tylubourne, I suppose," the ex-wizard said, filling a kettle from a copper pipe that somehow produced clear water when he twisted a handle on it.

"I... would indeed." Fraenk kept his voice even, not wanting to divulge his ignorance or stop the elf from revealing something important.

"You have to understand that I was unwittingly set as its tutelary; I knew not Lady Horgoeth nor her litany of diviners. I was hardly even a token member of the society of scholarly luminaries and never requested a guardianship of— you have no idea what I'm talking about, do you?" Valthor broke off.

"No, but keep going," Fraenk shrugged. The ex-wizard sighed.

"Assume you know nothing?" Valthor sighed.

"Safe assumption," Fraenk confirmed.

The ex-wizard lifted the whistling kettle and poured steaming water into cups, then, taking a nearby pouch, he sprinkled herbs into each.

"Give it a minute or two for the flavor to emerge," he said, handing Fraenk a cup. Then he sat in a stuffed chair with his own.

"The necklace that was until recently in your possession is the Ynne es Tylubourne, which means Circle of Intent. I call it the Mind Thief. Its powers you seem to have discovered on your own. It was quite difficult to piece that human's brain back together, I must say—especially as a bird. I had to slip in at night and—"

"You mean Joeth," Fraenk realized with a twinge of guilt. "That was an accident."

"I don't have to explain just how dangerous and destructive it can be. It's no plaything. And in the wrong hands, it's completely devastating. As in— it can destroy the city and turn a populace into an unstoppable army of mindless savages who will fight without reason or mercy.""It can do that?" Fraenk took a quick sip of the tea.

"I thought you preceptors were good at imagining man's capacity for evil."

Fraenk's cup chattered in its mismatched saucer as he set it down. His mind conjured images of Arathes' population in the throes of a blood-crazed bedlam.

"That seems like a... less than desirable outcome." Fraenk said carefully.

He watched Valthor with new suspicion, trying to puzzle out what manner of elf would create such a terrible apparatus. He seemed bookish and experienced, which was probably fertile ground for how it came to be.

"It's what I've been trying to prevent," the ex-wizard replied.

"So, how'd you come to own this… Jimmy's Tambourine?"

"Ynne es Tylubourne. And I was never its owner. In fact, it has a particular aversion to those with strong magical powers. Hence, the avian state you found me in when we met," the ex-wizard said, rising from his chair. "Biscuits. This calls for biscuits. It's been ages since I've had food that wasn't crawling on six legs."

He set about rummaging through jars and boxes on his shelves. As he did, Valthor continued his lecture.

"The wizardess who created it was named Lady Caterine of Horogeth. An expert in apperaturgy and making the wrong animal hatch from eggs. But most famous for hosting lavish parties, heavy with enchantment. You'd be served drinks by a crew of pirate specters or there was one where she turned everyone into centaurs and—" Valthor blushed and cleared his throat. "I've been to one or two— not really to my taste, but they were certainly creative."

He found a jar with oblong discs of fuzzy green and dark brown in it. Valthor fished one out and crunched it—then spat it on the floor.

"Ugh. Moldy." The ex-wizard continued to spit the offending bits to the floor. He laced his fingers together and articulated an odd set of gestures. The biscuits inside shivered and vibrated. Then a moment later, they sucked the fuzzy mold back inside and brightened to a golden brown. A gentle puff of aromatic steam rose off them. He picked the same one up and nibbled again.

"Much better! Would you like one?"

"Where's the mold?"

"Oh, they're not moldy yet. Chronologically."

He offered the jar to Fraenk, who, deciding it would be rude to refuse, accepted a biscuit and took a small bite. He was pleasantly surprised at how good it tasted.

"Where was I? Oh yes, Lady Horogeth. For being one so social, or maybe because of it, she was surprisingly paranoid. She was always worried about what others thought of her. So she devised the Mind Thief as a way to peer into others' minds in order to read their thoughts about her—which is a bad idea, I can tell you that. I don't care how good of a man you are, Neversleep, no one likes you all the time."

"Huh. Most people don't like me pretty much all the time. You get used to it," Fraenk remarked. He popped the last bit of biscuit into his mouth and took another one from the jar.

"Well, Lady Horogeth didn't. When she found out her friends didn't always adore her with their every waking thought. It only fed her fears. Soon, she was adding more power into the Circle to make it stronger. She found ancient and obscure magic—old magic. Then began adding protections to the stone so no one else would wear it or even want to look at it— especially another wizard."

"Let me guess, she eventually went completely insane, and she killed all her friends in some fiery gambit of doom," Fraenk set his empty cup down.

"No, she's fine. Lives in a cottage off the coast of Solopolis. Bakes meat pies for the local village."

"Wait. Really?" Fraenk asked. The ex-wizard gave him a sardonic shake of his head. "Oh, no. I was right about the whole kill-all-the-friends thing."

"Took an entire detachment of Arcane Lords to end her terror. Left a scar on the foothills of the mountain that still smolders with green ash," Valthor said. "Then a year later, I get a sealed box with a letter describing where to find the Mind Thief— as well as a grave warning to never touch it. Suddenly, I was made its guardian, all because I was nice to her at a party before she decided everyone was out to get her."

"So, how'd it get here?"

"Your Lynblood friend could tell you better than I," he said, rising from the chair. "But I'm no longer its protector. I can't touch it without... repercussions. When I first discovered you possessed it, I had my reservations about you being its bearer. But I now think you'll do fine."

"Not me, friend. I've got a job. It'll be safely under guard at the museum," Fraenk said without much conviction.

"Neversleep, anything can be stolen back," the ex-wizard stated. "I've met Lord Malgraye Fernbrook on several occasions. He's cunning, persistent, and ruthless—whatever plans he has are not to make the city better. You can't let the necklace fall back into his hands."

"What do you suggest?"

"I just said—_anything_ can be stolen back. You heard me say that, right?"

Fraenk stood with a groan and a stretch. He was surprised by how sore he was. That short respite off his feet seemed to let the fatigue back into his body. It was about time to take the healer's advice and get some rest for a while.

"Thank you for the tea. And the fire gizmo," Fraenk said and started towards the door.

"Neversleep? What is your plan?" Valthor asked, his voice edged with concern.

"A hearty breakfast at the estate and then a few dozen hours of rest, then it should be breakfast again. I'll go from there." Fraenk opened the front door.

"And the Ynne es Tylubourne?"

"That's your problem, not mine. You seem like a much more capable handler anyway. I'm just a human with no magic. You're an elf wizard with…" Fraenk gestured to the room. "…whatever all this is. You'll figure out a way to keep it safe."

"I can't touch it, I told you. And Lord Fernbrook will stop at nothing—"

"Let me ask you something," Fraenk growled, turning back to the elf. "You said you're an ex-wizard, yes?"

"That's right," Valthor said.

"Why did you quit? You're obviously good— two Arcane Lords couldn't breach your defense spells on this place. And you're an elf, which means you've had years to study and master your trade. And yet here you are, making lots of things that can incinerate, apparently. Why did you give it up? Tell me that much at least."

The ex-wizard paused and seemed to ruminate for a bit.

"You have the right of it, Neversleep. A keen mind, as I expected. I was, as you say, a master of my trade. I spent entire human lifetimes in the study and practice of magic. I'd exhaust the knowledge and skill in one area and go someplace else. But one late evening as I was turning the final page of an ancient tome— the last volume of a great hidden library, buried for centuries, that I discovered—I saw a footnote. It was a simple footnote. And it referred to a volume of a book I'd never heard of in another undiscovered library. I made the most important revelation that day— the thing about wizardry and magic is that you can reach what you think is the peak and find more mountain still. So I burned the library and buried it under a thousand feet of rock, then decided I'd try my hand at building gadgets instead."

"Then you should understand when I say this case is over for me—the last page of the book." Fraenk said. "The thieves were caught, and the stolen magical item returned. My friend who was killed has already had more justice than many humans get when an elf wrongs them. If I steal that necklace now, it just starts everything back up again and there will be no end to it. And I'm tired."

"Fine. Go on your way. Ignore the footnote," the ex-wizard said. He turned to his workbench and began to organize it. The surface was truly in a state of chaos. Valthor seemed immediately frustrated and overwhelmed.

Fraenk pulled open the door and was just about to step out.

"What about the Fernbrooks, Neversleep?" Valthor called over his shoulder, not looking up. "You may be done. But have they closed the book on this too?"

28

W HEN HE GOT BACK to the kitchens of Blackroot Estate, Fraenk was ravenously hungry. The ex-wizard's tea and biscuits only seemed to remind his body that it hadn't consumed any kind of substance without an alcohol content in... well, he wasn't quite sure.

There was that flame-roasted pig served during the overnight festivities in Rounderville, which he saw others enjoying, but he had no appetite for. This was prior to the incident when he had nearly melted Joeth's brain. Fraenk was relieved to hear that the man's mind wasn't at least somewhat repaired.

Which reminded Fraenk of another little detail from that evening—Valthor must have been spying on that moment as well if he was handy to help the man afterward. Sneaky bird, indeed.

Pollard was too busy when Fraenk arrived in Blackroot's kitchen, so he was handed off to a very thin man with dark, intense eyes. This chef seemed to take Fraenk's hunger as a personal challenge and prepared a large plate of scrambled goose eggs with peppers and blood sausage and delicately battered pan-fried herrings with blue-collared mushrooms and seaweed noodles. Everything was rich and savory, salty and heavy with cream sauce and pungent goat butter.

Fraenk wanted nothing more than to sit and enjoy his meal. He was hungry, to be sure. The alcove where he sat was fairly quiet, and he was alone. No one rushed up with another urgent matter. And yet there was an unquietness to his spirit. His thoughts still seemed to be churning inside his head. Fraenk realized he was still going over the case.

He really wanted nothing more than to shake this whole affair off—just turn his mind over and dump it all out like those annoying pebbles that sometimes get trapped in the bottom of a boot. Fraenk told himself that he'd done all he could. This was over. Like he had justified to the ex-wizard, this tale had as much closure as any case could reasonably expect. Nothing ever concluded with a clear and definite end point.

Fraenk promised he would talk to the curators of the Royal Museum and the Arch Preceptor of Graysage district about posting extra guards nearby—especially in light of the recent burglaries. No one needed to know about the true nature of the Mind Thief; they just had to prevent it from being stolen from now on and for the next several hundred years. At least until the elves of the Fernbrook family all died or became so senile they forgot about it. Fraenk admitted that the situation was less than ideal, but it wasn't the first dangerous item to require an eternal guard henceforth. Perhaps it could be destroyed instead? He may have to ask the ex-wizard about that.

There were still an abundance of questions he had about the necklace itself and how it fit into Lord Fernbrook's overall scheme. Fraenk assumed the old elf was using it to win at cards and defraud Lady Blackroot of her territory. That seemed like such an unsophisticated plan for an elf known for his cleverness. But perhaps simpler was better? Then again, how long would the High Lords continue to play with an elf that appeared to be cheating? No, there must have been another play—something involving the necklace's power. But that could be so many things, Fraenk realized. Who could know other than the Fernbrooks?

Fraenk's imagination had a brief fancy where he was using the necklace to force a room full of Fernbrook elves to reveal their dirty schemes to him, and they were powerless to stop.

Then a stab of guilt hit him as he remembered someone who might actually know. Someone who was responsible for getting the necklace to the Fernbrooks in the first place. And it also stood to reason that the one whose actions, in stealing the necklace back, set off the chain of events that got Miken killed. He wanted to be mad about that. Their carelessness or greed... or perhaps just foolish retribution. Whatever their reason, this was why Fraenk could no longer get a fresh, steaming loaf of brown bread from his friend anymore. He couldn't go talk with the man who was like a father to him, after what his own father had done—

Then a deeper guilt hit him. How long had it been since Fraenk and Miken had spoken? And wasn't their last conversation a heated argument? A screaming, curse-filled fulmination from a teenaged Fraenk that ended with him storming off, vowing never to look back? The foulest thing was that he couldn't rightly remember what it had even been about. Hadn't Miken wanted him to take over the bakery? Now it seemed like a reasonable idea, and that Fraenk had been the irrational one, wanting to be a soldier or one of the men who ventured out to slay monsters. All he recalled about that exchange was a blinding anger and a sense of betrayal. The next time he properly saw his friend was when Miken lay slain, an old man nearly unrecognizable. Another face Fraenk tried to scourge from his memory, like the face of his true father.

If the woman thief, Kyla, was to blame for Miken's death, then Fraenk bore some blame himself too. He'd let too many years pass without apologizing. Let moments of anger and then years of shame keep him from making amends.

And didn't she help him out? When the moment came, she played her part and kept the necklace from falling back into the Fernbrook's hands. Was Fraenk truly going to pay her for that favor with most likely a long prison sentence? He had no pull with the High Council of Justice. Even his friend Arch Partisan Brightrock would only have limited influence. Once in the system, it was a bureaucratic hellscape of long delays and administrative procedure. He might not be able to get her set free, but he could go talk to her at least. Maybe thank her for what she did. And who knows? She might know something of the Fernbrook's plan...

Fraenk stopped himself. What was he doing? This entire line of thinking was digging back into the case he closed and put away. Nothing good could come of it, and many terrible things were instead likely to happen.

He dropped the fork he was holding, which had a fat sausage skewered. His fingers slowly clenched into a fist.

Fraenk reached inside his cloak, removed the bottle, and took a long drink.

"You're a fool, Fraenk Neversleep," he said aloud. "Keep after this, and you're going to die."

The road to wherever she was being taken was a long, tooth-rattling ride on the floor of a wagon in the blackout hood. After her exhausting performance for the partisans, Fernbrook goons and Fraenk Neversleep, Kyla was immediately re-hooded and hauled away with the departing force. She, of course, knew why the partisans were there, and the Fernbrooks—that sniveling rat, Dandrikan—had sold her out the moment she left him standing in a pool of his own piss in that alley. The thing that bothered her then and is still unclear now was why Fraenk Neversleep had been there. Not just present for her arrest, but in the thick of it. He was somehow deeply involved, but in what way? She had also backed his gambit with the necklace. He'd at least had enough sense to keep it out of the Fernbrook's hands.

Kyla could hear the idle chatter of the partisans seated on the benches surrounding her. Their excited recollection of the previous events gave her a picture of everything she didn't see while she was literally kept in the dark. There were the bumbling Arcane Lords trying to breach the tower with ineffectual spells. Neversleep riding in, all in a huff about them rightfully doing their job in his district— as if they needed any permission from the likes of that glorified Blackroot elf-pet. But moments later, the rowdy partisans were guffawing about Neversleep's horse, who had set upon Arch Preceptor Gingerglade's arm like a stray dog with a beef bone. The feeling of dislike for the elf seemed pervasive and general. Gingerglade had a reputation for misusing the partisans in order to settle personal grievances but was now making their lives miserable by raising alarms on what turned out to be inconsequential enforcement matters all over his district. They were so busy, in fact, they had little time to serve effectively elsewhere.

Kyla listened, keeping silent and still. She did not want to draw attention if she could help it. A few of the partisans made suggestive comments about her, but thankfully, their superior officer barked an end to that jabber—he would not have his men speaking coarsely before a Lynblood lady. Whether it was chivalry or piety, honor was not entirely dead in this city, she observed.

As they bumped along in the cart, Kyla tried not to hear the thump and scrape of the small, desiccated body that also rode on the floorboards with her. That shriveled husk was not her Posuu. She would cry for him later, but right now, he would need her to be strong for what was to come.

In her experience with the law—which had only been a total of four times so far— this was the hard part and often the most dangerous: the intake procedure for becoming a prisoner. It varied by region, of course, but the broad strokes were quite similar: arrest, removal of all possessions, and assignment to a cell—with a more than zero percent chance of interrogations, beatings, or a mixture of both throughout this process. She had to keep her mind on that. If she let the grief take over, she'd do something stupid that would really get her in trouble—like give up hope.

But Kyla did feel like giving up. Her Posuu, childhood friend and closest ally. Her confidant and strength. How would she continue without him?

Then a mummified claw brushed against her foot, and she recoiled so sharply, the partisan guards nearly thought she was making an escape attempt. A tense moment ensued when she heard their clubs slide out of loops, hovering ready to send down a rain of blows. She cowered, trying to raise her cuffed hands to shield her head and neck. Then one wheezed with mirth.

"Aww, I think he just wants one more cuddle, honey," a partisan said, getting a laugh from the squad. They settled back into their seats; their large bodies radiated heat and were both fortress-like and claustrophobic around her. The air soon grew stale with the odor of rank male musk and her own sour breath coming back into offended nostrils. Kyla curled her knees to her chest and held herself until the wagon finally came to a creaking stop.

She was brusquely hauled out and to her feet, then dragged into a large, echoing building, where their boots whacked the polished marble like the strikes of the justice mallet. She let them bear her weight across a series of ever smoother stone floors. There was no more time for sorrow now. She had to be strong again. Kyla forced all her grief and despair down inside her, tiny and far away. She straightened on the bench, easing her shoulders back. They wanted a tough master thief ringleader; they were about to find out how hard she could be.

Kyla was handed off to a pair of female partisans and was taken to a mildew-smelling room with a moist floor. Still hooded, they stripped her of all her clothes, pouches, and everything she had on her, then splashed her with buckets of shockingly cold water that smelled intensely medicinal. Then she was thrust a set of rough fabric robes and ordered to dress.

She was again marched down a twisting set of corridors and stairs until finally being deposited on a rough stone bench, her manacles secured to a ringlet set into an imposing slab table. The female guard tugged once on the manacle chain to make sure it was secure, then began her standard recital of the rules—a speech she had given so many times, the words had just become an automatic series of sounds that she made at this point in the process.

"No shouting, swearing, or pissing yourself. Obey the guards at all times. Break any of these rules and you will be whipped. Disrespect a guard, and you will be whipped. If you attempt any violence or escape during your time in confinement, you'll be—

Kyla shot her hand up to its short length, clinking the chain. "Can I guess?"

A loud *woosh-WHACK!* sound, accompanied by a searing pain across her bare forearm, made her bite back a scream.

"First one's free, human," came the voice of the other guard, a man. "They always wanna test you."

"Your confessor is..." The female paused. " ...Slategrove?"

"Yeah, I think he's up," the male replied.

"Partisan Confessor Slategrove. You will address all statements and admissions to him. Do you understand?" "*Wait!*" Kyla said, sounding urgent. "Is he cute?"

She braced for another hit on the arm, but the shot that came whipping stung her cheek, twitching her head back to the side. Even through the hood, the bite of the guard's leather crop burned and made her eye water. She breathed heavily through the pain."Eh, he's not bad," the female guard replied. "But he don't have a good sense of humor like me."

Kyla felt the guard give her two playful taps on her shoulder with the crop, like their little repartee had been an amusing game they both enjoyed. She waited for the two guards to close the iron door behind them before she checked the stinging red welt on her arm— no bleeding or any permanent damage.

As much as she didn't want to instigate the guards, it was important to do for a few reasons. The primary one being it informed her on how strict, lackadaisical, or sadistic they were. Misjudging this at the wrong moment could have disastrous consequences. So even though it hurt, the knowledge it yielded was far more valuable.

Her secondary reason to take a shot or two was related to a thesis she had formed about interrogators. They never seemed to trust the answers of someone who was uninjured. Whether true or lies, the word of a suspect was automatically deemed a fabrication until they had been punched, kicked, cut, or otherwise mistreated enough so that they begged to give an honest confession. Certainly nearly everyone but a paladin bound in service to the seven above would lie to keep themselves from pain, but Kyla had to wonder if there were no better methods for getting to the truth. Until such a thing existed, she'd have to keep subjecting herself to some mistreatment. It was better to take it from a couple of guards, who were busy with other duties, versus the interrogator, who had nothing but time and creative new methods for getting their questions answered.

Kyla began to wonder if the two hits she had taken would be enough to look suitably roughed-up in the eyes of this Confessor Slategrove. The faster she could get through the interview while giving away the least amount of damning information, the better she would be.

She heard footsteps coming up the hallway.

"And so it begins..." She whispered, steeling herself.

Kyla heard the door unlock and someone enter the room and then close it again. She sat motionless, waiting for the opening gambit. Would this one come at her loud and fast or drawn out and calculated?

The hood was jerked suddenly from her head, ripping out strands of hair with it.

"Hello, Miss Gracefire..." A familiar voice purred.

Her eyes adjusted to the light, and she jerked back to the extent of her chains. Seated across from her was not Partisan Confessor Slategrove, nor any other partisan, but the wolfish grin of the Arch Preceptor of Fernbrook, Farathiel Gingerglade.

"... anything you'd like to confess?"

29

No one seemed to notice that the Arch Partisan of Arathes had dark brown eyes. If they had, Fraenk's plan would have gone bad faster than week-old slime eel through a spotted gull.

But as it stood, the guards and partisans who worked at the Council of Justice's detention cells had taken their typical demure approach to the sight of the city's highest law enforcement officer, busying themselves with this urgent task or the other.

Fraenk received a few curious glances, as he was an uncommon sight in the upper levels, but the mere virtue of him striding into the building shoulder to shoulder with Olwynn Brightrock gave him instant immunity from any challenge.

"I would like to state for the official record that this is a terrible idea, and I was opposed to it from the start," Brightrock whispered low enough for only Fraenk's ears.

"Noted and disregarded," Fraenk replied in tone.

"How does he even speak with this craterous ruin?" The ersatz Brightrock sucked back spit from the open, scarred grimace at the corner of his mouth.

"You mean, how do *YOU* speak with it?" Fraenk corrected. "Now keep it together, or we'll both find ourselves having a much longer stay here in the cells than we anticipated."

"Your plan is to just speak with this woman, right?" Brightrock went on. "No other heroics I should know about?"

"Well, when the explosion goes off, just keep your head down and act surprised."

The Arch Partisan shot Fraenk a horrified look. "I'm joking. Take it easy," Fraenk smiled. "You've certainly nailed the uptightness about the old dragon."

"I swear if you ever make me do anything like this again, there will be stabbings..."

"I just have some questions about the Fernbrooks and what they planned to do with the necklace. Get me in the holding cell with her for a few minutes, and we're gone."

Olwynn Brightrock's dark eyes glared at him.

"Yes! That's exactly the *'I hate you, Neversleep'* look he gives me all the time. It's uncanny," Fraenk winked.

They moved briskly and with purpose through the building. Fortunately, Fraenk had been here enough times to know the layout. They made their way past the main administrative area and out to the detention cell wing. Despite having no side windows in its tall, featureless walls, the building managed to stay well illuminated in the day by the large hexagonal skylight windows in the ceiling. That architectural feature, along with the building itself crawling with an army of partisans, earned the Council of Justice and Partisan Administration Headquarters the nickname "The Hornet's Hive."

Fraenk and Brightrock approached a partisan half-elf woman with rat-brown hair and dull green eyes, who sat at the reception desk for the detention cells. She was reading a small book, its cover stamped with a silhouette of a strange-looking tower rising from between two hills, which she hastily clapped shut when she noticed their approach.

"See? What did I say? Got here with no trouble at all," Fraenk whispered.

"Helmar? Helmar! Get out here. It's the commander!" Rat Hair squealed out to someone behind her.

From around the corner where the latrine closet was located appeared a round-bellied half-elf man with a thinning sweep of dark hair and a weak chin. He was tucking his uniform shirt into his gray trousers and had a city news scroll crooked in the elbow of an arm.

Both looked too out of shape for any partisan job other than knocking around defenseless criminals on the detention wing.

The moment the lieutenant saw Arch Partisan Brightrock, an almost fearful expression passed over his face, and then he snapped to attention.

"Good afternoon, Arch Partisan, sir!" He barked. Rat Hair stood as well, but was less enthusiastic about it.

"Be at ease, Lieutenant..." Olywnn Brightrock said. The lieutenant relaxed his stance somewhat but continued to shoot worried looks at the female partisan.

"Ashblossom, sir. Helmar Ashblossom. We've met before," the partisan supervisor answered, a slight hint of recrimination in his tone. He then gestured to his counterpart. "And that's Sgt. Pinesprig, at your service."

"Very good," Brightrock replied stiltedly. An awkward silence began to stretch as Lt. Ashblossom waited for the commander to say or do something else. There seemed to be further protocol here, but whatever it was, Fraenk was at a loss. And to his trepidation, the half-elf supervisor seemed to tell something was amiss. Perhaps their faux Brightrock was being— *what? Too nice?*

"And what is the nature of your unexpected visit, sir?" Lt. Ashblossom inquired.

"Well, uh... We need to see a prisoner, Lieutenant. For questioning," Brightrock said, adjusting the seam of his uniform.

"Our interrogators are already seeing to that, sir," Ashblossom replied in a tone that suggested everything was in order and required no further attention.

"And who is your guest, sir?" Pinesprig gave Fraenk a suspicious once-over.

"Unfortunately, we're not allowed to have visitors in the detention wing. Matter of security," Ashblossom said, not even looking at Fraenk.

Fraenk could see the situation slipping out of hand. Somehow these two vermin were getting the better of him and the visage of the Arch Partisan. They needed to reassert authority here, but his counterpart seemed unpracticed in wielding unchecked power.

"I'm the Arch Preceptor of Blackroot, if you must know," Fraenk raised his voice. "And I am accompanied by your commander. I'm sure you can make an exception for him."

Brightrock stood silently, without picking up on Fraenk's obvious opening.

"No worries, sir. Just an oversight, I'm sure. We'll have him escorted out for you." Ashblossom shot his counterpart a sideways glance. "Sgt. Pinesprig, please call the duty partisan and have this human removed from the detention wing."

Pinesprig gave Fraenk a petulant smile and then waved her hand overhead to flag the attention of the guards down the hall. Fraenk shot Olwynn a worried look. The old elf seemed to be just standing there and smiling in a way that a boiled skull might.

"Neversleep is with me, Lieutenant," Brightrock said low. Ashblossom sighed as if he was just asked to carry a crate of fresh horse turds up the hill to the White Palace.

"Sir, we would need an authorization document stamped by the duty officer as the rules state—"

"And who makes those rules, ass-bottom?!" Brightrock snapped, spittle flecking from his open mouth. Ashblossom gaped in astonishment. It was Pinesprig who was still not grasping the situation and decided to stupidly wade in next.

"Well, the council of detention typically votes on—" She intoned.

"I make the rules, you troll-faced gobbet of Tiamat-scorched skywhale fat!" The Arch Partisan blazed.

Fraenk suppressed a laugh, quietly pleased to see Gwen finally settling into the grizzled elf's skin, so to speak.

"Now, we will see the prisoner without delay. Am I understood?" Brightrock glared at each of them in turn. The partisans both looked suitably admonished.

"Yes, sir," Lt. Ashblossom looked down in a sort of nervous, unhappy manner.

"The thief woman that was brought in this morning. What cell is she in?" Brightrock repeated.

From where he was standing, Fraenk noticed the woman give a furtive dart of her eyes to the detention cell's hallway.

Meanwhile, the lieutenant squinted in an exaggerated indication of recollection. Now Fraenk had the distinct impression that *these two* were the ones acting strange.

"Not sure as I recall anything about that, sir. Maybe she came in while I was away from my desk. I'd have to check our logs," Ashblossom said in a drawn sort of way.

He made an almost sluggish walk over to the desk where a large tome lay open and spun it towards him. There was definitely something odd about his behavior. Then Fraenk realized why.

"He's stalling," Fraenk murmured under his breath.

Brightrock could see it too. "Fraenk, check the book yourself."

"Sir, I-I really must insist that—" Ashblossom began to stammer out something and folded the book closed. Fraenk snatched it from his grasp and began quickly paging back to the open section.

"Hey! He can't do that!" Pinesprig protested.

"Not another word out of you!" Arch Partisan Olwynn Brightrock rounded on her.

Fraenk scanned quickly, but the entire day's entry logs were blank. Neither the name nor a description of her could be found. There were no entries at all, which seemed quite odd.

"She's not listed. There's apparently no one in the cells." Then Fraenk noticed something else. The page itself looked new and unmarred by inky smudges or stray marks. He shoved the book back at the red-faced half-elf.

"Where is she? Where's the woman?" Fraenk demanded.

The partisan guards exchanged a nervous glance with each other.

"So help me, if you don't tell me now, I'll have you manning a solitary watchtower in the Pale for the rest of your natural life!" Brightrock growled.

Pinesprig glared defiantly. Fraenk could see the threat had made an impact on Ashblossom, however. He understood the implications of a duty on that arcane frontier.

"Cell nine. But you're too late—" He blurted.

"You fool!" Pinesprig spat.

"You're relieved of duty. Both of you. Done!" Olwynn Brightrock snarled. "Leave your badges and get out of my sight! NOW!"

Ashblossom and Pinesprig both looked completely shocked. They both stood slowly, almost waiting for Brightrock to change his mind. But all they got was his searing glare and spittle blowing from the ruined hole in his mouth.

As Ashblossom passed him, Fraenk snatched the ring of keys from his belt.

"You have five minutes to be outside The Hornet's Hive, or I'm sending a squad to put you in cells with your least favorite prisoners," Brightrock snapped. That seemed to convince them. Both partisans took off down the corridor.

"What happened to not causing a scene?" Fraenk asked, coming out from around the desk. He paused, noticing a familiar folded pile of clothes beside the female guard's desk. "It occurs to me that it's way more fun to be the Arch Partisan than a scullery maid," Brightrock grinned.

"Don't get too comfortable," Fraenk said. "Come on. There's something foul going on. We need to hurry."

And they both took off down the cell block.

Kyla's vision was closing in and darkening around the edges. The rope ligature being pulled at her throat was cutting off nearly all of her circulation and breathing. She had fought at first. Thrashed. Tried to scream. Tried to fight. Her manacled hands were raw at the wrists where she struggled to pull free. Her feet thumped the floor, restrained by another chain loop, which kept her from standing or kicking out at the elf who was now choking her to death.

All she could do was tense the muscles in her neck and turn her head, trying to keep her airway open. Only a faint wheeze of air made it through, but it was enough to keep her conscious for now. She wanted to spit in his face, claw at his eyes, and destroy him entirely, but she was trapped. Her body tried to panic, or cry, or just shut down— but she knew she could do none of these things... not if she wanted to live. If this craven elf had been stronger, she might have been dead already, but she was determined not to be yet another victim of the Fernbrooks. Not after everything they did to her.

Bound as they were, her hands could only pull at the manacles that kept her from rescuing herself. She fought back in other ways, shifting her body position and keeping the thin elf from getting leverage on her. She was not going to make this easy for Farathiel Gingerglade.

"Stop moving... and die!" He grunted, struggling with the rope. One of his hands seemed to lack the strength to properly grip its side of the garrote.

Kyla wanted to scream and cry out, maybe bite a chunk out of his neck. Whatever she could do to stop him. But the toll and loss of oxygen were wearing her down. She would soon pass out, and he'd be able to finish her once and for all.

"We can't have you... telling them... what you know!" He strained. His thin fingers turning purple from the rope digging into them.

Her vision was growing dark and narrowing into a small circle. The strength in her body ebbing away. Her breath began to slow. And a strange feeling began to creep in. Like, maybe, it was time to relax. Stop fighting so hard. Accept it, and it would be all over. There was warmth in the darkness.

The sound in the room was growing out of focus, like everything was far away and underwater. She could hear pounding that could have been running footsteps. The dull metal jangle of keys and perhaps the lock clicking unlatched. Maybe that was all her mind's work, imagining somehow someone would come to save her.

Kyla felt the rope suddenly zip out from around her neck. Cool, sweet air immediately filled her lungs. She gasped and pitched forward. All she could do was breathe. Huge, gasping chestfuls of air. In and out. Tears streamed from her eyes. She coughed and gagged.

Then the noises around her began to pull back together. The door to the room was open, and someone was talking. He sounded older and familiar—not exactly a friend, but someone she could trust.

"... Gingerglade?!" an older man's voice exclaimed. The sound was sharp and painful to her ears.

"Sir? W-what are you doing here?" Farathiel stammered. "I should ask the same for you. What were you doing to that woman?"

"I-I was..." He cast about for an explanation.

If she could speak, she would have told the other person that this cowardly phalet was trying to murder her. But it took all her effort to just get air back into her body.

"—She was choking, sir. Tried to end her life instead of facing the council's justice."

"Is that so?" The older man's voice asked.

"...actually, can I have a private word, sir?" Gingerglade pitched his voice low and conspiratorial.

"You'd better explain yourself, and fast!"

She heard the two men's voices leave the room and trail off down the cell block.

They didn't shut the cell door; Kyla's thief instincts couldn't help but notice. If only her hands were free, she could escape. Or at least try. Anything was preferable to being quietly disposed of in this supposed sanctum of justice.

Then someone's hands were grabbing the manacles at her wrists. Kyla almost screamed. Then she had the giddy notion that she had somehow conjured a spirit to release her. Maybe this was Skylae, come to tilt the scale back in her favor. Or at least in the balance of order. She'd done way too many bad things to receive a random favor from any Power.

The first manacle clicked open, and she finally had the strength to raise her head to see who her unlikely rescuer was.

"Neversleep?" She rasped, her voice sounding raw and ragged.

"Sorry it took so long to pay you a visit. And about getting you tossed in here in the first place." Fraenk said, unlocking the other one. He took to opening the ankle chains on her as well.

"Gingerglade tried... to kill me..." She rubbed at her throat where the rope had dug into her skin.

"We need to talk, but we're out of time here." Fraenk said, checking back toward the door.

She stood, unsteady at first, but she could feel her strength quickly coming back to her legs and arms.

"So... You're my noble knight, come to rescue me?"

"Maybe just repay the favor for saving my life," Fraenk replied.

"I don't think they're just going to let me walk out of here. I tend to attract attention."

"I'm working on that. I wasn't prepared for a jailbreak." Fraenk tapped his lip and cast about the room, as if the answer was set in one of the blank corners. Then he looked at the bundle in his hand.

Fraenk set her folded clothes down on the interrogation table, followed by a familiar small bottle that they sold in the healer's temple. She immediately picked up her charmed boots and clutched them protectively. Then rifled through and made sure the gloves were there too.

"I've seen you climb." Fraenk said. "Can you make it?" He pointed up the smooth stone walls to the open skylight in the roof above.

Kyla was hurt, exhausted, and emotionally drained—but if there was one thing she could always summon the last bit of strength she possessed, it was for her to escape.

They met up two hours later at a rooftop apartment overlooking The Hornet's Hive that Fraenk rented under a false name from a senile elf woman who enjoyed feeding all the local skrates. It was her years of conditioning them into a semi-tame state that convinced Fraenk the wild creatures could be trained for his purposes in the first place. And when he had lulls in his day, he would often come here to work with them on the difficult task of seeking out different scents, based on where he wanted them to go.

This was also another secret place where he came when he needed to rest. Being _the_ Fraenk Neversleep took hard work and meant maintaining unusual hours, as well as showing up in different parts of the city at any given time. But keeping everyone guessing where you might appear next, not to mention the fear and doubt it created for those attempting to get away with something nefarious, was well worth it.

Fraenk poured himself a healthy glass from one of the decanters he had stashed in the room and sipped slowly on it as the afternoon rolled by. His favorite skrate, Keeks, arrived at some point and curled up to sleep on Fraenk's chest. He could feel a fresh breeze from the lake, carrying many smells of the city with it. Smoke, cooking meat, and roasting fish. Salt and spices like cinnamon, rosemary, dragon's tongue, and sage. Even hints of some of the less appealing odors, like manure and dung, moldy wood, and the sweet tang of rot. That was the city, though. Good and ill. Light and dark. Those who choose to see one or the other could find it. And for all that this place had put him through and all the times he nearly died because of it, Fraenk found himself feeling an appreciation, joy even, for Arathes. He loved it here and couldn't imagine living anywhere else.

When he had last seen the counterfeit Olwynn Brightrock, he was having Farathiel Gingerglade strip-searched by a squad of partisans before slipping away on some other supposedly urgent matter. And not a moment too soon because Fraenk had passed the real Arch Partisan just as he was making a quiet exit through the main lobby.

"Welcome back, sir," The partisan at the reception counter gave the true Brightrock a surprised double-take as he passed. Fraenk had just enough time to slip into the back of a group of elven bureaucrats on their way out the doors. Arch Partisan Brightrock nodded to the one who greeted him, then moved on without breaking his stride. Although nothing on his gnarled face suggested he noticed Neversleep was there, Fraenk didn't breathe easy again until he was two blocks away from the Hornet's Hive.

Back on the rooftop with the skrate rumbling contentedly on his chest, Fraenk felt like he had just closed his eyes, letting the warm rays glow red on his eyelids, when a tall shadow blocked out the sun.

"I thought you never sleep. Hence, the name." Kyla said.

"It's got a better ring to it than Fraenk Sleeps-on-Occasion-But-He's-Still-Vigilant." He quipped and popped one eye open to look.

"I see your point." She stepped out of the way again, and Fraenk was blasted in the eyes by sunlight. He visored his face with a forearm and sat up. Perhaps he had slept. He definitely felt rested. Keeks was already gone.

Fraenk saw she was wearing her dark suit—the one she had been arrested in—but also had a drape of fabric over it that was the same tan color as the surrounding buildings.

"What's with the drapery?" Fraenk asked. "Less noticeable when I'm climbing up the side of a building," Kyla took another glass from beside the decanter and tipped herself a healthy pour.

"Makes sense." Fraenk drained his last bit and matched her.

He examined the cup for a moment, then looked over at her. Her face was in rougher shape than the last time he'd seen it, but she was still incredibly beautiful.

"Are we drinking to something?" He asked.

"The fiery death of every Fernbrook—chopped into small chunks and fed to dogs, their district burned, leaving not a single stone stacked on another, their names stricken from every scroll or book ever written."

"Pretty thorough. I mean, I would have settled for us winning and them losing—maybe Farathiel getting a bad case of 'dagger to the lungs.'" Fraenk shrugged.

"They deserve it all and worse!" Kyla said with a fiery intensity.

"I can't argue," he said, raising his glass. "And may the skrates use the ashes for their kitty soil." Kyla actually cracked a smile at this. They clinked glasses and drank. She then sat and looked him directly in the eyes. He did his best to match her gaze, but it was difficult.

"How did you know so much about us? At the lighthouse. You knew we stole the necklace back from the Fernbrooks."

"Made sense, I guess," Fraenk said, feeling a flush of pride. Shockingly, few people appreciated his work, despite how they benefited from it—but that also was a function of the job itself. "Why else would the Fernbrooks be putting so much effort and expense into finding some kobold?"

Fraenk saw her expression cloud over, and she looked away. There was a much deeper story there than he could imagine.

"You... loved him," Fraenk said, not unkindly.

"Not like some might suggest, but yes," she said and took another drink. "He helped me when I needed someone most."

"Where did you get the Mind Thief from in the first place?"

She grinned mischievously. "That part is a longer story for another time, I'm afraid."

Kyla drained her glass and then added a bit more.

"Then what convinced you to do the job?" Fraenk asked. "The Fernbrooks must have said they needed it for something."

"Old Fernbrook is too clever to involve himself directly, but this is unmistakably his parade," she said somberly. "We cut the bargain with an intermediary to Gingerglade and thought it was enough to keep us safe, but they found the broker. And then they knew where to commence."

"To what purpose, though? We need to figure out why he wanted it. More importantly, what he planned to do once he had his hands on it," Fraenk said, tapping a nail on the rim of his cup. "His plans are still in motion, Neversleep. Or he wouldn't have risked killing me in the Partisan cells just now."

"This goes beyond that blistered old spike in possession of a magical trinket. His dark purpose still uncoils itself. And he'll keep piling up bodies to get to it." Kyla pulled a black ribbon from her wrist and began to truss up her golden hair. "I suppose the only thing we can do is stop him."

"Oh no you don't!" Fraenk set down the glass and gave her a warning look. "You've been in enough trouble lately. I think you need to sit back and let me handle this."

Kyla crossed her arms and smirked.

"So, where is the Ynne es Tylubourne right now?"

"Right where I want it. The Royal Museum of Arathes."

"Where in the building? What wing? What display? How many guards? Have you ever even stolen anything of this value before?"

"I lift Lady Blackroot's booze all the time. Her distillery room is a treasury of liquid gold," Fraenk arched a mischievous eyebrow.

"You need my help."

"I can't be responsible for putting you in danger again. You're free now. They don't even know to come looking for you because in his effort to kill you, the fool Gingerglade had them keep any record of you off the ledger. You can just walk away," Fraenk said, standing. "I'll just have to figure it out on my own."

"Neversleep, why do something poorly on your own when you have an expert thief offering to help do it right?"

"Yeah, and what would the expert suggest?" Fraenk asked. Kyla Gracefire only smiled and slipped on her enchanted gloves.

Part VI

30

"**N**ow, let's go over this one last time. We're in the Main Hall here. The loop is the connecting hallway, where each of the twelve elven families has their own dedicated atriums—don't worry about those. Upstairs are paintings, sculptures, and other artwork, including divinely inspired statuary. To the rear, the armory and war spoils, including arms and armor of legendary heroes and enemies of old. Blink if you're still with me— close enough."

"Here's where *we'll* be: the downstairs levels where all the treasures, priceless artifacts, and items of an arcane nature are kept— including the museum's most recent acquisition, the stolen necklace of Fernbrook courtesy of Arch Partisan Brightrock. It is the most heavily guarded portion of the building. Each exhibit is checked every hour, and patrols every half hour, without fail or exception."

"The only way in and out is these stairs; this place might as well be the bank. According to official records, no one has ever successfully stolen from the Royal Museum of Arathes. And it's our job to make sure it stays that way. Did you get all that, Leafwater?"

Doran Leafwater nodded. His face must have shown how completely lost he was because Guard Sergeant Summersbane fixed him with a skeptical look and then shook his head.

"This ain't Dwarven engineering work on the Main Lift, Leafwater! It's guard duty. I'm sure you'll figure it out." Summersbane barked and gave his bristly mustache a tug—an unconscious habit Doran noticed about this imposing and unpleasant half-elf— then turned on his heel and marched briskly towards the stairs.

"... or your mother can land you another choice job somewhere else." Doran heard him mutter under his breath.

Doran was still taking in the impressive main hall, which featured massive carvings of the first four monarchs of Sarmatti and one of the original ballistas used to fire giant arrows down on the invading human army in the famed elven defense of the city centuries ago. It looked in surprisingly good shape, possibly even ready to fire, with a wicked-looking barbed shaft already loaded in the trench. Leafwater briefly imagined himself up there all those years ago, lining up an ugly human in the foresight and sending a bolt down to crunch through armor, flesh, and bone. Suddenly realizing he was alone, Doran turned to see the sergeant wasn't waiting for him and was already starting down the stairs. He scampered to catch up.

Doran Leafwater, former lieutenant of the Arathes partisans, Blackroot District, was now in his new role as Guard Third-Class, Royal Museum of Arathes. His training supervisor, Sergeant Summersbane, enjoyed being a monocratic blowhard, living vicariously through the history of his betters and their artifacts around him. Nevertheless, Doran was finding this position overall more to his liking. At least he no longer had to deal with the insufferable Hobb or that equally repugnant preceptor who somehow managed to bring calamity in his wake wherever he went. He took an unfair share of scrutiny after that deranged elf—who was in custody already for a crime—was killed under Doran's watch. Then proceeding the incident with the two blackhounds, which he was very nearly killed by, and no one else seemed the least bit sympathetic; half of them didn't even believe him. Doran decided he needed to find a different and much safer line of work.

There were aspects of the partisan service that he did enjoy. The instant and unquestioned authority over others. The stylish uniforms. A presupposed respect for him as an individual from anyone he encountered—this last bit was probably the most elusive still. Nevertheless, Doran found that being a guard would still cover the aforementioned benefits while giving him the calm assuredness of patrolling a quiet, dusty, unfrequented museum. No one cared about history anymore, it seemed. This, he found, was actually much preferable to being a partisan and all that, tolerating annoying humans with their pointless, needy calls for help all the time.

A change in occupation had been warranted for another reason, which Doran was unwilling to discuss with anyone else. He had become a laughingstock and a target of ridicule after a completely understandable loss of bowels in reaction to his near mauling by arcane demon dogs. Certainly anyone in that position might have done the same or worse. Nevertheless, he was unable to regain authority amongst his subordinates after that.

Doran suppressed his disgust and had to once again call upon the most powerful and formidable resource at his disposal—his mother. This was an indignity nearly equal to his accidental trouser soiling, but if he ever wanted to be taken seriously by his peers ever again, it was something he would have to endure. And given the way she relentlessly gnawed at him after he made his quite reasonable request that she use her influence to find him another equally or better job, Doran wondered if there wasn't a hint of the hellhound in her as well.

But in the end she came through and ear-pulled amongst her social circle until she secured him this choice spot on the museum guard staff. Granted, he had to take a serious demotion coming in, but considering the abuse he had to endure as a lieutenant partisan, having less responsibility was far better. The job itself was as untaxing as one could possibly find anywhere in the city. Perhaps only the attendants to the Monarch's Silver Eternity Tree in the Summer Palace had an easier job. Doran's duties included walking the length of a hallway twice an hour and enduring the insufferable prattling of a self-proclaimed historian supervisor. Leafwater hoped that at the end of his trial period, he'd be rid of this loquacious half-elf and his windbag expositions about *this* elven general or *that* clever politician— not to mention his downright near-treasonous dissertations on how the failed warlord Kreeg could have actually maximized his military's potential and swept the kingdom of Tigraen for himself. As if anyone in this realm or the next could have withstood the extra-worldly intervention of a deiform celestial in battle.

Doran found it best to make noises of agreement and wait until the storm of mule-sloss abated. Then he could get back to his own thoughts of where he might eat at the end of his shift or when it might be suitable to approach Lady Bellspire about a potential courtship with her sixth daughter, Siphanien. While she did bear that distinctive, overly large, pointed nose and fierce brows that some uncharitably dubbed her the 'Egret of Justice,' Doran felt like he could overlook these superficial exterior matters to really get to know the dull and humorless person she was inside. It was certainly preferable to living with his mother—even in spite of what his friends had hurtfully suggested: he'd essentially be marrying another version of her. *What did they know?* They were jealous because he had prospects of marrying above his station. They should all be so lucky.

Doran caught up to Summersbane at the bottom level of the museum. He was just wrapping up some mindless prattling story, which Doran had missed the entirety of. Perhaps it had been a retroactive critique of how Tiamat, the nine-headed dragon, could have bested the giant, Gromm, and kept the world forever plunged in endless darkness and chaos. Doran doubted it was important.

"...which is why we never venture into that corridor, unless you want to be dead. Did you get all that, Leafwater?" Summersbane snapped, turning to find Doran dutifully beside him.

"Got it, sir," Doran lied. Whatever the half-elf had been going on about, he'd probably pick up eventually or, more likely, never really have to deal with. It was best to placate the sergeant until he grew tired of lecturing. If it really mattered, the sergeant was sure to repeat it many, many times.

Doran glanced down the hallway where orderly rows of busts and pedestals, all bearing magical artifacts, were kept. They glittered or gave off a faint sheen under the flickering light of the torches in sconces on the wall.

"This is it then, sir?"

"Greatest public display of magical items anywhere," Summersbane boasted. "Go on. Have a look."

Doran walked down the corridor amongst the surprisingly prosaic exhibit of magical or cursed artifacts on display. Each bore a placard with a mundane explanation of why it was present in this collection. A large jeweled necklace was noted that kept its wearer young in appearance. An enchanted coin pouch that magically retrieved any coin taken from it. A brass cube with arcane writing that is said to be a doorway to a world of monsters. An ordinary pipe-whistle is rumored that if you play it, every rabbit in the forest would come seek you out. Further down there was furniture, mirrors, and even the silhouette outline of a statue of a woman. It made Leafwater wonder what impish inclination possessed wizards so they would create such strange objects.

"What if people try to... touch them?" Doran asked, knowing immediately from the sergeant's expression that it was a dumb question, but one he answered more often than any other.

"If someone's got wandering fingers? *Ho-ho*. What do you think? What do you imagine happens? Maybe you'd like to try it and see? Go ahead, Leafwater. Take the ring right there. It'll make you as strong as five men. Go on! I won't bark."

Whatever this pedantic exercise was, Doran Leafwater was already disliking it. But he also knew the sergeant wouldn't let up. Doran slowly and reluctantly reached out. He could see nothing there between his fingertips and the item, but before he could touch the ring, a thin wall of energy appeared, sending a lively jolt up his arm. Doran jerked his hand back as Sergeant Summersbane cackled.

"Warding spells on each one! You should see the sparks fly when the society elves bring their little gooey-fingered brats in here. *Ho-ho-ho!* Gotta pinch yourself to keep from laughing, I tell ya!"

Doran did not find it amusing to be shocked and then laughed at. But he supposed that answered more of what he was really interested in: could someone walk up and steal one of these items? If he was supposed to be guarding them, how difficult of a task was this going to be? Would Doran be constantly having to keep an eye on each tiny bauble or trinket? That seemed maddening. He was relieved that the museum did employ the latest and most secure methods of keeping valuables from theft. As far as Doran knew, warding spells of protection could only be defeated by a powerful wizard.

With that concern out of the way, something the half-elf had said bubbled to the surface of Doran's mind, perhaps by virtue of the fact that it happened in the district where he formerly served. And it would hopefully distract the boorish oaf from his continued mirth at Doran's expense.

"Sergeant, so what's this about a stolen necklace? Was it the one that was nicked by a Lynblood woman and her kobold in Blackroot? I used to work there, you know..."

"Ah, so you have been paying attention," Summersbane smiled, equally pleased and impressed. Inexplicably, Doran found himself warmed by this man's approval. The sergeant leaned in and began to whisper conspiratorially, despite the fact that there was no other guard in view or within earshot.

"But you've got the details all wrong, my boy," Summersbane continued in an excited tone. "So as I hears it... Old Lord Fernbrook takes up with this half-exalted mistress. Sparks and sorcery! But the old long toes ain't good enough—can't keep the points of his ears up, if you follow my trail. She's got a wandering eye and an inferno between the shanks. *Ho-ho!* So, the mistress catches an eye for their dimwit <u>kobold</u> servant, if you can believe that. She tricks the little glob into stealing the lord's family treasures so as they can abscond to distant shores. The partisans catch up with them in a love nest at the lighthouse tower, and there's a wizard's duel like no other! The kobold firin' bolts of thunder at the two Arcane Lords who come to subdue 'em. They hit him with spell after spell, but he's gotta be possessed by a warlock specter or something. Finally, they go with the heavy old magic that they're not even supposed to use— *but this kobold won't go down.* They combine an explosive flame spell with an arcane blood retraction... and *BOOM!* Chunks of kobold go flying everywhere! The lady half-exalt sees her lover die right in front of her, spattered in his gore, and goes completely mad. She tosses herself right out of the tower onto the jagged rocks below. Two young lives meet a violent end. All because of the necklace."

"A kobold used magic?" Doran asked, skeptical. "He... was one of those trained ones..." Summersbane blustered after a pause. "Astounding," Doran admitted. He was aware that a small portion of what the sergeant had said was most likely a fabrication, but still a compelling yarn nonetheless.

"And so the Arch Partisan himself comes in with the necklace and tells us it most likely belonged here in the first place, and we were to keep it secure," Sergeant Summersbane said with no small amount of bravado.

"And we've got it on display," Doran said, looking impressed.

"Brand's Bond," Summersbane drew a circle over his heart and tapped three times.

Curiosity already had its claws into Doran, and the complete story only made it more compelling. He had to see this fabled jewelry that could fracture a High Lord's house and cause such a dramatic end to two lives. He perversely hoped that it made no end of trouble for that nasty human preceptor who worked there as well. If they never crossed paths again in the half-elf's significantly long lifetime, it would be far too soon.

Doran started down the hall through the exhibits.

"Ah, don't worry about it now, Leafwater. Rounds aren't for another twenty," Sergeant Summersbane said irritably.

"I just want to lay eyes on it."

"Find your way, then," the half-elf said but made no further exertion to dissuade his subordinate. Instead, he propped himself in a chair with a dusty tome about the decline of the Pileusian empire and lit a long-stemmed pipe.

"So it's where?"

"Down at the far end of the hall there," he replied, irritated to be interrupted.

"Past the woman statue?"

"There's no woman statue, ya slab."

The sergeant was right. The dark woman's statue was not there— although Doran could have sworn he'd seen it earlier. He strode down through the torchlit hall, visually noting each item in more detail and moving on when it wasn't the one he was looking for.

Then he arrived at a polished stone bust in the shape of a disembodied upper torso without a head. There was no placard or signage for this item. For a long moment, Doran wondered what kind of cursed or magical artifact this marble section of a body might be. He finally realized, upon seeing more identical carvings all proffering necklaces and jewelry, that it was merely an empty display bust. This one had been set up to display something, but whatever that was, the necklace in question wasn't there.

"Sergeant?" Doran Leafwater called down the corridor. "Are you sure it's supposed to be here?"

"Ho-ho, Leafwater. Very droll," Summersbane called without looking up from his book. "You make the same jest that every greenie recruit does in their first week. *'Oh, something's been stolen. Help!'* and expect me to jump up and come running. Try harder than that!"

"You don't care then?" Doran called. "What if it was actually stolen?"

"Don't be daft! Now, if I have to get up and come down there. Pray to Mersey that you are correct, Leafwater!" He shot back, tugging so hard at his mustache that Doran expected it to come off in his hand.

"Very well, sir," Doran replied. "I'm only trying to do my duty."

Doran received no acknowledgement but could tell that his dropping the issue entirely was more irritating than if he persisted. The sergeant stared at his book for several moments, unable to read, until finally snapping it shut.

"Fine! I will look. But may Gromm help you if you're japing me, Leafwater."

The sergeant stomped down the hallway up to where he was standing. He angrily scanned Doran head-to-toe first before turning to the empty display bust.

"This is incorrect," Summersbane said, nodding too fast for it to be friendly. "Well, where is it??"

"I—I don't know," Doran stepped backward as his supervisor seemed confused and irritated. He looked around the floor below the pedestal. He checked the other displays, apparently thinking the necklace had just been misplaced.

"WHERE IS IT?" Summersbane shouted, ready to explode. He was pulling so hard at his mustache that hairy fibers of it began to come off in his fingers.

"I—I don't know!"

"You're not playing some jest on me, boy, are you?!"

"I'm the one who told you it was missing!" Doran shouted back, suddenly angry at being blamed for this calamity, whatever it was. As the sergeant was scouring the floors, Doran noticed beside the display bust a small brass item that looked like an orb with several spokes coming off of it in a circle. He reached out to touch it.

"Careful, you fool, you'll hit the—" Summersbane began to say, but Doran's fingers passed right inside the area where the ward spell should have been. Nothing happened to him. The ward was not there.

"Sir, what happened to the ward?" The sergeant asked, incredulous.

"What is this?" Doran picked up the brass orb. It was warm in his hand.

"Let me see that!" Sergeant Summersbane snatched it from him.

"Sir, what if someone did steal the necklace?" Doran dared to ask.

"But... we've *never* been robbed!" Summersbane replied in disbelief.

Doran watched him expectantly. There should be some Royal Museum Guard protocol for this— if there was, it had not been shared with him yet. If Doran had still been in the partisan service, he would have blown his whistle and brought the reinforcements. But the Guards had no such whistle. They had clubs and lanterns. Neither seemed suited for raising an alarm.

"It makes no sense!" The sergeant pinched the orb in his fingers. "How did they defeat the—"

A bright flare of light and release of electricity surged from the metal ball. Sergeant Summersbane's body went completely stiff, and he grunted like a man trying to hoist a barrel of wine.

"Sir?!" Doran began to reach for the half-elf but then thought better. Jolts of energy were still flooding through his body, and Doran did not want to be the next victim. Doran pulled his wooden club and tapped up underneath the man's hands. The ball went sailing upward, and Summersbane was released from the electricity's effect. He collapsed on the floor, smelling faintly of burnt hair.

"Sir! Sir, what do we do?" Doran asked more forcefully this time. But the sergeant could only mumble incoherently.

Just then a cry— a scream, to be more precise—came from somewhere above in the museum. Doran looked up.

"Help! Someone! HELP!!" Doran shouted. He took his club and whacked it loudly against the wall as he ran back toward the stairs. He hoped the sound would carry up to the other patrolling guards. And they would know what to do.

But he skidded as he arrived at the foot of the staircase. A strange, thin mist of fog was billowing down, slow and inexorable. That definitely wasn't supposed to happen here. A sickly fear and panic hit, making his bladder clench uncomfortably. He fought the sensation back.

"HELP SOMEONE! SUMMERSBANE IS DOWN, AND WE'VE BEEN ROBBED!" Doran bellowed up the large open staircase.

He heard shouts above. But they were indecipherable. Like a man commanding something, but his authority sounded nervous and unsteady. Rising like it was trying to stave off a—

Another scream and a different sound that was much deeper and more animalistic. Then came the echoing clatter of a wood club on the stone floor. Then heavy thumps, like a sack of flour being tossed against the wall. The man's cries became faster and more urgent, then stopped very abruptly.

"Someone's up there," Doran realized in sickening fear. "Someone... or some*thing*."

His mind conjured images of the blackhounds. Maybe they were back and coming for him. Doran turned and looked around for a way to escape. Of course, this was the museum, and there was no other way out.

"Sergeant?!" Doran looked down the hallway and saw his sergeant was still lying on the floor, moving weakly.

Someone had to do something, Doran thought. But who would catch the thieves? Who could stop whatever was happening on the floors above? Who could save him?

But then a strange calm settled over him at the realization— no one was coming. No other person or force would sweep in to protect him from this. The only one who could do anything now... was him. *Doran SKARKING Leafwater.*

Then a resolute voice inside him said, *Live or die, you need to do something.* "Don't worry, sir. I'm going for help," Doran said with a giddy, reckless confidence.

He gripped the club and raised it. Charging forth through the mist, Doran Leafwater ascended the stairs and into that unnatural creeping fog.

31

Despite the panic and his pounding heartbeat, Doran Leafwater felt a bit ridiculous as he charged up the stairs bearing only his small cudgel. He just left behind an entire collection of magical items—of course they were all secured by those annoying ward spells, so he wouldn't have been able to wield any of them anyways. And come to think on it, what was he supposed to do against whatever assailant awaited above—appear eternally youthful? Perhaps attack with an army of adorable bunnies? Perhaps there were more substantial weapons on the floors above. He did see a wicked-looking trident on the wall near the entrance.

The ominous fog only became denser as he ascended. Doran quickly realized that he probably should have some kind of plan for when he reached the main hall. It wouldn't do to arrive and stand there, stick in hand, deciding what his next action would be.

Remembering his partisan training, the first rule was whenever a situation arose that required more than a sharp word or tap with the club to settle, then it was time to get others involved. The partisans' strength was not in the individual but the might of the collective. The Royal Museum guards had to be the same. Perhaps even now, the brave and intrepid souls who worked here were rallying a—

Another scream from above and the sound of a man dying. Doran's legs gave an unconscious wobble. His imagined scenario where he mustered the guards and bravely led a sortie out to smash the unfortunate miscreant intruder was quickly being replaced with a plan that involved far less heroics and a lot more of him sneaking his way out the nearest exit.

None of these crusty artifacts seemed worth losing his life over. Yes, running away was a clear winner as far as ideas went. And it wasn't really an act of cowardice but merely a strategic retreat. A chance to regroup and return with a show of force. Maybe bring along a few paladins or Arcane Lords. Then they'd have numerical superiority. And best of all, he wouldn't be in charge anymore.

Then he remembered: the Royal Museum had its own dedicated Arcane Lord. The old coot was as ancient as half the items in the place— so old, in fact, that some of the things there were probably his. They could have set the wizard up in a vestibule and considered him part of the permanent collection. Granted, the only time Doran had met the elf wizards, he was asleep at his writing desk, his long, thin, silvery hair spread out, looking like actual cobwebs on an old piece of furniture. Doran hadn't even gotten the fellow's name— an oversight he was going to correct the moment this fracas was over. An Arcane Lord, no matter the age, was not one to be trifled with.

So what if the venerated elder had slipped into a more scholarly role at the museum? Doran believed he must still be able to cast a searing fireball like the rest of them. Even an Arcane Lord put out to pasture, so to speak, must still be dangerous. One had to maintain their license and annual competence test with the Registry to even be allowed to use magic, let alone bear the title of Arcane Lord. He may be old, but he was still a wizard, and _he_ would know what to do.

Doran rounded the corner and had one more set of stairs to climb. He could see a thick fog in the main hall flowing down like a gray, ethereal river. He could hear sounds above, heavy clumps and a reedy hissing. There was also a metallic *hsscht, hsscht* of plate armor in motion. Had an armored knight also arrived to mount a defense? That gave Doran even more fortitude. A knight and an Arcane Lord, battling some nefarious foe. This was something Doran wanted to see.

He quickened his pace, taking two stairs at a time, eager to not want to miss a sword blow nor a spell of this duel. Then his foot came down on something round, like a soft helmet or a mossy stone, and Doran stumbled. He landed hard and barked his hip against the nosing of the step. Wincing in pain, he looked back in time to see a head with pointed ears and trailing bloody strings of silvery hair go bouncing down the stairs and disappear into the fog. It brought to mind the old Arcane Lord.

"Huh. I didn't know wizards could take off their heads like that." Doran mused distantly.

He rose again, limping this time, and came to the main level.

The entire scene was vastly different from when he'd first arrived earlier that night. All the torches were extinguished, casting the entire Main Hall in an eerie bluish pallor—the bioluminescent blue mushrooms that grew in small clumps on the walls and ceiling preventing the room from being plunged into total darkness. The heavy mist or fog that he had experienced on the stairs was now thick up to a man's chest in this room. It had a fishy, lake water-type odor to it, acrid and tinged with a hint of algae. It gave every surface it touched an off-putting moistness.

Doran scanned over the foggy room for ally or foe. There were the tall statues, the ballista, and the other exhibits and displays—a stand holding the famous trident, Thunderspike, spear of Theomar Skywillow; the beautiful set of star-weave robes from Queen Gwencalon Silverstream; and the Frost Armor of Ulast Stonethrower, a fearsome half-giant general who led bloody raids into Sarmatti. The dim light revealed not a living soul, but he could still hear the slide of the armor and a sort of snuffling, wheezing bellows. It sounded like the labored breathing of the oxen that pulled the carts laden with stone from the depths of the city. Enormous lungs pumping air in and out.

If he could find that knight, maybe he knew what had transpired and what they should do next.

"Sir?" Doran called. "Good sir knight. We need your help—"

A hand clapped hard over his mouth. Doran had just enough time to see the half-giant's armor rise and turn suddenly before he was jerked bodily off his feet and back into the mist.

When he was finally convinced that the young elf had calmed his thrashing and attempts to scream long enough to listen, Fraenk slowly peeled his hand away from Doran Leafwater's mouth. He raised two fingers to his lips again, reinforcing the imperative to remain silent. When Doran registered who had grabbed him, his eyes went wide.

"*Neversleep!*" He hissed in a whisper. "By the Powers, what are you doing here?!"

"That doesn't matter right now. Keep your voice down, or that thing is going to find us." Fraenk growled back.

They heard the large creature's weight shift, feet thumping and armored plates sliding on each other. Fraenk and Doran both silently turned their heads to look.

Across the Main Hall, the normally unoccupied Frost Armor of Ulast was being worn by something. The particular dimensions of its body were not the same as a half-giant— it was broad at the shoulders and arms but tapered down to thin wrists and ankles with pointed, spidery digits. The creature had a flat, wide head that was owl-like with two massive luminescent eyes that glowed a faint pink, each one the size of a man's head. Beneath them, a segmented jaw rocked open and shut, full of triangular, serrated teeth, stained and dripping with blood. A smoky mist rolled off the armor itself as the warm, humid air was being actively turned into fog.

Both men remained crouched, motionless, as the creature scanned the Main Hall. The surrounding fog seemed particularly thin. They were caught out, like mice in a field, as the falcon soared above. Long moments passed. The creature cocked its head, scanning with all of its senses. Then, after an elf's lifetime, the beast finally turned and clumped off into the darkness.

"What is that thing, Neversleep?" Doran breathed, more terrified now than accusatory.

"I can't be sure, but I think it's an eldritch shadescourge wearing haunted armor," Fraenk replied.

"But what is it doing in this museum?!"

"I don't know! I don't work here!" Fraenk shot back. Both men crept backward until they could safely hide behind the enormous carved marble figure of Monarch Broridir Bluemount, perched jauntily on the deck boards of a ship.

"So what exactly are you doing in the museum at night, Neversleep?" Doran demanded.

"I got word about a possible theft, so I came to investigate," Fraenk said. "And I'm offended by any implications to the contrary."

Just then, a dark female form melted from the fog beside Fraenk. She was dressed head to toe in her thieves' gear, complete with the mask that hid all but her eyes.

"Fraenk, I got the necklace! We have to get out of here! But there's a huge—" Kyla whispered quickly, then looked over to see the guard, Doran Leafwater, on his other side. She pulled her mask down and smiled sheepishly. "Hello, who's your friend?"

"Doran Leafwater. He's a guard now... apparently?" Fraenk said. "Doran, this is Kyla. She's an independent nocturnal jewelry appraiser. We came to make sure all the valuables here were authentic. Did everything meet your approval, Kyla?"

"I'm satisfied. Impressed even," She nodded.

"But she's dressed like a thief." Leafwater said accusingly. Looking at her eyes, Fraenk noticed his scowl soften. Apparently her effect worked on others too.

"We'll just be going now. Good luck with the shadescourge, Doran. I hear the claws and absolutely everything else about them can be quite deadly."

"You can't just leave me here!" Doran locked onto Fraenk's arm in a panicked grab.

"Well, we might be able to help you, but we're really not supposed to be here this late. We could get in trouble."

"I won't say anything! Please!!" Doran pleaded.

Fraenk gave Kyla a look—*do we trust this guy?* She considered and then shrugged.

"Very well, Leafwater," Fraenk said. "But if we get busted, I'm telling everyone you were in on it too."

"Thank you, Neversleep! Thank you!" he breathed, almost collapsing from relief.

Fraenk poked his head out and looked around. He heard a crash and clatter come from the Hall of Heroes. The shadescourge was somewhere back there, destroying valuable pieces of elven history. He turned to see Kyla spying with him. There was something magical about the way the blue glow of mushroom lights danced across her face. She was inexpressibly lovely. Her eyes found his, blinking large and luminous. Her dark lashes, like the delicate wings of a butterfly.

"You're staring again."

Fraenk blinked, quickly looking away. He silently scolded himself for getting caught up in her alluring charms. It had to have been some magical influence that the Lynbloods possessed, which entranced any who gazed upon them for too long.

"I wasn't staring. I... was just wondering if your entire heist plan consisted of leaving me behind so you could go steal the necklace alone?" Fraenk demanded.

"Naturally. You only would've gotten in my way. And I got it, didn't I?" She patted the pocket at her hip.

"You know, there is such a thing as teamwork..."

She smirked back at him, giving one of those annoyingly cute smiles.

"So what do you think, Fraenk? What's a shadescourge doing here in the city? I've only read about them in books."

"As have I. They've supposedly got a weakness to large amounts of spriteweave flower extract."

"Simple then. I'll go pick the flowers, and you fire up the distillery," she quipped.

Another loud crash echoed through the hall. They could hear an empty helmet go clattering across the floor. The shadescourge unleashed an otherworldly howl.

"Hmm. As much as I like that plan… any other possibilities that are actually feasible?" Kyla asked.

"Well, sometimes the simple is what's best. I say we make a run for it. The beastie is way over there. We just head right for the door. He can't viciously dismember all three of us, right?"

"I don't like this plan!" hissed Doran.

"You're only saying that because you're the slowest," Fraenk replied.

Just as Fraenk was finished speaking, another figure appeared at the top of the stairs. It was a disheveled older half-elf guard with a mustache that was curiously thin on one side.

"Hello! Who's there??" The guard bellowed, his voice caroming off of the cavernous ceiling and walls.

"Sir! No! Be quiet! It will hear you!" Leafwater whispered as loud as he dared.

But it was already too late. Fraenk watched as hateful, glowing pink orbs emerged through the fog. The guard saw it as well. He stammered something high-pitched and incomprehensible and then made a heroically tragic headlong dash for the main exit. The shadescourge caught him in three easy bounds. The fog hid most of it, but there was screaming, and it didn't last for very long. Fraenk and Kyla looked at each other.

"What's our third option?" She asked.

For long minutes, the trio waited in silence, listening to the terrible creature feed. Fraenk's eyes continued to go back to the oversized crossbow-like elven ballista on display in the main hall. It was centuries old. It could just as easily break as actually fire a bolt. Perhaps the curators had even disabled its ability to launch an arrow at all. But if anything had the power to stop that unhallowed creature, it would be this weapon.

Fraenk was fairly certain he could creep out to it without alerting the beast. There was a bronze-pointed wooden shaft that looked like a man-sized arrow already loaded in the trough. Unfortunately, the bowstring was in the forward slack position, meaning he would have to carefully and quietly ratchet back the draw. Then it would be ready to fire. He'd still need to aim and pray that the ancient bolt could actually punch through magically enchanted armor. Oh, and he'd also need someone else to help work the two-man crank on the ballista's ratchet mechanism.

"Whatever you're planning to do, I don't like it," Kyla said, watching him.

"You're staring again." Fraenk said and winked at her.

"I'm serious, Fraenk."

"Doran and I are going to have a talk with Frosty. Ask it politely to leave. You get the necklace to safety, got it?"

"What? That's a terrible plan."

"Just wait until it's distracted and go. Maybe send for help if any of us are still alive."

Fraenk turned to his other side and grabbed Doran, who was fixed on the gruesome scene, silently gibbering to himself.

"It ate the sergeant... it ate the sergeant..." Doran murmured in shock and terror.

"Good news then, Doran. You've been promoted." Fraenk replied, pulling the elf in close. "Listen, I think we can best this creature, but I need your help. We may both die, but I promise to let it eat me first."

"*What?*" Doran's mouth curdled.

"Just listen. We're gonna shoot it with that huge arrow right there. See it?" Fraenk pointed the elf's head toward the ballista. "I just need your help drawing back the bowstring. Rotate the handle, and I'll do the rest."

"You can kill this thing?" Doran whimpered.

"We'll nail it to the door! And *you'll* get all the credit." Fraenk gripped his shoulder encouragingly. "A hero! Savior of Arathes... or at least the museum. They'll probably dedicate a new wing to you, Leafwater. Everyone in the city will be hailing your name."

"They will?"

"They won't unless you help me. Now, let's go," Fraenk said, and was heartened to see Doran crouch low to follow him. Fraenk looked back to confer with Kyla, but she was already gone. He quickly scanned the room, but with the dim light and all the fog, it was impossible to see where she was. And besides, there was no time—the creature would finish its meal soon and they would be next.

Fraenk motioned to the elf and they both crept out into the middle of the hall. They could see through the fog where the creature was tearing chunks of flesh from the unfortunate sergeant. It ate with energetic gulps, tearing away new bits with its fearsome jaws.

Without prompting, Fraenk and Doran fell in on either side of the ballista and grabbed their respective handles together. Fraenk nodded, and slowly, painfully slowly, they began to apply tension on the gear. It gave easily at first, drawing in the slack on the old ropes. They seemed tremendously frail to Fraenk's eyes, like they could snap at any moment. But it was all too late to stop now.

Fraenk and Doran drew steadily on the handles until finally the gear began to get hard to turn. Instinctively, they both pulled steadily, slowing as the first gear ratcheted into place. It made a loud *CLUNK*.

Everyone froze. The shadescourge. Doran and Fraenk. All listening for what they heard or might have heard. But after a moment or two came the wet sound of the creature resuming its feeding. Fraenk had no idea how many more times he could keep this process going. But Doran nodded encouragingly at him, and Fraenk realized they had to try.

Again, they leaned into the crank handle, slowing at the peak of tension. This time, the ratchet dropped almost soundlessly to the next tooth in the gear. *Maybe this could be done,* Fraenk thought.

Sweat was already beading his brow when they had gotten to the nearly last ratchet. One more and the string would be behind the bolt knock. They heard the beast move back from its meal and make a few assured barks. The creature was about to resume its hunt.

Fraenk nodded urgently at Doran, and they pulled, not caring about stealth or noise. This was the moment. A loud click as the bowstring locked into place. Fraenk stepped behind the ballista and shouldered the machine to him as Doran crouched back into the fog. To Fraenk's surprise, it was precisely balanced and moved naturally under his control. There was true craftsmanship in the ancient elves' work, Fraenk noted. Squinting one eye, he could see a brass pin with a ring that rose up—a reticle for the presupposed impact point of the arrow.

Fraenk shifted his weight, moving the machine until the sight fixed upon a spot between the beast's glowing eyes. He just then realized the shadescourge was looking directly at him. There was no time left. Fraenk grabbed the trigger and squeezed. Nothing.

A firm tension remained on the trigger. Some preventative safeguard was keeping the machine from firing. Fraenk realized he needed to release it quickly because the beast was now turning and coming towards him.

He tried pulling harder. That clearly didn't work.

If he had a moment to look, Fraenk was sure he could find the release, but the creature was now opening its drooling mouth and coming faster. Fraenk panicked as the beast charged.

"By your right hand!" Doran shouted from somewhere in the fog.

Both Fraenk and the creature reacted at the same moment. The creature, spying Doran standing defenseless in the mist, changed its target. Fraenk quickly slid his right hand up and felt a lever. He pushed until it made a satisfying CLUNK.

Seeing that the creature was coming for him, Doran recoiled in terror. The shadescourge crouched and was just beginning to launch itself upward as Fraenk's hand pulled the trigger. The machine's draw released the taut bowstring, and the ballista jumped with a mighty *Faa-THWACK!*

32

T HERE WERE PLACES ALONG the High Street where the walls still bore fist-sized pits and pocks in the stone, where it was said that the arrows of the elves had struck during the siege of Arathes. As a boy, Fraenk found it hard to believe that any weapon could cause such damage and had chalked that prattle up as a lot of rooster-crowing and lies from the other kids, for what kind of arrow could actually be fired with the kind of force that could carve out craters from granite or dwarfstone?

He now had his definitive answer, apparently.

The ballista-fired bolt moved almost faster than could be seen, but the wind from it blew an open channel in the mist with looping curls on either side that swept outward in a wave. Fraenk had lost track of the sight in his haste to fire, but fortunately his target was large and not far away. The projectile caught the beast right as it leapt and reversed its momentum entirely, tumbling it backward twenty feet. It made a surprised yelp as it was struck, then lay motionless in a dark heap near the main doors.

"Sweet Mersey, we killed it!" Fraenk exclaimed, elated. Doran stopped screaming, lowered his arms, and looked as well. It took a moment until he saw the crumpled body of the monster, then released a giddy, insane-sounding laugh that echoed across the cavernous museum.

"We're *alive?*" Doran Leafwater cackled. "We're alive!"

"I'm surprised this old warhorse held up." Fraenk patted the ballista. He saw a long crack running the length of the wood grain. He gingerly pulled his hand away, hoping no one else noticed that.

"Good sirs..." A voice called from above them both. Kyla was perched atop the statue of Monarch Broridir Bluemount. She was peering out over the fog.

"I mean, I know how I appear to everyone," Doran muttered, turning dour. "I get it. *Here comes Lieutenant Mud-bottom. Everyone laugh! Oh, look! The farcical lordling in the maroon tunic that dies in the play and makes everyone cheer.* But here I am!" "Alright, Leafwater." Fraenk clapped him on the shoulder. "Well done."

"Boys?" Kyla said more urgently. "You might want to belay your celebration. It's gone."

"What is?" Fraenk asked, still smiling.

"The beast."

Fraenk and Doran snapped around to where the shadescourge had fallen. The creature's presumably dead body was no longer there. All that remained was a hollow of mist that was already filling back in on itself. Icy dread gripped Fraenk. Both men swiveled, straining to look through the fog.

"Where is it?!" Fraenk squeaked.

"I don't know. I saw it limp off in that direction. I think you made it mad," Kyla said, pointing to the completely dark section of the side hall. They could hear heavy shuddering breaths and irregular footfalls moving across the floor. It released a low rumbling growl that sounded paradoxically very far away and way too close.

His mind raced with questions. How injured was the beast? Was it dying or regaining its strength? Could they outrun it now? Without being positive about any of these things, Fraenk had to imagine it was just as deadly as ever, maybe even more so, now that it knew they were there and was now apparently hunting them.

Fraenk immediately crouched down, and Doran followed an instant later. Soundlessly, he met Doran's terrified eyes, and they both seemed to have the same idea— the ballista. But how could he warn the elf that there was a huge crack in its frame? And would it hold up for one more salvo? Fraenk once again found himself running out of time and with few good options.

The ballista was worth one more attempt. With a nod to Doran, both men moved back into position on the war machine. Judging by the general direction of the monster's low breath, the implement was aimed in the wrong direction. Fraenk dipped under the shoulder brace and eased it up onto its pivot. It gave a long whine of protest as Fraenk stepped it around.

The shadescourge must have heard this as well, because it went completely silent. Fraenk and Doran froze. All he could hear was his own heartbeat pounding in his ears. Fraenk couldn't see the creature wherever it was, but he knew its malevolent senses were honing in on them.

He stole a glance back up at Kyla. What he saw scared him more than anything. Kyla was waving her arm wildly and pointing out beyond them. The look of sheer terror on her face said everything.

"Now," Fraenk exhaled to Doran. They grabbed the crank handles and pulled. The ballista creaked and groaned uncomfortably as they turned the gear, once again ratcheting back the bowstring.

Two malevolent orbs rose from the mist, much closer than Fraenk had imagined it would be. Doran began to make a thin, high-pitched sound that was somewhere between a grunt and a cry. The shadescourge took a limping hop-step closer. It was definitely wounded. Fraenk could see the fletchings of the bolt sticking out from between the armor plates of the chest and shoulder. It opened its jaw, and a thick pink foam spilled out. The bolt must be in its lung, Fraenk realized. Despite the injuries, the shadescourge only looked enraged. Its fierce claws screeched awfully as it stepped again.

"Go! Hurry!" Fraenk said. And they began to crank faster. Immediately, the wood in the ballista's body gave a strained series of cracks.

"Easy. Slower," Fraenk said. His eyes darted between the approaching beast and the expanding crack in the wood. "Neversleep?!" Doran exclaimed. "Not now, Doran!" Fraenk shouted back.

"Neversleep! What are we supposed to fire at that thing? Sharp words?!" The elf said.

Fraenk looked. And sure enough, the arrow trough was empty.

"Well, that's not good."

He tried to scan the room for more bolts, but he couldn't do that whilst watching the beast and making sure the ballista didn't snap.

"Kyla! We need ammunition!" Fraenk shouted up to her. "Do you see anything?"

"No," she called, but she didn't sound sure. "Wait. Hang on."

"Hang on?!" Fraenk blinked.

He heard her land softly and catlike behind him.

"Just don't let that thing kill me," she said, then took off straight for the shadescourge.

"How are we supposed to do that?!"

Fraenk could only watch as she closed the distance to the creature. Its large eyes caught her movement, and it swiveled its head. Kyla angled out toward its wounded side. The beast tried maneuvering into a position where it could swipe or bite, but it was slow and cumbersome. She tacked again, moving directly at it. The shadescourge tried lifting the arm where the bolt was lodged, but the joint was locked and useless.

Desperately, it slashed at her with the other paw, but Kyla tucked one leg under her and twisted her hip, sliding down into the fog. The thin black claws sliced the air just above her, and it snarled in frustration.

Clear of it on the other side, Kyla sprang back onto her feet and was running for the far wall.

The shadescourge had a moment of confused indecision— would it chase after her or keep coming for Fraenk and Doran? It seemed in favor of this new target.

"Keep it busy, Fraenk!" He heard her shout across the hall.

"HEY! *HERE*, you ugly, black-blooded, skark!" Fraenk taunted. "You're nasty enough to be a Fernbrook!"

"And... your mother was a fat... overbearing, busybody who ruined your whole life!" Doran Leafwater added, drawing an arched eyebrow from Fraenk.

The shadescourge whipped its head back in their direction and gave a wet hiss.

Fraenk leaned into the crank and felt the bowstring tick back another careful notch. One or two more, and it would be ready to fire. Provided they had another ballista bolt to use for ammunition. The wood gave an angry, protesting series of cracks. *Please hold,* Fraenk prayed silently. They turned again, and finally the latch popped up, holding the bowstring in firing position.

He dropped his hands away from it as the ballista tensed like a coiled viper, more volatile than ever.

"Kyla, we could really use that shaft now!" Fraenk yelled. The monster lurched forward, sensing their fear. It was close, and it gave them a hateful glare with its enormous eyes. Then it looked at the ballista, seeming to actually regard it in some dark way. They could smell its rancid breath, tinged with the coppery scent of blood.

"Fraenk! Use this!" Kyla's voice echoed from the other side of the room.

Then, with a sound like a sword point being dragged across stone, a golden, spearlike object came darting along the floor through the mist. Like some ground-based bolt of lightning heading right for him. Fraenk stepped down on top of it and felt a solid rod of metal underfoot.

With a howl, the monster suddenly rose up onto its back legs like a bear. While the half-giant's armor didn't fit the creature well as it walked on all fours, in this new attitude, everything fell into place like barding. It was some kind of dumb luck that the first bolt didn't glance off of one of the thick metal panels with the initial firing. Was there any hope of landing a hit now? But the creature seemed to be having trouble breathing, its enormous lungs laboring as air whistled out with bubbling blood from around the bolt in its shoulder. Somehow, being upright was giving it the respite it needed to recover strength. It continued to glare with hot, malevolent eyes.

Keeping his focus on the creature, Fraenk reached into the fog and retrieved what Kyla had sent— a beautiful and ornate golden trident, Thunderspike, spear of Theomar Skywillow.

"What am I supposed to do with this? Broker a peace with the ocean kings of Drialadon?" Fraenk asked, dumbly. The shadescourge snarled and tilted forward in a charge. Its dying strength was spent on ending Fraenk's existence.

Fraenk looked at the empty ballista, and then he knew.

"Kill it, Neversleep! Kill it!!" Doran screamed.

Fraenk slammed the trident into the arrow trench. It's wicked—triple points sticking out beyond by a foot. The beast was bearing down. He had no time to aim, but there was no need. Fraenk pressed the locking lever in and slapped the trigger handle.

A quick series of sounds happened nearly on top of one another. The low twang of the bowstring, a massive crash of the ballista coming apart in the subsequent release, and the shadescourge barreling headlong into the machine— then into Fraenk and Doran.

Fraenk was tumbling, getting battered by wood, metal, and beast.

Then everything stopped. All he saw was darkness and smoke... and something blue glowing far away. He realized he was on his back. There was a sharp pain in his calf, and another hard block of something was pressing on his spine—or rather, he was lying on something hard.

When he realized he was sprawled out on his back, Fraenk sat up. He was looking directly at the black fur of the shadescourge. He froze, waiting a long moment to see if it would get up once again to terrorize them, but this time it did appear to finally be dead.

He tried to move and again felt a painful pull at his calf. Fraenk looked down to see one of the beast's claws poking through his trouser leg and into the flesh. He gingerly removed it and bandaged the flow of blood with a clean wrap that he kept inside his cloak. Fraenk found his shirt was soaked and smelling of his favorite spirit. Sure enough, the bottle had broken in the calamity.

"Fraenk?" Kyla's voice called, concerned. He saw her rush through the thinning fog and darkness toward him. "The trident worked?"

"Put a fork in him. He's done." Fraenk sighed.

Kyla shook her head and grinned.

"Where's the other one? The guard," she asked.

"Leafwater," Fraenk said. He stood gingerly and looked around the carnage. The shadescourge was tangled up in the broken remains of the ballista, but they couldn't see the elf.

"Frnnnkkk Nwrrrsleeefff! Hellllffff!" A muffled voice shouted from somewhere in the pile.

"Doran? Where are you?""Eeess eeeeffeeenng mah head!" Doran cried out again.

Fraenk and Kyla exchanged a concerned look and made their way around to the other side of the wreckage. Limping, Fraenk got there a few moments later to find Kyla doubled over laughing. Then Fraenk looked, and he started laughing too. The shadescourge, dead with a golden trident buried between its eyes, had somehow in its fading throes managed to catch onto Doran's head in its horrible segmented jaws. But it had expired before it could bite down. And so there flailed the arms and body of the wispy elf guard, thrashing and screaming in an attempt to free himself. The combination of relief and exhaustion, mixed with the ridiculousness of Doran Leafwater's predicament, Fraenk and Kyla laughed until tears streamed down their cheeks.

"Geff me outta heeerrrre!" Doran shouted angrily.

"Sorry, Doran. Let's see if I can... " Fraenk hobbled in close and grabbed onto the monster's bloody, slimy jaw. It squished disconcertingly in his hands. He pulled, regripped, and pulled again, but the jaw would not move.

"Kyla, grab from the other side..." Fraenk looked up. The Lynblood woman was halfway to the entrance doors. A pit formed in the middle of his guts. He knew immediately what this was.

"So that's it? After all this, a simple backstab?"

"I'm sorry to do this, Fraenk," she said, not slowing. "I need the Ynne es Tylubourne. It's valuable, and I have to start over somewhere new. Don't worry. I won't let the Fernbrooks get it."

"*That hunk of dross??* What happens when they send another one of those beasts after you— or something even worse?" Fraenk tried to catch her, but he couldn't run. The pain in his leg was getting worse.

"They'll never find me."

"And they'll never stop looking, either. You'll live with your head always turned over one shoulder. Always checking the shadows."

"That's been my life! It's all I've ever known," she snapped. He could hear emotion rising in her voice.

"But it doesn't have to be," Fraenk said gently.

Kyla paused with her hand on the door. Fraenk stopped too, letting himself rest. He needed something for the pain, but that had to wait.

"And then what? Fall in love? Get married? Maybe you just want half-Lyn-blood babies?"

"Fine! You wanna go? The Main Gate's open! I won't stop you," Fraenk growled. "But the necklace stays with me."

"So that was all you've ever wanted," she scoffed. Kyla fished the pendant out and dangled it in the air. It seemed even more dull and oppressive than he had remembered— almost black in the dim light. "Have your last look, Fraenk Neversleep. You'll never see it or me again."

She dropped the necklace back into her hip pouch and pulled the door open. In the time it took for the door to swing back shut again, she was outside and into the night.

"Hells!" Fraenk cursed and started after her.

"Nvvvvrrrseeepp? Ooo still hrrrrr?" Doran's voice called, soft and muffled.

"Oh yeah. Doran, hang in there! I'll bring some help. We'll get you out! Don't move," Fraenk shouted as he hop-shuffled to the main entrance door, leaving Leafwater to do more of his screaming and thrashing. He grabbed the tall handle that was still faintly warm from Kyla's touch and jerked the door open.

"Kyla!" He shouted.

She was there in the courtyard. But she wasn't alone. She and the dark figure were standing close. At Fraenk's call, they both wheeled together like dancers to face him. Then Fraenk recognized the other man. He had tall black horns and the face of a demon. His one hand gripped her wrist out, hyperextending it painfully back. His other hand was clutched at her throat.

"Brimblade!" Fraenk snarled.

"Thank you for delivering the Ynne es Tylubourne to me, Neversleep. You truly are not to be underestimated. " He smiled with gleaming, pointed teeth like the infernal demon Shalokar himself.

33

"Listen, friend, you can let her go now and walk away or become the second ugliest thing I've killed tonight," Fraenk said, carefully brushing back the cloak on his shoulders to expose his brace of throwing knives.

"Yes. Arathes certainly does have a problem with *Iznesete* monsters slipping in."

"And with you opening the door for them," Fraenk shot back. "I'm pleased to put an end to it."

"You have me cornered, I'm afraid," the helltouched said, keeping Kyla between himself and Fraenk. "Don't kill me until you at least hear my offer, *štit.*"

Fraenk realized he had never heard the man speak before. His words were not inflected with the coarse, roughback Tigranean accent that was typical of his foul lot. There was something educated and entirely foreign about his pronunciations that made him even more sinister. Even his posture and comportment were suggestive of a quality and expensive tutelage. But to Fraenk, it told him that this one was smart and not to be underestimated.

Brimblade was dressed in a fine black high-collared robe with ornate orange stitch work in a familiar weaving leaf pattern that Fraenk recognized— the fern. He also still had on the metal collar with the large emerald gem, which did not complement the rest of his ensemble, but indicated that this trinket was something the helltouched never removed.

"Ease up on my friend's neck, and I'll hear you out," Fraenk replied. Brimblade adjusted his grip, but did not release Kyla. Fraenk realized she hadn't said a word since this exchange began, but she was watching him with large, terrified eyes. "So it was you in the shadows that day with the wizard," the helltouched said. "He got to you first, or we might have been allies. Or at least be at, uh, *za zaštita*... common cause."

"I don't caper and dance for the Fernbrooks. I've seen how they treat their servants," Fraenk retorted.

"We all serve some master—" Brimblade winced and grunted as light danced in the emerald at his neck. He looked like he might lose his grip on Kyla as well, and Fraenk quietly slipped a throwing blade into his hand. He just needed the man to move away from her a bit more, and he could throw it with confidence that she wouldn't get hurt.

But Brimblade recovered and composed himself, smiling more malignly than ever.

"Whatever the wizard told you about the Mind Thief is a lie, *na mojata*. He is not its guardian nor protector. He hired these rogues to steal it from my family. I'm sure he told you of my good lady mother, who was deceived into commissioning it from him in the first place. He was the one who created it."

That wasn't what Valthor told him, Fraenk noted.

"Then she went mad and killed all her friends, from what I hear," Fraenk replied.

"A genuine tragedy. And one that will someday be avenged. But for now, *raka*, I need to return with the Ynne es Tylubourne, where it will be secured, never to be used again."

"You're just a fetch-dog for Lord Fernbrook. You'll lay it in his claws the first chance you get."

"His alliance was necessary for my presence here in the city. And in exchange, I've allowed him limited use of the necklace's magic for his purposes. Afterwards, it shall be placed in trust."

"And just what does he plan for it?" Fraenk asked.

"I'm not allowed to say, unfortunately," Brimblade made an ingénue frown. "But let's just say that the city will be better for it."

Fraenk saw Kyla's face was starting to brighten. Her mouth was moving, but no words came out. Something was wrong—she was trying to warn him. What was she saying? *Smell?*

The helltouched seemed to be up to something, but if it was beyond holding Kyla hostage and revealing the details of his own scheme, Fraenk couldn't figure it out. Brimblade had been slipping extra words into his sentences, which could have been him translating from his original tongue. But he was also making odd twitching motions with his fingers. Whatever it was, Fraenk knew it was dangerous to let the helltouched continue.

"Get to your offer then, Brimblade," Fraenk said, impatient.

"Oh yes. Of course. It's this—" He rattled off a series of words that made light zigzag up his clawed fingers and into his arm.

Brimblade quickly drew the curving dagger from his belt and jabbed it into the front of Kyla's thigh. She shrieked in pain and surprise. Brimblade released her from his grip, stepping back. "You have a choice before you..." Brimblade snatched the pouch from Kyla's hip that contained the necklace. "Pursue me and the necklace, or save your friend's life. The Serpent Blade of Seothen is charmed with a magical poison that is quite toxic to all but my kind. Without a cure, I'm afraid she won't last long. The temple healers *might* be able to mix a cure, if they have an Arcane Lord's help."

Brimblade had stepped far enough back that Fraenk had his clear shot. He sent the first, then three more blades whistling through the night at the helltouched. Brimblade countered with a wave of the magically infused hand. The knives sparked angry white-purple off the arcane shield that hung in the air in front of Brimblade.

"Nice try, but you're wasting time, Neversleep," he said, and took off running from the courtyard in a flap of robes.

Instinctively, Fraenk started after him but saw Kyla buckle to her knees. She was holding her leg, which appeared to have completely given out on her.

"He's casting a spell," Kyla grunted. "I tried to warn you."

Fraenk tore open the hole wider where the blade had cut and checked the wound. She jerked in agony.

"How bad?" She asked through gritted teeth. Already it was beginning to turn black, with raised tendrils of decay pushing slowly under the surface of her skin.

"I think you know," Fraenk said. He stood, scanning the courtyard for help.

"Go after the Mind Thief. I'll get myself to a healer," she said; already her voice was losing strength.

"You can't even walk!" He shouted in frustration. "You'll be dead before a healer even

figures out what this is!"

Fraenk caught sight of a tavern across the courtyard, with lights still ablaze and jaunty music pouring out. While he didn't hold out hope that any of the drunk occupants inside would be useful, the saddled mare lashed to the hitch out front certainly was.

Without a pause, he ran. It only took him less than a minute to reach the horse. He slashed the reins from the post instead of untying them. Fraenk stepped up into the saddle and wheeled the horse around, spurring it into motion.

By the time he got back to her, Kyla's leg was much worse. She looked at him with dull eyes. The poison was moving too quickly.

"Kyla. You stay awake, understand me? I'm gonna get you help!"

Fraenk got her up onto the horse with him, thankful she wasn't too heavy. He found himself frozen for a moment of indecision. He knew the temple healers were good, but Brimblade said they'd also need an Arcane Lord. But the ones Fraenk knew inspired no confidence. He needed a powerful wizard who knew what devilish poison Brimblade would use. *But who could he trust?*

The front door to the lighthouse kicked open with a bang. Fraenk entered, sweating and holding an unconscious Kyla Gracefire in his arms. Valthor was bent over his workbench, focusing intently on some project. The loud noise nearly made him drop the complex brass and glass apparatus he was carefully fitting together.

"Mind the sudden noise, Fraenk," the ex-wizard said calmly. "I'm right in the middle of a delicate procedure."

"Valthor, I need your help! Now!!" Fraenk barked.

The ex-wizard used the pincers he was holding to carefully maneuver the smaller, long glass tube filled with a murky liquid inside a larger circular orb that had clear fluid inside. It clicked into place, and he removed the tool. He sighed with relief.

"Valthor! It's urgent!" Fraenk almost shouted.

"Yes, I heard you. But I'd prefer not to immolate everyone on this side of the city, if it can be avoided." Valthor secured a lid on top of the glass ball, and a light began to come from the inner glass tube. The whole contraption reminded Fraenk of his lost glow orb. But he had no time to reminisce.

Valthor finally turned to look at his guest—or rather, guests. He was wearing some multi-lensed contraption on his brow that reminded Fraenk of a spider's eyes.

Fraenk could feel his arms shaking from fatigue. He hauled Kyla's frame up and used her to shove the scatter of items on Valthor's table off onto the floor with a clatter.

"What is this?" the ex-wizard asked, annoyed.

"She's been poisoned. Serpent dagger of some such. Magical poison. You have to help her."

Fraenk pulled open her pant leg to expose the wound. A nasty black fluid was now draining from the cut, and her entire leg was woven with dark veins. Valthor blinked and didn't get up from his stool.

"Valthor, did you hear me?" Fraenk barked. "She needs your help!"

"The thief who stole the necklace and caused all this trouble in the first place? I think no," he said coldly.

"What? Why?!"

"So the world has one less thief in it," he replied matter-of-factly. "This one unearthed the tomb; let her lie in the cold grave."

"She was helping me take back the necklace—which YOU told me to do!"

"And did she then try to steal it from you at the first opportunity?" Valthor asked. "Almost immediately," Fraenk conceded. "—But that's only because she was scared. And in danger from the very thing you created! Oh yes, the hell-touched told me what you did."

Fraenk saw the ex-wizard's eyes briefly go wide. So that much of the story had been true.

"Where did you hear that?"

"I met the scion of the family. He was on a quest for vengeance against you specifically."

"He's lying about that. The family is all dead, Neversleep!" Valthor said bitterly. "And I am the cause. So I would be fine with one less thief out there stealing the Ynne es Tylubourne and causing more deaths because of it."

"You'll still bear the burden of one more death if you don't save her now." Fraenk put his hand on the elf's shoulder, then turned him to finally look at her.

The elf blinked at her through the lenses that made his eyes look comically large and bulbous. Then he finally really looked. Valthor's expression turned grim. He brushed the apparatus off his head and closely examined the wound in her leg.

"How did this happen?" He asked.

"From a dagger belonging to a helltouched named Brimblade. Magic poison."

"I know that one. He's a thrall. A dark master pulls that puppet's strings." Valthor rummaged through his shelf, gathering bottles of potions into a low wooden crate. He carried everything over to the cauldron in the fireplace and stepped on a wooden lever that was attached to some gears and armatures that disappeared into the stones of the hearth. Immediately, a flame sprang to life, igniting the logs on the grate.

"At least you've recovered the Mind Thief." He said, pouring out amounts of liquid from various bottles into the cauldron.

"Yeah..." Fraenk said gingerly. "Unfortunately, he also has the necklace as well."

The ex-wizard shot him a surprised look.

"Well, it was either go after the necklace or save her!"

"Always go after the necklace, you fool!" Valthor scolded and whacked him with a wooden spoon.

"I can't change it now. She's here. Can you save her?" Fraenk growled.

"Save her? The poison has progressed too far. There's no saving her. You'd be doing this woman a kindness if you just put a dagger in her heart right now." Valthor said.

"Then what's all this?" Fraenk shouted, pointing to the boiling pot.

"This, yes. Well, I'm going to try at least. I just wanted to set your expectations so you wouldn't hold out hope." Valthor stirred and sprinkled in some powder that crackled as it hit the liquid.

Fraenk wasn't sure what to say to that. He had felt his hope like a small ship being smashed by the storm and waves of despair. In his mind, it was the only thing that was keeping her alive.

"What can I do to help?" Fraenk asked.

"This is nothing you'll want to witness, Neversleep," Valthor said, gravely. "She will be in more pain than a soul can bear. And even then she may die. Several times. This poison also attacks the spirit. She may also return mindless and hungry. That is sometimes the hardest one of all."

"I'll stay," Fraenk said. "Just tell me what to do."

"Very well. It is what you have chosen," the ex-wizard nodded. "And what will you do about the Mind Thief?" "I'll get it back. I have a good idea where it's going to be."

The child was running through open fields of long grass that waved in the gentle breeze. The sun was warm on her face, and she had felt joy and peace in a way that she had never experienced. There were other children there, also running. They seemed to be playing a game with each other, touching one and then giving chase to the rest. They laughed and sang; each moment felt wonderful. The child could have played like this forever, she felt.

But soon the game began to move toward the gates of the city. The children all knew there would be food, and those who loved them were waiting. The child wanted to go as well, but something warm was on her leg, and it hurt. She didn't like the feeling and tried to brush it away, but her hands couldn't reach it for some reason.

The child thought there might be someone else to help, but none of the other children remained around her. They all seemed to be inside the gate. She tried to call them, but her voice was too weak. Perhaps she could go inside the city and find someone, but somehow she knew she could not enter— not with the dark stain on her leg.

"Child, are you hungry?" She heard a woman call. It sounded like her mother's voice, but that wasn't true because she didn't know her mother. The child turned to see the source of the voice: a beautiful woman with golden hair was standing beside a tree. The child approached cautiously, for this woman looked very sad, and the child did not want to cause her to cry.

"I am, my lady," the child said.

She reached up and plucked a white apple from the tree, handing it down to her.

"Then eat. And afterward you may enter."

The child closed her eyes and took a bite. The taste was sweet.

34

"Y ou're... staring," a frail voice spoke from the ex-wizard's bed.

Fraenk had been sitting in an overstuffed chair watching her.

He was exhausted, but he couldn't allow himself to rest—just in case. Sometimes, she was so still, her lungs rising so little, that he thought she had stopped breathing. But then she took a deeper, sighing breath, and he could see it again. The tiny ship of hope was battered by the storm and even feared lost too many times for his ragged emotions to deal with, but somehow he held on.

Hope was all he had.

"No, I'm not," Fraenk said, palming away the delirious tears that had sprung unbidden from his eyes. "I was... just waiting to tell you how foolish it was for you to steal that necklace from me."

"It wasn't... yours to be stolen," Kyla murmured.

"We stopped the poison. It was really bad and you almost..." Fraenk broke off for a moment and cleared his throat. "Valthor said when you had a chance to rest, he'd take you to a temple and get healed the rest of the way. That is, if you're actually still alive and not one of those returned dead, hungry for human flesh."

"I already ate," Kyla cracked one eye open, and her mouth pulled tight in an attempted smile. Fraenk could see her visibly returning back to herself with each passing moment. Then she asked, "Who's Valthor?"

"He's the ex-wizard who lives in the lighthouse. He also was the one who created the Mind Thief."

Both of her eyes popped open, panicked and unfocused. She made a feeble effort to pull the blankets off her and get up, but her body had no strength.

"Stop struggling. You'll just wear yourself out," Fraenk said.

"...can't be here..." Kyla managed to squeak before falling back, exhausted.

"He knows you stole it, and he helped you anyway. I'm sure you'll have a few things to discuss." Fraenk said, standing. "I'll be back to check on you later."

"Where are you going?" Her eyes were closed, and she sounded ready to fall asleep.

"I left a few tasks uncompleted and a hell-touched still breathing." Fraenk swept on his cloak. He paused to watch her for a moment. Eyes closed, her chest gently rose and fell. He couldn't tell if she'd drifted off already.

"Kyla?" Fraenk said softly.

"Mmm?"

"I need you to hear my words. As soon as you're feeling well, I want you to leave Arathes. You said it yourself, there's nothing here for you. I'll get you some coin to start over wherever you like, but it can't be here."

She made no reply. There was only the soft tick, plink, and burble from the various brass tubes in the room and the continuous low rumbling grind of the gears that drove the lighthouse lantern above. Fraenk wasn't even sure she was still awake to hear him, but then a single tear rolled from the corner of her eye back onto the pillow.

He turned and headed to the front door of the lighthouse. Fraenk looked back and was surprised to see Valthor sitting quietly at his workbench. This time he wasn't bent over some contraption but looking at Fraenk. The ex-wizard bore a grave expression. Their gazes met. Fraenk looked hurt and haunted. But Valthor's eyes were etched by years of wisdom and pain; he understood and gave Fraenk a curt nod.

Outside the lighthouse, Fraenk took a moment to tighten the saddle and tack of his stolen mount. Even though he told himself he was planning his next action, Fraenk was really just stalling. He wanted to go back inside and tell Kyla—

What?

What would he say? What did he even feel? No. How he left things was how they needed to be. No past and no future. If you have nothing, then nothing can be taken from you. That was his sworn oath, sacrosanct as the pledge of any paladin.

"I'm sure your rider is going to step outside and wonder where he parked you," Fraenk patted the horse on its shoulder and smiled. Then, kicking one boot into a stirrup, he swung up into the saddle. With a gentle prod, he spurred them forward, back down the jetty and towards the city. The air was brisk and seemed to cool that hot, tightening feeling in his chest that was trying to build the further he got from the lighthouse.

He rode past the docks and harbor, cutting through an alley and negotiating the horse up a flight of stone steps, which he seemed to be more nervous about than the steed. Fraenk was still forming possibilities on how he could both recover the necklace and bury Brimblade when a group of filthy children emptied out into the street in his path. Fraenk reined up hard to keep the horse from trampling them.

Their de facto leader was a tall, skinny boy appropriately dubbed "Stick," whom Fraenk remembered as the one who tipped him off when this whole bloody affair began.

"That's a good way to take a hoof, lads," Fraenk said when he'd gotten the horse sidled to a halt.

"They's eye'n for you, Neversleep," Stick said, apparently unconcerned for his safety.

"Who is? And for why?" Fraenk found himself unconsciously slipping into their street patois.

"Look at the big thumper. All nerv-sies!"

This drew laughter from the other kids.

"Oh, I know it and you don't," Stick jutted out his jaw— a defiant-looking gesture that merely meant he asserted the truth of his words; the further the stretch was, the indication of the strength of its verity. Then he uncrossed his spindly arms and stuck out a hand. Fraenk knew something was going down if the alley rats had news of it. But what exactly they might be referring to was anyone's guess— at least until their toll had been extracted. Stick curled his fingers in a 'gimme' motion.

Fraenk made a show of deliberation, hesitating to be squeezed of valuable coppers just for a few words of knowledge. That was the game after all, and both sides had to play their part. But inside, he delighted in any opportunity to press a coin into their scrawny hands. Fraenk would have paid them if they came to him with the basic information that the sky had been blue, or water was wet, or that the streets of the city at night were cold and hard to sleep on. But the alley rats were a tough lot, wild as any skrate and probably even more untamable. They trusted no adult, especially the ones who came with generous offers of food, money, or warm beds under a roof. The fools who fell for those lies didn't last long on the street.

Finally, after the appropriate amount of reluctance, Fraenk flicked two copper coins to Stick and cinched his coin purse string tight again—signaling the end of negotiations. The boy frowned and shook his head at the money, but Fraenk could see a pleased smile threatening to bloom on his face.

"Well? What is it?" Fraenk demanded.

"Your mommo's eye'n for you," Stick said, making the entire group of children sound a scandalized, you're-in-for-it *"Ooooooh!"* They laughed and elbowed each other, but Fraenk felt his heart almost stop.

For an instant, Fraenk saw a brief but perfectly clear image of his mother's face. He couldn't even remember her name, and he thought he'd lost her visage years ago, but somehow he could now see her. She was giving him that sad smile like the day that she sent him to town with Henrietta the sow...

"Neversleep?" Stick was watching him warily, ready to flee if he needed to.

Fraenk saw he was gripping the coin purse in a clenched fist.

"What did you say?" Fraenk asked carefully.

"Your mommo. Queen elf lady. They's asking about you. Got her house clubbies out eye'n for you n'everything."

He felt himself exhale.

"Oh. That's not my mother. She's Lady Blackroot, and—wait, she's looking for me?! Why?" Fraenk asked, but the kids were already spooked. They scrambled away through a narrow alley where the horse couldn't follow, whooping and jostling one another. It was best to let them go anyway; they wouldn't know much else.

But now Fraenk had a much more urgent situation. Had something bad happened to Lady Blackroot, or perhaps the district, while he was out dealing with this infuriating necklace situation? He realized it had been far too long since he had last briefed her on his work. And if he was honest, she was not likely to be pleased about what he had been busying himself with lately. Altercations with the Fernbrooks. A near kobold riot in Rounderville. His direct involvement with a prisoner escape at the Hornet's Hive. And this latest fracas at the museum—

Fraenk then just realized he left Doran Leafwater with his head in the mouth of that beast. Too late to do anything at this point. The morning guard shift would have found him by now anyway.

As much as he hated to leave Lady Blackroot out of the circle, Fraenk needed more time to recover the necklace and stop Lord Fernbrook's diabolical scheme— assuming he could figure out what it was first. If Lady Blackroot knew about any one of his troublesome yet perfectly-reasonable-at-the-time actions, she might not look so favorably on it and do something rash, like demote him or have him sent to the black cells with his old friend Carax the Cutthroat. Fraenk decided that the best thing was to continue to avoid her entirely until he could at least thwart Lord Fernbrook by getting the Mind Thief back in hand. Then he could weather whatever tempest she threw at him.

With that much resolved at least, Fraenk turned his borrowed horse on the cobbles back in the direction of the Royal Museum, where he might pick up the trail of Brimblade and also hopefully return the mare to its rightful owner without much fuss.

"Arch Preceptor!"

Fraenk cringed. How had they found him even before he got going? He briefly weighed the idea of spurring the horse on and pretending like he had not heard, but that was likely to ignite a greater response from the Blackroot guards. Fraenk was fine with wasting his own time on apparently frivolous quests for magical mind-destroying jewelry, but to put more of a strain on Lady Blackroot's guards was irresponsible and dangerous. So, biting back his annoyance, Fraenk wheeled the horse around to face the approaching man.

Fraenk recognized him immediately as one of the men who was nearly assigned to his security when Fraenk first rode out the gates, ready to draw an assassin's arrow. The man looked relieved to see him.

"Arch Neversleep, sir. I'm so glad we found you," he said.

"Yes... *Woodlarch?*" Fraenk tried to recall the man's name.

"Woodmire, sir. You're needed back at the estate, sir. Something urgent for Lady Blackroot—"

"What did she say?"

The guard adjusted the spear in his grip and shifted uncomfortably.

"Well?" Fraenk asked.

"I... I can't repeat it this close to a holy temple," Woodmire said. Fraenk could see the spire of Kyleria's cathedral was a good five blocks distant over the rooftops.

"Huh. That bad, eh?"

Woodmire nodded.

"Well, what's the version of it you could say in front of a paladin?"

"Her Ladyship is requesting your immediate presence for a matter of great urgency. And you're not her favorite human at the moment. In fact, you're a no-good, feckless, foul..."

...skarking idiot, a sloss-covered three-legged cruk with gout. A black-blooded, skyte breath and a mountainous pile of wet horse skit on a rainy day. Let's see... I think that's everything her ladyship said about you, sir." Woodmire finished just as he and Fraenk entered the gates of Blackroot Estate. Although they had ridden horses, the journey from the district in the lower level to the estate in the Uppers had still taken enough time to fill a small tome with the almost poetic long-form cussing that one could acquire over centuries as an elf.

"And that's the clean version, you say?" Fraenk asked.

Woodmire nodded emphatically. "I wouldn't dare repeat the other stuff."

"Huh. Alright, Woodmire. As you were. I'll find my way from here."

Fraenk had no sooner stepped indoors, when he was collected by an altogether humorless guard that refused to let him refill his empty hooch bottle and then by the ancient house matron whose pinched, disapproving countenance always made Fraenk wonder if the woman ate enough greens to facilitate a healthy digestive schedule. This time, instead of being tossed bodily before the dame and council of Acherons, Fraenk was delivered to Lady Blackroot's personal chambers.

When he entered, she was seated in front of a three panel mirror and wearing only an elaborately stitched robe over her underthings, while her maidservants flittered about her picking up various other garments that were scattered about the floor. Fraenk held up a hand to shield his eyes.

"Whoa. Surely nothing I've done deserves this kind of punishment!" Fraenk quipped.

"Where have you been, Neversleep?!" Lady Blackroot snapped. "Still very droll, I see."

"Well, I was—"

"Save your excuses for someone who might actually believe them," she said. A maidservant approached, carrying a billowy dress stitched with delicate silk flowers. Lady Blackroot considered it for a few moments, then waved it off with a flick of her hand.

"No, no. That won't do. Too pink. I'll look like I'm wearing the bung of a land kraken."

Fraenk had already made his way to her various decanters of spirits and grabbed the first bottle at hand, pouring himself half a glass.

"Go light on that, Fraenk. I need your wits about you. We have a problem."

"Lord Fernbrook," Neversleep guessed. Judging by the look she jabbed his way in the mirror, he was correct.

"So you know already?"

"I know my side of the tale. What is it on yours? Another invitation to gamble away part of the district?"

Lady Blackroot fixed him with a cold glare that made Fraenk lower his glass. Perhaps he had overstepped too far this time. He nearly began to apologize when another maidservant came forth bearing a dress even more whimsical and impractical than the last one. She waved this one away sharply as well.

"Bad news, I'm afraid. High Lord Whiteleaf has invited us to a grand gala at his residence in the Summer Palaces," Lady Blackroot said tersely.

"That is bad news," Fraenk said, raising a curious eyebrow. "So the boy prince stirs in his golden cage. I'm surprised the High Council of Elves even allowed our beloved Warden of the Pale and Protector of Arathes to make that kind of big decision."

"Of course not! My ladies informed me that Lord Fernbrook was seen leaving the High Lord's residence yesterday, and come the morning we have a fresh invitation waiting for this delightful surprise. If we had any warning about this, we would have stepped on it harder than a brown grease beetle."

Fraenk added another splash to his glass and began to pace.

"All the High Council will be there? And Lord Whiteleaf?" Fraenk asked.

"We would not be so rude as to refuse our Lord's generous offers," she said with venomous courtesy.

"Don't go. Find some excuse. Fernbrook's planning something big, my lady. I don't know what exactly, but I'm afraid he now has the means to pull it off."

"Oh, I won't be going," Lady Blackroot said and turned in her seat to face him with a devious smile. "*WE* will be going together."

Part VII

35

F RAENK KNEW SURPRISINGLY LITTLE about the elf who sat as figurehead over Arathes and Gwyndaer Province. High Lord Krispen Whiteleaf was the nephew of the Sarmatian Monarch Boridir Bluemont himself. He held the title of Warden of the Pale and Protector of the City, but the actual governance of the region fell to the High Council, which consisted of the ten prominent district leaders. They were the ones who decided collectively as a quorum on matters of policy and administration—ostensibly until the High Lord himself came of age to be able to rule in his own right, but the timeline for such a transfer of power was unsurprisingly open-ended. The High Council seemed to always have some important matters of state that required their wisdom and experience. But whenever confronted directly, they made all the right noises about how eager they were to be rid of this burden and ready for Lord Whiteleaf to rule on his own. Of course, that was the same story that Fraenk had heard for years.

As far as his day-to-day activities, the High Lord elf lived in the insular luxury of what was dubbed the Monarch's Summer Palace— a lavish estate at the very peak of the city which the Monarch himself rarely, if ever, visited. So Lord Whiteleaf had nothing but time to pursue any endeavor he fancied, so long as that interest wasn't the administration and leadership of the province itself.

The young elf was widely praised as an accomplished practitioner of dramatic arts, such as theater, poetry, writing, and music. He was said to be very skilled at the more civilized martial pursuits of horseback riding, swordsmanship, and archery, which were highly prized among elvenkind. He received the finest tutoring from learned sages and master instructors of nearly every subject. Lord Krispen Whiteleaf was said to lack for nothing—except possibly friends.

Fraenk pulled at the high collar of his formal doublet. Already the impractical attire required for the gala was an irritation, to say the least. Although he was no stranger to wearing nearly any style through the course of his duties as preceptor— from a beggar's rags to the theatrical plumes of a Caladanian folk dancer—the elves seemed to take particular insidious delight in creating garments that resisted the comfort of the wearer in favor of clean lines and decorative embellishments.

After being left with no other choice than to accompany Lady Blackroot, Fraenk was placed into the unyielding custody of the house matron and her battalion of servants, whose job it was to get the man to the nearly impossible state of 'being presentable'. This consisted of a near-scalding bath and a scourging from rough sea sponges, bodily grooming for parts of himself that even he'd never see, and finally being doused in enough fragrant oils and smelly perfume that made him almost miss the funk of the black cells. Then he was whisked away to the Blackroot's personal tailor, where his form-fitting garment was practically stitched up around him.

Fraenk stopped, staring out the window of the carriage that was now transporting them up the hill towards the Summer Palace. When he looked back, Lady Blackroot was watching him with a bemused smile.

"I like this disguise on you, Fraenk," she said. "It gives one the false impression that you're a respectable gentleman. I hardly believed such a thing was possible."

"I promise to be out of these cursed garments before any of their foul influence takes hold of me," Fraenk returned with a wry grin.

He had been so used to taking shortcuts to get everywhere in the city that Fraenk had forgotten just how long the journey to the very top actually took. Of course, that was the point of the Grand Procession—to slowly weave your way through the streets in embellished carriages pulled by great teams of horses and trailing an entourage of servants, so any and all of those unfortunates without an invitation could coo jealously as they watched you pass by. There was nothing elves liked more than to remind everyone lower than them of their status.

Fraenk had seen many of these processions growing up and often wondered what it would be like to be the person inside one of the golden conveyances. They were like the gleaming coach of the sun transporting a divine into the heavens. But actually being inside one was a disappointment that somehow transcended the experience by not meeting whatever expectations he may have carried. The ride was somehow both rough and jouncy. And the air inside the closed space was hot and pungent, with a mix of overpowering perfumes clashing with one another. Perhaps that was better than sweat and odors of the body, but it soon began to send a spike of pain into the space between his eye sockets.

He could tell that Lady Blackroot was uncomfortable too, but she bore it much better than him. She had calmed much since her earlier tirade. His mere presence around her seemed to have that effect. She had once told him, after one too many cups of wine, that she trusted him. Certainly a flattering sentiment, Fraenk thought at the time, but it seemed to imply that he might be the only one. She was surrounded by servants and advisors whose jobs and lives revolved around preserving her as an institution. They could not love her because they couldn't choose not to. Her peers, the other High Lord elves, lived more or less the same. And they, too, sought their own interests and that of their lineage. Fraenk had sworn his service to her, but he was only riding in the golden carriage to the top of the hill; Lady Blackroot lived in one.

During the long ride, Fraenk had time to give her a more detailed but still selective version of events since they had last spoken. He realized he couldn't fully explain without telling her about the necklace. To her credit, Lady Blackroot controlled any angry outburst she felt during the telling, instead asking a few direct questions and waiting for Fraenk to finish.

"So now you believe this Blackblade gave the necklace to Lord Fernbrook," she said.

"Yes," Fraenk replied without bothering to correct her on the helltouched's name. "They've got some scheme involving the necklace, but I haven't uncovered it yet."

"If it is as powerful as you say, Fernbrook could certainly cause trouble for us all," she said, thinking. "But he's begun to play his cards already."

"How do you mean?"

"This last-minute party, thrown by the High Lord himself, was most certainly sanctioned by Fernbrook. Probably placed the idea as well," she explained. "Now you have a very public event with the High Lord, all the High Council, and anyone else significant enough to receive an invitation. What he's planning requires an important audience."

"And we already know his ambitions. He's going to roll the dice again—and this time he plans to take the entire city," Fraenk concluded.

"So we must stop him," said Lady Blackroot resolutely.

Fraenk looked at her and understood her meaning. She wasn't telling Fraenk to handle this himself. She intended to be a part of this.

"My lady, I can't put you in danger. My job is—""*Skark* that, Neversleep! I gave you your job, and we're all in danger. I'm going to help." She gave a fierce glare.

Fraenk nodded, knowing better than to argue with her.

"Fine. If we can get the necklace, we'll stop Fernbrook's plan. How would you feel about seducing him?"

"Oh, be sensible, Fraenk," she waved an irritated hand. "I'd utterly destroy him."

And they both nearly burst their outfits laughing.

For the next hour, Neversleep and Lady Blackroot discussed, planned, and schemed various options for how they would first have to find where Lord Fernbrook was holding the Mind Thief and then how they might relieve him of it. The best they could come up with was for Lady Blackroot to engage him in an argument, and Fraenk would use one of his pickpocket techniques to lift it from him. Assuming that Lord Fernbrook would have it on his person.

By way of plans, this might have been the flimsiest one he'd ever concocted, but the look of life and excitement on Lady Blackroot's face somehow made him feel like it was stupid enough to actually work. And of course he had his alternate plan, which he did not share with her just in case Lord Fernbrook used the necklace's magic to read her mind. She couldn't divulge a secret she wasn't aware of.

Throughout their discussion, Fraenk saw glimpses of the younger elf that she had been many years ago, and it was something of a revelation. Here was the vibrant elf who had purpose and adventure—not the dusty old crone propped up in a chair over a dying district.

It occurred to Fraenk that he had never pressed much into Lady Blackroot's history beyond what was common knowledge. Her late husband, Lord Taener Blackroot, had died three hundred years prior of a rare, slow-wasting disease that happened to affect only elves. During his downturn, he had taken the unusual step at that time to prepare his wife for leadership of the district instead of his eldest male heir, which was the custom. This had led to a deep and bitter rift between mother and son, which culminated in her son leaving, and he had not returned to this day. His name, in fact, was forbidden to be spoken aloud.

Lady Arice's younger son, Aerlith, was a surprise baby born at the very last of her fertile years and whose parentage itself was shrouded in mystery. He had been doted on his entire life—so much so that many within the district whispered concerns about his ability to govern someday when his mother was no longer around and even questioned if an alternate successor was in order. Lady Blackroot would hear none of this, however, and was determined to make him ready to rule by having him spend time with the various district Acherons.

Fraenk had done his part to instruct the young elf but found him to be as equally precocious as he was frustrating to instruct. The boy had no interest in learning or leadership, let alone the dicey world of espionage and diplomacy. The lad was cheerful and sweet, but much more content to wile away his day with friends at the theater or listening to poetry and music in the square. But such was nearly every other young elf of his status and station.

And yet, amongst the older elves, there had been many a furrowed brow and wrung hand over this generation, who had apparently gone tender instead of tough. They did not understand struggle, for prosperity was gifted to them. How could they make difficult decisions if they'd never been tested? Fortunately for them, the perfect opportunity arrived with the rebellion of the warlord Kreeg. Now these young elves could march into glorious battle and have their mettle tested. They would ride forth as boys and return as men. Even Lady Blackroot, after much consideration and private tears, had sent her remaining son to be counted amongst the true and noble guardians of virtue—the Holy Army of Arathes.

Fraenk could see the toll it took on her, however. And between the worry for her son, the troubles of managing the turbulent district, and her failing health, the battle of life had turned into a siege. Just how much longer could she hold out?

Seeing her now gave Fraenk hope. Here was Lady Arice Blackroot, ready for another quest. Her eyes glinting with mischief. Fraenk couldn't help but wonder if this might be her final adventure. She was as old as any elf he knew. Any day, she might begin what they called the Twilight— an end-of-life malaise that takes hold of elves in their declining years. Progressively losing interest in talking, interacting, eating, drinking, and eventually just being. They pass into the grace of beyond shortly after. Lady Arice Blackroot was already well at that age. Some fatalistic part of Fraenk wondered if this might be her swan song. One last blaze before the fire went out.

He suddenly had another flash of memory. The face of his mother. The bravery she had right before—Fraenk stopped himself. He never wanted to think of that day again.

"You can stop making that sour face now, Neversleep. We've arrived," Lady Blackroot interrupted his thoughts. She had an inquiring, almost concerned gaze. He blinked, trying to mask whatever expression he had been making. Fraenk looked out the window just as the carriage began to roll thunderously across the first of three sets of drawbridges that led to the palace. The scale of the place was absolutely enormous, and it was more beautiful than any building he'd ever been within the walls of. Every surface seemed to be embellished with intricate carvings or patterns in the ancient elven tradition. It was surely a wonder, even if it was a veritable prison for the young High Lord Whiteleaf.

Lady Blackroot's carriage was one of dozens arriving in a line that snaked up to the portcullis, and then the empty carriages were sent back out to wait for the gala's conclusion. When it was their turn to debark, Fraenk stepped out of the coach first, as custom dictated that the most honored guest was revealed last. A crisply dressed army of servants lined the entrance and applauded after each guest. Fraenk noticed none of the staff were human or even half-elves. All were full elves, and yet none looked bored or irritated to be forced to do the bidding of others.

"The Arch Preceptor of Blackroot, *Fank Neverspeak*," A tall elf with a parchment boomed when Fraenk set foot on the stones.

There was an anemic smattering of perfunctory applause. No one here knew him or even cared to. Fraenk noted how the elf butchered his name, however—which was not a mistake that the finely trained personal staff of the High Lord Elf would make out of error. There were plenty of elves that did not like humans, ones that were outright hostile, and the rest who showed their displeasure in other ways. And they seemed to be in greater numbers the higher one went up in the city. There would be many here who would freely express their contempt of Fraenk being at this event to begin with— even if he was the personal guest of Lady Blackroot. If it was meant to be a slight, Fraenk let it go; it was not likely to be his last one of the evening.

"Lady Arice Blackroot, High Lord of Blackroot district and widow of Lord Taener Blackroot," the servant announced as she now stepped out. There was a much more enthusiastic applause from those in attendance. She hooked a thin hand around Fraenk's elbow and waved to the crowd with the other.

"They love to remind me of my dead husband," she said through her clenched smile.

"Don't worry, my lady. At some point in the night, I'm going to stab that guy with a fork," Fraenk murmured back. She gave him an amiable squeeze.

The two burly personal guards stepped from the departing carriage, and they fell in behind Her Lady and Fraenk. With their entourage now complete, they stepped forward toward the entrance gate.

An odd sensation came over him as they approached the doors. Aside from the many servants lined up and an overly effusive greeter who was lavishing compliments and well wishes upon each guest, there was another figure just behind them who looked distinctly out of place for this event. He had black hair and a neatly trimmed beard. His eyebrows and regular expression gave him a scowling visage at all times. He also wore the black and red ornate robes of the Order of Arcane Lords. The feeling Fraenk realized he now had was dread.

"No weapons, no magic," the Arcane Lord recited as each guest approached.

Fraenk watched with increasing alarm as the Arcane Lord was casting some type of continuous spell that produced a faint blue sparkling mist. It delighted the already drunk wife of Lord Seawind, who clapped and tittered as she passed through the magical vapor. The wizard did not look like he was conjuring this spell just for the pleasure of the High Lord's guests, however.

And as if to confirm Fraenk's suspicions, he watched as Lady Seawind's face began to change in the glittering miasma. Whereas before, she looked young and lovely, with hardly a wrinkle on her skin, after passing through the cloud, her youthful appearance seemed to return back to the way she naturally looked.

"My dear, your face!" Lord Seawind noticed the change first and did a poor job hiding his disgust. Lady Seawind gasped and probed her cheek folds with curling fingers. Her geriatric metamorphosis might have gone unnoticed by most of the guests had she not suddenly begun to shriek.

"What is the meaning of this?!" Lord Seawind demanded angrily. The Arcane Lord did not respond directly but called out to someone standing just inside the entrance.

Arch Partisan Olwynn Brightrock stepped out, along with several partisan guards behind him. He, too, was dressed fancier than normal, but his attire was still that of an Arch Partisan. Apparently, his duties also included coordinating security with the palace.

Fraenk felt his stomach drop. This was bad. *Really bad.*

"Brightrock? What is all this?!" Lord Seawind bellowed in outrage, his words slurring to suggest he too had been drinking. They weren't close enough to hear what Brightrock said in reply, but they didn't have to. Lady Seawind was having trouble keeping a quiet tone and broadcast her indignation to everyone in the vicinity.

"What do you mean, 'no glamors'?! That's not dangerous magic... It's absolutely necessary! Can't you see?"

"My good lady wife spent a prince's fortune on getting that done, only to have this *CRUK* dissolve it! It's an OUTRAGE!" Living up to his surname, Lord Seawind was blowing like an ocean gale. But they were like the wind and waves against a cliffside. As the saying amongst the partisans went, "There's *no stone harder than Brightrock.*"

"Our orders are not to allow anyone inside with weapons, magical items, or any magical enhancement. That includes glamours. For the safety of our beloved High Lord of Arathes," Arch Brightrock replied, snarling back. "I'm sure you understand this precaution. We've had some imposters around the city lately."

Arch Partisan Olwynn Brightrock turned then and looked Fraenk dead in the eyes. Fraenk almost tripped in his sudden attempt to look innocent.

"Is the boy king going to compensate me for this?!" Lady Seawind shouted, pointing at her wrinkly face.

Brightrock gritted his teeth and glared for a moment. He then extended his hand, jabbing two fingers out, and then briskly made a beckoning gesture. The lead servant clapped his hands, and several of the servant elves darted off from the end of the row into the nearby carriage house. The sweaty, red-faced elf immediately realized he and his lady wife should have held their collective tongue.

"Uh. That is... I... we... on better thought, it's not necessary. We would be well pleased to enter the gala as we are, sir. Wait. What are you doing?" Seawind stammered nervously. His wife began to cry. One of the High Lord's smaller carriages, ornate with polished white enamel and gold inlay, came trotting out to a halt beside them. The servants smoothly and firmly moved the uninvited guests inside.

"Enjoy your evening down the hill, my lord and lady," the head servant simpered. And with that, the Seawinds were carted away from the palace in a pall of shame that they might never fully recover from. They would have been the most gossiped-about scandal if not for what happened later that night.

Before they could get to the entrance, Fraenk put his hand over Lady Black-root's own and made a show of seeming to recall something important. The two guards paused right behind them on either side.

"Um, I'm afraid I must once again beg your forbearance, my lady. I seem to have made another miscalculation," Fraenk said, smiling but keeping his voice low. She gave him a squinty-eyed stare.

"How could you possibly have gotten yourself into trouble in the carriage ride up here, Neversleep? I was with you the whole time," she asked, incredulous.

"Well, my lady... I had concocted a backup plan just in case we were not successful in acquiring the necklace ourselves. It involved someone from our house using a glamor to get inside and later pose as one of Fernbrook's retinue in order to steal the item."

"I see. And what depraved fool would you have enlisted into such a misguided scheme?" "In my defense, we're typically quite the crack team, My Lady," Fraenk said. "And she's become quite the expert in wearing faces..."

The burly guard to the lady elf's left shifted dark brown eyes, then gave her an apologetic look. Then Lady Blackroot recognized him... or rather *her*.

"So, you're in on this too, Gwen? Mersey save me from my preceptors."

36

FOR A LONG MOMENT, Lady Blackroot gave him a pinched look, which seemed to suggest she was preparing to use whatever life remained to her in order to take whatever life remained of Fraenk.

"Burning *skarking* hells," she said finally, then sighed. "I must admit it was not a bad contingency. I should know better than to underestimate you, Neversleep."

"If we pass through that mist, they're going to uncover our deception, and we'll have some uncomfortable questions to answer," Fraenk said. He didn't add anything about their earlier escapade of impersonating the Arch Partisan himself in order to break a thief out of custody. But the nervous look that passed between himself and Gwen said everything.

"We need to get her out of here without being obvious about it, or they'll know we're up to something," he concluded.

Fraenk shot a quick look over at Arch Partisan Brightrock and his guards, who were now ushering more dignitaries and guests through the glamor-stopping cloud, including some of Blackroot's own elite. Some waved or bowed to Lady Blackroot, while others gave confused glances in their direction. All of this loitering was calling some very unwanted attention to them. Fraenk had to do something.

He was just about to propose a half-formed idea when Lady Blackroot suddenly began to raise her voice and shout.

"What do you mean you don't have it, Neversleep?!" she shrieked, drawing surprised looks from everyone around them—none more surprised than Fraenk himself.

"I– I–" Neversleep began to stammer.

"I told you three times not to forget, but what do you do?"

"I apologize, my lady..." Fraenk picked up her cue and began to follow.

"Well, don't just stand there! Go and get it. It's probably back at the estate, yes?" She clutched her hands in exasperation. Several of the nearby lords and even a few servants gave bemused smiles at this sudden dramatic outburst.

Fraenk started to turn, but she grabbed his sleeve.

"No! You stay here. I'll send someone *competent* this time. Credelle, go and fetch us our invitation to the gala. And be quick about it." Lady Blackroot grabbed the young brown-eyed guard and shoved him forth. He gave a curt bow, an eye-roll to Fraenk, and then took off in a sprint back down the three-part drawbridge. The whole farce was crude but effective. Brightrock and his partisans already seemed to have had their attention drawn back to another not-so-young elf, who was finding his own chiseled square jaw going soft and his toned body was now puffing out of his tailored clothing like so much rising bread dough.

"They'd never keep you out for a lack of invite," Fraenk said to Lady Blackroot, keeping his head low in a display of contrition.

"Oh, but you forget... I'm just a confused old woman," she replied, head raised and shoulders back. Her dignity was ironclad. "If you let them underestimate you because of who you are, it's better than any glamor."

Just then a loud clattering sounded from the bridge as a team of six massive black horses came drawing an opulent long carriage up to the entrance. Its polished black wood was embellished with silvery green leaves coming off in long, looping strands. On its door was the familiar sigil of their recent nemesis, House Fernbrook.

The carriage halted, and footmen pulled open the double doors. Since the sun was already low on the horizon, it made the coach dark inside. But Fraenk already knew who would soon be emerging.

"Lord Farathiel Gingerglade, Arch Preceptor of House Fernbrook." The servant announced, as the spymaster stepped out first to a tepid applause that rivaled what even Fraenk received. While it could have been a general disdain for this loathsome gutter rat, the crowd's reaction seemed to be more of a general bewilderment at Gingerglade's ensemble.

Instead of the ostentatious formal robes that everyone else was wearing, Farathiel was dressed incongruously understated for this event. Tunic and doublet were both in a matching murky green. It did have the gold-stitched Fernbrook sigil large on the chest; the rest seemed barely enough to be considered formal, but it lacked any of the form-fitting lines and restrictive collars that were to be expected for a gala. It was blossomed and roomy at the body joints, which gave a rather comical, almost jester-like appearance. One might assume that the Acheron of Ceremonies in Fernbrook was negligent in his duties, preparing this poor elf for the gala. But Fraenk's trained eye saw a much darker purpose for Gingerglade's attire. He had on a suit built for movement— he was most certainly up to something.

Fraenk watched him smile at those around him. Smug, like he had a secret that no one else knew about. Like he was getting away with a crime right before their very eyes, and they were too stupid to recognize it. Something impish came over Fraenk then. Perhaps it was desperation or frustration. He didn't know if they would be able to stop Fernbrook's scheme. The city itself might be left wide-eyed and gape-mouthed at the end, when the dust had settled and Fernbrook stood victorious over them all. But the voice inside—the one that sometimes sounded like Miken but now was sounding a lot more like his own mother— that voice was telling him not to stop. Not to quit. Not to give up. And if Gingerglade thought he might just gloat over everyone for their having failed to uncover the deception, Fraenk Neversleep wanted him to know that he wasn't so easily tricked. There was one fool here, and Fraenk wanted everyone to know it.

"Lord Gingerglade, will you be entertaining everyone with some tumbling later? Perhaps some capers or juggling?" Fraenk called out. A burst of laughter went up from the crowd. Farathiel turned red-faced, craning his neck to see who had insulted him. The laughter would have continued if not for the loud voice of the head servant, nearly screaming over the top of the noise.

"The honorable Lord Malgraye Fernbrook!! High Lord of Fernbrook district and special guest of tonight's High Lord's Gala!"

Applause and cheers went up from those gathered around the entrance as all watched a thin, elegant elf with swept-back silver hair and high cheekbones step from the carriage. Lord Fernbrook did indeed look stately, but he had a pervasive curl to his nose that made him appear as if the entire world had a smell that offended his nostrils.

So here was the elf who had casually condoned the murder of his friend Miken the baker for no better reason than he was in the way of the elf's ambitions. Fraenk watched him with an icy glare as he strode forth toward the palace entrance.

"What's this *special guest* business?" He heard Lady Blackroot mutter under her breath. "The other lords will not be pleased, I assure you."

Several burly personal guards also stepped forward from the carriage. Fraenk thought he recognized the one with curly orange hair and a fading bruise on his cheek, but he couldn't be sure. The guards quickly encircled Lord Fernbrook as he approached the entrance, scattering the lesser elves who were already there.

"How can he get through with the necklace?" Lady Blackroot whispered the question that was already in Fraenk's mind.

They soon had their answer as Lord Fernbrook and his entire entourage, including Gingerglade, moved through the blue vapor without incident.

"He doesn't have it on him." Fraenk's brow furrowed. "He's smuggling in the Mind Thief some other way."

Fraenk and Lady Arice look at each other. *This was interesting.*

"Is there a problem, my Lady Blackroot?" The simpering head servant asked when they approached. Fraenk could tell that as much as this snobbish and bitter elf might privately enjoy the scorn and public humiliation of a human, his duties were to keep the guests flowing in and not to foul their evening before it began.

"It seems my servant here has forgotten my official invitation," she said in exaggerated annoyance.

"So hard to find decent help these days," he preened, giving Fraenk a side-eye. "I won't even allow a human on staff here for just those very reasons. Besides, they die of old age before you can even get them properly trained."

He tittered at his own wit, and Lady Blackroot obliged him with a tight smile.

"Of course, your invite isn't necessary. You and your... _underling_ are welcome guests of High Lord Whiteleaf." It was not lost on Fraenk how the servant slipped into elvish when he used their word for peon. He clapped his hands, and a nearby elf, who had surprisingly wide shoulders and a strong jawline, stepped forward and held out gloved hands.

With practiced ease, this escort hooked his hands under her arm and at the small of her back, drawing her toward the entrance in a sort of dancer's embrace. It was completely ostentatious and excessive— and made Fraenk renew his vow to not leave this party until he'd skewered any or all of these pretentious skarks with some type of dining utensil. Fraenk followed a pace behind as the group of them passed through the Arcane Lord's magical blue mist.

He felt a prickly coolness on his skin as they went through, and the air smelled faintly of lavender, as well as another bitter scent. Fraenk kept his eyes down so as to avoid any unintentional eye contact with Arch Partisan Brightrock, should he be nearby.

His caution was unnecessary, however, as Brightrock was already far up the wide path of the grounds that led past the many fantastically carved topiaries in the shapes of mythological beasts and into the palace itself. Soon they all were moving along it and towards the magnificent structure ahead.

Entering the grounds of the Monarch's Summer Palace, Fraenk wanted nothing more than to hate this place. It was a shining beacon to their supposed benevolent protectors, these elves who lived for centuries and believed they were personally blessed by the Lyn-Tyrians themselves. And yet for all their claims of virtue, even putting their lives at peril to fight wars in the name of peace and justice, they still spoke with open disdain for humans and allowed the absolute squalor of kobold town. How could they be such a powerful force against evil in other parts of the world and be blind to the suffering within their very walls?

But here in the Summer Palace, he had his answer.

Fraenk found himself— impossibly and in spite of every negative feeling he could muster against the elves— in awe. The palace was an absolute wonder of architecture, art, and engineering all working together in a beautiful harmony that seems to have in many ways improved upon the rugged mountaintop where it was constructed. Every line, every curve, and every surface, placed with a purpose and to evoke a feeling. The use of space was deliberate and organic. Fraenk could even make out where foundations and walls of the previous fortifications were now flawlessly merged with the palace as an apparent physical embodiment of their eternal glory and their assuredness of that conviction. And who would argue with the ones who could summon divine power to destroy their enemies on the battlefield?

When they were less than a dozen steps from the palace's tall doors, Lady Blackroot extracted her arm from the elf's grip.

"I think I can find my way from here," she said, irritably, and sent the elf servant away.

She turned to find Fraenk staring up in sheer wonder at the main palace, or rather the entrance to the wing that contained the ballroom.

"Close your gawp, Neversleep. It's just a building," Lady Blackroot said, pulling him off to one side before they could enter. Her expression had gone serious, and he could read worry in her eyes.

"Once we go inside, I am no longer your friend; I am your master. You must guard your tongue and show deference to your betters— which in this place is pretty much everyone. Now, I too must pay my respects to Lord Whiteleaf, and during the gala I will be seated amongst the elders, so you will be on your own."

"Are you warning me to stay out of trouble?" Fraenk asked.

"Neversleep. I've always trusted you to do what must be done, but I'm telling you in no uncertain terms that if you get put in a spot here, there's not a thing I can do to save you. I won't even try."

There was no malice in her voice. Just a simple statement of fact. How many times had she shielded him, protected him, and saved him? Not just in these past few weeks, but ever since he came into her service? Fraenk didn't know why exactly, but he meant something to her.

"My lady, that Arcane Lord's counter-magic cloud has given us a chance. It's forced Fernbrook to get the necklace in by some other means. I believe that Gingerglade will be the one to retrieve it. If I can intercept it—"

"Then waste no more time talking to me, Fraenk," she gave him a smile that was almost gentle, wordless with the layers of significance that one person could mean to another.

Then, Lady Blackroot took the arm of her remaining guard, and they moved into the grand ballroom. Fraenk reached for the bottle in his cloak and found that he had neither. In his current outfit, he was carrying less than when he was disguised as a monk—no knives or bottles or tinctures of any kind. He felt a hard lump in his breast pocket and realized he was still carrying the small brass flame-starting device given to him by Valthor. Somehow it had not alerted the Arcane Lord as a weapon or even as being magical. It was a defective gadget after all and probably not of much use.

But he still had his wits, and that would have to be enough.

Fraenk fell in behind a procession of brightly and theatrically dressed elves of Lord Gallais Amberflax's entourage. Amongst their number, he was hardly noticed at all as he slipped inside the grand ballroom of the summer palace.

Fraenk found Farathiel Gingerglade right away amongst the crowd in his buffoonish clothing. He appeared deep into a tale of daring with a group of bored-looking elven maidens, who all looked hopeful for the story's conclusion. Fraenk would need to wait for him to slip away; that would be the sign that their plan to collect the necklace was unfolding.

What did surprise him was to see Doran Leafwater here. And unlike Gingerglade, he was surrounded by a large cluster of mesmerized elves who were entranced and hanging off his every word.

"The vile beast was mortally wounded, but still it sought my blood. So I cranked back the ballista again. And just as it lunged, mouth open to swallow me whole... I fired!" Doran dramatized, acting out this confabulated tale to the transfixed audience. They squealed excitedly as he reached the story's climax.

"*Heh.* Looks like you made it out just fine, Leafwater," Fraenk chuckled to himself.

A small orchestra was set up where the room curved into a natural concave shape to project sound out into the ballroom. They were well into the third movement of a famous elven waltz as Fraenk entered. He watched for a moment, transfixed as dancers capered and swirled to the music, switching partners and returning back. Bowing and raising delicate hands into the air, all in beautiful unison. There was joy on their faces. And blissful abandon. It reminded him of his ill-fated excursion into kobold town before it all went to Chard and they had to run for their lives.

It was not in the contrasts between the elves and kobolds, but how much they were alike. Here was music. And dancing. The joyous faces. How similar they all were when it came right down to it. At the soul of each was someone who wanted to enjoy a song, step lively in a dance, eat, and perhaps even love. But then it all seemed so ridiculous. Could he even imagine elves dancing in the mud around a smoking cook fire? Or kobolds dressed in finery, curtsying to the High Lord here in the Summer Palace?

He scoffed at such a preposterous thought. Then again, hadn't Kyla found favor and kinship in the kobold Posuu? And she was a Lynblood, which put her in a status even above elves. If someone like her could find something worthy in the lowliest creature that most others still considered to be monsters, what did any of this mean? Was it all artifice to keep elves in power and make sure the likes of humans, dwarvenkind, and kobolds were always in the mud?

This was the place, after all. The Summer Palace, formerly the outpost where the elves stood and fired their terrible ballistas down on humans. Fraenk knew the damage those weapons could do on a shadescourge, let alone a human. The reminders were everywhere. Reinforcements of elven superiority. Even now he could see it— not carved into the walls as a subtle bas-relief, but as a huge painting hung on a wall. The Siege of Arathes rendered in all its glory from the perspective of brave elves standing on the ramparts with bows and siege weapons. In the painting, they didn't look like heroes— they looked like gods.

Fraenk's throat suddenly felt very dry. An odd dizziness hit him, and he could feel his heart thundering in his chest. He knew exactly what it required in such a situation. The answer was the liquid there in tall bottles behind a suave, brown-haired elf that was serving at the counter.

With a thin sheen of sweat beginning to form on his brow, Fraenk weaved through the crowd in the most direct path over, while still keeping an eye on Farathiel Gingerglade. The server quirked an eyebrow upon seeing his approach. There were already tall flutes of a clear, sparkly wine set out for guests to take as they liked, but Fraenk ignored them entirely.

"What's in those?" Fraenk asked directly, pointing to the tantalizing row of ornate decanters, each with a different color of intoxicant— from dark brown, amber, almost blood-red to perfectly clear. Any one of which could quench this thirst.

"Those?" The server's mouth playfully curled up at one corner. "Oh, you wouldn't like those. They're... intense."

"That sounds like exactly what I'm looking for," Fraenk replied. "Splash one out and we'll see how it bends."

The server stepped back and seemed to size Fraenk up for a moment before making some internal decision. He pulled the bottle of bronze-colored liquid and issued a healthy pour into a crystalline glass. He slid it toward Fraenk— a look of challenge on his face.

Fraenk took the glass in hand, inspected the liquor, gave it a swirl, and then a smell. It was smoky and warm. He took a tentative sip, and all the sound seemed to go out of the room.

It was perhaps the best booze he'd ever tasted. Smoother than summer silk. Fraenk took another sip, then downed the remainder with a gulp. When he looked up, the server seemed in awe because he had backed away wide-eyed and then gave a deep, deferential bow.

"If you think that's impressive, you should see me with a bottle of the cheap stuff. This is good, by the way. Very good. I'll have another," Fraenk said, setting the glass on the bar top. The server didn't move, however, just continued to stare deferentially at the floor.

"What is it, pal?" Fraenk asked, eyeing him curiously. Then he noticed how quiet the entire room was. The small orchestra had stopped playing, and no one seemed to be speaking.

Then Fraenk felt something touch his ear. Two warm fingers had gripped the helix of his outer ear and were rubbing against it. Someone was behind him, and they were _feeling_ his skin.

An immediate revulsion hit him. A deep and primal instinct shot up like a lightning bolt from a black corner of his brain. Fraenk didn't think; he just reacted. Pivoting, he wheeled quickly, slapping away the hand.

"Get your skarking hands off me—!" Fraenk started to shout but then stopped when he realized just whose hand it was.

Although he had never seen him before, there could be no mistaking the regally dressed elf with the golden sigil of pale foliage and garland of delicate silver leaves on his head. The elf who now stood opposite him with wide eyes.

It was the Watcher of the Pale, Warden of the West. His royal eminence, the elven High Lord, Krispen Whiteleaf.

37

A COLLECTIVE GASP WENT up, and High Lord Whiteleaf recoiled, cradling his hand like it had been bitten. There was a long, terrible moment where Fraenk and the High Lord stood staring at one another, both in equal amounts of surprise. The entire room was so quiet that all Fraenk could hear was the battering ram rhythm of his heart trying to knock its way out of his rib cage. Then came the echoing words of Lady Blackroot's final admonition— if he got into any trouble she would not come to his rescue.

And now, what was the first thing he did when he was left unsupervised? Slap the young elf ruler of the entire region. Well, perhaps they'd give him a swift death...

High Lord Krispen Whiteleaf's face suddenly burst into a smile, and he began to laugh. It was an infectious, high, clear sound that made Fraenk also grin.

Fraenk's smile curdled when he saw the hate glares from the contingent of house guards that were now forming a menacing semicircle that was closing in around the two men.

"I'm so sorry, my lord; I beg your great mercy," Fraenk said, bowing low, hoping he looked appropriately contrite. His entire course on how high lordly courtesies and behaviors from their own Acheron of Ceremonies had completely flown from his head. On the bright side, the High Lord didn't seem offended at all. He was absolutely giddy.

"You are a human, yes?"

"Uh... Yes, my lord. I am Arch Preceptor Fraenk Neversleep, at your humble service." Fraenk said quickly, bowing again for good measure. He made sure to leave out that he was from the Blackroot district. No sense in having his lady involved in whatever dark fate awaited him.

"How... delightful!" The High Lord exclaimed, still beaming with a brilliant smile. "I've never met a real human before. Your ears really are rounded, as they say. Fascinating!"

"That's right, my lord," Fraenk looked up at him, suddenly struck by what the High Lord said. "Wait. You've... never met a human?"

"You are my first!" Lord Whiteleaf examined him with bright, inquisitive eyes— like one might marvel at an exotic bird or one of the baby Shivan cubs that traveled in cages with the touring Curiosity Caravans out of Gazea-Gazon. It was an uncomfortable feeling, to be sure, but better than him being dragged off to be executed for assaulting the High Lord.

"I have so many questions," High Lord Whiteleaf said. "What do you like to eat? How do things sound in your round ears? Why is your body so thick? Is it hard to move?"

Now that he had recovered from the initial shock, Fraenk was acutely aware that here he was, speaking plainly with none other than the most famous and private elf in the entire region. The so-called 'boy king,' High Lord Krispen Whiteleaf himself. But he was no boy, like the rumors had suggested.

Whiteleaf appeared to be an adult elf and looked much like a human in his thirties. This was young in terms of the hundreds of years that elves lived, but he was nevertheless a grown man. He was quite handsome, and his body was thin and slender like most elves. He had an intense but not unpleasant gaze. And his demeanor seemed rather excitable and enthusiastic— *but how could one blame him?* Apparently having only seen fellow elves his entire life, he is now meeting his very first human. Too bad it had to be Fraenk.

And that was another little detail that itself struck Fraenk as odd. Roughly half the population of the City of Arathes was human, and he had never encountered a single one? They really did keep him sheltered in this palace. At least he was excited and curious to meet a human, considering the foul attitudes the rest of the elves at the top held.

A gaunt and waxy-skinned attendant slipped in beside High Lord White-leaf and murmured something about the 'other guests' and of his 'duties to the kingdom.' Whiteleaf's face looked wounded, but he willingly accepted his handling.

"We must talk again, Lord Neversleep," High Lord Whiteleaf said with a smile. "You interest me immensely!"

The High Lord was ushered away by his handler and the contingent of guards to greet an endless stream of revelers at the gala. He seemed to comport himself admirably, grinning and greeting his subjects with warmth and affection. But Fraenk read something of the caged Shivan cub in him as well. Trotted out before the crowds, made to dance and look winsome. Perhaps even the most powerful elf in the city was also trapped by it as well.

Fraenk wanted another glass of that booze but thought it was best to make sure Farathiel Gingerglade was in sight. Knowing how much he enjoyed licking boots, he was probably waiting for his turn to lap at the leathers of the High Lord.

But when Fraenk scanned the crowd, Gingerglade wasn't there talking to the uninterested maidens. Fraenk muttered a curse and struck off across the room. He must be somewhere else in the ballroom. The orchestra had taken a brief pause, but the party was still in full swing. But as he moved around from one side to the other, he couldn't find Gingerglade anywhere.

In fact, Fraenk couldn't see any of the Fernbrook guards either. Lord Fernbrook was standing by himself, looking fidgety and irritable near a small plinth displaying an ancient elven vase from the second dynasty. The remaining members of the High Council, including Lady Blackroot, were all conversing amiably in a tight group near the High Lord's seat. There was no sign of the remainder of the Fernbrook entourage. They must have used the distraction to slip out when Fraenk was talking to Whiteleaf. Now they were off somewhere else in the palace, most likely retrieving the necklace. He had to find them quickly, but they could be anywhere. And worst of all, Fraenk didn't have the first clue where to look.

He made his way quickly to the doors at the end of the ballroom that looked like they provided access to the rest of the palace. But the moment he approached, the two burly guards stepped politely but firmly into his path.

"Guests must stay in the Grand Ballroom, sir," The larger of the two said, gesturing back the way Fraenk had come.

"I was told I could tour the grounds," Fraenk tried, knowing before he even said it that the guard was not likely to relent. But if Fernbrook's men had passed this way, they would have had to contend with these guards as well. Fraenk wanted to be sure of their resolve.

"His Lord's residence is not a museum, sir." The second guard was more direct and far less polite. There was no way that Gingerglade and his goons got through this way.

"Why don't you enjoy the drinks and dancing, sir?" The first guard's suggestion could have had an "or else!" along with it. He pointed a sharp finger towards a long table where servers were now uncovering an unimaginable array of rich, delicious, bite-sized delicacies. Caramelized silver mushrooms garnished with pinflower. Briny radishes soaked in herring head jelly, lamb sausage, and fire onions on toasted hard bread; honeyjack jelly-braised lake snail skewers. Iced cabbage pudding bowls topped with oxblood curd. Wide leaves of gollen greens with a paste of shadewort berries—which the server assured was not poisonous because the toxic seeds were all painstakingly removed.

Shadewort and gollen greens. As Fraenk recalled, that was the exact combination of food used in the botched attempt on Lady Blackroot. One hidden inside the other. *Whose idea had that particular dish been?* Special request from the Fernbrooks or just an eerie coincidence? Whoever had attempted it, their plan had almost worked. The would-be assassin secreted an unconventional weapon amongst something ordinary, like garden vegetables. Hiding in plain sight— if only people knew what they were looking for. Then insight hit Fraenk like a fist to the face. And he knew how Lord Fernbrook planned to get the necklace into the party.

Fraenk watched the servers with the trays leave, and sure enough— while the other entrances and exits were all under close guard, the servant's entrance down to the kitchens was open and accessible. Perhaps there were guards somewhere down in the kitchens, but the priority seemed to be given to the long string of elves delivering new exotic dishes on silver trays.

Fraenk knew he had to get down there, but now that they were in full service, he would look sorely out of place if he tried to slip in amongst them. He noticed how the kitchen servants were all wearing black high-collared outfits, far less flashy but not too dissimilar from his own, only with a white apron cinched to their waist. He quickly scanned the room and noticed an elderly woman drowsing drunkenly on a settee. Her white silken shawl lay beside her on the seat. He quietly slipped in beside her and, when no one was watching, snatched the cloth up behind him. Then it was just a matter of tying it around his waist and ducking into the row of servants who had set down their trays and were now filing back down the stairs.

If any of them recognized that Fraenk wasn't one of them, none said anything. As Fraenk suspected, a single guard strode down through the kitchens, but he looked more interested in dipping a finger in and tasting the sweet and savory sauces than in keeping a close eye on the servants.

The kitchen was a hot dance of chaos, with orders barked and bodies in motion. They were clearly good at what they did, because somehow a steady stream of fresh and steaming trays continued back up the staircase to the ballroom. Fraenk noticed several of the servants wearing billowy white hats that covered their ears and quickly snagged an unattended one of his own in order to preserve his disguise.

"Get those leeches over to Colsuma!" Shouted a sweaty, round-bellied elf who was sautéing some cuts of vegetables and meat over searing flames. It took him a moment, but Fraenk realized the man was talking to him. Fraenk had no idea who Colsuma was, but it was best for him to blend in and look obedient.

Carefully, he hefted a nearby bucket full of fat black leeches in the direction indicated by the chef's wagging spoon. They writhed, making moist sucking sounds as he lifted them up, seeming to sense fresh blood nearby. Fraenk's gorge rose briefly, but he looked away and breathed. What possible unholy dish they were concocting for these vile creatures, Fraenk was sure he didn't want to find out. Elves truly had an odd palette. Sometimes they demanded cuisine of the most pure plants and fungus that nature could offer, and other times— especially when spirits were involved—delving into the depths of culinary depravity. Not that other species were much better. Fraenk had lost more than one of his trained skrates to a hungry human family's cook fire. Kobolds were even less picky, to the point where rats avoided their area entirely. At least the kobolds and humans were honest about it.

As Fraenk weaved his way between the sweaty bodies of the chefs and servants, he watched as one of the leeches was probing dangerously close to his thumb. Another memory suddenly came to him from childhood. Young Fraenk had just finished a swim in the pond not far from their house. He had felt something odd; there in his armpit Fraenk discovered a dark, wet body, engorged with blood. And he was screaming for his sister to pull it off, but she too was screaming and wouldn't touch it. He had to run all the way home before his mother could remove the tiny black demon parasite.

The heat in the room was suddenly too intense. Fraenk was breathing heavily, his vision separating and coming back together. He bumped into the back of an elf who was delicately filleting a white trout. The knife slashed down hard, cutting entirely through the fish. The chef cried out, aggrieved that somehow Fraenk had ruined the entrée, but he didn't care. Fraenk moved forward without stopping.

Then a glorious fresh breeze brushed his cheek. He panted, taking in the coolness that was somehow fresh and carrying a dizzying array of other scents. Somewhere ahead was an open door to the world.

Fraenk slipped around the end of the row of cookfires and past the domed oven where hot loaves of bread were rising. As he passed by one oven, he caught a flash of an image. Two pairs of children's legs sticking out of the oven's mouth, smoking and black, Fraenk pinched his eyes shut. He could feel the roiling alcohol gurgling in his gut. What was this stuff?

He fell back against the kitchen wall, gasping.

"Fraenk," he heard a woman's voice say in his mind. *"Keep going. Don't stop."*

The panic, fear, and noise that was boiling in his mind like a steaming cookpot began to settle. He slowly opened his eyes. Everything was much as it was, but somehow he felt like he was different—the way a stone feels in the stream with the water moving all around him. In the midst of the chaos, he was solid.

His attention turned to the open doorway to his left that was letting in a gentle breeze. A doorway to the outside. A way for the necklace to get in.

Fraenk took a moment to steady himself against the back wall. The kitchen was still a swirling hive, but none seemed to notice him there. He checked back specifically at the elf who had given him the order. He seemed to be in an argument with another elf, both of them shouting and gesticulating with sharp knives in hand. Fraenk took one more glance around, making sure there was no one watching, then slipped back into the hall. There was definitely cool air blowing, like a fresh wind wafting in from outside.

Then he heard a rhythmic rumbling and the creaking strain of ropes. Low voices muttering, which he couldn't decipher but carried the tone of illicit dirty dealings.

Fraenk stepped silently as the hallway opened into the dim storeroom. He gave his eyes a moment to adjust.

Inside was so full of provisions for the gala, it was downright claustrophobic. There were large barrels of ale, hanging links of sausage and cured ham, crates and boxes full of fresh produce, bottles of spirits, dried ropes of seaweed, bags of grain and flour, and pretty much anything the guests of the young High Lord might desire. As Fraenk had surmised, since the palace was not supplied by large, unsightly carts of goods rattling endlessly through the elegant main Summer Palace entrance, it must have some kind of service lift to bring in food and other supplies. That must be what was letting in the air now.

Although there were two lanterns lit, most of the illumination in the room came from an ethereal blue square of light glowing in the floor. It was a strangely incongruous place, an inverted gateway where it opened into the sky. Of course, the portal was where the elevator platform descended from. It was approximately the size of two side-by-side horse carts, with a fat rope that hung down from the heavy winch and pulley system above. One had to admit that it was quite an ingenious design. And best of all, it could only be operated by someone inside the palace, so no potential infiltrators could use the lift to gain access from without.

Fraenk crept into the room for a closer look, realizing he was still carrying the bucket of leeches, but now with no good place to set them down. Then, in one terrifying moment, a man's silhouette stepped out from a stack of crates in front of the hole. His outline was thin and had the unmistakable jester-like puffs at the joints. It was Gingerglade.

Fraenk froze in his tracks, not daring to move or breathe. He couldn't tell which direction the elf was facing until his head tilted, and it was clear that he was looking down and out the opening. Fraenk breathed a tight sigh of relief, then slipped behind the ale barrels, just to be safe. That was too close.

Peering around, he could see one of the Fernbrook guards now working at the elevator's controls, putting tension on the line that controlled the massive counterweight— slowing the ascent of the elevator platform. Two more of the Fernbrook men were on the other side of the hole, their faces drawn in sharp contrast of pale blue light and heavy shadow.

"Careful, you fool! You're going too fast," Gingerglade barked at the man using the controls. He pulled up slightly on the lever to compensate. "Now that's too slow, idiot!"

The guard at the controls— who Fraenk now recognized as the man who had beaten him bloody a few days ago, Sir Edwyrd. Fraenk recalled saving that man's life by keeping him from drowning. Now here he was again, looking ready to beat Gingerglade instead. Fraenk quietly reveled in that idea.

Farathiel Gingerglade turned his attention back to the rising platform.

"Do you have it?" He called down eagerly.

Fraenk didn't hear the reply, but judging by Farathiel's reaction, whoever was on the platform did indeed have the necklace.

This is it, Fraenk thought.

It was a relief to finally know where the Mind Thief was. Now all he had to do was get it away from his devious nemesis and the complement of guards— which looked to be yet another in a long line of complicated problems, which Fraenk wasn't exactly prepared for. There were some jobs that called for a careful, multiple-step plan, executed with clockwork precision, that left your targets wondering how you even pulled it off. Ideally, with weeks of preparation and lots of accomplices to make sure it executes flawlessly. These were well suited for ideal conditions. The street kid in Fraenk had a much simpler, albeit crude, method for getting his hands on the necklace... known in the streets as the alley rat special: "snatch and dash."

While the Fernbrooks were distracted, Gingerglade still criticizing how the lift operator was still 'doing it wrong,' Fraenk slipped from his hiding place and crept quickly up the aisle. The light in the room began to dim as the platform was nearing the top. The best weapon Fraenk had at the moment was the element of surprise— and also a bucket of leeches, which too would be their own surprise.

Then suddenly, a cold prickle crawled up his neck and across his scalp. The instinct he'd formed on the streets and sharpened as a preceptor told him something was amiss. And there he saw it. Rising up from the hole in the floor were two black points that quickly became horns. The platform continued to ascend, revealing another of Fraenk's least favorite people in Arathes, ascending from the underworld below like the demon that he was.

Sorzon Brimblade. The helltouched warlock.

38

H ER LEG WAS STILL a warm wave of discomfort as Kyla sat up on the healer's billet. The temple's nursing attendants, who she was told were supposed to be discreet and even dispassionate in their duties of the healing arts, were somehow anything but either. From the moment Valthor brought her in, the staff became uncomfortably fixated on her. The specific attendants, of which she seemed to have twice as many assigned as anyone else there, were constantly fussing with her bedding or coming in with a tray of savory cheese and salted fish for her. Others in the building Kyla would catch staring at her wistfully. The feeling was somehow both flattering and off-putting at the same time.

Then it occurred to her why this was happening. Kyla had been living in the shadows so long that she had forgotten the effects of her Lynblood birthright. Her caretakers had called it 'the Charm,' and it was quite the opposite.

Kyla experienced it as long, awkward gazes from strangers and their inexpressible desire to be close to her. This would soon turn to professions of adoration and love. And if it went on for too long, the effects became sinister, with aggressive advances and demands until Kyla would have to forcefully defend herself.

She sometimes wondered if other Lynbloods experienced this same thing, but she had never met another to ask. She was a most rare and elusive creature. Perhaps now that Posuu was dead and she apparently wasn't welcome in Arathes, she might venture out and try to find another like her. They could live in a beautiful estate together, sponsored by some wealthy lord who just wanted to gaze at living art— like they were human peafowl, strutting about with bright plumage. Just another beautiful _thing_ to be collected.

No. That would never do. She had fought for and earned everything she had— not that it was all that much anymore. And who did Neversleep think he was to dictate to her where she could and should go? He may have saved her life, but that didn't mean it now belonged to him. The next time she saw him, she would give him a healthy piece of her mind.

That thought made Kyla grind her teeth. She could not stand to remain in the building any longer, where eyes were constantly on her. Kyla decided it was time to go.

"Miss! You shouldn't try to move," the young attendant said the moment she noticed Kyla attempting to rise. She rushed over to the bedside and gently forced Kyla back down.

The attendant was a sweet-natured half-elf named Meerie, who had a plain face and golden brown hair woven into a spiraling braid that was pinned up on her head according to the temple's custom. Although she was annoyingly attentive, she was less so than others— which was good. Kyla also insisted that Meerie be the only one to see to her. And she'd insisted it happen at a much less frequent interval than the dizzying nurse schedule, which had someone intruding on her with what seemed like every other breath.

Meerie was still a nurse's apprentice, which put her on a closer to equal footing for differences in medical opinions. And Kyla would need that advantage now as she attempted to quit her current care.

"I thank you, Meerie. But I must be off. I need to— ugh!" Kyla grunted, unsuccessfully trying to keep her discomfort from showing in her voice.

"Oh no, miss. Don't get up," the attendant looked stricken. "We've only just bandaged and salved your leg. Plus, the tincture you've taken is going to make you woozy for a while."

"You can't keep me here."

"I wouldn't think of it, my lady. But you're so special. I'd hate myself if something bad happened and I didn't try to stop you."

Kyla squeezed her hand and gave her a smile. Meerie blushed shyly.

"You don't get many Lynbloods down this way, do you?"

"I never thought I'd get to actually see one in my life," she said excitedly. "What I mean is, you're a living gift of the Powers and blessed by—"

"Almost like I'm not a living person," Kyla said, an edge of sarcasm in her tone.

"Oh no, miss!" I didn't mean—" Meerie looked stricken.

"It's alright. I'm teasing you, sweet girl," Kyla smiled, swinging her good leg to the floor. "Help me up."

Meerie did as she was asked. Early on, Kyla had insisted upon a privacy screen, which made it somewhat easier for the two of them to get Kyla dressed. At least no one would be staring at her. She also took the added measure of covering her golden wavy hair in a hood and wrapping her face with a scarf. Meerie's enamored gaze seemed to diminish some, which Kyla was glad of. She wanted no further attention.

Before she was nearly killed by that demon-faced helltouched, Kyla had planned to sell the Ynne es Tylubourne and use the money to establish herself in a new city anyway— the pathetic entreaty of that rock-headed Neversleep notwithstanding. She had become notorious to too many people, not just the Fernbrooks, but now the partisans and Arcane Lords as well. Being famous was disadvantageous if one maintained a criminal lifestyle.

It wouldn't be too difficult for someone with her skills to find jobs somewhere else, but she'd need money to travel. Kyla needed to get the necklace back. And if she was able to extract a little revenge along the way, all the better, she mused with a dark grin.

But her bandaged leg reminded her how that prospect was dangerous. And not one she could do alone. She had no crew anymore and no one she could trust.

Well, maybe not *no* one.

"Where can I find the man called Neversleep?" Kyla asked.

Meerie seemed to find this funny, because she broke out into a warm smile.

"What is it?" Kyla asked.

"Well, miss, all you need to do is stick around here for a while. He's bound to be in soon with this or that injury," Meerie said. "They keep an open bed just in case he comes stumbling in."

It was Kyla's turn to smile. "That bad, eh?"

The young woman nodded and laughed.

"Never mind. I'll just be off. Perhaps I'll just walk the city and listen for the largest calamity. He's sure to be nearby."

Meerie suddenly gave her a serious look.

"You shouldn't be out wandering the streets of Arathes, miss. It's dangerous. The priest says there's a dark moon out and the stars are in a wrong position. I'm just a girl, so I don't know too much, but my nanna says it's a bad omen. Plus, there's men out there who hide in the darkness. They would *hurt* a beautiful lady like you."

"I'll be safe, Meerie. The Powers watch over me."

Kyla slid her small dagger out of its scabbard, showing several inches of honed steel. Then clacked it shut again.

"That's for the ones who need more convincing," she winked as she fixed the scabbard to her belt.

Once Kyla was on her feet, Meerie helped her to the door, looking heartbroken like she was seeing a dear friend depart on a long and perilous journey. Kyla found it endearing, in spite of herself.

"I thank you for your help, and you have my blessing," Kyla said, lowering her scarf and kissing Meerie on the forehead. It was a gesture she hadn't done in many years. An honorarium that was said to bring good fortune to its recipient for the rest of their days. But also one that her vile caretakers had turned into a paid service for her to perform when she was a child— and one she vowed never to do again. But now it seemed both right and good.

Meerie had tears streaming down her cheeks when she looked up. Kyla pulled the scarf back over her face and limped out the door.

Exiting the Temple of Mersey, Kyla chose a direction at random, just wanting to be away from there. Already the shadows were growing long, and the sun would be setting soon. Kyla saw the bare, tall masts of the ships at the docks ahead, not too distant, but still arduous considering the condition of her leg. The fresh air seemed to carry with it a new clarity.

A quiet, inner voice seemed to be urging yet another path. She could beg passage with a group of prioresses on pilgrimage, returning home to Bactropolis. Maybe she would even join their order— give up the life of thievery and take a vow of charity instead. They'd certainly welcome her to their simple lives of service to the divines, and she'd never go hungry again. No more revenge or life-threatening danger. And no more excitement, for that matter.

It made sense on a practical level. Perhaps this was the fresh start she actually needed.

As she began to move, Kyla found that her leg was already feeling... not better, exactly, but at least dull to the pain. It still felt heavy and stiff, and she moved like a woman thrice her age. But hobbling along like an old woman had one great advantage— all who passed seemed to completely ignore her. No uncomfortable stares or searching hands. She was effectively invisible.

"I should've become an old woman years ago," Kyla thought with an amused chuckle.

As she finally made it to the street that led down to the docks, a thin sheen of sweat had formed on her brow. She needed to rest, and the scarf was stifling.

Kyla was about to remove it when she noticed the two men heading her way. Her breath caught in her throat, and she nearly stumbled. It was the same two men whom she had spied on earlier in the tavern. Coming quickly in her direction were the shady broker Dandrikan and a haggard-looking Leos Muninger.

Rage, heartbreak, and fear all mixed together when she saw the man who was responsible for Posuu. Not even a thought, but an impulse flooded her, and all plans for a life of service and charity vanished in a storm cloud of hate. It was as if the dark fates had provided Dandrikan, and this was her chance to send him to Geth's Door.

Her hand dipped into her robes, grabbing the handle of the dagger in her belt. She would become that agent of vengeance, by the Powers. All she had to do was let him get close.

But as she stood, Kyla felt her hand begin to tremble as her adrenaline mixed with pain and fatigue. Could she even trust herself to strike true? She might as well have been an old woman, for in her current state, she couldn't run or fight. And the imposing bodyguard with the two-handed sword strapped to his back would surely hack her to bits, whether she killed Dandrikan or not.

Still shaking, Kyla decided now was not the moment— but her revenge would come. She lowered her head and tried to look hunched and elderly, hoping her disguise would hold. She needn't have worried.

The two men advanced quickly, oblivious to her presence. Dandrikan was rattling off a diatribe of instructions to Leos, who only appeared to partially register the words. He had dark rings around his eyes, and his face was pale. Something was definitely wrong with him.

"... get up there and be ready to recover the necklace. That's most important, hear me? And before you do, you must drink this..."

Kyla saw Dandrikan hand Muninger a bottle of black liquid. She barely had enough time to stagger to one side to keep from being plowed over as they passed. Muninger took the bottle and headed up the road back toward the upper city, while Dandrikan continued on toward the docks.

The Ynne es Tylubourne—Kyla thought. Dandrikan was still plotting to get his hands on it. She also noticed the tension in his tone. He was speaking like a man whose scheme could fall apart at any moment. Perhaps he had a buyer lined up and stood to gain enormously. Whatever it was, Dandrikan had just sent his bodyguard away to recover it, leaving him dangerously exposed.

Kyla stopped and looked up. She could see the tall masts of the ships in the harbor again. Ready to embark and take someone like her somewhere—anywhere else in the world. The possibilities were endless. She might journey to a place far away, where she could forget all the pain this city had caused her and start a new life. It would be the right thing to do and even honor the power whose own temple she had just been healed at. Forgive and move on.

That's what a Lynblood was expected to do. They were not criminals or schemers or plotters of foul deeds. They were exalted and pure. That was what everyone believed. But not all the Lyn-Tyrians were about charity and forgiveness. Some were agents of divine justice and retribution. Some destroyed entire armies with their fiery blades. Perhaps that was the type of Lynblood she was, too.

Kyla watched for a moment longer as a single gull cut an angle across the sky away from her. Then she flipped her hood back up and turned, following the shadowed path that led down after her condemned betrayer, Dandrikan.

Fraenk had just enough time to slip behind a crate of fragrant mushrooms before the elevator carrying Brimblade came to a stop. This new development certainly shoved a stick into the spokes of his poorly conceived plan. Perhaps they had done him a favor, however, and forced him to think for a moment before acting.

He could not see what was happening from his hiding spot, but it became clear that he didn't really need to. Brimblade and Gingerglade exchanged growled acknowledgements with each other before getting straight to business.

"Is that it?" Gingerglade asked eagerly.

Fraenk had seen Brimblade holding a wooden box, gripped protectively at his chest as he entered, and now heard the helltouched open it.

"Your master has use of the Mind Thief for one hour. *One hour.* Then it must be returned here to me."

"Yes, yes. You'll get your necklace back, when—" Gingerglade's dismissive tone was cut off.

"If it's not back in my hands in one hour, I'll come up after it with a few of my friends from below. And you most certainly don't want that," Brimblade warned malevolently.

"Release me!" Gingerglade choked, then began to cough. Fraenk wished he could see the scene of the helltouched squeezing the sniveling elf's neck but didn't dare move from his hiding place.

"You'll have it back. I swear," Gingerglade sounded angry, but there was fear in his voice as well.

After a pause, there was the sound of the box being opened.

"Not much to look at, is it?" Farathiel Gingerglade said, stifling a yawn.

"If you only understood its true power," Brimblade replied.

"And what dark scheme do you have planned for it, I wonder?"

"Go on, you're wasting time."

"That's right, you're not allowed to touch it, are you? You wizards and your traps..." Gingerglade chided derisively.

Fraenk heard movement, which must have been the elf picking up the necklace, for the next sound was the wooden box snapping closed.

"You, wait with the helltouched. The rest of you, with me. Let's go," Gingerglade ordered his guards. All but the large, bearded man at the elevator controls formed up around their Arch Preceptor, forming a tight phalanx. Fraenk's snatch-and-run plan was surely out of the question now.

They moved as a group up the row and toward the storeroom's exit.

"I'll be waiting," Brimblade called after them as a warning.

Fraenk tried to make himself as small as possible behind the crate of mushrooms. The group passed him without notice. Too intent on their own purposes.

He heard them go out of the storeroom and down the hall back to the kitchen.

Well, you've missed your chance to get the necklace, and now you're stuck in this room with a murderous warlock and Fernbrook guard, Fraenk scolded himself. If he didn't get back upstairs and stop Gingerglade soon, he'd never get another chance. But first he had to deal with these two.

Fraenk looked down at the bucket of leeches. One of them had crawled up and latched onto the back of his hand. Revolted, Fraenk quickly pulled it off and almost crushed it in his fist when suddenly he had an idea.

Sorzon Brimblade was pacing on the elevator platform and muttering dark curses to himself when Fraenk stepped out from the shadows, striding quickly down the row. The man's dark expression first looked annoyed— probably expecting Gingerglade— but then twisted into cold fury when he recognized Fraenk. His face then changed again to surprise as Fraenk slung the contents of the bucket into the air at the two men. A moment later, they were splattered with large, wiggling aquatic parasites.

At first, they didn't recognize what they'd been hit with, only turning to face their surprise attacker.

"Neversleep! I was hoping to have another chance to—" Brimblade sneered, reaching down to the sheath at his belt where he kept his unholy dagger. Then something squelched wetly on his doublet, turning his attention. It took only a moment for him to register the dark, writhing leeches. He began to wail in a high-pitched voice that seemed incongruous for this terrifying visage.

"Obscura Veinfiends!" Brimblade screeched, batting at them furiously. "How did you escape the underrealm?!"

The Fernbrook guard recoiled as well, either because of the leeches or the terrible cacophony of the helltouched.

Fraenk used the distraction, running quickly to close the gap between himself and the Fernbrook man. The guard looked up just in time to see Fraenk swing the empty bucket in a wide arc. It smashed against the side of his head, shattering in a spray of wet chunks of wood. He staggered backward, momentarily stunned. Fraenk kicked hard, hitting the guard in the side of his thigh— a technique he'd learned from his fight training. The effect was immediate. A nerve spasm shot through the man's leg, and he dropped to one knee with a grunt.

Fraenk turned, looking for something else to bludgeon this man with, when two mighty arms locked around his chest. The Fernbrook guard had caught him in a bear hug, with one arm pinned to his side and the other up at his chest. Fraenk felt the man's muscles engage, and the air *WHOOSHED* out of his lungs.

Fraenk tried to breathe, but he couldn't pull in anything. His hand instinctively went for the brace of knives at his hip, but of course they weren't there. He couldn't move or breathe. He had no weapons because of that cursed Arcane Lord's magical mist. All he had was—

The kindler.

If his arms had been trapped in any other configuration, Fraenk would have found himself constricted to death by this oversized man with his foul breath and long, orange beard. With his pulse thundering in his ears, Fraenk spidered his fingers into his breast pocket until they touched the cold brass block. He tweezered the gadget between his index and middle fingers and lifted it out.

Just then, the guard shook him, and for one terrifying moment, Fraenk felt the Kindler slip free. An instant later, it landed in his palm.

Fraenk flicked the cover open and mashed the lever, which called forth the flames.

Nothing happened.

His vision was starting to swim as his lungs burned for air. He tried the lever again. This time, several sparks shot out of its opening, but that was all. Fraenk pressed again and again, more frantic as panic flooded him.

Then the voice came again. *Her* voice.

"The flame is there. Be patient, Fraenk."

He stopped, then drew his thumb down on the lever slowly. He could feel the mechanism inside catch on another internal part with a satisfying 'click.' Then a fireball the size and color of the guard's head exploded from the end of the device. And an instant later, his beard was a fiery version of its former appearance.

He released Fraenk with a surprised scream, stumbling backwards and swatting at his face. The big man collided right into Brimblade, who had just flicked away the last leech and turned his attention back to Fraenk. The two men collided and fell into each other's arms like some farcical tryst of two unlikely lovers. They landed in a tangle on the elevator platform floor.

Fraenk coughed and gasped on his knees. He knew he needed to get up, but at this moment was just grateful for breath.

Brimblade and the guard quickly separated, scrambling back up to their feet to face Fraenk, red-faced and enraged. Brimblade pulled his dagger, and the Fernbrook guard raised his two massive fists. It looked for a moment like there might be a competition for who would get to be the one to kill Fraenk.

Fraenk rose quickly to face them, but a wave of dizziness sent him wobbling backwards toward the elevator controls. His hand landed on the brake lever of the elevator platform. The two men realized where they were standing much too late.

"Going down?" Fraenk asked, then shoved the lever forward. Immediately, the platform dropped, taking a wide-eyed Brimblade and the guard with it. The rope keened and smoked through the block as it unspooled at a furious rate. The platform dropped fast, its hardware not allowing for complete free fall, but it was certainly not anything Fraenk would want to be on when it came to its terminus.

He moved to the opening to watch it reach the ground with a distant crash. Both men bounced off the platform and tumbled several feet. They lay dazed on the ground, moaning. Not dead, but it would be a while before they would be able to give him any further trouble.

"And just to be on the safe side..." Fraenk flipped the counterweight lever and let the elevator platform rise again. These two would have to go around to the main gate if they wanted back in to the party. And the helltouched man in particular would not be a welcome guest at all.

Fraenk had no time to revel in his victory, however. Gingerglade was probably moments away from placing the necklace in Lord Fernbrook's hands. He only hoped he wasn't too late to stop them.

39

TIME WAS ONCE AGAIN Fraenk's enemy, and subtlety would be its first casualty. Certainly, a careful and stealthy exfiltration of the storehouse and palace kitchens would have been optimal, but Fraenk had no moments to spare. He would have to go all out and hope he could get to Gingerglade and Fernbrook before they could act.

Sprinting past a surprised kitchen staff, Fraenk took the stairs three at a time to get back to the Grand Ballroom. He could hear a distant, thunderous round of applause, then a man speaking— the voice was that of High Lord Krispen Whiteleaf. He seemed to be making some address to the crowd.

The ballroom itself was empty but for a few guards standing near the outer doors. The hallway that led deeper into the palace, which was previously blocked by guards, now stood open and was where the sound of the speech was coming from.

Fraenk moved towards the voice as quickly as he could without looking too suspicious— just another late arrival to the High Lord's speech.

He had no time to admire the beautiful construction and artwork in this new section of the Summer Palace. Everyone seemed to be gathered ahead in the hall, even bigger than the ballroom. This one had eleven thrones set up, where the Lord Elves of the High Council now sat. Krispen Whiteleaf stood in front of the centermost and largest throne, where he was now addressing the gathered crowd.

His words became clear as Fraenk slipped into the room.

"...have benefitted from not only my education from the finest minds in all of Sarmatti and the world beyond, but I have been under the care of the wisest and most prudent gathering of elven minds anywhere in the world."

Whiteleaf gestured to the seated elves on either side of him. As another wave of applause rose, the elven lords nodded back dutifully and otherwise looked stately and serene.

"I have long sought their guidance for all matters of governance, for the city and beyond. I bestow upon them my highest honor for good and faithful service."

Ten servants, who had been positioned at the front of the crowd, now stepped forward. Each held out something in front of them, which they now passed to the members of the High Council of elves. When the servants stepped aside, Fraenk could see that they were small, delicate silver leaves encased in a dome of glass. He had never seen anything like them, but whatever they were, the crowd exhaled an awed gasp.

"I present the leaves of the Borellean Silver Tree. The oldest mortal living being in the known world," High Lord Whiteleaf said. "May your goodness, loyalty, and nobility continue long after the last leaf has fallen and blown to the horizon." Another huge round of applause and cheers went up.

"Those are worth a fortune," Fraenk heard a thoroughly drunk elf beside him remark.

As High Lord Whiteleaf's speech continued extolling the virtues and achievements of the High Council, Fraenk moved through the back of the crowd forward towards the dais. He could see Farathiel Gingerglade right up front across from the throne where Lord Fernbrook sat looking smug and devious. Fraenk couldn't tell if he had the necklace in hand, but he certainly sat with the confidence of one whose plan was in order. And if he was in possession of it, then Fraenk wasn't quite sure what to do next.

Stop him if he tries to use it.

He had to get closer to do that. So Fraenk continued to weave his way through the crowd. A nervous, excited energy seemed to be in the air as Fraenk caught snippets of conversation from the elves he was moving past.

"—What is he doing?"

"—he's declaring his ascension." "No, he's already High Lord."

"—promoting someone new to the High Council?"

"I heard he's formed a new alliance with the Tyrant."

"My lady's maid said he's getting *betrothed*."

Fraenk was actually a bit surprised by all this wild speculation. The elves were notoriously tight-lipped about each other and almost never speculated in front of humans about their High Lord. This kind of reckless rumor-mongering was reserved for behind closed doors and after they were well into their cups. But then he realized that was the exact condition he was in now, only they didn't expect Fraenk to be among them.

Fraenk quietly slipped in directly behind Gingerglade just as High Lord Whiteleaf appeared to be finishing up his speech. A kind of breathless hush fell over the gathered elves, and Fraenk realized he'd been too focused on Fernbrook— he missed what the High Lord had said.

Whatever it had been, all the High Council looked shocked. A cacophony of mutterings and whispers went up from all gathered. Krispen Whiteleaf began to shout to be heard over the voices.

"You have heard me right, my lords and ladies! From this day forth, I am officially disbanding the High Council of Arathes so that the kingdom may grow, and I along with it. I do not make this decision lightly, and this is not a punishment nor a rebuke for those who have served me well. The province, the city, and I will be forever grateful for their service."

Now it was Fraenk's turn to be shocked. This was the last outcome he expected from this event. Fraenk stole a glance at Lord Fernbrook, who was red-faced and looked completely blindsided and enraged. Obviously this wasn't part of his plan either.

Good. Fraenk thought. Take away the elf's power, and it wouldn't matter what he did with that necklace. Perhaps for all the skulduggery and murder, Lord Fernbrook's plan would unravel without Fraenk even having to lift a finger. Life never seemed to be short on irony.

But when Fraenk looked at Lady Blackroot, expecting to see her with some kind of reaction, she was staring straight ahead impassively like nothing had even happened. Then Fraenk noticed all the High Council were doing the same thing— all except Lord Fernbrook, who had a look of grave concentration on his face.

"I would like to take this time to announce that... that... " High Lord Whiteleaf suddenly faltered, like he'd forgotten what he was about to say. His eyes seemed to go dull, and his voice lost all of its inflection. "...that I will be abdicating my position as High Lord of Arathes and Warden of the Pale."

"No, my lord!!" One of the white-clad servants exclaimed, so shocked and despondent that he abandoned all official decorum. The gathered audience was too stunned to notice. But Lord Whiteleaf was not done with his surprises yet.

"And I will be naming as my successor... Lord Malgraye Fernbrook."

Whatever personal cost he would bear for it, Fraenk couldn't let this farce continue. Fernbrook was somehow using the necklace to dominate the mind of Krispen Whiteleaf. All the Lord elves stared off distantly, as if they had not heard or didn't care. And given how vicious and contentious some of their meetings were over some of the most trivial matters. They would have been on their feet battling such a sweeping proclamation rather than looking completely uninterested.

It was when the other elven lords of the High Council began to clap their hands mechanically for Lord Fernbrook, without raising any protest or objection— Fraenk knew their minds were also under his control.

Lord Fernbrook did his best to look both surprised and reluctantly delighted. He waved out at the crowd, who, slowly and hesitantly, began to clap for him. The applause built to some kind of lukewarm enthusiasm. Whether the crowd was too stunned or just not pleased by the notion of a High Lord Fernbrook, it was difficult to say exactly. But there was one person who didn't clap at all. He knew this had been Fernbrook's plan all along. It was how he could take over the entire city without anyone knowing or being able to prevent him. Everyone here, all the most powerful and influential of the elven aristocracy, was present to bear witness. The High Lord chose his successor, and the High Council raised no objection. In a few moments, Fernbrook would accept his lofty new position as High Lord of Arathes and Gwyndaer region. Any hope of getting him back off the throne would be nearly impossible.

Fraenk had to stop this— somehow.

From his own experience using the necklace, it required one's focused attention and concentration. If he could distract or interrupt Lord Fernbrook, perhaps the effect could be broken long enough for Lord Whiteleaf and the others of the High Council to return to their senses. It was his only option.

Without a second thought, Fraenk shoved past Farathiel Gingerglade and plowed right into Lord Fernbrook just as the stately elf stood to accept the honor. The two of them fell back onto the throne he had just been sitting on, tilting it backwards and spilling both of them to the ground. Yet another gasp rose from the crowd. They were certainly getting their fill of surprises this evening.

Fraenk knew he only had moments before the elf would recover and activate the necklace's power again. He had to find where Fernbrook was holding the Mind Thief on his body and lift it from him like an experienced pickpocket.

"Get off me, fool!" Lord Fernbrook roared, indignant. "Guards! Get him off me!"

"Sorry, sir!" Fraenk, he slurred. "A thousand pardons, my lord."

Fraenk quickly pat-searched Fernbrook's hands, neck, and pockets, making it look like a fumbling attempt to rise and get off of him. But there was a problem— he couldn't find the necklace anywhere. How was Fernbrook using it if—

He felt several sets of powerful hands suddenly wrench him to his feet. Brawny palace guards twisted his arms until they were bound painfully up behind his back. Fraenk looked up, and the entire room was now staring at him. The crowd looked the same way one might if a stray dog had hopped up onto their banquet table and unloaded its bowels in the midst of all the food. For most there, Fraenk could see whatever seething animosity or dislike of humans had been completely reinforced. This might be the last time any human was ever allowed inside the Summer Palace.

His failure was so comprehensive at this point, he would most likely have to board a ship for the farthest point he could reach— if he was allowed to leave at all. There was a very good chance he would be thrown back into the black cell with Carax the Cutthroat, in actuality this time.

Yet for all that transpired and every effort he had made, Fraenk felt the worst about failing Lady Blackroot. She had trusted him to save her and the district. Now it was very likely that they would become the new High Lord's next victims.

Fraenk scanned down the row of elven lords, hoping to communicate his contrition to her with his eyes, if nothing else. He saw all the lords of the former High Council looking at him, but in the way one might stare at a rather uninteresting plain bowl of cold porridge or perhaps an empty patch of dirt. Even the High Lord Whiteleaf was watching the scene with listless impassivity.

In fact, Lord Fernbrook seemed to be the only one on the dais having a strong reaction to Fraenk's collision— understandably so. But the way he cursed and blustered, raging at this drunken human idiot and the utter indignity he suffered because of him, Fraenk realized that there was no way he could be using the necklace's power at the same time.

That meant someone else was. And Fraenk cursed himself this time for being the idiot. The answer was there staring him in the face— literally.

Farathiel Gingerglade had a thin sheen of sweat on his brow and a look of grave focus on his face. Fraenk was the only one who noticed a growing bristle of delicate frost forming on the outside of the elf's pocket. The Arch Preceptor of Fernbrook was somehow using the Mind Thief's power to control most of the elves on stage. The strain on him must have been enormous because he could only stand and stare straight ahead.

Fraenk needed some way to break Gingerglade's concentration, but he was too far away and the guards holding him were too strong.

"Fart! Hey, Fart!" Fraenk shouted. Gingerglade made no reaction.

"Silence him!" Lord Fernbrook shouted to the guards.

"I know what your treasonous plan is, and you're not going to get away with it," Fraenk snapped back at Fernbrook. The old elf gave him a devious smile.

"Get him out of here. I don't want a human present when I accept my new duty as High Lord of Arathes. In fact, they're going to find the city much less to their liking in the days to come."

Fraenk felt a firm hand on his shoulder and saw that it was Arch Partisan Olwynn Brightrock.

"Olwynn. Stop that Preceptor Gingerglade right there!" Fraenk, she pleaded. For a moment, he had a sickening feeling of dread that Farathiel had Arch Brightrock in his thrall as well, for the look he gave was calm and without as much of the loathing glare that Fraenk had become so accustomed to.

"Skark that, Neversleep. You're in enough trouble already," Brightrock growled, digging his fingers painfully into Fraenk's shoulder.

"Thank the Powers you're alright!" Fraenk winced. "Please, you have to listen—"

"Let's go." Brightrock said to the guards, and they began to frog-march Fraenk out of the room.

"No! Wait!" Fraenk cried as he was forced away. He had one last opportunity to do something before it would all be over.

"Fart! How'd you like the strip search?!" Fraenk shouted over at Gingerglade. He saw the elf's brow furrow for just a moment, but it was the reaction he was looking for.

"Did you like that? It was _my_ idea," Fraenk continued. Gingerglade's face twisted in anger.

Then something else interesting happened. Lady Blackroot and Lord Cullor Mosswater suddenly shook their heads and began to blink. They looked like someone had just woken them up— or pulled them out of a trance. It was working.

"What about when I ordered my horse to bite you, Fart?!?" Fraenk chided. "You cried like a whelp! *'Ooo, me arm! He broke me arm!'* I'll be laughing about that jolly nibble as long as I live!"

Gingerglade twitched again, seeming to recoil from the memory of Jimothy savaging his arm. This time, Lady Illse Coldfrost blinked back to her senses and looked about like she was unsure of how she'd even gotten here.

Fraenk had one final gambit. He hoped it would be enough. "And the Lynblood girl you tried to strangle? I *saved* her, and she told me your entire plan to take over the city," Fraenk announced. The crowd of elves were all watching him now, keenly interested. Even Arch Partisan Brightrock paused his guards so Fraenk could continue. "Get him out of here!" Lord Fernbrook shouted from the stage.

"Let's hear what the man has to say," Lord Kallan Hardoak cut in. He was now free of the necklace's effect as well.

"You hired them to steal the Ynne es Tylubourne— the wizard's magic pendant that can bend one's mind. When it came time to pay, you tried to stiff them. But you didn't know they had an inside man... or rather an inside kobold. They stole it back. So you sent that psychopathic Bas Greenbriar to hunt it down, and he slashed his way across the city trying to get it back. You set her up at the lighthouse, then used your connections at the Hornet's Hive to slip in and try to silence her. You failed, though, Fart. And now it's over!"

Farathiel Gingerglade screeched in rage, surprising everyone around him.

"You think you're clever, huh, Neversleep?" Gingerglade's smile twisted into a look of pure, venomous spite. Then his eyes rolled back, and he cupped his hands together in front of himself. A glaze of sparkling ice suddenly encased them.

Fraenk looked around nervously. Gingerglade was using the necklace on someone, but who?

His answer came a moment later. The *whooshing* sound of a blade was followed by a heavy whack that sent a hot spray of liquid across his face. The guard standing to Fraenk's left released his pinned arm, and his head pitched forward way further than normal anatomy would allow. Then his entire body went boneless in a gurgling splash of blood.

The fallen guard revealed another figure standing just on the other side, holding a blood-covered silver sword and grinning like a maniac.

"I challenge you to a duel, Neversleep!" High Lord Krispen Whiteleaf screeched.

40

Although trial by combat was extremely rare in elven society, there were several instances throughout their history that suggested it did have a precedent. In each case, they were the deciding factor in weighty matters of great import, such as which brother a particular princess would marry, an exiled lord seeking justice over a stolen birthright, or single combat between two honorable commanders to save the bloodshed of their armies.

On the other hand, duels were far more common amongst humans, who seemed to use them for dispute resolution in matters both great and completely petty. Fraenk recalled an instance in his own district where a man was stabbed over an argument regarding how 'brown' a particular stray dog was. The answer: medium brown.

Fraenk had never personally participated in a duel. He believed himself to be smart enough not to allow himself to get drawn into one. Usually he was able to resolve a conflict one way or another before matters degraded to the point where single combat became the deciding factor. Most often another round of ale was the most effective way to disarm any argument, and if that failed, preemptive violence.

Duels were another matter entirely. They expected participants to follow a set of rules to make them fair—which Fraenk considered any fight where he did not have the clear advantage not worth the risk. And they nearly always resulted in bodily injury for one or both parties at a minimum and quite frequently death. And what did one win in such risky contests? Typically, it was a slight increase in one's own nebulous concept of "honor" or just bragging rights over beating a dead man—which that and a few copper coins could buy you a roll in the sheets with any girl in the Canal Street joy houses. All were solid reasons why it was a pastime for fools.

And yet, for all his caution, here Fraenk found himself... in a duel... with the High Lord of Arathes himself.

As he recalled, there were many regional variations on how to conduct one-self in a combat trial. Sometimes the winner was the one who drew blood first; in others, points were given for each successful hit. Since there seemed to be no officiant or oversight of any kind for this sudden and unexpected contest, Fraenk had to assume that things automatically defaulted to primal fight rules, of which there were only two.

The first and really most important rule was to 'not die'. This was fairly self-explanatory and easily understood. Being alive was generally the condition that all aspired to remain in, and it made things a lot easier if one wanted to brag about being a successful disputant afterwards. It was, unfortunately, the rule that half of the participants could not uphold.

The second rule was just as easy to understand but a lot more challenging to perform. It was simply to 'kill the other guy.' Or, short of that, maim, disembowel, disarticulate, exsanguinate, incapacitate, or otherwise force them into complete trouser-wetting submission. It was this second rule that now put Fraenk in a most unusual dilemma.

How was he going to win a duel against the High Lord of Arathes? The answer was quite simple: he wasn't.

"I yield, my lord!" Fraenk said immediately and raised his hands as fat drops of blood crawled down his cheek. Krispen Whiteleaf stared back with wild, unfocused eyes that followed him but didn't seem to see Fraenk at all.

"I challenge you to a duel, Neversleep!" He cackled and waggled the point of the blade at Fraenk's chest. Neversleep stepped back out of reach of the sword as Whiteleaf laughed again, high and crazed.

"I YIELD!" Fraenk shouted more insistently. Then twice more at all the gathered elves, who by then had backed away to the far corners of the hall and away from the sword-wielding maniac. Even the guards in the room looked at a loss for how to handle this—torn between their duty to both protect and obey the High Lord elf. No one seemed eager to put a stop to this mad display. No one except Brightrock.

"My Lord, you've had an eventful evening—"

Fraenk heard the Arch Partisan say from behind him in a soothing voice that he almost didn't recognize. It was so disarming that Fraenk almost lowered his own hands and turned to gaze astonished at the grizzled old elf. But Whiteleaf would not be placated by words.

Whiteleaf slashed the air with the blade and nearly took the tip of Fraenk's nose off.

"SILENCE, *Br*-ort-*ick!*" Lord Whiteleaf stuttered. He seemed to falter when recalling the elf's name, but he recovered quickly. "Against the wall with the others. I want to duel with Lord Neversleep! A proper duel— to the death."

Fraenk's heart sank as he heard reluctant footsteps recede back from him. He was truly alone now.

"My lord, I unfortunately can't duel with you because..." Fraenk said, trying to find some valid reason.

"No, you can't, can't, can't!" Krispen Whiteleaf's smile was all teeth. "Not without a weapon! Get Neversleep a proper sword!"

Fraenk wasn't sure who, but someone— that Fraenk promised he would take revenge upon later— then slid a sword that came clanking and jangling across the floor to his foot. It reminded him of the trident that Kyla had passed him when he was facing off against the shadescourge. He nearly wished that was what he was facing right now. His rules of engagement would at least be clear.

"*Pickituppickitup!* Pick it up!!" Whiteleaf gestured excitedly with his own blade. Fraenk hesitated, casting about the room for anyone who might come to his defense or even a mere suggestion of how to proceed. Even lifting a weapon in the direction of the High Lord was big trouble— especially for a human. The royal guards, Olwynn Brightrock, and even the High Lords all watched him, but none made a move to end it. No one seemed to want to interject themselves into any part of this. Especially not after seeing the near-headless guard lying in the middle of the floor. The general consensus seemed to be to just let the High Lord kill Fraenk... And then, afterward, maybe a light dessert?

Krispen Whiteleaf grew impatient and slashed the air in front of Fraenk's face, chopping away a small bit of his collar. That was too close.

"Take the blade, or I'll kill you where you stand!"

Reluctantly, Fraenk stooped and grabbed the sword, keeping his eyes fixed on the young High Lord, whose head was now tilted to one side and a thin string of saliva was spilling down from the corner of his mouth. There seemed to be nothing of the polite and curious elf he had met earlier in the evening. Gingerglade's magical influence had twisted him into some kind of monster.

Fraenk quickly searched for his true enemy amongst the crowd while trying to keep Lord Whiteleaf in his periphery. He caught just a glimpse of Gingerglade, hands still frosted over and standing between the Fernbrook house guards.

"Fraenk, watch out!" He heard an older woman shout as the High Lord launched himself forward with a wild series of swings. Fraenk was only passable as a swordsman and barely managed to completely parry three of the four attacks. He felt pain in his side, and an oozing warmth made the fabric cling to his body. The High Lord was young and fast. He had clearly been receiving top training in martial skills.

"Good show, sir. You've drawn blood. You are the victor," Fraenk grunted, giving a slight but cautious bow. He kept the sword point down but ready to counter.

"That's just a drop, Neversleep. I want ALL OF IT!" High Lord Whiteleaf screeched. He swung again, but Fraenk stepped back out of range.

"Don't hurt him, Fraenk!" He heard the old woman call to him again and realized it was Lady Arice. She and the High Council lords from her side of the dais had moved back to the far side of the room, but she was at least trying to help.

"I wouldn't think of it, My Lady," Fraenk called back. "You're not suggesting that I throw this duel, are you? He's trying to kill me!"

"There's worse things than a quick death, boy!" Lord Fernbrook chimed in. "You'll discover all of them if you harm our beloved High Lord."

"YOU–!" Fraenk stomped towards Fernbrook until Whiteleaf slid directly into his path.

"I *ch*-challenge you to a... *duelllll!*" The High Lord shouted again. Fraenk saw there was something wrong with one or both of Krispen Whiteleaf's eyes, for they were pointing in different directions. He smacked his forehead hard several times, and they straightened again. Whatever Gingerglade was doing, it was wreaking havoc on this poor elf's mind.

Fraenk knew he needed to put an end to this and quickly, or the High Lord would end up vacuous, like the human gang leader Joeth. But it wasn't going to be easy.

As if to emphasize this, High Lord Whiteleaf shot forward with a blistering series of slashes, cuts, and jabs. His form was flawless, and his years of instruction from the best instructors were on full display. Fraenk's own sword could not keep up, and he staggered backward with half a dozen fresh cuts on his body. The look Krispen gave him said what they both knew— he could have easily killed Fraenk right there. Then Whiteleaf capered backwards with a series of whimsical hopping steps that might have been amusing if he wasn't on the verge of committing a murder.

"This is FUN! Are you having FUN, N-Neversleep?" Whiteleaf asked, spittle flecking from his lips. He attacked again. But this time his coordination was off, like he was drunk. Whiteleaf was struggling much more now. His swings were slow and telegraphed. Sensing his opening, Fraenk pressed this advantage. He parried two cuts, then two more, before side-stepping an awkward overhand chop that left Whiteleaf wrong-footed. Fraenk swung his own blade as Krispen Whiteleaf turned, wide-eyed and defenseless.

Fraenk's sword edge sang right for the High Lord's exposed neck. Whiteleaf's hands were down at his sides, and he stood, blinking and looking confused. Fraenk realized this at the last moment.

He fought the momentum of his own swing, somehow miraculously stopping the slash inches from High Lord Krispen Whiteleaf's skin. Several people in the onlooking crowd shrieked or gasped. The high elf sucked in a breath, looking confused and scared. It was that moment when Fraenk realized Gingerglade had released his hold, giving the High Lord back his mind at the moment when he would have had his own throat opened by the first human he'd ever met. It was diabolical and malevolent.

Fraenk dropped his sword with a clatter. This was madness.

Then, to his horror, Fraenk watched Whiteleaf's eyes roll back again and the rictus smile peel back from his teeth.

"Oooh. I thought I had you with that one, Fraenk." Gingerglade's words came out of Whiteleaf's mouth.

"You'll die for this," Fraenk growled. "Come and get me, Neversleep," the puppetted elf began to laugh.

The crowd seemed to have recovered from the shock and were now a chorus of angry shouts.

"He tried to kill the High Lord!"

"Assassin!"

"Guards, arrest him!"

Now all the guards who had previously stood back while Fraenk was nearly cut to ribbons rushed forward to the defense of their sovereign. *Where was this enthusiasm minutes ago when Fraenk was the one begging for intervention?*

"It's your *t-t*-time to die, Fraenk," Whiteleaf began to say, his eyes rolling wildly in their sockets. Something was very wrong. The elf's mind was about to break. He needed to hold together for a bit longer until Fraenk could figure out how to save him.

Just hold on.

Suddenly, Fraenk had an idiotic idea that was probably going to get him run through with that silver sword. Before the High Lord could lift his blade again and Fraenk could second-guess himself, he launched forward, wrapping both arms tightly around Krispen Whiteleaf.

"Wh-what are you doing, Fraenk!?" He heard Lady Blackroot shriek from across the room. All the guards stopped in their tracks, unsure of what was happening. It wasn't an attack necessarily but more of an enthusiastic hug.

"What? What is this? Unhand me!" Whiteleaf struggled. He still clutched his own sword but couldn't swing it with his arms pinned tightly to his sides. At least Whiteleaf was unable to hack him to death like this, but how long could Fraenk hold onto him?

Then the second part of this bad idea came to him. Fraenk certainly couldn't best the elf in a sword fight; he was much too slow and severely outmatched in swordplay skills for that. But in a contest of wrestling, Fraenk's size and strength did put him at the advantage. And there was nothing he loved more than an unfair fight, especially when it was in his favor.

"My Lord, may I ask for this dance?" Fraenk smiled, then lifted the elf off his feet. They spun together like some mockery of performers, Krispen Whiteleaf screeching and Fraenk stepping lightly on his toes. The elf's sword point swung in an arc with them, backing off the encroaching guards. Fraenk moved them together across the floor, heading directly for his intended target: Farathiel Gingerglade.

The Arch Preceptor of Fernbrook had his eyes pinched shut, but he must have been able to see through Whiteleaf because he faltered when the bizarre couple spun towards him. Fraenk timed his steps and movement. He would only have one chance at this.

As he anticipated, the Fernbrook guards saw their approach and stepped back, leaving Gingerglade standing by himself. All Fraenk had to do was let go of the High Lord at the right moment of the turn and trade him for a new dance partner. One that he was planning to destroy, if the fates would allow it.

Then the moment came, and Fraenk opened his arms, allowing High Lord Whiteleaf to spin backward, safely and a bit dizzy, out into the open space of the Grand Hall. The first movement of Fraenk's dangerous dance was executed perfectly.

Fraenk spun again, stepping quickly, and caught sight of Gingerglade. His hands reached out to grab the elf— to grip his neck and squeeze until cartilage snapped and bones broke.

But something awful happened. Fraenk's feet stopped moving. Then his hands too were frozen. His entire body refused to obey any command. It was like he was paralyzed, for nothing he did, no matter how hard he tried, could make himself move.

Then something much more unnerving occurred. Fraenk felt his body move, but he was no longer in control of it. He stood straight up with his arms hanging loosely at his side.

"Nice try. But it looks like I'm the one who has you, Fraenk," he heard the delightedly sinister voice of Farathiel Gingerglade say inside his mind.

41

WHEN THE EX-WIZARD VALTHOR had told Fraenk that he didn't understand the true power of the Mind Thief, it was not as if he didn't believe the old elf because he had already seen and used it. But channeling the necklace's power to read someone else's thoughts or even to split open their mind was nothing compared to what it was like to have it turned upon you.

Fraenk Neversleep found himself standing in the Grand Hall of the Monarch's Summer Palace, staring into the face of his mortal enemy. Every action to get here had been his own. Every choice, every thought, and every move was a result of applying the significant power of his own mind to resolve the problems of a district and his sworn-to lady. But now he was at a complete loss of autonomy. Fraenk could feel the magic surging to every corner of his brain, a deep and powerful thrum that asserted its own commands with almost no effort. Any attempt he made to regain his own mind or even try to command some part of himself to move was batted away as easily as one swats a fly.

More terrifying still was that Fraenk could fully feel the presence of Farathiel Gingerglade inside with him. The elf was like a ghost, moving through walls, unlocking secrets, and uncovering everything that he believed to be the only place in the world that was truly safe.

Fraenk suddenly felt pressure on his chest and an urgent need for air. But when he tried to inhale, his lungs wouldn't obey. *Was the Mind Thief powerful enough to make a man suffocate himself?* Apparently so, because no amount of effort would allow Fraenk to get himself a breath.

Then he felt something shift, and he was gasping for air.

"Oh, sorry about that, Neversleep. I can't have you dying on me that way," Gingerglade's voice came again from inside his head. It was loud, like the elf was standing right beside his ear.

"LET ME GO!" Fraenk screamed back with his own thoughts.

"I don't think I will. I'm still going with my original plan to have the High Lord hack your ugly human head off with that sword. But he'll get to you in a moment. He's a little dizzy right now."

So the state of the other's mind can affect the one using the necklace, Fraenk thought.

"That's right. You definitely wouldn't want to use it on someone who was insane or diseased," Gingerglade's reply came a moment later, and Fraenk had the terrible realization that there was no private thought, no internal plan—nothing was safe from Gingerglade's reach.

"I think you finally understand now, Neversleep. I <u>possess</u> you. Any dirty scheme you come up with, I'll know the moment you concoct it. There's nothing you can say or do to save yourself. And I'm going to make you stand there and stick out your neck while he swings the blade. Won't that be fun?"

A wave of panic and fear washed through him, and he could feel Gingerglade's delight.

"That's right. Be afraid. I want your fear."

Fraenk forced himself to be calm. There had to be some way out of this, even if Gingerglade could see and hear all of his thoughts. Some way to best him—

"You're welcome to try," the insufferable elf cut in again.

"Be quiet and let me think, Fart!" Fraenk shot back and was pleased to feel a ripple of annoyance from his enemy.

"Your mind is a fascinating place, Neversleep. So many juicy secrets in here. So much information that I can use. I wish I had more time to explore. Look at this—"

An image popped up in Fraenk's memory of the lighthouse and the Lynblood woman. *How was Gingerglade doing this?*

"I can dig through every part of your mind. See? Now I know where the girl is. You've shown me right to her. I'll make sure we kill her this time. Oh, yes... and thank you for tipping me off about the fool ex-wizard who lives there. We'll definitely be prepared when we storm the place with enough Arcane Lords to turn it to ash and cinders."

Fraenk's thoughts and memories were flying faster now. And every time he tried to hide or conceal something, Gingerglade smashed through like a savage wolf tearing apart a bunny.

"What else? What else? What about your district, Neversleep? Where is it vulnerable? I can see all your secret hiding places. Your stashes of booze and your many hoards of gold. Don't worry, I'll make good use of it all."

Images of locations all over his district flashed in his head. Every secret Fraenk had was being violently ripped out of him. Fraenk was breathing faster. He had to stop Gingerglade from going any further, but there was nothing he could do.

"And your Lady Blackroot? Where is... Oh. This is interesting. She's so weak and frail. And so many ways that misfortune could befall her— I can see them all because you've thought about each one. And you've been worried she's going to die. Aww, Neversleep. You actually _care_ about her. I didn't think you cared about anyone but yourself. A pity you never took the opportunity to tell her. How sweet that would have been," Gingerglade cooed malevolently.

Fraenk suddenly felt himself stand up straighter. His body took three steps and turned all the way around, so he was now looking at the opposite side of the room. All eyes were still fixed on them.

"Shall we go over and tell her now before you die?" Gingerglade asked. "No, never mind, I don't care."

Fraenk could see High Lord Whiteleaf standing steady now. He waved off his palace guards, who would probably all find themselves reprimanded and reassigned after their failure to intervene in this evening's events. Not that it would do him much good with his head chopped off and rotting on a spike outside the city gate.

An odd sensation washed through his mind as Fraenk felt the magic shift. It weakened its hold somewhat, and he felt another presence. He watched as Krispen Whiteleaf stiffened. Once again, Gingerglade took hold of the High Lord's brain. Fraenk could feel their three minds all linked in some way.

High Lord Whiteleaf turned stiffly and started walking their way. He smiled and waved at those present like he had done something heroic or was about to. Whiteleaf gave the air a few experimental chops with his blade, then fixed his eyes directly on Fraenk.

Even though Gingerglade remained in firm control of the magic, there was something about this connection that Fraenk felt could be exploited. Now, while he was distracted with the elf, it was Fraenk's only chance.

"LORD WHITELEAF, STOP! DON'T DO THIS!!" Fraenk forced his mind at the space where the new presence had entered. The effect was immediate. Krispen Whiteleaf staggered backward and clutched his head like he'd been struck. The control of Gingerglade, too, lost its intensity, and Fraenk could suddenly move on his own.

But then his body froze as Gingerglade came slamming back into his brain more intense than ever.

"NONE OF THAT NOW!" The elf roared. Fraenk felt his body go rigid as all his muscles spasmed at once. The pain was total and blinding.

Fraenk wasn't sure how long it lasted, but when he could see and breathe and think again, High Lord Whiteleaf was standing right in front of him. He had the sword resting on Fraenk's shoulders and was staring at him with a sort of sad, apologetic look on his face.

Fraenk felt a wave of exhaustion. The exertion—and also the bleeding—made him want to collapse, but of course he couldn't. And now he was going to die.

"I didn't want you to miss this part, Neversleep," Farathiel Gingerglade's inner voice said viciously. "I'll be sure to let you go at the last moment. I wouldn't want to have my mind shattered like you did to that poor human in Rounderville. That would be bad for me."

Then Fraenk felt an acceptance that this would be his death as he looked back at High Lord Whiteleaf. They were both powerless in all this by forces beyond their control. He returned a baleful look. It said to Krispen Whiteleaf that this was not his fault. And furthermore, that Fraenk forgave him for what he was about to do.

It could have been the same look that the pig Henrietta had given him when he was a boy. Tears sprang into his eyes. For sorrow. For regret. For grief. He could hear an angry voice that sounded like Gingerglade trying to scream at him, but it was distant and unimportant. This memory, so primal and powerful, sent a wave of indescribable emotion through him.

Fraenk could see the effect wasn't just with him, either. Whiteleaf was crying as well—fat, round tears that spilled down his smooth cheeks. Fraenk couldn't see Gingerglade, but he could feel the elf flailing and battered by a storm of anguish and sadness.

Then another memory came from that day, unbidden but even more powerful. It started as a sound and sent an icy wave of fear through him. It was the unholy squeal of a pig. The traumatic memory that he had kept locked away, wanting never to think about again, was coming for him, breaking down the door of his mind, just like it had done in his childhood home.

"No, Fraenk! Stop! What are you doing? What is this?" Gingerglade's panicked voice cried out, terrified. Fraenk had seen this before, so he knew what was going to happen, but the elf was totally unprepared. The squeal of the boar was loud and close. Just on the other side. *Boom!* Fraenk could hear the impact clearly in his mind. A cold sweat covered him, and his mind rebelled, wanting to be anywhere but here— to recall anything but this. He knew he had to keep going, though. It was the only way he would be free.

Fraenk could see Whiteleaf too was experiencing this as well, for the look in his eyes was wide with terror. But there was nothing to be done about it.

In his memories, Fraenk Neversleep was once again the small boy huddled in his house with his mother and sister as the monster outside smashed its way in. His own terror flowing through him and out into Gingerglade, who was making a high-pitched keening whine. There was nowhere he could go to escape the beast that was now coming through the door towards them. The monster with the body of a man and the head of a hog. Whose eyes glowed red, and blood dripped from its butcher's apron.

Its inhuman squeal became a man's scream— or rather a chorus of screams as both elves shrieked. Farathiel Gingerglade's frosted hands shot up to cover his eyes, releasing the necklace. Fraenk felt the hold on him immediately fall away, and his body collapsed. Which was very much to his advantage, because High Lord Krispen Whiteleaf had raised the sword over his head and was swinging it down with all his might.

Fraenk thought the blow was aimed at him initially and flinched as the screaming elf charged forward. But he leaped over Fraenk's collapsing body and went straight for the one behind him.

Farathiel Gingerglade lowered his hands just in time to see the High Lord lean his entire force into a vicious downward slice. The sword cleaved through cloth, flesh, and bone of Gingerglade's shoulder, stopping in the middle of his chest, right at the point where the elf's heart was now taking its final flailing beat.

The Arch Preceptor of Fernbrook made a gurgling sound as red blossomed and spilled from the cut. Fraenk turned to catch Gingerglade's eyes, wide with terror and confusion, before he dropped to the floor.

A collective mix of gasps, shrieks, and shouts all erupted from the crowd at the same time. Lord Krispen Whiteleaf turned to look at Fraenk. There was a wild, untethered expression that seemed to suggest something was definitely wrong with him.

"I did it, Neversleep!" He breathed. "I killed the Mad Boar! I killed the Mad Boar..."

A moment later, a mass of bodies crashed upon both men. Palace guards were all scrambling to stop this calamity from going any further. Fraenk had no energy to resist as he was thrown roughly onto his belly and thick iron manacles locked around his wrists. He took a few punches and kicks as he was pulled to his feet.

"Throw him in the cells. He'll be hanged in the morning!" A red-faced captain of the palace guard shouted.

"Wait!" Arch Partisan Brightrock broke in, fighting his way to the middle of the scrum. "This man is *my* prisoner!"

"And what is his crime, captain?" Fraenk heard Lady Blackroot's stern voice shout as she also approached, mean as any shadescourge.

"Attempted regicide! Assaulting the High Lord!" The captain barked back. "And this is a matter of the palace, my Lord Brightrock."

"You're not even questioning any of this?! There's foul magic at play!" Brightrock leaned in and snarled through his broken mouth.

"Impossible! You yourself oversaw security, Arch Partisan."

"The necklace..." Fraenk said weakly.

"That's right. They smuggled in a magical amulet. Right there!" Lady Blackroot jabbed a finger at the individual who had just picked it up. Lord Fernbrook had somehow slipped into the crowd, found the Mind Thief on the floor, and his hand was just about to close around it. When all eyes fell on him, he raised it up in the air, pinched between two fingers like it gave off a redolent odor. Olwynn Brightrock snatched it from him with an accusatory scowl. He held it out for examination. The stone was flat and dull. Its unburnished chain had not even a hint of shine.

"That's nothing. A trinket? It doesn't even interest me," The captain's eyes barely looked at it.

"He was using it to enter my mind," another voice said, and all went silent. They turned to see High Lord Krispen Whiteleaf stepping through the parting sea of guards.

"My actions were... not my own. I didn't want to—" Whiteleaf broke off, looking down to where the body of Gingerglade was soaking in an ever-widening pool of blood. "He made me... kill. And..."

Krispen Whiteleaf trailed off, his voice haunted.

"One has to wonder what other actions my High Lord was unwittingly compelled to do!" Lady Blackroot shot Lord Fernbrook an accusatory glare.

"The High Council will certainly investigate." Krispen Whiteleaf reached out suddenly, putting a hand on Fraenk's shoulder.

"Sir. I'm so sorry. I—" He said, then turned quickly to the captain. "Release him. He saved my life."

"But my Lord—"

"Another word, captain, and I'll create a new lowest rank just to demote you to it." Whiteleaf snapped.

Fraenk felt the cuffs come off him, and the guards let him go. High Lord Krispen Whiteleaf extended his hand to him.

"I will not soon forget what you've done for me, sir. I'm told this is how humans say 'thank you,'" the High Lord said.

"It is, my lord," Fraenk replied, taking his hand. Whiteleaf gave Fraenk's arm a quivering wobble, like the dying throes of a Silverbow salmon. In spite of his weariness, Fraenk couldn't help but smile.

"Shake hands. Did I do it right?" Krispen asked.

"Perfect."

Part VIII

42

THE NEXT HOUR PASSED in a blur from the immediate aftermath of the death of Farathiel Gingerglade. For Fraenk's mind and body, both damaged and in exhaustive fatigue, time was slippery—passing in jumps and starts or speeding by too quickly.

After being administered to by the palace's healers, Fraenk was given a draught that he could have sworn to seeing his wounds stitch closed right before his very eyes. He was a bit addled at the time, however, and it could have all been a function of his overtaxed mind.

All the while, the High Lord of Arathes himself had briefly spoken to him before being whisked away by his personal guards to rest in his dedicated wing of the palace. Already his handlers were laying the explanatory groundwork to exculpate the High Lord from any wrongdoing in the deaths of a guard and the Arch Preceptor of Fernbrook. The dutiful Head Servant stepped forward to proclaim that Lord Whiteleaf was regrettably unwell and needed time to rest, even as behind him the two bodies were quietly removed, floors scrubbed to an unnatural shine, and any trace of the death of two elves completely expunged.

Nervous guests were quickly herded back into the main ballroom like startled barn fowl, where they were plied with strong drinks and sweet confections in a vain effort to at least temporarily placate them from the traumatic events they had just witnessed. Some seemed to want to process everything immediately, but for most others there was a general feeling that the less said about these events, the better. And by tomorrow, perhaps this would all seem like a bad dream. Nothing would stop the rumors that would forever swirl about this night for many years to come, no matter how hard the official speakers for the palace might proclaim otherwise. Elven memories might only last for a hundred years, but gossip, it seemed, was eternal. And while the revelers were told they could stay and dance for as long as they wanted, many were already making hasty arrangements with their carriage drivers to be taken back down the hill.

There were none who departed the gala faster than Lord Malgraye Fernbrook and his entourage— now short one member. Fraenk was still in a mental haze at the time, but he could vaguely recall the elven lord shouting and cursing some villainous human to blame for his own Arch Preceptor being butchered in front of everyone. For once, it was a relief to not be the focus of Lord Fernbrook's rage, but Frank didn't envy the poor sap who was.

The tirade quickly died, however, when other members of the High Council aimed some pointed and uncomfortable questions directly at Fernbrook regarding his own involvement in this scheme. Questions about if Farathiel Gingerglade was acting alone or at the behest of another. Statements were made just shy of accusations, which heavily implied Lord Fernbrook may have been more closely involved than he appeared. How could he *not* know what his own man had been doing? And wasn't it he who would most benefit from this scheme of stealing the High Throne of Arathes? That was a black-hearted plot that sounded dangerously identical to treason.

Lord Fernbrook's already pale complexion turned a waxy gray. And he was suddenly beset with an urgent magical-necklace-related illness, which necessitated an immediate departure. Not even waiting for his retinue, he slithered out of the gala and back home to where he could avoid further accusations. And most likely to begin to plot further mischief anew.

Lady Blackroot had attached herself beside Fraenk for the remainder of the evening. She spent the time shielding him from the curious, besotted, and dim-witted, all of whom wanted to impose themselves upon the impertinent human who disrupted the otherwise lovely event.

The advantage of having Lady Arice at hand was that she was ready to strike like a viper that spit profanity at anyone who tried to disrespect Fraenk. The first to find out was Lord Brydor Longgrass, who was no doubt the vanguard of a forthcoming Fernbrook smear campaign. He suggested to all listening that perhaps Neversleep was somehow complicit and might, in fact, be the scheme's true author. Lady Blackroot unmanned him with a verbal disemboweling so complete that the elf went scurrying away on the brink of tears, perhaps to live out the remainder of his days behind a wall tapestry.

"I thank you, my lady," Fraenk grinned after she had finally chased them all away. Someone had given him a generous pour of a dark brown liquor in a crystalline glass, which he sipped very slowly, savoring it. This libation might have been the best thing he could remember tasting, but it might have had something to do with the fact that he somehow survived the night.

"Careful, Fraenk. I think those fancy clothes are beginning to twist your mind. Or perhaps that necklace left some lasting damage to your brain," the elderly elf said and winked at him.

"I do feel a bit bad about Gingerglade," Fraenk lamented. "I wanted to chop that miserable skark in half myself."

"Well, I'm sure you'll make other mortal enemies. It's a big city, and you're a very unlikable human."

"Your enemies are mine, my lady."

They clinked glasses and drank.

A moment later, their moment was yet again interrupted. Arch Partisan Olwynn Brightrock approached through the crowd. His face was making some kind of hideous, snarling upward curve that Fraenk finally recognized as a smile.

"Egad, sir! You should warn people when you do that." Fraenk said.

"Do what?"

"Smile."

"Amusing, Neversleep. Perhaps I'm just relieved you didn't kill the High Lord of Arathes," Olwynn said. "I will say this: in five hundred years, this was the most interesting party I've ever been to."

"I would be careful announcing that kind of thing, sir. We've already had one lord elf's reputation sullied this evening, and I'd hate for vicious rumors to get started that you once had fun."

Olwynn snorted, then turned to Lady Blackroot.

"Lady Arice," he said in a tone that was almost demure. And then a look passed between them that Fraenk recognized. Stunned, his eyes shot wide as the answers to many great mysteries were finally being revealed— in particular, why a hardened soldier like Olwynn Brightrock would be convinced time and again to show favor in his dealings with Blackroot district. Apparently, there was a more *intimate* history here than he had ever suspected.

"*I*-I didn't realize that you two..." Fraenk stammered dumbly.

"Neversleep!" Lady Blackroot snapped, color rising in her cheeks. "Keep your secrets, or you'll be buried with them."

Fraenk lowered his head in a show of contrition and fought back the creeping smile that threatened to be his forthcoming cause of death.

"What can we help you with, Arch Partisan Brightrock?" Lady Blackroot said so primly that Fraenk almost burst out laughing right then and there.

Fortunately, she elbowed him so hard at the cut on his arm that the pain made him forget all about it.

"Actually, we were about to transport the necklace up to the Registry, where it will remain under the eternal protection of the Arcane Lords. I was wondering if Arch Neversleep would like the honor of accompanying us," Brightrock answered.

"Seems like the best place for it," Fraenk said. "They're not tempted to use it themselves?"

"The wizard I showed it to seemed utterly uninterested. But he said they'd keep it secure in a special vault for that kind of thing. What do you say?"

Fraenk was about to refuse him, but Lady Blackroot answered for him.

"Of course he's up to it, my lord. Neversleep, I bid you my leave." Lady Blackroot said, allowing Fraenk to help her up. "We'll have much to discuss back at the estate. And in the meantime—"

"Find more trouble to get into, yes, my lady, I will obey." Fraenk bowed carefully to kiss her hand, but she swatted him in mock irritation.

"Don't worry, Lady Blackroot. He'll be with me," Brightrock said confidently. She barked out a laugh that surprised even her, then nodded.

"As you say, Arch Partisan. Go in the Light of Tolwyn."

The old elf arched a curious eyebrow at the sudden invocation of the Lyn-Tyrian but accepted with a solemn nod.

"Well, Neversleep, let's be off. I know we'll have our own enlightening discussion of recent events along the ride, won't we?" He turned to fix Fraenk with a reproving eye.

"This 'honor' is feeling very much like an ambush," Fraenk said, swallowing the last of his drink and his mind beginning to pleasantly swim. "I'll have you know, I wasn't even at the museum the other night."

"Wait. You were involved in that too?!" Brightrock growled.

"Um... *no?*"

After Fraenk had seen Lady Blackroot into her carriage with a robust contingent of Blackroot guards and nearly all of his preceptors— except for the notoriously absent Nim Stonebridge— he felt safe enough to send them off from the Summer Palace back down the hill to the Estate. He was confident that

Lord Fernbrook had played all his cards and wouldn't be any further trouble, at least for this evening. There were still many unsettled matters, but all that would have to wait. For now, the most important thing was to get the Mind Thief down to the Registry of Magic, where it would cause no further trouble.

Fraenk felt an odd feeling mounting up with Arch Partisan Brightrock, the fiendish looking Arcane Lord from earlier and four sturdy partisans who acted as Brightrock's personal escort. They formed a loose column, riding with the partisans at the very front and rear and the wizard trailing a respectful distance back from where Brightrock rode abreast with Fraenk.

They waited for the last carriage to clear the road before departing back out of the drawbridges and down the main avenue.

The evening's events continued to swirl in his mind as they rode. He had trouble thinking in terms of victory and defeat, but the resolution to this long and sordid story of greed and magical necklaces somehow ended with Fraenk still being alive and thwarting the plans of the powerful Fernbrook family. He shook his head, marveling at how he somehow managed to duel the High Lord without being killed.

"I should be writing all this down," Fraenk mused to himself.

But not everything had ended so cleanly. He had made himself an even greater target for those with ambitions for Lady Blackroot— of which there were plenty. He didn't miss the looks some elves gave her at the gala. She had been strong for many years, but she was fading in strength and influence. There would be more like Fernbrook who would see this as an opportunity to take what was hers, by force or by cunning.

On top of that, Fraenk had dangerously elevated his own profile. There were others who would see Fraenk in the same way that the gang leader of the slums, Joeth, did—a human with ambitions to rise. And if he wasn't going to be a political player in the City of Arathes, he would become a pawn.

And Fraenk was not the only one who had announced himself as a target in this world of power and influence. The young High Lord seemed to be ready to break the bars of his golden cage. Although he had been under the power of the Mind Thief during the violent outburst, Fraenk had seen the look on Krispen Whiteleaf's face just prior when he had said he was dissolving the High Council. He appeared to be genuine in his sentiment. Whiteleaf was ready to announce his own ascendancy; that he would rule Arathes and the province of Gwyndaer on his own.

Paradoxically, having met the elf and also nearly been killed by him, Fraenk nevertheless had a good feeling about him. High Lord Whiteleaf left him with the impression that he would be a fair leader, possibly even a great one.

Whiteleaf's unusual fondness for humans was a curiosity. It was certainly nothing he acquired from the devious and hateful servants who surrounded him. Perhaps Whiteleaf could have brought about a new era of cooperation and equity between human and elfkind. But the cynical part of Fraenk knew that was too much to hope for.

It was a moot discussion in any regard. The High Council had already quickly convened on the spot and determined that the High Lord was completely under the necklace's powers. He would need several dozen more years of observation before they could be sure that it had no lingering magical effects. Only then could the High Lord begin to study the lengthy subject of governance and law—the first step in the process of taking full power of the land. It seems there had been another coup this night, and the High Council had successfully defended itself from an incursion by the city's rightful lord.

The hour bell rang as they rode through the darkened streets. The sound of horse hooves echoed through the beautiful plazas of the upper city. None felt the need to fill the beautiful quiet with insipid small talk. That wasn't Olywnn Brightrock's style in any case.

As they went, Fraenk's mind drifted back to the preceding events. He wanted more than anything to sign his name to the bottom of the scroll and seal it with wax—end of the case. But there was something floating just beyond his awareness that nagged at him in all this. What was it? Why couldn't his exhausted mind let it rest?

Then his thoughts went to the woman. He couldn't help but wonder how she was faring. He trusted the ex-wizard to see her back to health, but then what? Perhaps she had done the exact thing Fraenk had told her and booked passage on the first boat downriver. Fraenk knew it was the right thing for him to tell her to do, even though it was difficult. She wouldn't have been safe and still wasn't safe as long as the necklace was anywhere it might pose a temptation for her to steal. Soon it would be over and done with. The Mind Thief was almost to its new home in the magical vault at the Registry, which was beyond the reach of even the most talented burglar.

And then a new thought occurred to him— one that was giddy and delirious. With the necklace safely put away, did Kyla still have to leave? Perhaps it would be fine for her to stay in Arathes after all. She could find other work. Put down roots. Maybe he'd see her out on the streets one day and—

"Neversleep. Your mouth is hanging open," a raspy voice snapped him out of his thoughts. Olwynn Brightrock was giving him an odd look.

"The mind wanders," Fraenk said quickly, straightening in his saddle.

"It looked like yours was on a long voyage over the horizon."

Fraenk chuckled. Another moment passed, and Brightrock cleared his throat.

"In light of everything that's transpired, you might be tempted to think of yourself as some kind of hero, I suppose. You're imagining that you bravely saved the kingdom or prevented a great calamity. Maybe there should be a great parade up the high street for you with flower petals and fairy lights. You should be given coin and have a house that looks out over the lake. The theater should be making plays and writing songs of your exploits."

Fraenk looked over. *Was Olwynn Brightrock about to say something nice?*

"But let me smash that notion for you right now. You're the same person you were when this all started. They'll never love you because you're human. And soon all of this will be forgotten. Whatever thanks you've got by now is all you'll ever receive— and it's a great deal above others far more deserving."

The old elf paused, then looked Fraenk in the eye.

"However... you conducted yourself with honor, which is the most I can ask of any man loyal to the High Lord—human or elf. And so you've earned my respect."

The words hit him harder than he expected, and Fraenk felt a small lump in his throat. His mind reacted instinctively, sending forth sarcasm as the antidote to sentimentality.

"... which I can *trade* for a house or gold," Fraenk replied, grinning.

Arch Partisan Brightrock shot him a dark look, then snorted in a very un-elflike way.

"That's the last time I ever try to say a kind word to you, Neversleep."

"Good. It doesn't suit you at all."

Then Brightrock reached into his vest and fished around with his fingers. Fraenk was half expecting him to pull out a coin or perhaps a parchment, but when his hand emerged again, it was holding the Ynne es Tylubourne necklace. Fraenk tensed, unsure of what was about to happen next. He'd been betrayed far too many times for reasons surrounding this very item for this to sit right with him.

"I dislike magic," Olywnn Brightrock said, letting the stone pendulum before him. "Many see it as a short path to getting what they want. But its purpose is always dark. Even those with the purest heart and best intentions can get twisted by its seductive ways."

Brightrock suddenly pointed with his other hand to the ruinous hole in his mouth.

"Magic did this. I'm sure you wondered how it happened."

"I've never asked," Fraenk replied.

"Someone I cared about... *someone I trusted*—" His voice broke off. He swung the Mind Thief back into his palm, squeezing it in a fist. His voice suddenly dropped until Fraenk could barely hear him over the sound of the horse hooves.

"This is too dangerous to exist— even at the Registry. Too many know where it will be and they won't stop going after it, one way or another. The wizards can't guard it forever. You more than anyone understand that."

Fraenk met his steely eyes.

"You have to destroy it. Find a way. But whatever you must do, it is *your* responsibility."

An echo of the ex-wizard's words coming from Brightrock's mouth.

"*What?* I can't—" Fraenk tried to protest.

"You must. I have a decoy that I'll give to the Registry, but the Mind Thief is now yours."

Fraenk watched him slip off his leather gloves and subtly drop the necklace down into the fingertip of one.

"Take my gloves then if you're cold and stop complaining, Neversleep!" Brightrock said in a tone louder than a conversation level. He held them out like a promise of certain doom.

Fraenk hesitated, wanting to do anything but take charge of the necklace again, but the moment was drawing uncomfortably long, and Brightrock's glare gave him no way to argue. Reluctantly, Fraenk took the gloves and carefully slipped them on. He could feel the cold rock at the center of the pendant against his palm, and a chill swept up his arm like an ill premonition. Then a feeling came into his mind like dark, murderous intent— as if someone nearby wanted him dead. Fraenk saw a thin layer of frost was beginning to form on the palm of his new glove.

Alarmed, Fraenk immediately looked over at Brightrock, whose mind only felt relieved to not be holding the item any longer. The murderous feeling was from somewhere further away—someone directly in front of them.

Just then, the urgent voice of the lead partisan called out.

"Sir! Something's in the street ahead!"

Fraenk felt his hair crawl with dread. Before he even looked, he knew what would be waiting. That unresolved thing that his brain was trying to warn him about earlier. The missing corner to the map of misfortune, which was his life. Somehow dismissed and then forgotten after the events in the storeroom, but Fraenk chastised himself for letting it drop— or perhaps not letting him drop hard enough.

The dark figure who stood in their path on the roadway had long horns that curled up to the sky and a faint glow of green at his throat.

"Who is it?" Brightrock demanded. But Fraenk knew they were wasting valuable moments with this confusion.

"He's come for the necklace," Fraenk said urgently. "Get the wizard up here. Now!!"

But by then, vile, hellish magic ignited in the darkness, and all turned to chaos.

43

O LWYNN BRIGHTROCK HAD JUST turned to call for the Arcane Lord when the dark figure's hands suddenly flared into swirling balls of purple light. The hellish face of Sorzon Brimblade was illuminated for just an instant before he posed his body in two quick movements. His hands chopped forward, sending the wicked, crackling orbs of energy out in quick succession. They found their targets with grim accuracy.

The closer partisan who had initially called the warning was struck in the middle of his chest and went tumbling backward, propelled by the exploding magical ball. He tumbled and landed, crisp and smoking, on the stones.

The second elf had just enough time to wheel his horse around before the ball struck his mount. The resulting blast took the mount's head off in a flare of light. Horse and rider hit the stones on top of one another. The partisan was not killed immediately but lay pinned and bleeding badly from the fragments of the horse skull shrapnel that dotted his chest and head. He let out an anguished cry, which turned to a wet gurgle.

"Phielax! We're under attack!" The Arch Partisan shouted, but the wizard was already thundering past on his steed, leaving the caustic wisps of vapor from his own spell in the air. The Arcane Lord sent forth a heavy blast of power that seared and crackled off the shield spell that Brimblade managed to raise just in time.

The Arcane Lord launched skyward from the horse's back and landed down powerfully on the street, his force leaving a small impact crater of cracked stones. Phielax's fingers curled and began to glow. Whereas he looked bored casting an anti-magic charm on the endless vapid guests of the gala, the wide smile on the wizard's face said this was something he'd been waiting for his entire life. A true test of his skill.

Fraenk was not one to freeze up in the heat of action, but there was no way he could help in a wizard battle. All he could do was rein up his stamping, panicky horse. And now with two guards down, he couldn't help but think they were woefully unprepared and undermanned for this guard detail.

"Fraenk, get out of here!" Brightrock shouted at him as another scream rose in the night air. This time it was from behind them. Fraenk had just twisted in his saddle as a riderless horse came barreling out of the darkness. It checked Fraenk's mount with its body, sending them pitching sideways. He nearly caught himself, but a surge of raw animal fear flooded his mind as the Mind Thief caught the fleeing beast's thoughts.

He was weightless for a moment, then something hit him hard in the shoulder. Fraenk opened his eyes and saw he was on the ground. He scrambled to his feet, grasping for his own horse's reins, but it too turned and disappeared after the other in a clatter of hooves. Then more sounds came from the street behind them—shouted curses and the clang of metal in the darkness.

The mounted partisan was circling a figure on the ground, jabbing at him with his spear. But the dark assailant was armored and swinging a massive two-handed sword. Although he was slower and lacked the height advantage of the mounted elf, there was something inexorable and dangerous about the way this man moved. He was military trained and he knew combat. He could sense when to avoid the darting spear and when to let it clang ineffectually off his armor.

And when the armored man countered with the massive blade, the partisan elf could only wheel the horse back out of reach.

He cannot keep this up. That dark warrior is too strong.

And as if his thoughts could manifest the reality, Fraenk watched helplessly, in horror, as his premonition came true.

The mounted partisan rode forward, attempting an overhand jab, aiming for the open seam at the armored man's neck, but the warrior ignored it entirely, countering with his own powerful, angular cut. The tall blade came down diagonally, splitting the spear, arm, and body in one ugly blow. The partisan grunted heavily, then cascaded to the stones with the thumping sound of falling wet meat.

The dark warrior hefted the dripping sword to his shoulder, turned, and stalked towards Fraenk and Brightrock. There were sounds of cracking energy and flares of light behind him as Brimblade and the Arcane Lord spelled and countered each other, but Fraenk couldn't take his eyes away from the approaching nightmare.

Beside him, he heard Olwynn Brightrock slip from his saddle to the street and move up beside him. He pulled a beautifully ornate pair of twin swords from the sheath on his back. They were thin with delicate curved line work in the elven tradition; the metal was silvery and pale and looked impossibly sharp. Fraenk had never seen a weapon so beautiful, let alone a matched set. Fraenk didn't know how well he'd do in another sword fight— especially with this monster— but perhaps if they worked together, they'd have a chance.

"Right. So I'll go from one side and you—" Fraenk reached out to take one blade from him. Brightrock immediately pulled it back with a look of indignation.

"I don't think so! I've seen your swordplay," Brightrock snapped. "You take my horse and get to the Registry. Summon the other Arcane Lords and then rally all the partisans you can find!"

Fraenk tried to protest, but Brightrock maintained his aura of being very difficult to argue with. The old elf didn't wait for Fraenk's reply. With a sword in each hand, he charged forth toward the dark warrior.

For being over five hundred years old, the Arch Partisan was shockingly agile. He attacked using a fighting form that Fraenk had never seen before, both swords moving in tandem, sometimes synchronized and other times coming at opposing staccato, leaving bright hatches all over the man's heavy armor. The large combatant seemed downright sluggish in comparison, taking wild sweeping chops at the old elf, who effortlessly sidestepped and danced in for another salvo of attacks.

"Go on, Neversleep! Get out of here!" Brightrock grunted, jumping clear of another powerful stroke. There was something about the way the old elf was sweating that Fraenk didn't like. He also noticed how the elven blades were just as ineffectual as the other partisan's spear had been. Fraenk wasn't about to abandon Brightrock now. Somehow, he had to help.

Fraenk needed a weapon. Even a metal rod or discarded board would do. If he could distract the large man, maybe Brightrock could get behind him and land a blow on a more vulnerable part of his body.

But as Fraenk cast about for anything to use, he could only see how pristine the streets around him were kept by the legions of elven servants in the upper city. Even the white apple trees that lined the road were swept clear of any fallen fruit. The bodies of the fallen partisans were a short distance away, and both had weapons—spears and the iron-knobbed clubs that the partisans always carried. But retrieving them would put Fraenk perilously close to the raging wizard battle that was now devolving into aimlessly fired bolts of electricity as the two magic users wore each other down.

He felt something slip inside his glove. Fraenk almost cursed his own stupidity. In all the excitement, he forgot about the incredibly powerful weapon that had just been used against him—the Mind Thief.

Closing his fist around it, Fraenk stepped forward and focused its power on the big man-at-arms. A crystalline crust of frost immediately formed on the glove.

"Neversleep! What are you doing?" Olwynn Brightrock shouted. There was a cut along his left arm that was bleeding dark black in the moonlight. "I'm— Give me a moment and I can stop him," Fraenk strained, raising his open hand toward the fighter. He focused his mind on pulling energy from the necklace and felt a surge move through him. An intoxicating buzz hit his brain, making it feel alive and like he wanted to talk to everyone in the city, all at the same time. Or maybe make someone's eyes bleed and head explode.

Stop. Focus. Fraenk told himself. He searched out with his mind for the dark warrior, who continued to swing the massive sword and never seemed to tire. But instead of where he would find all the memories, thoughts, and intentions, there was nothing. In fact, there was a complete absence of all of it. There was a void instead of a consciousness. Fraenk drew more power from the Mind Thief, probed deeper, searching every dark corner of the man.

But there was no mind to grasp. His head was a black pit, a void of darkness.

"That's not possible," Fraenk whispered.

"Did it work?" Brightrock called as he dodged another vicious swing.

"No! I... I don't understand it!" Fraenk shouted back, moving closer and pulling more from the necklace to no avail.

"I can see that, you fool. That was—*ungh*!—sarcasm." Olwynn replied, ducking under another cut.

The helltouched had used magic to summon creatures from the under realm before; perhaps this man was drawn from the other side as well—some kind of infernal warrior, hollow of mind and soul. But Brightrock ducked under a flat cut and this time aimed a flurry of attacks at the warrior's legs. A small spray of blood spilled out from a cut at the dark figure's knee joint. If it could bleed, then it could die.

"Maybe the helmet is blocking me!" Fraenk said. "It could be enchanted."

"Well, kindly ask him to remove it.""You're being sarcastic again."

Fraenk heard an agonized groan behind him and glanced back without thinking. The first partisan who had been hit by the energy ball was moving slightly. Somehow, he was still alive. Fraenk could only imagine the pain he was experiencing. Beside the man's outstretched hand lay his spear.

He needed that weapon, but there was no way he could run over, grab it, and get back in time to save his friend.

But he still had the Mind Thief, and there was a way it could help. Fraenk nearly refused to consider it, but the dark warrior landed a vicious kick to Brightrock, sending him sprawling backward onto the street. The old elf was slow in recovering and could only manage to crawl on his hands and knees.

Fraenk had no time to think of the ramifications. He forced his way into the injured partisan's mind—and immediately regretted it.

He felt a full-body wave of searing fire, like all his nerves were being ripped out of his skin. His teeth clacked together, and a scream surged through him. The sensation was like nothing he had ever experienced before. All he could think of was some way to make it stop. The agony. The suffering.

MAKE. IT. STOP.

And then the pain turned to smoke. A cool feeling of relief almost brought him to tears. The partisan must have also been experiencing the same thing, for he relaxed as well. The necklace could somehow keep the elf from feeling his pain, which was a powerful mercy.

Fraenk could feel the elf's mind clear, and he was filled with an overwhelming gratitude.

"Am I going to die?" The elf asked calmly, more a question of fact than fear.

I need your spear. Fraenk sent his thoughts to the partisan, whose name he suddenly knew as Draver. The elf was confused in his thoughts, however, somehow not understanding why he was on the ground and unable to stand. Fraenk pressed again, more insistently. He knew with each moment that the malevolent warrior was advancing on Brightrock.

Draver, throw it to me. Fraenk demanded from the partisan.

"Burn a prayer for me in the temple of Brand, that I may comprehend the knowledge of what is beyond," Draver said.

"Please! The spear! Your Arch Partisan needs you."

The elf moved mechanically, disassociated from his own body. His badly singed hand could barely grasp the weapon with several fingers missing. Anyone else would have been experiencing agonizing pain, but the elf seemed more irritated by his body's difficulties in getting the spear to Fraenk. But soon, he managed to haul back and toss the spear over.

Yet again, Fraenk found a weapon had come clattering to his feet. He was ready this time and hooked the toe of his boot underneath, flipping the haft up into his grip. Fraenk charged forward, drawing the spear back in two hands.

The dark warrior was striding in toward Brightrock, who was in turn scrambling back, trying to avoid the next overhand chop. Just as the man raised the blade, something hit him hard in the side of the head, sending his helmet flying.

The warrior wobbled two paces to the side, apparently stunned. He stopped in the middle of the street and turned. The dark tangle of sweaty hair shrouded his face. Then the man let the big sword point fall, and with his free hand, he pawed furiously at the side of his head. He began moaning and beating his skull like there was a fire in his brain and he had no way to put it out. There was something oddly sinister and familiar about this, Fraenk realized.

Now with his helmet gone, this was Fraenk's chance to stop him for good. He quickly set the butt of the spear shaft on the ground and reached out again with the Mind Thief.

Gritting his teeth, Fraenk gripped the necklace and pulled from its power. He could feel a hard crust of ice enclosed around his fist. The energy was like nothing he'd ever felt before— raw and primal. Whoever this fiend was, Fraenk was going to stop him right here and now.

But the moment he reached out for the warrior's head, Fraenk realized he had made a terrible mistake. Fraenk was expecting to find one man's mind, but instead there were _thousands_.

The things he'd found were not human at all, and they were hungry. They didn't possess thoughts or reason—only an urge to devour. Immediately, they sensed Fraenk's mind touching them, and they surged towards him, latching on with psychic mouths like leeches.

He tried to pull back, but somehow they held him. Fraenk tried to command them away with the Mind Thief, but there were far too many. He felt a strong gnawing sensation at the edges of his sanity, like his own thoughts and memories and just the possibility that the world could be a right place ever again were all being eaten.

Then Fraenk heard himself laughing, mirthless and loud, jarring to his ears. He wanted nothing more than for the sound to quit. It was starting to drive him mad. _But it was funny, wasn't it?_ Not funny, but terrible and joyous, and they all were so hungry. He couldn't stop—Fraenk had to FEED them—

HE MUST FEED THEM!

"Neversleep? Neversleep! Get a hold of yourself," Olwynn Brightrock's voice was distant.

But Fraenk was surrounded in the black pit of sorrow of his mind. Everything was quickly slipping away. He tried to force his will toward the sound. But the creatures were heavy and weighed him down.

Then he heard a sound—a voice that was both elemental and clear. A song rose in the air, sung in Elvish. It was like the shining beacon of the lighthouse, cutting through the darkness. Fraenk turned toward it with his mind and grabbed on.

He never expected the Hymn of Lost Souls would be sung for him.

It was everything he could do to pull back from the man's void of a head where the chorus of hungry dark creatures fed. Fraenk tilted and fell sideways to the street. Brightrock's song trailed off.

"You have a beautiful voice, sir," Fraenk said from the ground.

"This is no time to have a lie down," Brightrock shouted back "He's coming for you!'

The dark warrior must have felt Fraenk's incursion into his mind. Slowly he turned, the point of his blade dragging along the cobblestones and making a sanity-fraying *SKREEEE* with the edge. Fraenk was expecting a swirling void of nothingness in the place where the man's head was. Instead, what he saw was far more disturbing.

The front of the man's armor was battered and war-tested, but now that he was closer, Fraenk could recognize a familiar design painted on the metal. It was the sigil of a major house of Arathes. And not just any house—it was the sigil of Blackroot. *Why was this inhuman creature wearing the armor of House Blackroot?*

Fraenk looked into the dark face of the warrior and realized to his horror that he knew this man. Leos Muninger had been his friend. And now something was terribly wrong with him, because when he smiled, hundreds of tiny black worms fell out of his mouth.

44

"*D*ON'T MAKE SUCH A *fuss over a few dead vermin,*" the voice of Bas Greenbriar rang in his memory. It was followed by the horrifying image of children's legs sticking out of the smoking oven. Then Fraenk saw the black worms crawling across the elf's terrible smile.

Another voice, this time the Arch Partisan, was saying, *"Bas Greenbriar had a head full of black worms."*

And now here they were, spilling down the breastplate of Leos Muninger's armor.

"No..." Fraenk whispered. "Leos. No!"

The big man seemed to regard him for a moment; his eyes were hollow pits of darkness.

"Fraenk?" Leos said as if recognizing him for the first time. He grunted in pain and shook his head, making drops of sweat fly from his slick hair.

"Fraenk. There you are. I've been looking for you," he said ominously.

The big man hauled the sword up over his head in an almost lazy motion and brought it crashing down. Sparks jumped where the blade glanced off the ground. Fraenk rolled to keep from getting chopped in half.

"What are you doing? Stop this!" Fraenk shouted.

Leos swung again. Another overhand cut sent more sparks up and rang in the air like the toll of a bell. The big man didn't seem to be trying too hard to kill him, but Fraenk had to keep agile to stay out of the path of the blade.

"Leos! You're sick. There are black worms inside your brain. They're controlling you—"

"CONTROLLING ME?!?" Muninger screamed and slashed the air with a series of slices that Fraenk never would have been able to avoid. He felt the rush of air on either side of his face. "They don't control me, Fraenk! They *protect* me. From you."

He leveled the two-handed sword point right at his face. Fraenk crabbed backwards, then felt the shaft of the spear under one hand. He snatched it and brought the point up defensively. But Leos was walking away from him now.

"I tried to make amends. Tried to earn absolution. But there can be no forgiveness, can there, Fraenk? You'll never let go of the past, and I'll always be held in bondage to you."

"You don't owe me anything. What's past is done and gone," Fraenk said, standing. "Just stop this and we—"

"Then have you forgiven me?" The big man turned back suddenly.

Fraenk hesitated too long before uttering an unconvincing assurance that he did.

"A lie!" Leos shot back. "You always lie. That's what you do. You live to manipulate and control everyone around you."

"I never—" Fraenk started.

"—*tried to exploit me?!*" Leos Muninger howled and rubbed furiously at the side of his forehead. "*They* told me you just did. My little friends said you wanted to reach in and hurt my mind. But they stopped you. You can't reach me with the necklace when *they* are protecting me."

"They're eating your mind, Leos." Fraenk said imploringly. "I've seen it already. They're going to destroy you. I know you can feel them in there."

"Neversleep. Kill him..." Olwynn Brightrock was standing unsteadily with one sword raised. His other arm was bleeding freely and hung loose at his side.

Fraenk moved closer, keeping the spear point aimed at Leos' head.

"Leos, we can get you to a healer. They can help you. Cure you of these things," Fraenk said, hoping he was right. Either way, he had to get his friend to put down the sword.

"Give me the necklace, Fraenk," Leos said plainly. "Give it to me now, and I won't kill your friend."

Whatever Leos thought was going to happen, Fraenk was certainly not going to let him hurt Olywnn Brightrock. If that meant stabbing Leos with the spear, he'd do it.

Then a flare of light and an anguished sound came from Fraenk's right. He turned just in time to see the two wizards grappling together in some sort of arcane wrestling contest. Sorzon Brimblade had the Arcane Lord Phielax by the neck with two glowing hands, and the man was trying to pry the helltouched's grip apart with his own magical counter. Blood was pouring from Phielax's neck and shoulders, and he was crying out in anguish. Then the spell on his hands flickered briefly and finally went out.

The next instant, Brimblade pulled the man's head completely from his shoulders in a mess of bloody carnage. The Arcane Lord's body jerked, then tilted forward and hit the street.

Fraenk's shock was only surpassed when he felt the spear suddenly jerk from his grip. When he looked, Leos had it now in hand. Without a pause, he hefted it up into an overhand grip and sent it sailing in a deadly path through the air.

It hit Olwynn Brightrock in the abdomen, launching him backward and pinning his body against the wooden gate of one of the wealthy estates along the street. Brightrock gasped and dropped his sword, clutching at the spear lodged in his side.

"Nooo!" Fraenk roared in anguish.

"That was *your* choice, Fraenk," Leos warned. He grabbed up his sword again, stalking toward the old elf. "The necklace, Fraenk. Or I have your friend's head."

Leos Muninger stood aside the elf with the blade in both hands, poised like an executioner ready to do his grim task. He let the point rest on the back of Brightrock's neck. Olwynn looked out with steely, resolute eyes.

"Wait." Fraenk stepped forward, raising his hand.

"Go, Neversleep," Brightrock said, a fresh spatter of blood on his lips. "Get the Mind Thief out of here. Don't look back."

"I guess this friend doesn't matter much to you either. A pity." Muninger raised the blade high over his head. "This is what Neversleep's acquaintance gains you..."

"Have it!" Fraenk shouted, stopping the big man before he could swing.

Leos paused, then turned as Fraenk pulled off his glove and held out the Ynne es Tylubourne.

"You want it, it's yours! Here. Let no more lives be lost because of it."

He let the necklace dangle from his hand. Leos fixed upon it, and his eyes went dull. It seemed to take the fight entirely out of him. His grip on the sword loosened, and he let the point drop to the ground. Then his mouth curled downward like someone about to cry.

"What is happening?" Leos asked.

Fraenk saw tiny flecks of black drop from the man's nose and mouth. He seemed to notice them for the first time. Leos' hand touched his lip, and he looked down at his fingers in disgust. But the moment his eyes left the Mind Thief, the hateful sneer began to return.

"Come on," Fraenk said, holding the necklace out to catch his focus. "This is what you came for."

Something in the item's charm was affecting the worms, loosening their grip on his friend. Leos took a step towards him; the two-handed blade fell from his grip and clattered to the ground.

Good. Fraenk thought. *This was working. Just draw him in.*

Leos started towards him in slow, plodding steps. Closer. Fraenk balled his other fist, ready to drop his old friend as soon as he was in range. Leos' big hand scratched his ear. His fingertips came away slimy and black. A terrible realization dawned on his face.

"Fraenk? I think there's something wrong with me."

"Come on, old friend. Keep your eyes on this. We can get you help."

Fraenk kept the necklace held out. Leos' was almost to him, and Fraenk was already trying to plan his next move. Get Leos to the temple of Mersey or perhaps Valthor knew a cure for—

"I will take that!" A blood-covered glove snatched the necklace from Fraenk's grip. He turned to see Brimblade holding the Ynne es Tylubourne, smiling in victorious savagery. He dropped it quickly into a pouch.

Fraenk began to launch himself at Brimblade when the helltouched held out his poisoned dagger in his face. Fraenk jumped back.

"Careful, Neversleep. You have no one left to carry you away for the cure," Brimblade warned. "How did she do, by the way... Did the Exalt live? I hope they didn't have to saw off her leg to save her."

With the Mind Thief no longer in his sight, Leos blinked—its effects losing all sway over the worms. He turned to Brimblade as if he might help.

"They're... in my head," Leos whimpered. "I... I can feel them crawling."

"You have one more unfinished task before you— kill Neversleep. I will bring this to the Master," Brimblade commanded.

"Please help me," Leos said, his voice very small.

"You are beyond help. He will never—" Then the green gem in the collar burned brightly on Brimblades's neck. His voice sounded doubled, like two men speaking the same words. "The Sign of the Under One is upon us. The hour of cleansing is here! Once you finish up here, then you may join us for the summoning."

What fresh hell was this? Fraenk wondered.

Brimblade coughed, then stepped back. Despite his clear exhaustion and battered appearance, the helltouched had more plans ahead. He gestured and uttered arcane words of magic that sent a swirling blue-green fire up from the ground that surrounded and engulfed him entirely. When the flames diminished, Brimblade was gone.

Leos' expression went slack. He strode back to pick up his huge sword. He adjusted his hands on the grip and raised the blade. Fraenk looked around at the obliterated partisan guard detail. Brightrock had slumped against the wall, unable to collapse to the ground, pinned as he was.

It was now just Fraenk and Leos standing in the dark, empty streets.

"Leos, your mind is poisoned. You're not thinking clearly," Fraenk insisted.

"Dandrikan said you were tricky, Fraenk."

"Dandrikan?!" Fraenk's eyes went wide.

"He said you had an item of unimaginable power, and he would give me something that would protect me."

"He gave you the worms?"

"He cultivates them. In the plague house. The men there don't mind... they're dying anyway," Leos said.

Fraenk's brain was reeling. Questions and conclusions were crashing against each other like a frothing sea. Did Dandrikan send these two after the Mind Thief? Dandrikan wasn't a mastermind. He was a charlatan. A backstabbing traitor at best. Yet if he was getting a soldier and a helltouched to do his bidding, Fraenk realized he underestimated him. Dandrian must have bigger plans for it than to sell it for some coin. But what?

"Leos, what is Dandrikan going to do with the necklace?" Fraenk demanded. "Sell it? Make everyone like him?"

"He will awaken the Under One. The Under One will cleanse the city of its sins." Leos recited blankly.

That was the same religious babble that Brimblade had said as well. It seemed familiar somehow. Where else had he heard that? Then the words of the bald street preacher sprang into Fraenk's mind. The cult leader of Nim's supposed 'Palewood Brethren' was preaching something very similar to that. What would Dandrikan be doing with the Mind Thief and a doomsday cult? Fraenk knew he probably wasn't going to like the answer to that.

"Who is this Under One?" Fraenk asked. "Is it Dandrikan? Or that Tigranean preacher?"

"Bultzoaan the Great Leviathan. The gateway to the arcane realm will be opened, and they shall call forth the netherdemon. He shall drown the city in blood and fire."

"Netherdemon?!" Fraenk exclaimed. "Those aren't allowed in the city."

"They've already begun the ceremony."

"You're serious." A wave of dread washed over Fraenk.

The big man stopped in front of him and reached up with his free hand. After struggling for a bit, he got one, then the other shoulder plate unbuckled, letting them fall to the stones.

"Leos! Please. If what you're saying is true, then something very bad is about to happen to everyone in Arathes, and it'll be pretty hard for me to stop it if you kill me."

Leos unclasped his breastplate. It dropped with a clatter, leaving him with only his rusted ring mail shirt. He wiped his mouth, leaving a dark smear across his cheek. Then Leos took the sword in both hands.

"This has to end now, Fraenk. I'm sorry."

Fraenk pinched his eyes shut. If he was going to get sliced in half, he didn't want that to be the last thing he saw. He heard the faint swish of the metal links of the chain shirt move. This was it. Without thinking, Fraenk just began to speak.

"Leos! Leos!! Wait. Don't do this. I forgive you. What happened when we were kids doesn't matter now. You can't change it. I held onto it because I was bitter. But you deserve better. You can only change what you do now. And if you kill me, it won't change anything. You can't move on until you forgive yourself."

There was a pause. Fraenk cracked an eye open. And was surprised to see Leos was not poised with the sword raised above him.

He had the hilt sitting on the ground and the point of the blade under his chain mail shirt. The sword tip pointed right at his heart.

"I'm sorry, Fraenk. For everything I did. I know I was a bad kid, but I wanted change." Tears were in his eyes, and the small, hateful black worms were spilling out from his mouth. "I guess it's too late."

"Wait, no. What are you doing, Leos? Stop!"

"I don't want to hurt anyone else. Dandrikan is at the docks. Pier four. There may still be time to stop him."

Fraenk screamed and tried to grab the blade, but it was too late. Leos Muninger leaned forward with all his weight. He groaned as the sword cut all the way through him and came splitting out through the mail on his back. He collapsed sideways and watched Fraenk for a few more moments before the shine left his eyes.

Falling backward onto his seat, Fraenk unleashed an anguished wail. Everything around him was collapsing and turning to darkness. Despair threatened to engulf him. This necklace was a magical force of pure destruction. He could see why Brightrock wanted it gone.

He sat there for a moment in the silent darkness, wishing he had a bottle of something with which to numb himself.

"Neversleep... why are you... sitting there?"

Fraenk could hear the voice of the Arch Partisan now calling to him from beyond, just like Miken had done. Perhaps he was bringing sage wisdom from the realm of light.

"Neversleep, *you cruk!* Get up... or Gromm strike you... by the Powers!"

The voice was loud and had an unusual amount of swears from someone in the beyond. Then Fraenk saw the old elf's hand raise.

By some gift of Mersey, Brightrock was still alive.

In an instant, Fraenk was up, scrambling over to Brightrock. He looked at the wound, unsure of what he could do.

"Sir, hang on. We'll get you to the temple healers."

Brightrock grabbed Fraenk's shirt with surprising strength.

"Don't worry about me. Get down there and stop those men!"

"But—" Fraenk tried to protest.

"Neversleep. Really listen to me this time. If you let those skarks summon a Netherdemon into this city, I'll kill you myself. Probably with this very spear."

"Yes, sir," Fraenk acknowledged.

"Take my horse and go. And Powers give you strength," Olwynn Brightrock said.

Fraenk ran to the only horse who hadn't fled the carnage— a steely-spined stallion who seemed to have taken on the disposition of the Arch Partisan himself. He took one last look at Brightrock, who pointed to the spear shaft, then to Fraenk's head.

"Do not fail," was the last thing Fraenk heard the elf say before he spurred the horse on. And they rang mighty galloping hoofbeats through the otherwise dark and quiet streets of Arathes.

45

BULTZOAAN THE NETHERDEMON BEGAN the day much like he did every day for the thousands of years before it—with the screaming and the madness, the feasting on souls of the damned, some light stretching and jogging in place, followed by bearing malevolent witness to the dead ones dreaming in the endless void. Of course, 'day' was a relative term in the timeless expanse of the unsanctified underrealm— one had to just decide on a span of time and go with it.

Now, if one was being honest, his name was not actually Bultzoaan—it was just an ominous sobriquet that he had picked up along the millennia by the many cultish admirers who sought his malign presence, then also by the other ones who were decidedly less enthusiastic about the insanity and carnage that he wrought and wanted to banish him from their plane of existence. Either way, the name had stuck and at least made it easier when the other Netherdemons wanted to wish him a jolly commemoration of his unholy birth. Not that anyone asked him, but he actually preferred the name Winston.

Bultzoaan was just relaxing into a fiery pit of unimaginable despair when an odd prickling feeling came over him. It felt very much like the sensation of being dragged interdimensionally across to the plane of reality where the concept of 'happiness' was rumored to exist. It was Winston's least favorite place to be.

As he understood it, many believed that Bultzoaan was a singularly evil entity who was bent on pure destruction, but this was not strictly true. He had other interests besides widespread madness and bathing the landscape in blood— like contemplating the eons and impending existential destruction of all things, for one, and also fishing. Suffice it to say, he had a full and active life that didn't involve just sitting around malevolently waiting to be summoned to run rampant on a world of hapless, scurrying lesser beings. And yet, they had an annoying habit of periodically drawing him forth to do just that. They were certainly gluttons for punishment because while some of Bultzoaan's contemporaries used false promises or trickery to slip over the middle realm, he was very clear every time what the outcome of his arrival would mean— a lot of property destruction and people generally not having a good time. Sure, he was an eldritch Netherdemon, but he did have integrity at least.

When the summoning first began, Winston mistook the trans-dimensional draw as a bit of indigestion. Earlier, he had been devouring the souls of some sour, miserable humans who lived out a bleak existence in a cold and hostile land, which they were puzzlingly proud of and quite defensive about. He decided he'd never understand humans. It was best to hold one's taste receptor orifices closed and swallow them with as few bites as possible.

But when he felt the summoning sensation again, Winston knew what was happening. It couldn't have come at a worse time, either, but here it was. The doorway of light, the chanting, arcane runes written in blood. He wasn't even sure how they managed to figure out how to keep doing this— or why it even worked. Winston had been pretty thorough about killing all who summoned him, which he *thought* would be a logical deterrent from any further foolhardiness. Yet these creatures were nothing if not self-destructive. He would have to oblige them yet again. They could be so annoying.

And so with a sigh of resignation, Bultzoaan tucked his arms, legs, and tentacles in tightly—getting flung across time and space could be dangerous—and he prepared to enter the realms of man.

"Whee!" called the blasphemic leviathan monstrosity as he hurtled toward the light.

An Editorial Footnote from the Wise Scholars of Graysage:

With sincere apologies, the transcribers of this adventure must pause briefly in the telling of the tale of Fraenk Neversleep, for it should be noted that no events from the precedent section are strictly or even partially true.

This is for two reasons: The first is that it is impossible to truly know what the average day of a netherdemon would consist of, so a fair amount of artistic embellishment was applied by a bored novice of Amberflax with an overactive imagination and a flair for the dramaturgical in the realization of this part of the story. The second, and far more dire, reason is that if a human were to slip inside the mind of a netherdemon like Bultzoaan, one would be quickly driven catastrophically and irreversibly insane—for the foul and malignant churnings of an outer being's thoughts are so putrescent and evil, your delicate human psyche could not handle it. It was a lesson hard learned, with several of our scholars bearing the consequences. The readers of this account have been spared a horrible fate and are left to simply enjoy the story without fear of being driven mad by even tertiary contact with a void creature of interdimensional despair. You are welcome.

Please enjoy the remainder of Fraenk Neversleep's tale without further editorial interruption.

Trying to keep up with Dandrikan had been an exhausting and frustrating task for Kyla. Despite her aching leg, she managed to find him at the docks, but just before she could gift him with a dagger to the ribs, he was met by an imposing bald man and his cluster of filthy, rough-spun-robed acolytes. She had no choice but to slip behind some cargo crates and pray to the Powers she'd get another opportunity.

That chance would not come.

They traveled in a group to pier four, where shipping operations were ceased while a major renovation was underway with the construction of a longer dock and more of the large cargo cranes. The carpentry crews were a mix of humans and elves from Drialadon who were apparently specialized in their trade but took a leisurely approach to their jobs. They arrived late to the site and went home at dusk, unlike the Arathenian longshoremen, who worked endlessly loading and unloading the cargo ships, which often ran late into the night.

By the time Dandrikan and company arrived, pier four was almost entirely deserted, which was precisely why they had chosen it. She could see that they desired a certain amount of privacy for what they were about: some kind of illicit dockside ritual.

The difficulty for Kyla was that the entire area was wide open and provided her with no place to hide for a stealthy approach. The pier's boarding was new planks of gray cypress and recently laid down. They were clear of anything set upon them whilst being conditioned for the harsh aquatic environment with a mixture of olive oil, tar, and several other ingredients, which were a closely guarded secret.

Dandrikan seemed to keep to the open and within the middle of the action. His redolent friends—whom she quickly figured out were some kind of religious cult—were going about the preparations for an elaborate rite or ceremony. Dandrikan fussed and quibbled over every minute detail, often requiring a particular setup to be done more than once. For whatever reason, these acolytes obeyed without question, which Kyla imagined was one of the benefits of having a cult of mindless followers. It reminded her of the so-called guardians who raised her and the people they'd exploited over the years, willing to do anything for the favor of a Lynblood.

When it was clear Dandrikan would not be stumbling into the point of her dagger anytime soon, Kyla withdrew to the upper level of the nearby dry docks, where a massive Pileusian galleon was suspended up on blocks and being overhauled for some imaginary future war, using gold that could have been better spent in a myriad of better ways. She had to admit the ship was impressive, however, and quite beautiful— with three tall masts that a grown man couldn't get his arms around and weighing in the hundreds of tons. It certainly must have made an impression on any others it approached on the sea. Although the behemoth ship itself was as cumbersome and unwieldy as the Pileusian government was said to be.

Kyla was eager for justice but forced herself to wait it out. As her friend Posuu had often said, "Haste makes the target flee; patience serves them up for tea." The memory of him made her smile and stung her heart at the same time.

This would end eventually, and Dandrikan would unwittingly wander somewhere alone and unguarded, an ignorant little mouse venturing out into the open while the watchful owl circled overhead with claws at the ready. Kyla knew how to hunt the likes of this rodent.

And so she sat up in a pile of folded sails to watch the proceedings and wait. With her leg still a dull cloud of pain, she began sipping from the second health drink she covertly picked up at the temple. The flavor was nothing appetizing, but it left her head in a warm buzz and her limbs feeling pleasantly heavy.

Time could be a tricky thing— as anyone with children or currently afflicted by lycanthropy could tell you. One moment a person could be watching cultists drawing out arcane symbols and lighting tallow candles; the next they could wake several hours later to the ululations of a dark ceremony well underway.

Which is exactly where Kyla found herself: groggy, sweaty, and confused, with her body tangled in the waxy canvas sailcloth.

Kyla unwound herself from the salt-stenched coverings, letting the air cool her sweaty skin. There was flickering light reflecting off the side of the building, and a terrible sound carried on the breeze from the pier that she realized was a chorus of rising and falling voices. She looked down and saw them in a large circle. The acolytes had shed their smelly robes and were cavorting and gyrating in filthy linen loin wraps. The firelight from a ring of braziers cast their wiry bodies in contrasting shapes of orange and black. There was a strange structure assembled on the very edge of the dock looking out over the lake—it was a crude, triangular scaffold of wood and hung with what looked like dried human bones. The fat, bald priest stood before it with hands raised and led the dark invocation.

The followers replied with agonized chanting in a language she did not understand but really didn't need to. Cults never got a ceremony going this elaborate unless something terrible was about to go down.

And this looked bad on a level that could only mean either a mass ritual sacrifice, indiscriminate killing frenzy, or methodical door-to-door proselytization—all were cause for great alarm.

Kyla scanned the figures in the circle, looking for Dandrikan. She was sure he'd be the ringleader in the middle of all this madness, given how he had fretted over every detail of preparation, but she didn't find him anywhere in the hokum. Panic gripped her, fearing that she had somehow missed him and allowed the rotten skark to slip away while she was asleep. Then she saw him pacing impatiently along the edge of the firelight, and relief washed over her.

"Thank Skylae," she said with a dark smile. "He's finally ready to meet my dagger."

Kyla was pleased to notice that her leg was feeling much better as well. Unintentionally taking the advice of the temple nurse had actually worked. She tested her weight on it, and sure enough, the medicine and possibly resting for a few hours did yield positive results.

Perhaps she might be inclined to heed their insistent, annoying advice more often in the future. Then again, that didn't feel like a very realistic promise to make.

Using her enchanted gloves and boots, she quickly scaled down the side of the building, spider-like. And also, like a spider, she began to stalk her prey, ready to catch him in her web. Kyla moved around the stacks of crates, building materials, and piles of rough lumber that were being used for the dock's renovation. She kept one eye on Dandrikan and seemed to grow more agitated with each passing moment. As she got close, Kyla could see he was agitated and muttering to himself. Something had this man in great distress. If she were to guess, it probably had something to do with the plans he'd made earlier with the big soldier. If things were going badly for him, all the better. Kyla smiled, reveling in his anguish.

"No better time to end him than when he's most tortured," she said, slipping the thin dagger from her leg sheath. He paused, with his back to her, close to the shadows of a tall crate. She could kill him, drag his body off, and be gone before anyone else noticed.

As she moved in closer, her hand trembled. What was happening? Was this another effect of the medicine, or something else? Was her body betraying her when she was only a few steps away?

But her thoughts began to take over. Maybe it was the Lyn-Tyrian in her blood that was telling her not to do this. *Don't use pain as an excuse for doing evil.* Kyla may have been a thief, not a killer. Was she actually going to stab an unwary man in the back? She needed another moment to think about this. Killing Dandrikan wouldn't bring Posuu back, nor her other friends. But on the other hand, he appeared to be up to something nefarious with this cult. Maybe she'd be preventing some terrible thing from happening.

Watching Dandrikan standing there, he just looked pathetic and weak. Like a scared, insecure little man inflicting his chaos upon the world. And there were so many others out there just like him. Killing him would be like squashing a single nightbeetle, and would have about the same amount of impact on ridding the world of their kind.

Then another thought occurred to her. Kyla didn't have to kill him. She could do something much better than that. Something she had no moral quandaries about: she would simply kidnap him and drop him on the next ship headed to anywhere far away. See how this insect liked the sailor's life on the high seas instead of causing trouble in Arathes. This seemed like a very good plan indeed.

But before she could act, Kyla watched her opportunity for vengeance go up in a swirling blue-green fireball. A hateful dark figure with black horns stepped from the flames and fell to one knee.

"Finally you arrive!" Dandrikan shouted in equal parts anger and relief. "What happened? What kept you?!"

"Your old friend Neversleep nearly messed everything up! From what I was told, Lord Fernbrook wasn't able to seize power like he wanted because of something that human did. One minute the High Lord himself was about to kill him, and well—no one can say for sure. The partisans got the necklace and were on their way to lock it up again, but we got it back." Sorzon Brimblade barely had the strength to take the pouch from his belt.

Dandrikan greedily snatched the bag away from him and dumped its contents into his own palm. He held it up by the thin chain, and the small dark stone seemed to avoid reflecting any of the dancing firelight. Even though she could only see its shape, Kyla knew what it was.

"I never should have allowed that foolish old elf to use it. He nearly cost us everything! But the pure chaos he would have created for the elves at the top would have been glorious. They'd be too disorganized to mount a defense against what's about to happen."

Kyla listened, feeling serious second thoughts about not killing Dandrikan when she had the chance. "Where's Neversleep now?" Dandrikan asked, suddenly worried.

"Your hired thug is taking care of him as we speak. He was just about to finish it when I left," Brimblade replied, then reached up to the metal collar on his neck. "Sir, I've served you well, yes? You said you'd release me when—"

Dandrikan raised his clenched fist. The emerald ring on his hand blazed with light. The corresponding green jewel on the helltouched man's neck also flared. Heat waves and the sound of searing flesh came from the metal collar, and Brimblade cried out.

"*Don't tell me what I said!* You'll be free when I say you're done. And you have one final task: make sure no one can interrupt me once this all starts," Dandrikan seethed.

"I obey, Master! I will protect you with my life," Brimblade grunted in pain. Finally, Dandrikan released his fist, and the light in the ring and collar died.

Then Dandrikan said something that sounded like "Nimbus Obscura."

Kyla watched as the evil helltouched took a deep breath and exhaled a long string of syllables. The words seemed to turn tangible as they came from his mouth like a cloud of smoke toward Dandrikan. Brimblade continued the chant, while the other man slowly raised the loop of the Mind Thief and widened it to go around his neck. Then, he drew it back into the sparking cloud that surrounded his head. A muffled laugh came from within the cloud, and Brimblade let the spell die.

When the cloud dissipated, Dandrikan was wearing the Ynne es Tylubourne.
Kyla gasped. *How was that possible?* As far as she knew, the necklace couldn't
be worn by someone who wasn't a wizard and protected by very specific wards.

"Not good," she whispered to the night.

Dandrikan laughed—*cackled,* really. Giddy with some kind of powerful
high. Kyla's second-guessing about killing this evil worm had become full-on
regret. She was pretty sure one of the actual Lyn-Tyrians would have no trouble
preemptively ending this guy. Sometimes being preternaturally influenced to
virtuous acts was very inconvenient.

Then Dandrikan turned and strode back to the circus of cultists, leaving the
helltouched man to slowly recruit himself alone on the dock boards.

"I am ready! You may call forth the beast now!" Dandrikan shouted at the
bald priest, who returned an annoyed glare but didn't break in the repetitive
string of foul syllables that seemed to be making the flames in the brazier dance
higher and an eerie mist appear along the water. They were words of the darkly
arcane, Kyla recognized, and were unholy ones at that— for each utterance felt
like tiny cuts along her skin. This was older than Gorothkan magic—a primal,
ageless force that only wrought destruction. The fat, bald man raised his voice
higher as the sinewy dancers responded in kind, vibrating in ecstatic trance.
Dandrikan paced impatiently, his attention alternating between the cultists and
the dark waters of the lake. He looked like he wanted to whip them on but
seemed unwilling to risk breaking their concentration at this critical moment.
The fat priest's cries became high and shrill. His hands emerged from the sleeves
of his robes, and Kyla saw he was now holding a curved blade. The fat priest
turned and moved to the triangular structure, where they had a beaten and
bloodied man bound up to the frame—apparently he was meant to be their
blood sacrifice. Waves of energy and sparks of light were rising from the arcane
runes drawn out onto the dock boards, rising skyward.

She wanted to stop this, somehow, but rushing into the thick of everything
seemed like a good way to become the next victim. Kyla wondered if she had
time to alert the partisans, but in her prior occupation as a thief, success often
relied upon the slow and inconsistent response of the authorities. They might
still be looking for her as well. It was foolish to even involve them at this point.

The fat priest raised the blade, muttering some words of enchantment,
which made the blade begin to glow. He then slashed at the bound man, making
long, but shallow, cuts in his flesh and causing the man to wail in agony. Blood
immediately began to run from the gashes in his flesh. This was clearly part of

the proceedings, because a sour wind began to rattle the bones in the structure, and arcing tendrils of power crawled along the beams. They moved faster as more of the man's blood trickled down in dark drops.

Kyla couldn't let this continue. These gibbering yokels were up to some magical purpose, and it wasn't to summon an adorable puppy for each person in the city. Perhaps she could create some diversion or distraction to throw off their incantation. But by the time she'd figured out some sort of half-cocked plan, the spell had reached its apex. The energy rising from the markings on the ground rose to a point above the heads of the dancers and then seemed to get pulled together and directed out to the center of the lake. Like light being focused into a tight beam by a curved lens of glass.

There was a distant sound, like thunder, but instead of coming from the sky, it sounded like it was originating from far beneath the waves.

"Well, I really don't see how this situation could get much worse." Kyla whispered to herself.

As if some unseen, all-powerful force outside of her realm with a darkly ironic sense of humor was controlling what would happen next, Kyla's words were no sooner spoken than proved immediately correct.

A single wavering shaft of light shot up from the point where the beam had met the water—far out in the depths of Lake Ewyn—followed by a massive boiling froth of water that shot skyward. A shockwave of putrid air immediately followed, rippling over the water and through the docks. Ships thumped heavily against the pier, and it sent everyone wobbling unsteadily on their feet.

Then came a sound. Low and deep and hungry. A single note that sent a cold chill through her body. Something was coming.

Something immense and terrible.

46

"**R**IGHT. SO *THAT'S* HOW things could get worse," Kyla muttered.

The commotion on the pier had gone quiet. Everyone had their attention fixed on the falling plume out in the lake. Bodies frozen in an involuntary and primal dread.

Far out, a rippling wave began to move along just under the surface of Lake Ewyn, making a small hill out of the water. Something massive was gliding inexorably toward the city with some unknown purpose.

Kyla had the immediate feeling that she should run. But instead found herself fixed to the spot where she stood, gaping. She distantly wondered what it said about people that, in spite of every survival instinct telling them to escape, they had to stay and lay eyes on the enormous thing that was surely coming for them.

The Palewood acolytes' summoning ritual was all but forgotten as they also watched. They had been quite pivotal in this thing's arrival and had, up to this point, felt that summoning this monstrous beast was definitely something they wanted. But as they now witnessed the approach—at first with exhausted rapture, then with growing unease— questions began to form as to whether or not this had been a good idea. And as it drew closer, they had a better sense of its size and scale. There was also a certain malignant intent to its direct path toward the city. *Had they really summoned a large creature that was going to destroy the city—a city that they were still in?* And so the acolytes' delight for completing their lifelong mission quickly melted away, replaced by concern, fear, and finally mind-blanking existential terror.

Then, as if some enormous creature swimming toward the city wasn't disconcerting enough, something even scarier happened. For as the dread wave reached the outer limits of the harbor, the force causing it was suddenly gone. The wave rolled on without it. Faces looked around in confusion.

"Where did it go?" one of the men asked aloud the question they all were thinking.

"And now is a good time for me to go," Kyla whispered to herself. She stepped backward into the shadows and was moving stealthily up the dock when she heard the voice of the fat priest shriek.

"There! The great Bultzoaan has arrived!"

The natural human instinct to know the proximity of any nearby netherdemon took over, and as much as she didn't want to, Kyla stole a glance over her shoulder. She immediately regretted it. A huge scaly dome, like a tiny island, had just breached the water surface. It was much closer than she was expecting—probably ten ship-lengths from the end of the longest dock. And beneath the black waves, she could see a terrible asymmetrical constellation of yellow glowing orbs that rolled and blinked. The creature wasn't moving and just seemed to be watching the city. Kyla released an involuntary whimper, and the strength in her body wavered.

The Palewood Brethren all seemed to have the same terrified reaction. A ripple of shrieks and cries went through their ranks; they stood knock-kneed and trembling. Only Dandrikan stepped closer, raising his arms in triumphant welcome.

"Yes! He's here! Rejoice! For the Unhallowed One is upon us!" Dandrikan shouted, his gesticulations wild and manic. He turned back to the cult, who gave off the distinct impression that rejoicing was not about to happen. It was clear that they were all experiencing a significant amount of summoner's remorse. Many of the scrawny men were already stepping backward, out of the circle of runic symbols, heedlessly toppling candles and capsizing one of the braziers, which erupted in a burst of sparks.

"This is what you wanted!!" Dandrikan cried, sounding like he was trying to convince them. "Bultzoaan the Undergod is here! The punisher and destroyer! The time of cleansing. Punish the unworthy. It's waiting for your sacrifice."

Dandrikan grabbed the acolyte nearest to him, but the man shook free with a child-like whimper. The arcane dealer turned to the fat priest next.

"Welcome your god, priest! Finish the summoning!" Dandrikan shouted.

The fat man only shook his head, making his bearded jowls wobble.

"I-—I can't!" He stammered.

"You're a coward!" Dandrikan growled. He clenched his fist, and cold steam rose from his chest. "Tell them your true purpose, priest!"

The fat man's body stiffened.

"I'm not a true believer. My name is Jerome, and I used to be a cobbler. I saw them wandering and knew they needed a leader. I-I just learned their invocations from books so they'd trust me. So they would work to keep my belly full and my purse fat with coin," the false priest blubbered. "We were never supposed to actually get this far!"

Dandrikan released his mental grip on the big man, and he immediately covered his mouth, as if somehow he could stuff everything he'd spoken back inside. But it was too late.

The half-starved and haggard acolytes turned to fix their leader with poisonous, reproachful glares. Their thin bodies, a testament to all the hungry days and miserable nights in service to this greedy charlatan. And now they had helped him summon forth a great evil to wreak fiery death upon non-believers in a ceremony that would also soon require their sacrificial blood offering—somehow this had sounded like a brilliant scheme back during the late nights drinking sour goat milk liquor and commiserating over their hatred of everyone who wasn't them back in the swamps of Tigraen. Now, in the unholy light of the submerged demon's many eyes, a certain kind of clarity had taken hold. This was unequivocally a bad idea and not something they wanted to die for.

"Lads, wait!" The priest called. "This man is a demon. He sent a foul spirit to overtake my voice. It... was he who made me say false things! Destroy this man! And then we can cure me by casting out the spirit with fine foods and strong wine. Or—or your leader will surely be taken from you!"

"Stuff yourself on your own coin, you fat pig!" One acolyte threw a lit candle at the priest, which went out in midair but still splashed him with hot wax. Others spat and cursed at him. The priest tried to follow, but a man with black teeth waved a dagger at the fat priest, making him abandon his pursuit.

"Come, brothers!" Dandrikan called out to them. "I will lead you now. We must finish our work here. Your god awaits a sacrifice." His smile curdled as he clearly misjudged these men's appetite for further service to the cult. They shoved past him and continued to back further out of the summoner's circle.

When she was young, Kyla was always taught that cursed souls, those who worked in service of evil—either by birth or by choice—were tainted by it forever and would remain in thrall to its influence without redemption or remorse. But here in this moment, she was amazed to see that all it took to break the dreaded Cult of the Palewood Brethren was one fraudulent leader to finally admit their deception—that and the mixture of cowardice and terror created by an approaching netherdemon.

Although none had spoken it aloud, the Palewood Brethren had seemed to collectively decide to immediately disband and cease further association. They continued their cautious retreat.

"We must give it the blood sacrifice-—or it will abandon this realm!" Dandrikan pitched like a spoiled child.

"Spill your own blood and get *skarked*, you weasel!" The black-toothed man shouted at him and made an obscene three-fingered gesture.

Then the beast sent out another deep, trumpeting call that Kyla could feel low in her chest and back teeth. She was filled with a dark, atavistic sense that she was nothing but helpless prey and would be consumed not once but millions of times over a span of eons. The urge to throw up and empty her bladder at the same time was almost overpowering.

The terrified brethren broke ranks and began to run back down the docks in headlong panic.

"STOP!" Dandrikan raised his hands. The surrounding air seemed to swirl and crystallize into delicate flakes of snow. The cultists froze in place, their bodies motionless, like they were playing some kind of child's game.

He's using the necklace on them, Kyla thought and decided she was probably much too close to the action. In fact, if Dandrikan had some kind of wish to die by this summoned monster, then that was just another item off her list. She should really think about getting as far away from the city as possible. And there was no better time for that than now.

But when she tried to turn and go, Kyla also realized that she, too, could not move. *Why couldn't she move?* Kyla tried harder, but she was frozen in place.

"You faithless scum!" He shouted at the frozen men. "You claim you want cleansing for a city of decadence and fornication. To see your enemies cower in fear at the coming of the great destroyer, Bultzoaan. He is here now, but where is your devotion? I will remind you."

Dandrikan made another motion with his hand, and the acolytes reached down to their belts. As one, they raised crude daggers, knives, and bits of sharpened metal wrapped with rope handles and touched them to the corners of their throats. Dandrikan was going to turn this into a mass suicide after all. Kyla gasped in shock when she felt the blade of a dagger press up against her own throat—even more disconcerting was that it was held by her own hand.

She pinched her eyes closed, trying to force her own will back into her body. Break the connection to Dandrikan. Don't let him do this.

"Prove yourself to your Undergod!" Dandrikan shouted.

Kyla fought against the impulse. Her hand started to move but then struggled. There was a sharp feeling against the underside of her chin. She willed her hand to pull back and drop the blade. But she could also feel her own arm tensed and pulling the dagger towards her neck. Kyla wanted to fight it—tried to with all of her might—but it was like trying to spur a horse that she wasn't riding.

Kyly pinched her eyes shut and heard a grotesque sound: a squishing, slicing, and sawing that was multiplied many times over. Those with the sharp blades had it mercifully easiest, for their bodies fell first. The ones with rough, improvised shivs had to hack and tear at the flesh on their necks while making muted screams until their sacrifice was complete. It would be those sounds that would haunt her dreams.

As she continued to feel her own blade still pressed uncomfortably against her neck, it seemed to be suspended by two opposing forces. She only hoped whatever mental will she was using to abate that terrible urge could hold out long enough. The force controlling her was strong, and she felt the blade press harder. But there was something else, like a strong hand that kept the knife from cutting her.

Then suddenly it was over. Her dagger came away, and a warm trickle dripped down from where it had been. Kyla looked down to see that there actually was another hand on her wrist. It was what had stayed the dagger. There was also a body standing right behind her.

Alarmed, she spun immediately out of the grip of whoever had been holding her and saw the face of Fraenk Neversleep. He smiled at her and looked relieved. That made two of them.

"If you're looking for a shave, I know a charming little anura who does wonders with beards," Fraenk said. But something about seeing him now made her anger flare.

"What are you doing here?!" She demanded, then knew immediately what this was about. "The necklace. That's it, isn't it?"

"Sorry. It looked like you were about to do something drastic. I thought I'd help."

"I don't need your help," Kyla snapped back, wiping her own blood off the blade of her dagger and sliding it back into its sheath.

"You're bleeding," Fraenk shrugged.

She touched the thin cut on her neck. It was barely a scratch. He looked at her for a moment longer, staring again as a result of her Lynblood charm, no doubt. Kyla could feel herself growing impatient.

"About what I said before. At the lighthouse—" Fraenk started to say, but a raised shout turned both their attention back to the scene on the dock.

Brimblade had lowered the poisoned dagger that was positioned at his own throat. Somehow he too had resisted the urge to kill himself from the call of the Mind Thief. There was a deep, shiny gash cut into the metal collar on his neck, so perhaps he was not impervious to the necklace after all—merely fortunate to be wearing that thing. Either way, he was definitely not pleased about how he had been included in its influence in the first place.

He stepped around the bodies of the fallen acolytes, who lay in all attitudes of death. Their blood running in pools and dripping down into the lake below. Brimblade was shouting a curse at Dandrikan, who waved him off dismissively.

"I knew you were strong enough to resist it," Dandrikan began to explain, then seemed to realize that he was justifying himself to a sniveling subordinate. His expression curdled. "Be ready to defend me! I will require complete concentration for what comes next."

"Now's our chance. If I draw the helltouched away, can you get the necklace from Dandrikan?" Fraenk asked.

"I think we have a much bigger problem than that right now," Kyla pointed to the harbor.

"What? What am I looking at? A small island with eyes?"

Fraenk's brain did not seem to want to comprehend what he was witnessing out in the harbor, which was a perfectly reasonable reaction for someone seeing an eldritch netherdemon for the first time. But the monster tasted the traces of blood from its until-very-recently devoted followers, and its massive domed head began to rise... and rise... and rise, water cascading off it in sheets.

It had hateful golden eyes that seemed to be taking everything in simultaneously and two massively thick tentacle appendages that grew from either side of its face. A circular, fleshy pit of a mouth opened and closed in anticipation of its impending feast. The rest of the creature seemed somewhat humanoid in its structure, or at least mixed somehow with the unholy offspring of the spawn of the ancient dragon, Tiamat. The creature's skin had large scales the size of a shield and slick black skin that reflected iridescence in the moonlight. Standing up in the waters near the pier, its head was above the top of the nearest dockside buildings. The longer Fraenk stared at it, the more he felt his sanity eroding.

"So... this must be the netherdemon everyone keeps talking about," Fraenk muttered, rubbing his temples.

Kyla turned to look at him.

"You knew about this?"

"I'll just say it wasn't a complete surprise," Fraenk replied.

This impossibly long day that refused to finally be over was quickly turning into not just the worst day he'd ever had, but possibly the worst day anyone, anywhere, had ever experienced. Why did _he_ have to be the one having this spectacularly terrible day?

"Well, I just saved the city once tonight. I think I'm going to let someone else handle this," Fraenk said. His entire body felt exhausted. The incident at the Summer Palace seemed like hundreds of years ago.

"You are, huh?" Kyla planted her knuckles on her hips and looked fiercely at him. Fraenk crossed his arms petulantly.

"Fine. It's your city, Fraenk," Kyla shrugged. "Besides, I'm not even welcome. Not that I'd want to live here anyway. This city is infested with monsters."

"And it used to be such a nice place, too."

The creature raised its head back and issued a deafening blast of sound. Shrieks rose from the workers on the closest dock. Fraenk could see figures scrambling in all directions—fear and panic turning the situation into utter chaos. The monster raised its dual tentacles and smashed in the roof of the fishmongery, sending shattered timbers and a glittering silver rain of trout out as nightmarish projectiles. Fraenk stepped aside as one stray fish came whistling past his head.

Frank and Kyla watched helplessly as, a few moments later, some dockworkers, fishermen, and guards had mounted an impromptu defense. They charged in, lobbing barbed harpoons and flinging gutting knives at it. All of which bounced harmlessly off its thick, slimy skin. Although brave, the endeavor was ill-fated, for it ended with a single swipe from one of the creature's arms that smashed the docks to splinters.

"Hells!" Fraenk growled. "Why do I end up fighting every monster in the city?"

"How are we going to stop it?" Kyla asked.

"We?" Fraenk looked over at her with an arched eyebrow.

"Let's not argue about this again, Neversleep. It's tedious. I'm going to help you, and that's the end of it."

Kyla's eyes looked frightened, but her cheeks were flushed and she was smiling. Something about the way the light from the burning docks was dancing across her delicate features made her look quite lovely.

"Very well. But you've chosen a poor time to help. I have no idea how to defeat a netherdemon. We're probably just going to die," he said grimly.

"I figured as much. We can at least give him a fight. Poke him in one of those eyes."

"Maybe you could call in some help from your friends?" Fraenk pointed skyward.

Kyla scoffed derisively.

"We're not on speaking terms. Besides, I think I've used up any last favors with them."

Fraenk felt inside his cloak. While he did take the time to stop along the way down to grab his trusty Preceptor's cloak and his brace of knives, nothing amongst his many pockets seemed like a suitable weapon against an arcane creature of this size. Nothing seemed to be able to damage it. Maybe if he had a ballista—or a hundred of them—he might be able to bring the creature down. Or some type of banishing magic to unsummon this beast, but that would require competent wizards at the ready, of which he had none.

Then something stuck in his mind: What about Dandrikan? What was his role in all this?

Fraenk turned to see the wispy blonde man waving his arms and shouting at the creature. *That was an odd reaction to seeing a city-destroying leviathan.*

"Here we are, Bultzoaan! Come! We are here!!" Dandrikan shouted with nihilistic glee.

What was he doing? Fraenk wondered. It was as if he wanted the monster to notice them—which might be an even worse idea than the poor guards who had just tried to harpoon it. That was the rantings of a madman. For surely only someone who wished for death would invite such calamity. Perhaps those black worms he cultivated had gotten inside him as well and were now eating holes in his brain. That was the only explanation for why he could possibly want to court such pandemonium.

Fraenk saw the fat priest, who had somehow avoided being compelled to cut his own throat with the rest of his followers because he didn't have a knife. He rushed over and grabbed Dandrikan's robes, shaking him in a manic frenzy.

"This is not what we agreed to, Dandrikan! You said if we brought forth the Under One, we'd control its power," he screamed over the din.

"You thought you could control that?" Dandrikan laughed, pointing at the creature that was in the process of ripping through the hull of the cargo ship moored at the pier. It was taking on water quickly and listing severely to starboard. With another powerful smash, the ship split in two and sank so that only the tall masts were visible.

The priest stammered, trying to grasp the depths of Dandrikan's betrayal. But he had not reached the bottom of it until he felt a dagger ram hard into his belly.

"Only _I_ can do that!" Dandrikan sneered, releasing the blade.The priest groaned and staggered backward, holding the dagger's hilt. His face bore a shocked, dismayed expression, somehow still not believing that this unscrupulous dealer of cursed artifacts was capable of such evil. The fat man took three more small steps backward, almost toppling off the edge of the dock, then his arms pinwheeled and he fell forward onto the dagger. Dandrikan winced and stepped back as the fat priest wheezed out his final breath.

"Oh, brilliant. Why couldn't you just fall in the water like you were supposed to?!'" Dandrikan complained. He tried to push the man with a foot, but it was going to take much more than that to move him.

"Help me with this!" Dandrikan growled and waved over Brimblade for help. The two men struggled mightily to shove the whale-sized corpse into the harbor. Finally, they maneuvered him to the edge and tipped him in with a large splash. As if in response, a thundering trumpet from the creature sounded, and Bultzoaan the Great Leviathan turned to see them in all its terrible arcane grandeur. Its many eyes seemed to flicker with unholy delight.

Fraenk made a grim realization at that moment. Dandrikan was not mad at all—at least not in the execution of his scheme—which itself was as completely chaos-touched as only a recluse who lives in a plague house could devise. But this evil man was not compelled by dark parasites or a city-scaled suicidal urge.

This had been his plan all along. And it was working perfectly.

47

"FORGET THE MONSTER! WE have to stop Dandrikan!" Fraenk shouted, pulling Kyla back just as a length of shattered ship mast hit the pier beside them with a booming crash. She shot him a look like he was crazy. The netherdemon plowed its way through another section of docks and was on a direct path to where they were all standing. They had to escape. Call for the army of the city or the kingdom itself. They might even have to beg their neighboring kingdom of Tigraen for help in some kind of ironic reversal of fortune.

"Yes! Come closer!" Dandrikan perched at the edge of the docks. His face a wild, manic grin.

"Come on! He's going to use it!" Fraenk shouted.

Kyla looked over and saw Dandrikan raising his arms, a crystalline mist beginning to form around him. Then she understood what Fraenk meant—the fool was attempting to use the Mind Thief on this monster.

"That's insane," she gasped. "That won't work. Will it?"

Then she felt a terrible premonition that was no premonition at all. Her dreams—they had warned her this was coming. They had shown her a creature just like this one destroying Arathes. Thousands of souls screaming and dying in fire. Kyla understood, and it was like a door to a dungeon opening wide. The feeling made her blood run cold.

"Hurry!" Fraenk had already started running. Not back up the dock and into the city where he might be able to escape, but down toward the end of the pier—and the spot that was most likely slated for demolition by the monster in the next few minutes. It was quite possibly the last place anyone would want to be, but they had no choice, and she knew it.

Fraenk moved quickly toward where Dandrikan was standing in front of the arcane structure with Brimblade defensively behind him. Kyla was running beside him a moment later.

"You get the Mind Thief off of Dandrikan," she said. "I've got a little surprise for that hell-horned skark!"

He nodded and looked relieved to not have to face the helltouched warlock, but at the same time worried about how he would handle Dandrikan now that his adversary had the necklace. He did not want to end up in another Gingerglade situation.

Both of their foes were understandably distracted by the enormous creature incoming, and Kyla angled her approach away from Fraenk so she could come at him from as close to his periphery as possible. Hopefully, she could get there before the warlock noticed her attack.

Another mighty crash sent a shuddering vibration through the ground underneath them. They could feel a spray of water and had to dodge falling debris from the destructive rampage.

Fraenk was twenty strides from the end of the dock when Brimblade must have sensed their approach, for he turned his head and looked right at him. A purple glow of energy flared around his hands. Neither she nor Fraenk could get to the helltouched in time to interrupt whatever spell he was about to unleash.

But then something unexpected happened. The sacrificial man who was bound up in the arcane structure jerked to life, startling everyone.

"Phane's embrace!" The bloody man cursed aloud, thrashing in his bindings. It was a momentary distraction, but it was all he needed. Kyla saw Fraenk's hand shoot forward with a quick flash of steel. Brimblade raised one arm, and the shield spell managed to deflect the throwing knife from hitting him in the chest. Instead, it ricocheted sideways and lodged in Brimblade's shoulder muscle. He staggered backward, throwing the other spell wildly from his injured side. A wicked crackling ball hit the center of the docks and exploded, the spell missing a direct hit on Fraenk, but its shockwave sent him tumbling.

Brimblade wasn't even looking when Kyla leaped through the air, her legs tucked and dagger raised. She hit him full force with her knees, knocking him backwards. Her arm was a spiked blur as she stabbed over and over again.

"How do you like it!?" She screamed, landing on top of Brimblade as he thrashed and tried to defend himself. Kyla didn't know how much time she'd have before he would counter, but she hoped to do as much damage as possible.

She heard Brimblade utter a quick, arcane phrase, and a flare of power launched Kyla backwards off of him. Midair, her trained instincts immediately took over, and she twisted cat-like, using her momentum to turn her body and land in a crouch. She watched helplessly as her dagger bounced once off the dock and splashed into the water.

"Skarking hells," she muttered.

Brimblade was trying to pick himself up but found all of his new punctures made it difficult. Dagger or no, Kyla was ready to stop this cursed man once and for all. With a roar, she flung herself forward and slammed into him, just as he was starting to conjure a spell. They tumbled together, like iniquitous lovers. She hooked her strong legs around his midsection and braced one arm under his throat, pressing down until the green gem dug painfully into her forearm. Brimblade's horns stuck into the wood, keeping his head pinned in place. Kyla could hear him struggle for breath. His hands beating at her ineffectually.

Some commotion was happening behind her as Fraenk tussled with Dandrikan. Then the deafening blast of the behemoth's call, so close it could have been on top of them. Whatever was happening, she could only hope that Neversleep was handling it, and she would not let Brimblade stop him.

"Please. Don't kill me," Brimblade managed to gasp.

"I'm out of mercy," she sneered, pressing down harder. He made an awful choking sound. There was fear in his eyes.

A searing hot pain flared at her forearm where the green gem was pressing. Kyla pulled back, and Brimblade thrashed, releasing a wheezing shriek with his gasping breath. She could see the collar glowing hot and smelled the man's flesh sizzle.

"Get it off me!" Brimblade croaked. "Help me..."

Kyla stole a sideways glance and saw the green signet ring on Dandrikan's fist glowing. Agony on the helltouched's face as the emerald collar flared with it.

"You can't... defeat Bultzoaan... alone," Brimblade grimaced, his rough brow slick with sweat. Finally, the green gem in his collar went dark, and he gasped.

"He uses the collar if I don't obey him—I was forced to do his bidding. He would release me when it's over, but he's going to kill everyone. Let me help you."

"No. I think I'll kill you, and we'll take our chances," Kyla spat.

"I'm the only one who can send the demon back to the netherrealm. Please!"

Kyla found herself suddenly torn between the urge to choke off his airway again and some other part of her—the deeply Lynblood part, no doubt—that felt things like pity, hope and mercy. This foul creature had caused nothing but misery for her and Fraenk. And here he was at the end, begging for his life. But she read fear in his fiery eyes—and something that felt like truth. Maybe he was their only chance to get rid of this arcane behemoth. And maybe he was just trying to trick her into letting her guard down.

Kyla saw Fraenk's dagger, still lodged in his shoulder. With an animalistic cry, she grabbed it out and raised it to Brimblade's neck.

Fraenk was twenty strides away from where Dandrikan and his helltouched guard were standing, but he was closing fast. He had slipped a knife from his brace and was just about to send it into the side of Dandrikan's head when Brimblade must have caught the movement out of the corner of his eye and began to turn.

Brimblade's response was faster than Fraenk was expecting, especially considering all the magic he had expended in his recent wizard's duel. Both men reacted simultaneously, but then a shout from someone else turned everyone's attention. A blood-covered man bound up in Dandrikan's ceremonial scaffold that Fraenk had fairly assumed was dead.

"Fraenk! It's you!" He shouted, seeming to recognize him. There was something familiar about the other man as well, but he was covered in blood, and Fraenk had absolutely no time to think about how they might be acquainted.

Using the split-second diversion, Fraenk flung the knife just as Brimblade called forth his magic. He saw it strike the helltouched in the shoulder before one of his wicked energy spheres came humming far too close for his own liking. There was a blast—too close—and Fraenk found his legs pumping with no ground underneath them.

He tumbled to a hard stop on the docks a moment later. Fraenk turned to see if Brimblade was conjuring another one of those spells, which he was fairly certain that he wouldn't be able to dodge this time. But when he looked, Fraenk saw an angelic being flying through the air with a small sword raised in hand. She hit Brimblade solidly and immediately began furiously stabbing him. Fraenk blinked and realized it was Kyla.

He had no time to be impressed, however. The impact tremors from the creature were getting very close, and he didn't have to look to know where the monster was—for it was filling the entire side of his vision. Fraenk scrambled to his feet, drawing two blades.

He located Dandrikan standing in front of the sacrificial scaffold. He had both arms raised, and a vicious blizzard of ice and snow was swirling around him. Even the lake water underneath was freezing solid and forming a column of ice that was raising him up. Fraenk knew he had to stop this. He flung the first blade, aiming right for Dandrikan's head.

His arm made an anemic flop forward, and the throwing knife clanged harmlessly to the dock boards. Something was wrong with his muscles. Fraenk quickly tried again with his offhand, and the same thing happened. It was like his arms lost their strength whenever he tried to hurt Dandrikan. Then he realized *that was exactly what was happening*. Another cantrip from the Mind Thief.

Dandrikan unleashed an anguished scream, and a brilliant glow flared from the necklace. In response, or maybe because of it, the creature unleashed an unholy, deafening resound that vibrated the air around them. The twin sounds seemed to pitch and modulate for a maddening amount of time until their notes became one. Then all went silent. Dandrikan fell to one knee, gasping for breath. The leviathan stood motionless and staring with its many terrible eyes.

"Fraenk? Fraenk!"

The sacrificial man stirred again with newfound energy. Fraenk heard the man's faint but grateful cry. "You came to rescue me!"

Fraenk looked closer. Then, finally, recognition dawned. Although he was shirtless and his skin slashed in several places, not to mention covered in blood, Fraenk finally recognized him.

"Nim?!" Fraenk said, incredulous.

It was Nim Stonebridge, the junior preceptor of Blackroot. Fraenk just now realized he hadn't seen Nim in days. *Had he been kidnapped and tortured by the Palewood Brethren this whole time?*

He quickly rushed over to the man and began hacking away at the bindings.

"I knew you'd come, Fraenk. You must have figured out the Palewood Brethren were up to something, and then when I was kidnapped, you spent the last two days tracking me down." Nim said, rubbing his sore wrists.

"That's exactly what happened," Fraenk agreed. "Glad I found you in time. Can you stand? I need you to go get the partisans and—

Fraenk just realized Brightrock would not be coming to their aid.

"—get the Arcane Lords. The council of wizards. The army. Everyone. Wake the city. Bring every man who can hold a spear or fire an arrow."

"It's no good, sir," Nim said, clutching Fraenk's shoulder for stability. "I can barely walk."

"You have to try. I'll find some way to distract Dandrikan. Maybe lead the creature away from the city. "

Then a noise like a peal of thunder came from the sky. It almost sounded like a chuckle, but a most awful, unearthly bedlam that made one despair of ever knowing joy again. Fraenk saw both Dandrikan and the creature were laughing.

"Fraenk. How do you like my new pet?" Dandrikan shouted down from the top of the ice column. "That fool Fernbrook wanted the power of a king, but he could've had the power of a <u>god</u>!"

"You're still a small, pathetic man stealing magic from your betters!" Fraenk shouted back.

Fraenk saw the massive black appendage the thickness of a tree trunk come dropping through the air. He had just enough time to pull Nim out of the way before the monster's tentacle smashed a runnel through the dock boards.

"Careful with that tongue, Fraenk, or I won't let you live long enough to see your beloved city destroyed. Arathes is corrupt! Full of spoiled, entitled elves. For far too long, they have decided what is right. When they are as evil as any monster! They're no saviors—they only pretend to be righteous. They're meddlesome! Interfering in the Tigraen kingdom's affairs. Propping up the weak Tyrant who should have been left to be crushed by the mighty army of Kreeg. Only an iron hand like Kreeg can save the world—"

"Hey Dandrikan?" Fraenk shouted, interrupting him. "I don't care why you're doing this. You just sound insane."

Dandrikan's monologue faltered, and his expression darkened.

At first, Fraenk thought it was a reaction to his insult, but then another man limped up beside him. A very familiar and adversarial individual with dark red skin and long black horns. Fraenk nearly jumped out of his boots. He scrabbled for his knives but felt a calm, firm hand on his shoulder.

"Wait, Fraenk. He's with us," Kyla said.

"What?! Since when?"

"Since I'm no longer a slave to this," Sorzon Brimblade tossed the emerald collar down with a heavy clunk. "I've been in thrall to that fetid worm for too long. That's how he controlled me."

"You expect me to let all that other stuff go?" Fraenk narrowed his eyes. "You tried to kill me. And her!"

"I mean, we've all tried to kill you, Fraenk." Kyla winked at him.

"You're not helping," Fraenk said back.

"If you still have grievances, Neversleep, we can sort it out after we survive the netherdemon," Brimblade replied. Then they all turned as Dandrikan shrieked in rage.

"Faithless betrayer! You can all die together!" The blonde man shouted, his breath steaming around the necklace.

The Leviathan sprang to life—arms, tentacles, and body all thrashing itself at them. They ran back up the docks. Even Nim, who was in the worst shape of all, had channeled newfound strength from pure survival instinct. The creature's ponderous appendages crashed down just behind them as they sprinted.

"I can open a nethergate to send it across, but I'll need time to pour out a ferrosulfur circle big enough for it to fall into." Brimblade explained, between breaths.

"Won't that open a door big enough for a bunch of other monsters to pour through?" Fraenk shouted.

"I never said it was a great plan," Brimblade fired back. "If you've got a better method to banish an eldritch monstrosity to the void, we can do it your way instead."

"Fine. Kyla and I can help you with the circle. Nim, take my horse and summon the reinforcements. We're gonna need them," Fraenk added.

They made it up to the boardwalk and paused. The creature had fallen back as its progress was slowed by having to smash its way through the new construction of a more solidly built pier. After Fraenk made sure Nim was safely riding away back into the city, he took one of the fat pouches that Brimblade had on his belt.

"We start with a half circle. Once the creature is inside, we close it up and open the portal. Remember to use only half. Pour it thin and make it last." The helltouched man instructed. "It has to reach the other's line. If it's not a complete circle, the spell will fall apart."

Fraenk and Kyla exchanged a look as if to ask if they were really doing this. But they didn't have any other options.

They moved out until they stood in a wide triangle. Fraenk checked back over his shoulder to gauge if their dimensions would accommodate the Leviathan. Did he seem like a large or an extra large? It was so hard to tell just by eyeball. They started pouring out the contents of the pouch on the ground, hoping the circle's dimensions would be correct and that they had enough of the strange crystalline powder to go around. Fraenk stepped as quickly as he dared, easing out a thin stream from the bag.

Fraenk tried not looking at either his other two associates or the behemoth that was now getting closer every moment.

"Hurry, Fraenk! Get ready!" Kyla shouted. Fraenk looked and saw her side was prepared already. Brimblade stood at the top of the arc and had started muttering out the spell to open the portal. Fraenk felt his bag had about half left. He backpedaled away from the line and watched the monster approach.

"Wait for the creature to get close," Fraenk said. "Don't start it yet."

"Thanks, I had no idea how to spring a trap," Brimblade fired back sarcastically.

"Boys, do I have to start stabbing people again?" Kyla cut in.

The two men went quiet but shot angry glares at each other.

They all moved to the back of the circle just as Bultzoaan the Leviathan stepped up out of the water. It was coming straight for them. Fraenk could feel fear and panic rising as its heavy footfalls tremulated the ground underfoot. Without thinking, he whispered a prayer to a power that he hadn't spoken to in many years. Not that he was likely to answer at this point. Their lives were now in the hands of their former foe, and they had no idea if this scheme would even work.

They were about to find out.

The creature had just taken its first step into the circle when Brimblade gave each of them a nod.

"Pour it now! Go!" He shouted. Fraenk and Kyla shot forward, separating on either side of the beast. It seemed confused at first, unsure of whom to smash first. Fraenk found the end of the Ferrosalt line and began to pour from the pouch.

At the same time, Brimblade spat out the final part of the spell. He held out his arm, which was already bleeding from where he'd been stabbed by Fraenk's throwing knife and many more times by Kyla's dagger.

The moment his blood hit the Ferrosalt, it burst into multicolored flames. They ignited the powder in a run, moving quickly around where they had poured it. Fraenk saw it was catching up to where he and Kyla were attempting to meet in the middle.

As the flame leapt up, Fraenk could already see the world shimmering and starting to draw thin under the monster's foot. It was working. All they needed was to connect the circle for the fire to complete the door. With any luck, the beast would fall through into whatever hell waited on the other side. He would become their problem then.

"Almost there," Fraenk grunted, pouring and stepping quickly. "Just a few more seconds."

Fraenk felt his bag getting light—too light. He wasn't sure if he'd make it to Kyla with his remaining powder. Then an icy dread hit him as the last powder fell from the bag. The flames surged right up to the end of the line.

"Fraenk, move!" Kyla shouted from right behind him. Fraenk stepped aside just as Kyla finished her own bag, coming up to meet the end of his. The flames met, and the circle was complete.

A wave of relief and elation washed over him, and Fraenk felt emotion boil up in his chest. The ground inside the circle began to vibrate and waver madly, and an entirely new hellish landscape began to fade into view. Fraenk was so intent on watching the portal that he didn't see the beast was making a final desperate attack, its tentacles coming down from above with terrible force.

If the monster had chosen Fraenk and Kyla as its target, they would have been taken completely unaware. But, unfortunately for the helltouched man, he was the focus of its fury.

There was a moment where Sorzon Brimblade was standing, conjuring the portal to a netherrealm, and in the next instant, a massive black tentacle was there instead. Kyla saw it too and screamed. The portal fizzled away, and the magical prismatic fire turned to smoke—along with any hope that they would make it out of this alive.

"Skarking hells," Fraenk muttered.

48

"THERE'S NO ESCAPE, NEVERSLEEP," Dandrikan's gloating voice came from somewhere overhead. Fraenk and Kyla scrambled back away from the monster.

They both looked up to see the small man floating in the air towards them. He was nearly fifty feet up and just out of Fraenk's accuracy range for a thrown blade. Dandrikan was wearing some kind of belt made of clouds, which was apparently the reason he got so far up. He was hovering like some kind of storybook fairy.

Fraenk now recalled the same belt Dandrikan had on in the shop when he had first come for the Mind Thief's appraisal. Apparently this was another of his ill-gotten magical trinkets. And the power it held was giving the wearer a cloud-like lift. But Dandrikan looked wholly novice at its operation. He wheeled and swirled his arms forward, then back, trying to keep his balance. Then he twisted in a series of jerks to maneuver himself around to face them.

Dandrikan gave them a fierce scowl, obviously intending for this moment to be terrifying, or at least serious. It was anything but. Fraenk and Kyla burst out laughing.

"You should've practiced more with that. You look ridiculous," Fraenk shouted at him.

"So? It doesn't matter. The city is mine now. Even after I'm done with this loyal creature, I possess the Mind Thief, and I can enslave everyone in Arathes—including you!

"No one will ever love you if you force them to be your friend, Dandrikan," Fraenk retorted.

"Perhaps I'll keep you around so we can discuss how to properly run a true authoritarian government. Kreeg was just the first. But there are many of us in league across the world who are ready to seize power."

"You think I care to live just to hear you talk politics? No, thanks," Fraenk scoffed.

"Have it your way, Fraenk," Dandrikan shrugged.

They watched as the behemoth rose back to its full height, then delivered a huge overhand smash to the adjacent warehouse. It would soon be doing that to every building in the city, and they had no way to stop it. Dandrikan cackled.

"I think we'll go take a tour of Blackroot Estate first. I'll give your lady elf my regards before we crush her," Dandrikan sneered.

The creature turned to look at them for a brief moment, then waved its clawed fingers at them in an obscene mockery of a boyish 'goodbye'. Then it stomped off in the other direction, towards Blackroot District and the rest of the city.

"You couldn't just pretend to like him, then cut his throat later?" Kyla asked.

"I have my principles, shaky as they are. Besides, he was going to destroy the city and kill everyone regardless," Fraenk said.

"Fair. Also, what is wrong with you?"

They watched the monster lumber down the row, smashing and destroying indiscriminately. Fraenk could hear Lady Blackroot's voice lecturing him about how each warehouse and building was a valuable asset for not just the clients who had property stored but the district as a whole. And every destroyed building was a weakening of Blackroot itself—from which they might never recover. But all he could think about was his own failure to see Dandrikan as capable of creating such chaos. Fraenk knew he was unscrupulous and conniving, but this plan was more grandiose than he'd ever given the man credit for. Perhaps it was that mix of ambition and willingness to attempt something truly this ridiculous and risky. But by the Powers, Fraenk had to grudgingly admit, the fortunes were favoring his recklessness.

Fraenk watched as the creature smashed through the storehouse on the row, where hundreds of barrels of ale and packed crates of liquor bottles were waiting to be hauled off to the many inns and taverns across the city. A moment later, it erupted into a bright plume of fire that rolled into the sky. Fraenk balled his fists in anger. This had gone too far.

The unforgivable crime of destruction of booze aside, Fraenk knew he couldn't just watch this thing rampage. It could kill tens or hundreds of thousands of souls, starting with the other woman he had sworn to protect, Lady Arice. Without Brimblade or some other wizard, they had no way to properly fight this thing. Then an idea flashed, like the sweep of the beam from a lighthouse.

"Valthor the ex-wizard!" Fraenk said excitedly. "If we can get to him—""No, Fraenk." Kyla cut him off. "He-he's gone."

"What?"

"After he took me to the temple, he said he was leaving Arathes for a season. He said he had to atone for some things. He's not here."

"That's damn inconvenient," Fraenk grumbled, turning. "Maybe he's built some kind of flame weapon for destroying rampaging monsters. He seems to love making those— "

Behind them, he saw the massive dry docks where the Pileusian galleon had been for months. Fraenk recalled how Fenduin Tallowfrond, the Acheron of Harbors, complained in nearly every one of their meetings about the work stoppage on the ship due to a lack of payment. Despite many letters and sending personal couriers to the capital, Cirrusol, they were unable to find either someone to bring their account current or even anyone who was responsible for sending the ship in for repairs in the first place. How could an empire be so poorly managed and disorganized that they'd lose an entire war galleon and no one cared? Fraenk was sure that eventually some enterprising soul would uncover a parchment and follow the clues to the missing ship. Who knows if Pileus would even be a kingdom by then?

Then an idea began to form.

"Dandrikan doesn't know the ex-wizard isn't here, though," Fraenk said. "Lead the creature away to the lighthouse. It's protected by warding spells. Hold up there until Nim brings the Arcane Lords."

Kyla's brow creased.

"We'd have to run all the way to the end of the jetty, where we'd be trapped, and hope that the old coot's spells can stop an arcane netherdemon?" She looked at Fraenk as if he was the one now mad.

"No, not us," Fraenk said. "I'll go. You get out of here. Like you said, it's my district and my job to protect it. I can't let all these people die."

"That's very admirable. And I wish you the best of luck. We'll build a small, flat memorial statue in your honor."

Kyla met his eyes, her face grave. Then a smile curled at the corner of her mouth.

"Fine. Let's go do the worst idea you've ever come up with in the short time I've known you, which is sure to fail," she said. "Just how exactly are you going to get that thing to follow us?"

"Just watch," Fraenk said with a mischievous grin. He could see Dandrikan hovering behind the monster in a trail of wispy clouds.

"Dandrikan! You pathetic little whelp! You're going to fail at this, just like everything else in your life. Couldn't cut it as a wizard, and your parents shipped you off because they didn't love you. And I hear your older brother is far more smart and handsome—"

Fraenk wasn't sure if his taunts were getting through to Dandrikan at first, but the moment he had mentioned his older brother, both the man and the enormous monster halted.

"Oh, so that wasn't a lie. Your brother is your better. Dextur, was it? Shall we send for him to make sure your plan succeeds?"

The words had no sooner escaped his lips when the Leviathan turned completely around. They saw its many terrible eyes flare brightly before it began towards them, not at a slow plodding pace, but at a ground-shuddering run.

"That worked a little too well," Fraenk gulped.

It was Kyla's turn to grab his arm and pull him, sprinting toward the building behind them. Any hopes that they could outpace this beast in the open were shattered, like the warehouses it was now plowing through indiscriminately.

They slipped inside the cavernous dry dock building and were immediately looking at another massive behemoth—this one was made of wood, rope, nails, and sails. It was the Pileusian galleon, called the *Maerxis Gambit*, actually larger by half than Dandrikan's monster, and was currently under maintenance in the building. The ship was set up in a long, wide trench that could be flooded to float the ship in and out. Currently, the water was out, and the boat appeared to be set into the floor with its main deck level with the dock's flooring. Getting closer, one could see it was actually resting on massive blocks and fringed by an array of scaffolding that gave workers access to any part of its exterior. There was an elaborate yoke and pulley system rigged up to lift the vessel onto the blocks, just so they could service the parts of the ship that were below the waterline. It was truly a mind-boggling feat of Dwarven engineering, no doubt. Who else would be mad enough to build such a thing? The scale of both the building and the ship made Fraenk feel minuscule.

"It's too fast. We're not going to make it," Kyla said what Fraenk was already thinking.

"What do you suggest?"

"Maybe the ship has bolt throwers or some other mounted weapons?" She replied.

Fraenk didn't have the heart to tell her that all the armaments were removed during maintenance. There was a slight chance that something weapon-like was yet on board.

"Worth a look." Fraenk said, hoping to at least get her away from the path of the monster.

Kyla didn't wait for another word. She ran straight for one of the scaffoldings and scaled it, climbing the braces and then vaulting up the side of the massive ship—much in the same way she'd done with the wall when they were escaping the blackhounds. This time, however, Fraenk found himself grateful she was out of immediate danger. A moment later, she appeared back at the rails.

"There's no weapons, Fraenk! But I think there's something we can use..." Kyla shouted excitedly. "Get up here. Hurry!"

He couldn't imagine what she might have discovered there that might help, but he was willing to try anything at this point.

Fraenk eyed the scaffolding on the ship. Although she made the ascent look painfully easy, Fraenk realized his own climb would be nearly impossible. And adding to it, his body was starting to ache miserably from the continuous abuse it had endured. He tried unsuccessfully to find a part of himself that wasn't sore.

"Go on. I'll be right there." Fraenk shouted back.

But just as he stepped forward, the side of the building exploded inward in a shower of flying wood. Fraenk was thrown forward, tumbling bodily into the support scaffolding, which collapsed a moment later. He dropped down through two more levels of boards into the deep trench where the boat was positioned. The planks tipped him forward, and he rolled, coming to a stop halfway under the galleon in a shower of debris and dust. He found himself coughing and staring up at a keel that was wider than his arms splayed out to both sides—which they happened to be. Fraenk's head hurt, and his vision didn't seem to want to form one single image but was two slightly offset pictures that moved past one another.

As his eyes came back into focus, Fraenk noticed something in the hull of the ship. Thin, beautiful lines that moved and shimmered, running along the length of the wood. It brought to mind the other complaint that the master of docks had been bitterly lamenting. These large, important vessels were reinforced with warding spells and other seals of protection, which kept them seaworthy in a naval action against enemy spellcasters. Without them, the ships were vulnerable to any number of hazards, but it also made them notoriously difficult to repair. All the spellwork would have to be unwoven before boards could be replaced, then the wards added back again. It was as time-consuming as it was expensive. The wards were still active on this ship. That was a turn in their favor. The creature could smash through regular buildings, but could it get through a structure that was magically reinforced? There was one way to find out.

"Fraenk?! Where'd you scurry off to? We're not done with you," Dandrikan screeched as he floated through the new opening in the dock. The creature unleashed a deafening roar that rattled the very foundations of the building. Brilliant flares of colorful glowing tracery blossomed out from the hull as the ward spells seemed to deflect even the waves of air from the monster.

Fraenk got unsteadily to his feet. He could see where the scaffolding had collapsed along the side of the ship in both directions. There were metal rungs to climb out of the long flood trench, but that would just put him up on the floor in front of the monster. He had to get onto the ship, but on this side at least there was no way to do that. But first he had to make sure Kyla got to safety.

He ran out into the open area between the ship and the dock.

"Kyla!" He shouted up.

"I'm kinda busy, Fraenk!" She shouted back.

"Get below deck! The ship has wards. You should be safe!"

"Oh no, you don't!" Dandrikan was hovering up near the building's rafters and heard the exchange. A moment later, the monster's long tentacles were slamming down on the deck of the ship. Fraenk watched helplessly as the behemoth battered the galleon like some grotesque reenactment of Caladel's Kraken sinking the armada of the pirate Handsome Zaine. As it thrashed against the boards, powerful, jagged arcs rippled through the wards like bolts of rainbow lightning, giving off angry crackling protests.

The galleon itself seemed no worse for wear. Fraenk knew the spells would wear out from repeated abuse, but at least for a while, Kyla would be safe inside—assuming she survived the initial attack.

"Kyla?! Are you alright?" Fraenk shouted up to her. There was no reply. Only the face of Bultzoaan the Destroyer, looking down at him with its many terrible eyes.

"What are you doing down there, Fraenk?" Dandrikan grinned wickedly. "You're trapped! If you're not careful, you could get—*squished!*" The beast's arm shot downward towards him. Fraenk had to dive backwards to narrowly avoid the fate of Brimblade. But he had no time to recover because the creature was furiously sliding its clawed hand toward him, trying to grab, smash, or slice his body—whichever it could manage to end his life. An enormous barb dug into the stone floor right between Fraenk's legs.

"Not like that," Fraenk wheezed.

The beast tried to grab him again but was at the full extension of its arm. The massive appendage pulled back out of the trench as quickly as it had entered. A stupid part of his mind wanted to believe it was over, that the leviathan had deemed Fraenk to be out of reach and therefore worth no further effort, but of course he was wrong.

A moment later, the beast's flailing tentacles came spilling down like two massive, enraged black snakes. They whipped and probed blindly, searching for their quarry. Fraenk ducked behind the only hiding place available to him—one of the dozen massive blocks that were supporting the entire weight of the galleon.

The dark appendage appeared to his left, sweeping the ground for someone to latch onto and crush. The moment it bumped into the block, Fraenk had just enough time to roll under it as the tentacle coiled whip-like around it.

There was a deep splintering groan, and the support block was suddenly ripped out from under the galleon. Another shuddering series of creaks ran through the length of the ship, then the building's support timbers.

He looked up, holding his breath, hoping the massive weight of the galleon above him would hold. In a way, it felt like this moment encapsulated his entire life—standing at the bottom, the solid weight of everything above waiting to crush him, while monstrous snakes came at him from all sides, also trying to get him.

And yet, somehow he stood. Through it all and in spite of everything, there he was. He had no idea how. Fraenk would certainly not go as far as to credit one of the many unseen Powers that people seemed to beg when they needed help, blame when things went wrong and otherwise forget the remainder of the time. But there was certainly something unbelievable about everything he had been through.

He made a quiet promise to himself that he would put to paper everything that had transpired. If nothing else, it may be useful for his eventual successor to review the details in order to better know and serve the district. This was contingent, of course, on Fraenk surviving the giant monster, which was still trying to crush the life out of him.

A moment later, the whipping tentacles were back, this time probing deeper, searching for him. The monster had its head wedged between the galleon and the trench to allow further reach. Fraenk ran as the appendages snaked after him. He tried getting behind other support blocks, but the monster knocked them out of the way. And with each new one gone, more of the galleon's immense weight was held by the massive overhead rigging. Then the whole boat began to move sideways, giving the creature more room to get further down and its tentacles closer to grabbing Fraenk.

Stealing a backwards glance, Fraenk saw the monster now had its full head into the channel and all the support blocks were toppled. Worse still, the scaffolding on the opposite side had also collapsed. Fraenk had nowhere else to go and was running out of room to escape.

He backed away to the far side of the trench, trying to keep the ship between himself and the monster. But its probing appendages ran beneath the keel, searching hungrily for him. Then the creature lowered its head and looked sideways across at Fraenk.

The many terrible yellow glowing eyes found him there in the darkness beneath the massive ship. And although he tried to look anywhere else, his gaze was compelled to stare back. The netherdemon had him, and Fraenk saw in those eyes an ancient cruelty beyond madness. Eons of despair, insanity and the end of—

A rough coil of rope smacked him in the head from above. For a moment, he was stunned, like someone had slapped him. Then instinctively, like it was the most natural thing he had ever done, Fraenk grabbed hold of it and looked up.

A beautiful figure in a radiant halo of light was looking down at him from high above. For a brief, heart-stopping moment, Fraenk mistook her for an actual Lyn-Tyrian. But that was the malfunctioning of an over-worked mind. Still, he found himself smiling in spite of it all. Kyla laughed.

"Quit grinning like a low country Firbolg and hold on tight!" Kyla shouted from atop one of the galleon's yardarms. She kicked a fat chunk of timber off the opposite side of the beam. Fraenk saw it was tied to the rope he was holding and ran up through a suspended pulley in the ceiling.

"Wait, I'm not r—" Fraenk had just enough time to register both of the black tentacles flashing toward him before the rope went taut and he was jerked upward.

Fraenk immediately lost his grip, and everything twisted. An inverted world sped by him downward, and he realized he was the one upside-down with the rope looped around his foot.

He felt the blood thundering in his ears as he was pulled upwards by one ankle. Fraenk's head snapped back, and he looked down to see two large, dark, worm-like shapes surging up, seeking to pull him apart.

He heard something rush at him, then with a *THUMP*, his world went dark.

49

Awooo-OOOOO!!

The triumphant blare of horns sounded as the grand procession moved slowly through the streets. Crowds pressed in thick on all sides to catch a glimpse of their champion and savior. Not even the Monarch himself received such fanfare when he came to the city, but this was a singular celebration. Riding at the focus of the column, in the high seat of honor that was not only to the right but also above that of High Lord Krispen Whiteleaf himself, Fraenk smiled and waved to the throngs as they screamed his name over and over.

Fraenk felt euphoria, but under that was mostly relief. He had survived the impossible, and it was over. Now he could bask in the revelry and ride slowly through the city, letting the grateful populace have their chance to heap their adulation upon him.

"Take it all in, Sir Neversleep. This is for you. You defeated the creature and saved us all." Krispen Whiteleaf smiled, amiably shaking his elbow.

"I'm sure you're right, my lord," Fraenk said, struggling to recall the exact events. "But how did I do it? I can't seem to remember."

Whiteleaf only smiled wider and waggled a finger. "Modest as ever, I see. Just enjoy the praise. And have a look over there! They're already rebuilding your district. Blackroot will be better than ever."

Fraenk twisted in his seat and could somehow see down over the distance to the docks, where freshly hewn timbers were being framed into new buildings. He could even hear the faint *tok-tok-tok* of hammers setting nails into beams and saws cutting boards to length.

"How long has it been?" Fraenk asked, feeling more confused.

"We've been cheering your name every moment since. Ne-ver-sleep! Ne-ver-sleep!" Whiteleaf jostled him with even more joviality.

"Oh, and look, all your friends are here to celebrate you!" The High Lord elf added.

Fraenk saw a line of faces in the front of the crowd. Lady Blackroot and Arch Partisan Olwynn Brightrock, arm in arm. Kyla Gracefire stood with Nim Stonebridge and a dapper-looking kobold. There was Gwen—who wasn't in disguise for the first time Fraenk could remember—and her face was so unfamiliar, he began to doubt if it was even her. Then he saw his old friend Leos Muninger, who somehow survived his self-impalement, and for that Fraenk was very glad. Then even Lord Fernbrook, Bas Greenbriar, and Farathiel Gingerglade were in the row, clapping and cheering enthusiastically for Fraenk. Sorzon Brinblade was beside them too. He wasn't sure why that sight was strange to him. The old baker Miken and Doran Leafwater were there as well. Finally, Fraenk saw his mother and father. They looked much the same as they did when Fraenk was a boy, but they both seemed happy, and it made his heart break.

"I'm dead," Fraenk said in answer to his own unspoken question.

"What?! No..." Whiteleaf clapped him on the shoulder a little too hard. "You don't die quite yet, but soon. Terrible thing, that. Just enjoy your parade, for we love you and it will be all the recognition you ever get for your bravery! Now, sir, listen to those crowds cheer your name!

The throng had taken up a singular chant, saying it over and over.
NE-*VER*-SLEEP! NE-*VER*-SLEEP! NE-*VER*-SLEEP!

"Neversleep!"
Someone slapped him hard in the face. Fraenk opened his eyes to see Kyla leaning over him.

"Ow!" Fraenk's head throbbed something fierce.

"Get up, Neversleep. We have to move, or that monster's going to find us."

"I defeated it already," Fraenk said groggily. "The High Lord threw me a parade."

"No. The falling wood hit you. I think your brain is addled. Here, drink this."

He felt a curve of glass press to his lips, and a cool liquid filled his mouth. It tasted sweet at first, like honey and spring mint, but that was just to cover the bitter medicinal notes that hit a moment later. He nearly spit it out, but she pressed her hand over his mouth and made him swallow.

"Extract of Melonfire. You won't thank me in a few hours when it wears off. But I guess the upside is that we might not live that long," Kyla said.

"That's a cheery thought," Frank grunted.

It took only moments, but Fraenk suddenly felt a prickling chill run through his extremities. He sat up, oddly energized. The fatigue and pain in his muscles were being overrun with a dangerous new urge to get up and do more, along with the heady confidence that he definitely could.

Fraenk took a quick moment to look around and orient himself.

At first, he thought Kyla had somehow dragged him to another location because all he saw was a spider's web of thick chains crisscrossing in all directions. Everyone was pulled groaningly tight. In fact, the whole building seemed to creak and protest under some unseen labor. It was dark where Fraenk sat, but a shaft of moonlight was spilling in from a long row of open windows.

They were sitting up on a catwalk high in the upper section of the dry dock, where all the suspension rigging was built into the dock. Directly below were the galleon and the leviathan. Not yet aware of Fraenk's escape, its twin tentacles still thrashed and writhed, searching for him. He could see the entire ship moving slightly as the creature worked itself further underneath it. It made frustrated, pig-like grunts and snuffs as it forced itself deeper into the trench.

"We have our chance. Let's go!" Kyla urged, pulling him toward the windows, which led out onto the roof and to safety. But Fraenk hesitated.

The protesting metal of the chains and moving ship meant it was now held entirely by the elaborate suspension network in the ceiling. This crane rig was designed to slowly raise much smaller ships onto the blocks and was certainly not supposed to get knocked around by monsters. Fraenk's eyes followed the thick chains up from the four corners of the galleon, which eventually all met together at one enormous block and pulley wheel, which was itself the near dimensions of a small ship. The entire building was straining under forces that its craftsmen and engineers had never anticipated.

Down below, if Bultzoaan the Leviathan had been left to its own free agency, it might not have been continuing to probe for Fraenk beneath the hull of the ship. But under the yoke of Dandrikan's magic, it was still doggedly attempting to destroy him. Fraenk saw Dandrikan and his cloud belt, floating closer to the creature, as if to oversee its progress. There was something off about the way Dandrikan moved, mindless and open-mouthed. He also noticed thin red lines tracing down from the corners of the man's eyes and the openings of his ears, and Fraenk realized it was blood. The strain of keeping this monster yoked must have been enormous. More than one mind could bear.

"What are you waiting for? It's busy. Let's get out of here!" Kyla gave him another worried pull. Her expression showed what he was already thinking: if they didn't get out soon, this entire place would collapse on them.

Perhaps it was all his years on the streets, fighting for every scrap and facing danger for daily survival, but Fraenk grew very good at spotting an opportunity. And in the chaos of a dynamic situation, there were moments he could exploit to his advantage. There was one time he had stolen a guard's coin purse as he was being hauled away. Not only had he eaten better than he had in months, but his reputation on the streets had risen to the point of alley rat celebrity—if there was such a thing. So risk-taking became his trade, and seeing those chances coming was his study. Even the most dire circumstances could turn by a single twist of fate.

He could feel that something about the situation was one such moment. Fraenk located a set of ropes that led from the central pulley across the rafters, turned, and then went down to levers near the far wall. This was exactly what he was looking for.

"Fraenk!" Kyla pleaded.

"Go on. I'm right behind you," Fraenk lied, knowing he had to get her outside before attempting what he was about to do. She looked doubtful but started off toward the window.

Fraenk found the control ropes for the suspension rig. One would disengage the locking mechanism, the other held it in place, and he didn't know which was which. It meant he had half a chance to get this right. He reached for the last remaining throwing knife on his belt, but it was not there. He could have sworn he had one more—

Then a blade sank into his back.

Fraenk sucked in a breath of pain as well as surprise. He reached back for the weapon, pivoting to see who had stabbed him. His first thought was Dandrikan had somehow found him and was trying to kill him. But when he turned, only Kyla was standing there.

Stupidly, he almost asked her if she saw who had stabbed him, but then he saw her face and understood. Her eyes were unfocused, and she stood at a stiff angle. She lashed out with a flurry of hits that rocked Fraenk backward.

He reflexively raised his hands in a combat stance, ready to counter another salvo. But Dandrikan's voice turned his attention.

"F-f-f-fraenk. I thought we lost you," a hateful voice intoned. And then Dandrikan floated up into view. He wiped furiously at the thick tracks of blood on his cheeks, leaving a red smear. There was a red trail of mucus flowing from both nostrils.

"Dandrikan. You're dying," Fraenk winced in pain.

"You don't look so hot yourself, Neversleep," Dandrikan sneered back.

Fraenk saw on Dandrikan's chest the necklace, encased in a thick crust of ice like a frozen breastplate. Perhaps if he could break or somehow dislodge it, he could stop Dandrikan's scheme. He reached back, taking hold of the dagger's handle. A bolt of agony shot through his body.

"Oh, I wouldn't do that, Fraenk," he said. "Looks like it's in your kidney. Pull that out and you'll bleed to death in minutes. Actually, go ahead! I'm just going to kill you anyway."

"It would be worth it just to slit your foul neck!" Fraenk spat.

"Then this pretty thing dies too," Dandrikan purred.

Kyla turned mechanically and walked toward the edge of the catwalk. She moved one foot out over the edge, ready to step into oblivion.

"Wait! Stop!! You win, Dandrikan. Please. *Please* don't," Fraenk pleaded.

"Why shouldn't I?" He smiled cruelly.

"Because..." Fraenk started. "I'll tell you something you don't know about the Mind Thief."

Dandrikan looked skeptical at first, then intrigued. His curiosity always did get the better of him. He motioned with a hand, and Kyla stepped backward from the edge.

"Very well, Fraenk. What is it?" He demanded.

Fraenk sighed heavily. He felt his strength ebbing. Dandrikan's brows etched together suspiciously, but curiosity clearly got the better of him.

"Tell me quick, Neversleep. Or this one is about to have a terrible accident!"

"Wait!! Stop! It's simply this—" Fraenk sighed, then threw up his hands, defeated. "The necklace makes what one mind experiences happen to the other person as well. They are linked."

Dandrikan scrunched up his face in confusion— as if Fraenk had told him a recipe for blackjam scones or something equally pointless.

"So? And why would I care about that?" Dandrikan asked with narrowed eyes.

"Well, I'll show you."

With a grunt, Fraenk pulled the blade from his back. And in a single fluid motion, he flung it at the lift control ropes against the wall.

The knife struck with a satisfying clunk and splatter of blood, splitting the fibers nearly all the way through. One single tenacious strand hung on, but the rest of the strands unraveled, curling off perilously in both directions.

That one cursed strand held, pulled to the very limits of tension. Fraenk's heart sank. That was it. His last move. He could feel blood spilling from his back and his body weakening. That one strand of dull cord which refused to—

—*SPANG!*What was once a stubborn strand of rope one moment vaporized into a cloud of fibers in the next. And suddenly everything around Fraenk became motion and sound. The chains in the ceiling rattled out with great shuttering force through blocks and pulleys. Enormous counterweights set on all sides of the building began to rise, and the entire building shook violently, with a deep, primordial moan.

Fraenk had but a brief moment to worry that the entire structure might cavitate apart. A massive boom echoed through the docks, and a brilliant flare of light ran the entire length of the hull as the ward spell took a massive hit.

Then a sound issued from beneath the galleon that was so terrible, that if he had any blades left, Fraenk would have been tempted to cut his own ears off just to make it stop. It felt like the tortured chorus of a million damned souls, all wailing at the same time. The monster's tentacles stiffened straight out briefly, then fell with a numb, fleshy flop. They both slid over the side of the ship, leaving long, slimy trails. The deck shuddered violently as the beast thrashed its limbs and body against the hull. Its back arched and pulled—its tentacles now pinned under the immense weight of the galleon—as it continued to issue high, anguished barks.

Dandrikan cried out and clutched his nose; the monster's pain was an echo in his own body.

"You see what I mean?" Fraenk said. "His pain is yours now."

Dandrikan shrieked as Bultzoaan bucked mightily down below. The ship thumped in response. The creature was currently trapped, but that wouldn't last long. Fraenk saw the ship below him was teetering precariously on its keel. If it tilted over to one side, the Leviathan could free itself to continue its rampage unabated through Arathes. Given the way the beast was pulling, that seemed the most likely outcome. But Fraenk needed the galleon to fall the other way.

Fraenk looked down at the dizzying distance between himself and the main deck. A fall from this height would mean instant death. Dandrikan and his cloud belt were spinning out of control in the empty air above the ship, suffering with the creature. Fraenk felt a gush of warm blood running down his back, but it didn't matter. He knew what must be done.

Fraenk launched himself forward and off the catwalk. For a breathless moment he flew. Then Fraenk collided heavily with Dandrikan. They spun entwined, wildly, for several dizzying moments, dropping fast until Dandrikan managed to right himself. Fraenk grasped the buckle of the cloud belt and unlatched it. His foe uttered a pathetic shriek before they both dropped, accelerating fast towards the ground.

Fraenk grabbed Dandrikan close and arched onto his body just as they hit the boards of the ship. They both tumbled toward the gunwales. Then heavy blocks and pieces of the ceiling began to rain down. They smashed into the deck, nearly crushing Fraenk and Dandrikan.

Then slowly the ship began to tilt.

Fraenk turned as the deck skewed under him. Bultzoaan the Leviathan rose level with the edge of the main deck, its many terrible eyes fixed on Fraenk and its horrible wet mouth open to catch him as he slid. Dandrikan had grasped a loose rope and was holding on. He cackled as Fraenk slid ever closer to the open pit in the creature's face.

"Goodbye, Fraenk!" Dandrikan shouted.

Fraenk could do nothing but helplessly slide toward the terrible maw of the leviathan. Then its hunger suddenly turned to surprise as the galleon pinned the monster against the wall of the channel. Dandrikan saw this and knew it was bad. He scrambled to pull the necklace from his body but could only beat against the icy bulwark around it. The weight of the tilting galleon was pressure on the creature's skull, strong at first, but it grew by exponential magnitudes with each moment.

All Bultzoaan could do was scream. An unearthly roar of anguish—doubled by Dandrikan's voice. They both felt the monster's skull crack. Then its head shattered in a massive spray of viscera, blood, and brain matter.

Fraenk slid uncontrollably into a hot, pillowy mass of wet mazzard as the galleon hit the side of the wall with an earth-vibrating boom. A massive yellow eyeball fell into his lap, fixing him with a dull, questioning gaze. Fraenk yelped, scrambling backward out of the monster's destroyed head.

Then a body slid toward him, landing just within arm's reach. Dandrikan looked out with lifeless eyes, blood erupting from every opening.

"I warned you," Fraenk said.

He saw that the ice brace around Dandrikan's chest had shattered open. There at its core was the Mind Thief necklace, but it looked different. Then Fraenk saw why; the crystal at its core was splintered with deep cracks. Even looking at it felt different. Fraenk felt no aversion to seeing it. The Mind Thief no longer made him bored or want to look away. Somehow, its magical effects seemed totally gone.

Perhaps Dandrikan had pushed the item beyond what it could handle. Somehow beyond what it could bear. And now, it lay destroyed. Perhaps that was the best outcome after all. It was what Brightrock had wanted. And if Fraenk was being honest, something he had no idea how to accomplish on his own.

But, even though it was destroyed, Fraenk knew it wasn't the end of it. Others might try to recover it—possibly even repair it, given the chance. He would have to make sure everyone knew it was finally over—that the Mind Thief would never be active again.

As he lay, an uncomfortable pain dug into his hip, and Frank shifted, reaching for the offending item. Fraenk had felt a loop of chain and pulled it up into view. Then he began to laugh. Olwynn Brightrock had given him one more blessing. The decoy necklace he had slipped into Fraenk's pocket looked almost indistinguishable from its original.

Fraenk let it dangle in the light and smiled.

50

FRAENK SPENT THE NEXT two weeks recuperating in his private reserved bed at the healer's ward of Mersey's temple. There was no parade in his honor, and even the thanks he got were muted. More often, what he received instead were questions of *'why'* that were neutral in tone at first but became more accusatory—as if Fraenk was somehow responsible for all the calamity. Then after that, inquisition ebbed, and they were replaced by annoying faces with buzzing questions that only the Arch Preceptor seemed to be able to answer. He finally escaped one night and stole away to Valthor's lighthouse.

And even though he'd left a note that stated in no uncertain terms that he was well and not to send guards to scour every corner of the district for him, he only managed to make it three days before they did exactly that. But by then, his body's complaints had subsided to a level sufficient enough to allow his return to his tower in Blackroot Estate. And so, without much fanfare, Arch Preceptor Fraenk Neversleep was back on the job.

Very much to her credit, Kyla had found him in the immediate aftermath of the attack and staunched the bleeding in his back until he could be seen to by the healers—effectively saving his life. She even came to visit him a few times while he recovered.

These were late evening visits, after the bustle of the day had calmed and when they had the least amount of interruption. They drank tea (and sometimes stronger stuff) while munching on small cakes and confections from a new pastry shop she had found in the upper market. They talked a lot about what they both had been through. Both of them had nightmares, but Fraenk could never seem to fully recall the content of his own. They were impressions mostly. Large shapes with many eyes, still watching him and waiting. Kyla shared a few of her own dreams—ones that featured Fraenk as a subject.

The first was of a giant woman with blood dripping from her hands and hair, looming over the city, searching under buildings for Fraenk. Then another of a pale white horse and Fraenk as its rider, both dead, but raising an army of shadows as they moved. She explained that the images were difficult to assign any kind of meaning to and not meant to be taken at face value. Whatever reason she had to tell him all this, Fraenk found little comfort in knowing.

As a macabre way of lightening the mood, Kyla insisted upon hearing the full account of Farathiel Gingerglade getting halved by the High Lord. The joy she took in hearing it bordered on the pathological, but considering what he'd put her through, Fraenk figured she had earned the right to hear its telling as many times as she liked. Fraenk also shared that, according to his preceptors, the Fernbrooks were having some difficulty finding his replacement. Hard to believe, considering they could dredge the canal and find any number of mucousy eels equal to the task. That got a laugh from Kyla, but he also noticed her unconsciously touch the thin line of skin just under her jaw where the elf's cord had left its mark.

It was during her last visit, after a stray vanilla butter biscuit had fallen from their tray and she leaned forward to recover it, that Fraenk was not surprised to see the chain of the decoy necklace peek out from her collar. He brought up the Mind Thief later in the course of their conversation—about how his preceptors discovered it was unaccounted for and how the partisan and Arcane Lords were still trying to recover it. Kyla proffered the theory where someone had picked it up in the chaotic aftermath and probably found it so uninteresting that they threw it in an old trunk where it would live out the rest of its days, unremembered and out of action.

Fraenk made a show of vowing to doggedly track it down someday when he had recovered. The Ynne es Tylubourne was far too dangerous to be floating around the world unguarded. Kyla quickly promised her aid in its recovery as well. Whether or not she figured out that the one she carried was a fake, Kyla made no indication. And of course, Fraenk already knew exactly where the authentic one was: in a leather pouch he kept around his own neck. It was the only place he could be sure no one else had it.

In a quiet moment at night, he had experimentally tried to put it on and summon the necklace's power. But whatever Dandrikan had done to it seemed to have depleted the item's mind-dominating magic. Now, only its charms to appear entirely uninteresting were possibly still active. Or else it was just an ugly, cracked stone on a pitted, old chain. Fraenk kept it close nonetheless. It was a small burden to have to carry forever, but didn't everyone have something they always carried with them?

As the evening was drawing late, Fraenk wanted to say more to her, but he could never find the moment. They always seemed to be in the middle of a side-splitting laugh about Doran Leafwater with his head stuck in the mouth of the Shadescourge or in the silence when their eyes met while both were taking a sip of tea. Those moments created a feeling he could not put into words. He wasn't even sure what he would say or if there were even words to express the mix of thoughts that he held for her.

There were times when it looked as though she was about to say something to him as well, but her eyes veered off, and Kyla would mention the delicious flavor of the cake or how the city was overdue for rain. Their moment never seemed to happen.

Even though she said she was going to stay in Arathes, it would be a while before his paths crossed with Kyla again—at least until the incident with the cursed statue. But the account of that tale is written in another scroll.

The unfortunate incident in the palace regarding the High Lord having too much strong wine and losing his senses was overshadowed by the kraken attack on the docks. The new Arch Partisan was a much younger elf and a returned military hero who was just as humorless as his predecessor. During the commissioning process, the new Arch Partisan was verified as unaffiliated with any elven house by the elder council, but Fraenk's own preceptors did uncover certain familial connections that tied back to the Fernbrooks. It then came as no surprise to hear that the investigation into Lord Fernbrook's attempted coup had stalled out entirely. Fraenk knew the day was coming when Fernbrook might try again, but it would not be soon. Elves were devilishly patient when they wanted to be, and Fernbrook could wait until long after Fraenk was dead.

The leviathan's rampage on the dock turned out to be something of a hidden blessing for the port of Arathes and for House Blackroot in particular. The aging docks and warehouses that previously were beginning to rot on their posts were now being constructed anew along with a redesign of the entire harbor, which had more piers, warehouses, cranes, and berths for ships. The entire operation was heavily financed by all the High Houses, including by Lord Whiteleaf himself.

And when word filtered back to Pileus about how one of their prized galleons was rumored to have defeated a kraken in naval combat, they moved with surprising haste to find the gold required to finish the ship's overhaul so they could bring the ship home. Political stunt or no, the Acheron of Ports was more than happy to get the galleon out of his docks and turned back toward home.

Fraenk Neversleep sat on the stone bench in the garden of Blackroot Estate, much like he had been when he was first summoned to the scene where his friend Miken had been killed. It felt like an impossibly long time ago. And in other ways—in the freshness of his grief—like not much time at all.

The afternoon sun dappled the waters of the Ancestral Pool. He had decided to be done staring at walls, with their faded etchings of the past. No good ever came from staying embittered by history. What was done long ago could not be changed. Letting it fester inside would only destroy you, like it did to his friend Leos. Fraenk found himself thinking a lot about his friend, wishing he could have made peace with the man sooner. And when he started feeling too melancholy, Fraenk would visit him at the tomb he'd commissioned far beyond the city walls. Leos always liked to sleep outside.

As he sat in the sun, Fraenk heard a foot scuff gravel and was expecting to see Nim Stonebridge approaching. His underling had healed quickly and seemed to not bear any ill feelings about his kidnapping and torture. He was downright chipper most days, proclaiming to all who would listen about how his fortunes had changed. Although most attributed this newfound joy to his brush with near death, Fraenk suspected it had more to do with his almost unbeatable run at the dice tables—which Fraenk himself had secretly secured for him with the dealers on Canal Street.

When Fraenk looked up, he was surprised to see Lady Blackroot being helped along the path by her handmaids. She cursed and swatted at them as they fussed over her, unperturbed by her mild abuse.

"May I join you, Neversleep?" Lady Blackroot asked when she saw him watching her procession.

"It is your garden, my lady."

Fraenk slid to one side on the bench to allow space for her.

"Good. It took a lot of effort to get out here, and I'm not about to turn around now."

Her handmaids required several more minutes to get the old elf situated on the bench and get her dress draped in a pleasing way, until Lady Blackroot finally had to threaten them with a horsewhipping to send them scampering off.

"Who *skarking* cares what my dress looks like? It's just us out here."

"As you say, my lady," Fraenk chuckled. "I think they just care about you."

She watched him for a moment out of the corner of her eye.

"How is your friend's health these days?"

"He's finding retirement suits him well enough and is glad to be out of the city. He frequently tells me how pleased he is not to be cleaning up after another one of your messes. If only I had that luxury," she said with a wink.

"Give Lord Brightrock my regards and tell him I'm pleased to pay him a visit whenever he wishes."

"Oh, you're not allowed anywhere near the place," Lady Blackroot snorted out a laugh. Fraenk couldn't help but laugh, too.

"We've been through much, haven't we, Fraenk?" She said wistfully.

"That we have, my lady."

"Many have tried to kill us. The Fernbrooks. And before that, the Redthorns—who nearly succeeded..."

"Yes, I'm quite familiar."

"I got a letter today from my son's personal secretary. The one I sent along to—"

"Spy on him," Fraenk smirked.

"*Keep him safe.*" She paused and took in a slow breath. "Apparently, the main host of Arathes' army is on the march home. I'm told he's a different man than the one we knew. I sent him off in order to see him grow into a leader. But war has shaped him in ways we have yet to understand. We have many challenging days ahead, Arch Preceptor."

"I'm by your side until the end, my lady," Fraenk said.

"Mine will be coming sooner than yours, I fear."

Fraenk started to protest, but she quickly cut him off.

"Stop. I don't keep you around to lie to me, Neversleep." She looked directly into his eyes. "I will require your solemn oath that you'll watch over him when I'm gone. He is now my surviving heir, and I worry greatly for him. He will need good people to guide him. Blackroot still has many enemies."

Fraenk was a churning mix of emotions. But Lady Blackroot always spoke plainly with him, and her concern was evident. She would not relax until she wrung the promise from him.

"I will, my lady," Neversleep vowed and immediately felt an icy chill across his chest. And for a moment, Fraenk felt like he could read the old woman's mind. *It was fear... for her son or fear of him; he wasn't sure.*

Without thinking, Fraenk touched the leather pouch on his neck; it was cold to the touch and hard but quickly thawing. Fraenk's heart began to pound.

Lady Blackroot looked down at her reflection in the Ancestral Pool. Then sighed and grew very still.

"Do you know why we elves have these put into our gardens, Fraenk? Other than the fact that they're outrageously expensive and a pain in the kiv to upkeep?"

"It's where you dispose of meddlesome handmaidens," Fraenk said, deadpan.

Lady Blackroot barked a laugh, then her expression grew serious.

"We have a saying—well, we have many buildings full of sayings—but one in particular that goes: 'If you forget your father's face, you will repeat his sins.' These pools are to connect us to those we have lost, though we love them, to remind us not to make their same mistakes."

Fraenk could remember his father's face—at least the last one he wore. The terrible one with the upturned snout and glowing eyes. But he had one before that. There was a man underneath the monster. A troubled, broken man, one that meant well but lived too far in his cups to help the people he cared about. Was Fraenk repeating the same mistakes? He had no answer.

Fraenk was surprised when she took his hand suddenly.

"I must ask something significant of you, Fraenk," she said. "I need to see into the waters of your past."

Fraenk tensed and almost stood.

"What?! Why?" He asked more angrily than he had intended. She had no business there. She would not be safe poking around in his head, as both Lord Whiteleaf and Gingerglade discovered.

"I wish to name you as Lord Protectorate of Blackroot," she said. There was no mirth in her tone nor expression.

"You have a rightful heir, and he is of age," Fraenk replied. "I'm sure Aerlith would object."

"And it is for his very sake that I ask. Fraenk, you know what it takes to keep Blackroot district strong. The son who returns doesn't understand the workings of the city like you. The things that must be done in order to preserve our interests and keep our enemies at bay. The boy who left cared for nothing but plays, poetry, and the skirts of maidens. Now, I worry about what will happen to all that I've built if it's run by a fool."

Fraenk looked up nervously. The estate's guards were fairly distant, but if they overheard her, it could make his life very difficult. Some would judge even this conversation as treason and Fraenk as a round-ear usurper.

"You're too hard on him. You have to give Aerlith a chance, my lady."

"War seldom returns better versions of men. And the only battle he saw was from a distant hill," Lady Arice growled. "My mind is made, Neversleep. I want you to oversee the district as Lord Protector until you feel that Aerlith is ready. It will be up to you to make sure he's prepared for everything it means to be Blackroot."

"Even if we both agreed, no other elf in this city would allow it," Fraenk warned.

"If I could find even the most distant elf in your lineage, that would change everything."

He stared at her for a long moment, then smiled.

"Oh, well done, my lady!" Fraenk barked a laugh of relief. "You're having a jest at me for all the trouble I put you through. Fair enough. I deserve that."

Fraenk's smile faltered when he saw her stony expression.

"For the sake of my husband, Lord Taener Blackroot, and our family line going back to the Second Age. *Please,* Fraenk," Lady Blackroot begged. Fraenk saw how thin and frail she looked. "We only need one ancestor, and I can name you by law. *I need you to allow this.*"

Fraenk still hesitated. He could see many ways this could go very poorly for him, even if she found an elf somewhere in his past—which itself seemed highly unlikely. He had no wish to deny his patron, however. The woman had lifted him up in so many instances; why not let her try one last time?

"Come on, I shouldn't think I would have to beg someone to become the most powerful human in Arathes."

Finally, and with great reluctance, Fraenk nodded.

"Lean forward and let me look."

Lady Blackroot hooked her small skeletal hand in his arm, and they peered together into the Ancestral Pool. She began whispering something in Elvish that Fraenk didn't understand. As if in response, a slight breeze picked up, tossing the flaps and folds of their clothing. But instead of the water growing more choppy, it turned mirror-still.

For a long time she gazed. Fraenk only saw the reflected sky and their own images. Then finally she grew very still. Questions buzzed in his head, but he waited for her to speak. The silence drew out longer, and Fraenk began to wonder if she had somehow fallen asleep. But then finally she spoke.

"My son, Aerlith, shall succeed me alone as Lord of Blackroot."

The hope Fraenk didn't realize he had been holding onto collapsed like a warehouse being smashed by a leviathan. A twinge of bitterness twisted in his mind, but he forced it back. Lady Blackroot had already given him more than any human could ask, and he would be grateful for it all.

"I will serve him as well as I serve you, my lady," Fraenk said. "Long may he rule."

"He'll certainly have his work cut out for him." She smiled wearily. "Come, help me up, and let's go have a drink."

"A splendid notion, my lady." Fraenk said, taking her arm.

Fraenk helped Lady Blackroot back to standing. A fresh breeze moved through the estate garden, carrying the sounds of leaves, water, and the songs of birds. A rare and elusive feeling of tranquility came over him. For as long as it would last, he was determined to enjoy it.

"Fraenk. I am sorry for your parents. I had no idea," she said as he led her up along the gravel walkway, her dress swishing softly as they walked.

"Yes. I lost my family when I was very young." Fraenk Neversleep looked up to the wide expanse of the shimmering Lake Ewyn in the distance, countless points of light glinting like stars. Whatever word that was from his memories was gone, bleached away by time and now rewritten by a new destiny. The past held only hurt, so why not bury it beneath a mountain? The view from the top would look something just like this.

It was only when Fraenk stepped forward without her that he noticed that Lady Blackroot had stopped.

"What is it?" Fraenk asked, seeing that she bore a puzzled expression.

"Your family—"

"All dead. These many years. At least I think there is nothing left of my father. I'm not certain how that devilry works."

"But your sister."

"Her too. Killed alongside my mother." Fraenk said.

"But that's not true, Fraenk. I just saw her in the waters. She's alive."

THE END

Epilogue

Winston the Netherdemon found himself back where he belonged, in the dimension of eternal non-existence. It was not a bad place to live, but being a location outside of time and space made it somewhat difficult to receive written correspondence. Nevertheless, it was good to be home.

He was surprised to note that he had something of a headache—which was a novelty—and found himself rather enjoying it. It wasn't often that he experienced anything but ennui or hunger... and perhaps an occasional mild interest in pottery. But it didn't explain how he seemed to be unable to account for exactly what had happened from the time he was splashing along the shoreline in a lovely human world to this moment now when he was back in the netherrealm. Mortals were indeed a tricky lot. Perhaps they were more than just tasty souls to devour.

For now, all he wanted was a nice hot cup of jasmine tea (which was a comfort in any dimension) and a few biscuits laced with the undying screams of the eternally anguished. He curled up in a blanket of sorrow and kicked his feet up in front of the flames of torment. As far as relaxation went, this was the furthest thing from it and exactly how Winston liked to spend his eternity.

As he basked in the glow of cozy swirling madness, an odd thought occurred to him: perhaps in another time that was a very long, or perhaps incredibly short, span from now— it was hard to determine such things in the nonexistence—when they foolishly summoned him to once again run rampant in their terrible world, Winston thought he might spend just a bit of time getting to know them. Learn what makes them tick, to borrow their odd expression. Perhaps discover their hopes, desires and dreams... and also fears—yes. Tasty, tasty fears...

"Summon me again, foolish mortals," he thought. *"You'll find me in the arcane scrolls under the name... Bultzoaan."*

The Realm of Galhadria is wide and expansive with more stories happening elsewhere. The attentive reader is frequently rewarded with references, characters and extra details from these other books. For example, Fabreo makes an appearance in A Songbird's Tale and the Battle of Sauchvor is a key event that happens before the story Dueling Wizards begins. I highly encourage you to read the other books in the series.

A Songbird's Tale, by Tiffani Sahara

Dueling Wizards, by Dustin Ballard

Keep up to date on the latest news from our authors on Blacksteel Press Publishing. (blacksteelpress.com)